NO ORDINARY TERROR

NO ORDINARY TERROR

J. Brooks Van Dyke

Printed in the United States of America

For information address:
Mulberry Lane Books
10152 Banbury Avenue
Westminster, California 92683
714-222-8889

Library of Congress Cataloging-in-publication Data
J. Brooks Van Dyke, 1943

No Ordinary Terror / J. Brooks Van Dyke
Library of Congress Catalog Card Number: 2013903971
ISBN 978-0-9886033-2-5

Interior Layout: Sarah O'Neal | eve custom artwork
Cover Design by LINDSEY DESIGN GROUP, INC.
Interior Magnifying Glass Image © Elenasuslova | Dreamstime

www.mulberrylanebooks.com

Mulberry
Lane

DEDICATION

To My Wife
Judy
who is a constant blessing.

And to
Emily & John
whose lives of loving encouragement
are my constant pleasure

ACKNOWLEDGEMENTS

I am grateful for Emily and Annie, who constructively critiqued the manuscript.
And to Jan Roger, whose attention to detail saved me from embarrassment.

MAP OF ENGLAND, SCOTLAND & WALES

NO ORDINARY TERROR

CHAPTER 1

"Davies, I insist. Poison. Belladonna. Strychnine," Dr. Thornton had said in the young academic's office before morning classes.

Professor Henry Davies gathered his note papers, and again the words assaulted him.

Poison. Belladonna. Strychnine.

He left his laboratory at the University of London and went outside, colliding with a man carrying a barrister's case. The evening air was heavy with moisture, smelling of rain and wet bark. Mumbling his apologies, he secured his papers under his arm and walked quickly toward Mary's house. Early fog haloed the gaslights, dampening his spirits. A familiar fear touched his spine.

"Poison," Davies said as he walked. "Why poison? But the Huns'll kill me if I don't sell them my formula." He tried to focus on his bride-to-be in three weeks, Mary. Instead, Dr. Thornton's early morning tirade and the German thug's incessant death threats pounded inside his head. "Twenty-eight's too young to die," he said into the early fog.

Davies threaded around groups of chattering students.

"That's him... Dr. Davies," one of the girls said.

"Handsome," said another.

"Brilliant in class but tough at rugby."

Davies made his way through a jumble of lorries and omnibuses on Forbes. He quickened his pace eastward, thankful that a fresh wind was at his side. He eyed the shortcut to Mary's house that sliced through Beeton Park—a place he knew better than his own laboratory. Gusts plucked at the copses of elms, sycamores, and willows.

He checked his pocketwatch. Late.

Pedestrians watched him as he passed, coattails flapping. His thoughts plucked at him like the gusting wind.

Should I tell Mary? No. Richard, then. I'll tell Richard. It's madness! Thornton claims the Crown and Number Ten have high hopes for my formula...

talks of meetings. Officialdom. But when? And where? And those bloody Germans! How did they know about the formula? And their death threats. Fifty thousand quid for my formula. Sell it? Never. His stomach churned.

Davies edged by a family and received cross looks from the father and mother as they were tugged by their children towards Rundell's Toy Shoppe. Forced to stop at the Tynsdale and Cambria crossing, he welcomed the pause.

He stood behind a man wearing a bowler and glanced across Tynsdale. His stomach knotted. The traffic officer gestured and their small crowd moved forward. Davies edged around the others, getting past fancy-dressed couples headed for an evening concert at the university. He glanced over his shoulder. There! A German tormentor was keeping pace on the other side of Tynsdale.

The deadline's tomorrow. I need time.

He crossed Monarchy, then onto Beeton Park's squeaky grass. There he moved between the trees he used to play among with Richard and Emma when they were children. He avoided exposed roots and half-buried mossy rocks many centuries old. Then he moved faster, climbing a knoll to a dilapidated groundskeeper's shed. Atop the knoll Davies looked back. The German following him was lumbering across the carriageway like a great bear.

Battle him now! But his pistol...

He made his way over the path trampled hard from usage and along the weeping willows at the edge of the lake. Their usually languid branches were now driven by the wind. Geese and ducks took to the air as he passed.

Davies got back into the carriageway through an opening in the traffic. He groped for the papers under his arm. They were gone! Looking back, he saw the German splashing in Beeton Lake, gathering wet pages. He managed a smile.

My meeting notes. Get soaked, you fool.

It gave him time to think. Above all, the Germans must not connect him with Mary. He came to a crowded crossing and was again forced to wait.

Why does the Admiralty classify my discovery as top secret? How could a technique that delivers medicine through the human epidermis into the bloodstream be considered a national secret?

He crossed the carriageway and stopped at a milliner's window, watching for the pursuing German, but he was not in sight. Davies adjusted his appearance and walked two more blocks to Mary Palmer's sanctuary.

He struck the old door knocker. It rattled the broken bell inside. He dragged his comb through his hair then stood, nervously cracking his knuckles. Mary stepped into the hallway, gorgeous in her ribbons and best party frock of vermillion and black.

"Henry," she said, blond hair catching the meager light. "The Watsons are here." He swept her into his arms and raised her from the floor, her silk skirts rustling and flowing. "Put me down, you're wrinkling my clothes," Mary said, but clinging to him. The smell of lilacs and powder came to him as he kissed her neck. He lowered her to the floor.

"Come. They're waiting." She fluffed her dress and tugged at her skirts, leading him through the modest parlor towards the dining room.

"Here's Henry," she said.

He greeted Mary's parents and the Watson family and made profuse apologies for being so late.

"No matter, Henry," Mr. Palmer said, getting up and shaking his future son-in-law's hand. "We've enjoyed getting acquainted with Dr. Watson— Dr. John H. Watson, I should add. You've seen my collection of his accounts of Sherlock Holmes," he said with a nod towards stacks of *Strand* magazines visible in the parlor next to his favorite chair. Henry bowed and helped Mary resume her seat.

Mr. Palmer was normally austere and measured. His guiding principle was economy, as sparing with words as with money. But this night he was ebullient, thrilled that Dr. John H. Watson, M.D., second only to Sherlock Holmes, his hero, was dining at his table.

"Everyone, eat, but first, pray dear," Mrs. Ida Palmer urged. Her taffeta frock whispered and her corset stays creaked as she found comfort in her chair.

Henry forced aside the chase by the German and concentrated on pleasantries. "Richard, old chum, when did you return from France?"

"Thursday," Richard said, ladling peas onto his plate, some spilling onto the tablecloth.

"I see you're wearing an ascot. Not quite you, is it?"

"Don't tease him, Henry," Emma said. "He looks rather smart, doesn't he?"

"But can he keep it up, or will he go back to his bohemian attire?"

Richard smoothed his ascot and then finger-combed his scruffy goatee. His bright eyes went to his rugby chum and found anxiety dwelling on his face. He glanced at his sister. He saw her studying Henry too.

"I hardly recognized you tonight," Mary joked, joining in the teasing of Richard.

"Selfridges," Richard answered, gathering the errant peas.

"It's the most popular shop nowadays," Emma said with the blink of keen eyes behind her gold pince-nez. "It's causing a sensation. An American owns it... from Chicago. I bought this there last week." She fluffed the sleeve of her aubergine frock. "You could spend an entire day there."

"Richard, tell us about France," said Mary.

"He spent time with Auguste Rodin," Emma replied for her brother— his mouth too full to speak.

Mr. Palmer cleared his throat for attention. "Tell me, Dr. Watson..."

"Call me John."

"Imagine, two physicians in the same family," Mr. Palmer remarked, eyes wide.

Touching her father's hand, Emma said, "And working under the same roof."

"It must be confusing at times...ah, for the patients, the name Dr. Watson, that is, both of you, Dr. Watson, I mean," Mr. Palmer said. He watched this man, Sherlock Holmes's famous Boswell. To have such a man in his very home was a magnificent circumstance.

"At first it was confusing," Dr. John said, sipping lemon water. "We've trained all of our patients to call us Dr. John or Dr. Emma."

"You must be proud of her...John."

"Don't share that with Emma. Her patient list is almost the equal of mine. And she's been with me only eighteen months."

"Two years next month," Emma corrected, buttering her bread, glancing at Henry.

Henry watched Mary. He had to keep fighting back images of Germans, of his own murder, and the thug who right now must be hunting the neighborhood for him. He gulped his water and compulsively leaned towards Mary and whispered, "Why didn't you tell me about Nigel sooner?"

"Later."

"But you knew."

"I didn't want you to—"

"You've known for weeks. Mary, why did you—"

She silenced him with a dreadful stare. Then she forced a smile for the watching Emma.

"Dr. John, forgive my inquisitiveness," Mr. Palmer said. "Since Mary and Emma have become such close friends and, well, I know that you are the great Dr. John H. Watson..."

"Mr. Palmer, go ahead. And by the by, may I call you William?"

"Of course. I'd be honored, in fact. Anyway, it's like this. When we learned that Richard and Emma are your children, I wondered why you hadn't mentioned them in your Sherlock Holmes accounts?"

Dr. John's eyes shifted to the twins, then to his host.

"William, only our closest friends, and our patients, know about them," Dr. John said, cutting the lamb on his plate and spreading vinegared mint on it. He speared a small piece and forked it into his mouth. "My word, Mrs. Palmer, this is delicious."

"Thank you."

"William, early in my friendship with Holmes, I realized we were dealing with the foulest lot. Moriarity and his ilk, you see. After Richard and Emma were born, I decided to shield my family as best I could. Their mother, God rest her dear soul, and I decided that any references to our home or my medical practice would, for security purposes, be false locations. There could never be any mention of Emma or Richard. You understand—retribution... who knows what? Any references, you must surely appreciate, are wholly fictitious."

"By Jove, of course," Mr. Palmer said, waving his fork. His eyes took in Richard and Emma. "So you two were kept away from Holmes and Baker Street?"

"When their mother passed on," Dr. John said, "we moved in with Sherlock for a period. The children lived with Mrs. Hudson, bless her."

Richard added, "She's like a second mother to us...never knew our real mother."

Emma nodded agreement. "Mrs. Hudson's younger sister is our housekeeper...Mrs. MacIntosh. She was married once, but years ago her husband perished in an accident down at the docks... Lambeth. So Mrs. Mac—that's what we call her—Mrs. Mac has been with us ever since. Like a grandmother to us, she is. And a mother, too. We are blessed." She smiled but flicked a gaze at her brother. He nodded slightly, not looking at Henry.

"You were saying, Dr. John," Mr. Palmer said. He edged closer over the table.

Mary whispered to her mother, "I've never seen him like this."

Dr. John cleared his throat. "Well, living with Sherlock Holmes was a challenge. It took a year or more before he accepted the children underfoot. Then something occurred, something which I'm not at liberty to reveal, and from that moment on, Holmes warmed to them and appointed himself their unofficial uncle."

"We still call him Unca-lock," Emma said. "That's what we called him when we were learning to talk. Unca-lock."

Richard jabbed his sister's arm. "And Emma hasn't stopped talking since. All her suffrage speeches at Trafalgar and Hyde Park...a professional talker she is, I'd say."

"Stop it," Emma said. Henry managed a smile, but he was staring at a disturbing darkness in the window behind Richard.

Mr. Palmer leaned even more over his plate. "What could have transformed Holmes's attitude towards the twins?"

"I'm sworn to secrecy, William," Dr. John replied, "but I'll wager the turning point case is in your *Strand* magazines over there."

"Please, sir," Richard gently interceded. "Our father has pledged strict confidentiality to Sherlock."

Mr. Palmer deflated. "You must agree, it *is* intriguing."

"That it is, sir. That it is," Dr. John said with a smile and broke off some bread, raising it towards Mrs. Palmer. "I enjoy fresh bread, and this, my dear lady, is excellent."

"Yes, smashing bread...everything," Richard added.

Mrs. Palmer held the bubble and squeak over Henry's plate. He waved it away and nodded towards the lamb. "Lamb, please."

Mrs. Palmer passed the platter. "You seem starved, Henry."

Henry swallowed and said, "Thank you." Mary sent him a look, embarrassed by his excessive appetite. He glanced at her and she managed a smile.

Emma finally nudged her brother and whispered. "Something's troubling Henry."

"Richard, Mary tells me you're an artist," Mrs. Palmer said. "You graduated from Slade Art School. Becoming quite well known, I understand. And there you are drawing while you're eating. Do show us."

"Takes his sketchbook everywhere," Emma said, laughing. "To bed, I think."

Richard raised the sketchbook. Mrs. Palmer gasped and pressed her hand to her chest. "My word, it's me! You've drawn me."

Mr. Palmer exclaimed, "Remarkable... like a photogravure."

"It's just a rough sketch...a quick study. That's all," Richard said and carefully tore the page from his book. *"Beauty itself doth of itself persuade— The eyes of men without an orator."*

"Gracious. Shakespeare," Mrs. Palmer gasped.

"Lucrece," said Richard. "Here, Mrs. Palmer...with my compliments."

"Don't encourage him," Emma said, "or we'll be here all night listening to recitations."

"Ask him to sign it, Mother. You will, won't you, Richard?"

He autographed the sketch and printed the quote.

"He'd rather quote Shakespeare than talk about his art," Emma remarked.

"Or Lucrese," Richard said, interrupting.

"Sometime when you visit us, he'll show you his studio. Be warned, it's filthy." Emma jabbed Richard in the ribs, never missing an opportunity to remind him of his neglect. "He's a sculptor, too. His hammering shakes the whole house. Tell them about the sculpture you're working on."

"A bust of Lady Billington...in Carrara marble...from the same quarry Michelangelo got his Pieta marble," Richard said, hoping the topic would shift from his work.

"How perfectly fascinating. And your paintings, tell us about them," Mrs. Palmer asked in an attempt to keep conversation from Sherlock Holmes. Mr. Palmer let fly with an indignant snort and resumed eating.

"I've been experimenting with rather atmospheric studies of Beeton Park. I wish I could set up a tent and capture Beeton in the seasons."

"If you can stay away from Paris and the ladies long enough," Emma said. He tore a piece of bread. "We had good times there, didn't we, Henry?"

Henry did not answer. Grotesque images of the German, wading, gathering his soggy floating notes commanded his thoughts. Mary gave him an elbow. "What? Oh yes, good times. Yes, of course we did." He toyed with a piece of lamb. He felt suffocated, fear cloying at him. The window shadow...

Henry couldn't purge Nigel or the Germans from his thoughts. He had considered a visit to Scotland Yard about the threats. But he knew how inept the Yard was from past experiences with the Watsons and Sherlock. He had tagged along on several adventures and had discovered the truth that Lestrade was the best of a rather amateurish lot. He also knew Lestrade's son, Gordon, a personal friend and rugby chum, who had followed in his father's path at the Yard. But what could Gordon actually do? It was Henry's word against the German's. Scotland Yard could only act when a crime had been perpetrated. Like the Beechleas Grange case Richard and Emma had cracked. Everyone knew what would happen, but the Yard had been powerless to prevent it.

The moral dilemma concerning the use of his formula as an instrument of death froze him. Dr. Nigel Thornton and the Germans had insinuated themselves into his soul.

Emma drummed a finger on Richard's knee, a well-used communication. Neither looked at Henry.

"Henry, when will you tell the university about your engagement?" Mrs. Palmer asked. "Mary wishes to wear her engagement ring at university and not just for special occasions."

He looked up, missing a beat. "I'm sorry, Mrs. Palmer. What did you say?"

"I know the university has that rule about fraternizing with the staff. So, when do you expect to tell them about you and Mary? They see you together every day, don't they? They must know soon. Goodness, the wedding is only three weeks away."

"Soon, I believe. Very soon," Henry said. Mary glanced down at her ring and smiled, but sincerity was not in it.

"Glad to hear that," Emma said. "We ladies are going shopping this Saturday, aren't we? Maybe Selfridges, too."

"We shall have a merry time. Just the three of us," Mary said. "My wedding dress." She gently nudged Henry and went on. "We must talk to Geoffrey and settle the ceremonial details."

"'Tis a pity your Reverend Halsey couldn't be here tonight."

"Geoffrey sends his apologies," said Emma, "but he had to attend a ministerial conference in Cambridge, you know."

"Emma," Mr. Palmer said. "When will you and your Reverend Halsey become betrothed?"

"Father," Mary said, "that's none of your business."

Emma's cheeks were hot.

"I'm sorry, but you and your Reverend Geoffrey..."

"Ha," Richard said. "You'd think with the kind of pulpiting bombast Geoffrey delivers, he'd be unafraid to ask Father for her hand. But..." Richard shrugged.

"It's none of anyone's business," Emma said, sounding prim.

"I say, old chum," said Richard, "I chanced upon Simon and Reggie last week. They're forming a rugby team. It'll be fun... old times and all. Geoffrey and I signed up. Gordon, too."

Henry gazed at the darkness behind Richard. *Had there been movement?* "I don't think so. Considering my work and the wedding preparations..."

Richard's smile vanished like an innocent's hearing a guilty verdict. "You're daft, old man. That's not what you said when we were at the Five Nations in Swansea."

"Huh?"

"Last month. You were rather desperate to get back into the game."

"Wedding preparations, Richard," he said again. *No shadow, just darkness.*

"Wedding preparations? All you have to do is be at the church on time," Richard laughed, twisting the ends of his moustache, trying to understand Henry's sudden change of heart.

"Go ahead, Henry," Mary said, her voice brittle. "You've been working entirely too much recently."

"I better not. I-I might get injured, and then where will I be?"

Emma chimed in, "Oh, piffle, Henry. If you get injured, then I'll make you right, and besides, you're the one who causes the injuries, Wild Welshman," using the nickname he had not heard since his glory days at university.

"No, I mustn't. Too many people are depending on me."

Mary exchanged glances with the twins and received a rush of warmth from Emma.

"I say, old man, are you unwell? You have yet to smile."

Henry pushed away from the table.

"Where are you going, Henry?" Mary asked as he walked toward the window.

"It's nothing." The darkness outside was impenetrable.

"He's in rather dark water, I'd say," Richard said loudly, a challenge, glancing at his sister.

Henry said nothing.

After dinner Mr. Palmer invited the men to join him in the parlor for port while the women cleared the table. Mr. Palmer stopped Dr. John at his stacks of *Strand* magazines.

Henry grabbed Richard's arm. "We must talk."

"About bloody time, old chum. You have Emma and me on tenterhooks. What?"

Henry didn't know where to begin.

"What is it?" Richard said, reading the distress in his friend's face.

"I don't know where to turn. Mary told me that my boss, Dr. Thornton, has been taking the credit for discovering my formula. As his secretary, she hears things and well," Henry swallowed, "she heard him talking about it. Thornton even had the brass to order her to remove my name from my documents and insert his own name. Can you believe she did it? She did it!" Henry's fists bunched at his sides.

"Ghastly, old boy, and I do sympathize. But you know how political the university is."

"But what's more, Thornton ordered me to adapt my formula so it can deliver poison. Poison, mind you."

Richard's eyes hardened. "What kind of poison?"

"Any kind. Belladonna. Strychnine. Poison. But that's not the worst of it." Anguish twisted Henry's mouth.

"Steady on, Henry."

Henry leaned closer. "German agents visited me the other day... about my discovery."

"What? How did they hear about it?"

"They offered me fifty thousand pounds if I'd perfect the formula using... poison." Henry cracked his knuckles. "Nigel wants poison. The Huns want poison."

"Good God. What did—"

"I said no... absolutely no. But two nights ago, another German visited my flat and threatened my life if I didn't cooperate. I showed him the door."

"One for the home team," Richard breathed.

"But he's been following me everywhere and tonight, too...as far as Beeton."

The two friends broke off their conversation when Mr. Palmer and Dr. John joined them for their port.

"Tonight was the first time in days that I've seen him outside the university," Mary whispered to Emma. "But even there, he walks past me and doesn't acknowledge my existence." Her lip quivered.

"He's under pressure with his classes and research," Emma said, hand on her arm. "What a revolution his discovery will be to the medical profession!"

"No. There's something quite wrong. I can feel it. You see how he's behaving."

"I'm sure it's nothing more than overwork and maybe a little pre-wedding jitters we've all heard about," Emma said, breaking off as Mrs. Palmer entered the dining room.

"Perhaps you're correct. I still have doubts."

The ladies busied themselves whisking crumbs into a silver tray until Mrs. Palmer left again carrying dishes. Emma found herself admitting that Henry seemed especially disconnected tonight. *Another woman? Impossible.*

"Emma, do you think he's found another?" Mary asked, as if she had read Emma's thoughts. Her hand went to her hair.

Emma removed her pince-nez. "Tish-pish! Out of the question." Mary sighed, but her concern was etched in the softness of her face.

Mrs. Palmer reentered and led the women to the parlor, abruptly ending their discussion. The rest of the evening was spent chatting and playing

Whist. By ten o'clock, everyone exchanged farewells and Mary halfheartedly agreed with her parents' assessment that the dinner party had been a success.

"Yes, it was a most happy evening," Mr. Palmer declared. "Imagine, Mother. Dr. John H. Watson was here in our home." He trudged up the stairs in the dark carrying several *Strands*. Mary stared through the cracked parlor window at Henry running to his apartment, looking behind him as he went.

CHAPTER 2

"We shall straighten this out today. We must."

As Mary walked to the university, the early rays of sunlight fell across her cold determination. The more she thought about Henry's unacceptable behavior, the angrier she became. She clutched her purse as the school was coming to life.

Mary slowed when she saw a large throng gathered at the front entrance to the science building where she and Henry worked. She watched a coroner's wagon arrive and police controlling the crowd. She quickened her pace. Without warning a uniformed constable snagged her elbow and brought her to an immediate halt.

"Where ya goin' miss? Can't ya see we've sealed off this 'ere buildin'?"

"I work here. I'm Dr. Thornton's—"

"Which is yer name?"

"Mary Palmer."

He checked a small note in his hand. "Mary Palmer? Y'er one of 'em what's on the list what needs a talkin' to in 'ere. Foller me," he grunted, as if escorting her inside was the final indignity in a life of indignities.

"What happened?"

"Ye'll find out soon 'nuff."

He led her to the staff meeting room, where everyone from the department was assembled and noticeably distraught, their grief permeating the air like a sour smell. She glanced around for Henry. He was absent. *Where are Henry and Dr. Thornton?*

Evelyn Moxely came to her, sobbing.

"What's happened?" Mary asked.

"They didn't tell you?" Evelyn slumped into a chair, drawing Mary into another beside her. "It's terrible, terrible."

"What?"

"When I arrived this morning, I turned the lights on, which you know is my custom. All the lights."

"Evelyn, tell me," Mary said, pulling her chair to sit knee-to-knee with her work friend.

"I began to make tea for everyone, and while the water was heating, I went to the lab to turn on the lights and there he was, dead...on the floor! I knew he was dead." She snapped her fingers. "Like that I knew."

Mary forced down her fright. "Who's dead?"

"Dr. Thornton."

"How?" Mary asked, stunned, looking around the table.

"There was no blood, thank God, or I'd have fainted, for certain I would," Evelyn said, twisting her handkerchief.

Mary sagged into her chair.

"I called security and they brought in the police. They're in the lab. We're supposed to wait here to be fingerprinted and questioned."

When the thought came it frightened Mary, a thought so revolting that she dropped her head and shut her eyes tight. Shame flooded in, but the notion and its ugliness grew in parallel. *Did Henry do it?*

Had he become so angry with Nigel Thornton about the alteration of the documents that he killed him? *No, impossible.* Her mind skittered between hating herself for the trust she had placed in him, and hating herself all the more for considering his guilt. When she fumbled for her handkerchief, a man appeared in the doorway.

"I'm Inspector Swayne of Scotland Yard. I'll be with you shortly. Nobody is to leave," he said. Miss Moxely cried again as he strode towards the laboratory. Mary waited. The men sat, hands clenched on the table.

Inspector Swayne returned to the room. "I must question each of you in Dr. Gregory's office." He looked at Mary, his notepad and pencil in his hands. "Your name, miss?"

"Mary Palmer."

"Miss Palmer, what do you do here in the science building?" he asked, scratching his nose with his pencil.

"I'm Dr. Thornton's secretary."

"Would you like a glass of water?"

"No, thank you."

"This way, then," he said. Mary trailed behind him, overhearing Dr. Gregory, the head of the department, say, "Poor girl."

The inspector led her down the familiar corridor, and they walked past Henry's outer door. Seeing his name, it forced her to turn away. Passing Dr. Thornton's door, she smelled something particularly offensive, and unfamiliar, that in a building known for chemical smells of all kinds caused Mary to wrinkle her nose and hold her breath as she followed the inspector. Inside Dr. Gregory's office, Mary exhaled.

"Have a seat, Miss Palmer," the inspector said, motioning with his notepad.

She awaited the questions. They began immediately, comfortable ones at first. Then came, "Miss Palmer, do you know anyone, I repeat, anyone, who might want to kill Dr. Nigel Thornton?"

She looked at her hands.

Inspector Swayne repeated the question.

She said quietly, "I think...so. No...well, possibly."

"Tell me, Miss Palmer."

"I know that," she looked directly at him, "...that Dr. Davies discovered a very important technique...actually a formula. And Dr. Nigel Thornton asked...no, I am sorry, I misspoke." She drew her handkerchief to her nose. "Dr. Thornton insisted I remove Dr. Davies' name from certain documents relating to the discovery."

"Go on."

"He ordered me to insert his own name into those documents."

"Whose name, Miss Palmer?"

"Dr. Thornton's name."

"Why?"

"I should imagine so he would be credited with the discovery and not Dr. Davies," Mary said, gaining confidence.

"When did he order you to do this?"

"A while ago...a number of weeks. I do not remember."

"Does Dr. Davies know about this?"

"Yes."

"How?"

"I told him."

"When?"

"The other day, sir. I couldn't keep it a secret any longer."

"What was Dr. Davies' reaction to your confession?"

"He... well, he got angry at me and he said he would take care of Nigel, or..."

"What do you think he meant by that?"

She looked at her hands. "I don't know, sir. I assumed he would talk to Dr. Thornton."

Inspector Swayne waited. "I'm told Davies was a fine professor."

"Very popular, and he's considered the best we have."

"Do you think others would share your opinion of him, Miss Palmer?"

"I think so. Especially the students."

"But not the staff?"

"I don't know," Mary said and glanced around the office. "I mean yes, of course, the staff held him in high regard."

Inspector Swayne stared at her. "Did you see Dr. Davies again after you confessed the name substitution to him?"

"No. I told him about the matter at the end of work and I went home straightaway."

"Describe your relationship with Dr. Davies."

Mary felt utterly transparent before the inspector. She convinced herself that somehow he knew about their engagement. "What do you mean, sir?"

"Were you friends?"

"We had a wonderful, I should say, good relationship." Mary felt naked and cold—caught in a lie that was not a lie but felt like one.

"'Wonderful,' you said. What did you mean, Miss Palmer?"

"He's one of the heroes of the school. Dr. Davies is brilliant. He's an easy conversationalist...handsome, and...kind. A religious man. I doubt if there is a single woman on the campus who would not consider him wonderful." Mary stopped. She had said quite enough.

Inspector Swayne leaned forward. "Miss Palmer, I must tell you that in my business I meet every type of criminal in London. And the vilest of all are well educated, gifted, even religious, and for all their achievements they are corrupt. Your attraction to Dr. Davies is quite normal, and you share that with many women. But," he said, "many women attracted to this type of man are now dead."

Mary blanched.

"Thank you, Miss Palmer," Swayne said, closing his notebook. "You may go. But I insist you see Officer Plant. He'll want your fingerprints. I'm sure we'll have more questions as the investigation unfolds."

The inspector got up from Dr. Gregory's worn chair and asked to have Evelyn Moxely appear for questioning.

Mary stopped at the door. "Sir?"

"Yes, Miss Palmer?"

"May I ask what killed Dr. Thornton?"

"Some poisonous concoction applied to his skin... all quite preliminary, Miss Palmer. We have the top man from St. Bartholomew's in there now consulting with the medical examiner and our forensics man. Whatever the poison is, it's quite extraordinary."

Mary forced out her words. "May I ask who you think murdered him?"

Swayne allowed a cynical smile. "You already know our suspect. But I warn you, Miss Palmer, do not speak of this to anyone." He waved his notebook. "Go along now. Don't forget, Miss Moxely is next."

Outside, Mary leaned against the doorframe, the thought that Henry committed the murder weakening her. Then she presented herself to Officer Plant for fingerprinting.

Afterward, she looked into the conference room. "Evelyn, the inspector wants you in Dr. Gregory's office." Evelyn looked at Mary as she edged past, expecting further guidance, perhaps another word, an impression. Mary offered nothing. She stood for a moment, unaware that everyone was looking to her for a report.

"Dr. Gregory, I feel quite unwell. May I have your permission to visit my physician and not return for the day?"

Dr. Gregory walked her to the door.

"Of course you may, Miss Palmer. I'm rather shaken myself."

Outside she stepped through the crowd; voices pressed her with questions. She kept her head down, elbowing, aiming herself towards the Diagonal. A large man fell into step beside her.

"Vat's goink on?" His accent was thickly German.

"One of the professors died in the laboratory."

"Who?"

"I'm not allowed to say."

He left her and she walked quickly toward Henry's flat. She ran up the front steps and entered the dim lobby. A stout landlady stood picking her teeth with a pin. She gave Mary a stern look.

"Have you seen Henry Davies?"

"No, 'n' I ain't 'eard 'im neither," she said. "Ya know it ain't proper for a gil ta be seein' a man by 'erself."

The landlady crossed her arms over her bosom, a barrier between Mary and the stairs leading to Henry's flat on the second floor.

"It's urgent I see him right now, madam. Please, may I knock on my fiancé's door to see if he is there?"

"I'll do the knockin'."

She gripped the front of her plain skirt, and Mary watched her struggle up the wooden stairs. She heard several knocks from above and she prayed Henry would respond. The woman reappeared at the top of the stairs, shaking her head.

"May I give you a note for him?"

"Suit yursef. Put it in 'is slot up 'ere."

She watched Mary fumble in her purse for a scrap of paper and a pencil. She found only paper.

"I always have a pencil," Mary said lamely.

"Wait 'ere," said the landlady, waddling into her apartment.

"'Ere, take it," the landlady said, thrusting a short nub of a pencil at her.

Mary knelt on the stair step and wrote her message. She folded the note and slipped it in the pigeonhole bearing Henry's initials. Mary handed the pencil back to the landlady.

"Keep it. Ye needs it more 'an me."

Once outside Mary headed to the Watsons'. The landlady watched Mary cross the street and turn the corner. Then she grabbed the note and took it into her apartment. She pressed it flat against the kitchen table and read it.

"No carryings-on in my building...never." She returned the note to Henry's mail slot.

Mary had climbed the familiar stone steps to Emma Watson's home before, but never so heartsick. She opened the door marked with elegant gold lettering: Watson and Watson, Surgical Practitioners, John H. Watson, MD and Emma A. Watson, MD. The cold brass door pull sent shivers through her. She was thankful for the relative warmth of the entryway, and she looked through the inner glass door to the long stairs that led up to Richard Watson's studio and flat.

Mary entered the overcrowded waiting room and saw every seat uncomfortably filled—five old ladies, a senile gentleman, four mothers and six children were staring at her. She stood clutching her purse to her breast and considered leaving, but where would she go? Certainly not home... leastways not yet.

"Ya won't git ta see 'em docturs tah-day, dearie," one of the mothers said as she reached for her little girl and hoisted her into her lap. "'Ere, 'ave 'er seat. No use, mind."

Mary thanked the woman as the little girl squirmed on her mother's lap.

She closed her eyes and waited. Inspector Swayne's unrelenting gaze filled her mind.

She looked up as the doctor's door opened. A man in smithy's clothes limped out of the office.

Emma scanned the room and said, "Next." But when she saw Mary, her tweezed eyebrows arched in surprise. "Mary!"

One of the old women struggled to help her senile husband to his feet. Emma helped them, then glanced at Mary in silent inquiry.

As Emma passed, she said, "Wait in the dining room. Mrs. Mac is in the kitchen, no doubt."

Mary left the uncomfortable waiting room and walked down the hall towards the rear of the Watson home and into the dining room.

The modestly furnished space was familiar to her. The mahogany table and sideboard shone from years of Mrs. MacIntosh's careful polishing. Lemon fragrance still lingered from Mrs. Mac's morning once-over. The carpet was showing a path of wear from the inner surgery door. A mirror with gold leaf hung above the sideboard. Centered on the opposite wall hung two watercolors Emma's twin Richard had painted when he was ten years old.

By the time she approached the kitchen, she had given in to tears. Mrs.

MacIntosh heard her and came into the room, still drying a plate from the family's breakfast.

The housekeeper exclaimed in her Scottish burr, "Mary Palmer! What's a matter, dear gel?" She wrapped her arms around her and sat her on a chair. She went to the kitchen and returned with a glass of water and a fresh tea towel.

"There, there, gel. Don't say anything if ye don't want." Mary sipped a little water. The housekeeper dragged a chair beside her and pulled Mary towards her, drawing her to her bosom. Like Henry, Mary was an adopted member of the Watson family, and her need seemed grave.

Emma joined them. "Mary...Mrs. Mac. What's wrong?"

Mary looked up from her sodden handkerchief. Emma pulled up a chair. "What happened?"

"I can't find Henry," Mary began, her words running together in fright, "and they'll be hunting for him because they think he killed Dr. Thornton and he was found dead in the lab this morning and I've been to Henry's flat and he's not there and I think I'm going mad!"

"Dear God," Emma said. She looked at Mrs. Mac. "I'll get her something." Emma returned from surgery with a twist of sedating powder.

"Here, Mum, mix this with a small glass of water," Emma said.

Mrs. Mac loved to hear Emma call her "Mum"; it was an endearment the childless housekeeper treasured. She went to prepare the sedative.

"Mary, I want you to drink it all. Have a lie down in the parlor. I'll return as soon as I'm able." She looked into Mary's glossy eyes. "You relax. Richard and I'll need you with a clear head."

Mary nodded. "I'll try." After she swallowed the medicine, Mrs. Mac walked her to the settee.

"We sat here last week," Mary said, " talking to Geoffrey and Emma about our wedding."

Mrs. Mac fussed with Mary's pillow. "Ye rest now. I'll be in the kitchen. God'll make this aright."

Mary drifted into uneasy sleep.

CHAPTER 3

Henry checked the old clock that had once ticked on his parents' bed table when he was a child. He had overslept. It was nine-thirty, three hours later than his customary start for work. Then he remembered his first class had been cancelled. But then his troubling dilemma crowded in; the awful words came to him again from a dark and twisted place.

Poison. Belladonna. Strychnine. Death. Germans. Today.

"Good Lord, today!"

Scrambling up, he got to the washbasin, splashing water onto his face until his sleep-filled brain cleared. He dressed and headed for the kitchen. There he noticed a note on his table that hadn't been there last night. A steady, anonymous hand had printed:

Davies
Today answer yes or dead you be.

That Hun was here, by God! How did he get in? Henry examined the door. It had not been jimmied; no forced entry. He turned the note over and looked for any sign of authorship. *The drug company's agent? No. The thug, then.* He crammed the note in his coat pocket as he left his apartment. He took the stairs two at a time. *I must see Geoffrey.* He glanced at the slapped-together mail cubicle with his name on it and noticed a note in his slot. He left it for later, his mind taken up with the risks facing his formula as a poison.

Henry made his way quickly to Queen Street, hoping a hansom was in queue. He wove his way around women going to market with baskets, a fish porter carrying a tray, and a patterer gathering a crowd eager to learn of a death at the University of London. Henry noticed none of it. He halted at the crossing and hailed a hansom. The horse ambled towards him. Before he had stopped waving, a firm hand grabbed his shoulder. He turned. It was his tormentor.

"Dafies, today vee must haf answer, ja," the German whispered in his ear, keeping a secure hold of Henry's shoulder.

Henry twisted free of the German's grasp and jumped into the hansom. "Metropolitan Tabernacle, Elephant and Castle," he yelled, and immediately he realized the German would have heard his destination. "And hurry!" The German cursed and jumped backward to avoid the hansom's wheel. A flurry of blue telegraph paper fluttered from his pocket to the ground.

While the German searched the carriageway for a cab to give chase, Henry leaned back into his seat and wondered what his friend Reverend Geoffrey Halsey would make of his dilemma. And could he help?

Henry looked behind him before he dashed up the steps to the large, red doors of the church. He made his way into the church office.

"Henry Davies. How are you this fine day?" Thora Mansfield asked.

"Where's Geoffrey?"

"I'm sorry, Henry. He's over at St. Bart's making hospital visits."

"Oh. When do you think he'll return?"

"Don't know. Won't be long. Why not wait in his office?"

Henry waited inside his friend's bookish study, pacing and thumbing through several theological volumes before Reverend Geoffrey Halsey opened his office door. Henry's rugby chum looked grave. He quietly shut the door and stood there, tall and broadshouldered, in clerical black.

"Geoffrey, we must talk."

"I know."

"You know? You've talked to Richard Watson, then?"

"I walked past the university on my way from St. Bart's. I saw police at your building. I spoke with a constable, and he told me there had been a murder. I went inside to give comfort. I didn't see Mary, but I talked with Evelyn Moxely." Geoffrey fixed his eyes on Henry. "Thornton was murdered. You're the suspect, Henry."

"Murdered? But I simply wanted to talk to you about my work." Fear and confusion marked Henry's face. "I'm suspected? Why?"

"A constable inside the building said that they believed one of the professors did it," Geoffrey said.

"But why me?"

"According to Evelyn, your outer office door and the door between your office and Thornton's lab was unlocked."

"So?"

"And the fact that you weren't there this morning."

"But my first class was cancelled!"

Geoffrey studied him. "Evelyn said it was the way Nigel was murdered."

"What way?"

"Some type of salve applied to his skin. Something you and Nigel Thornton were working on together." Geoffrey sat down. Henry collapsed into his chair, speechless.

"He and I weren't working on a formula together."

"Why do the police think you were?"

"He had Mary forge his name on my reports, that's why I'm here, to talk about it, the ethics of it all, the morality...I daresay our names have been linked through her. I don't know." Henry was at the fulcrum between rage and terror.

"Look at me, Henry," Geoffrey said. "Did you murder Thornton?"

Henry's lip curled. "Not you."

"Did you?"

"No, absolutely not."

Geoffrey managed a smile for his rugby mate. "Tell me everything about this ugly affair."

Henry recited his story as fluently and clearly as he would recite the Apostles' Creed in church. He covered all the facts. Geoffrey scribbled notes while Henry purged his mind. Perhaps his recitation would offer Geoffrey an inspired notion that would rescue him from his fears.

Geoffrey didn't interrupt. But he was slack-jawed at the revelations. Henry handed his friend the anonymous note. "Here, give this a look." Geoffrey uncrumpled it, flattening it on his desk. "The Hun caught me before I came here this morning. He shadows me everywhere." Henry's fists were clenched. Geoffrey stared at the note. "Well?" Henry demanded.

Geoffrey glanced up.

Henry shouted, "Well?"

"You must go to the police," he said. "Tell them what you just told me. Nigel...the Germans...the threats...everything. This note, as well."

"Go to the police!" Henry started pacing. He had become an expert at pacing. "You've been with the Watsons and Sherlock Holmes enough to know about the police and the Yard."

"What do you mean?"

"Look, once the police find a convenient explanation, they hang on like a hungry dog with a piece of meat. They don't explore other options because they have too many cases and too few people. You know that, surely you must."

Geoffrey waited, partly because he knew Henry was correct and partly because he didn't know what to say next. He always felt pressure at moments like this, when practical reality collided with what was right.

"Henry, you must go to the police," Geoffrey said again.

"Geoffrey, I came to you to get counsel on the morality of the poison formula. Now you're insinuating I murdered Nigel." Henry leaned across his friend's desk. "Scotland Yard? Trust them? Turn myself over to them?" Henry went to the door, but Geoffrey stopped him.

"Keep your voice down. Now sit."

"I can't."

"All right, then...stand. Let's think."

"What's there to think about? I suppose you..."

"Listen, will you?"

The two friends measured the gulf between them.

"Do you think the German followed you here?"

"I might as well've handed him a map."

Geoffrey ran his palms over his temples.

"See here, Geoffrey," Henry said, calming his nerves a little. "I'm not going to the police. If I do, I'm a dead man. You talk to Richard. He'll tell you I shouldn't go to the police."

"Henry..."

"Talk to Dr. John. Emma. No, talk to Sherlock," Henry said, pushing by Geoffrey. "He'll tell you. They'll all tell you about the police. They'll tell you that I should hide."

Geoffrey went back behind his desk. "Very well, maybe you're right. Perhaps you should hide, at least until Richard and Emma can begin work on your case." Geoffrey knew he would regret his words. After all, he had preached on trusting God, even during the impossible situations in life.

"So, where should I hide?"

"My parents' cottage near Straithairn."

"Straithairn, Scotland?"

"If you're correct, Henry, the German is probably watching outside, right?"

"Straithairn," Henry repeated, indecision lining his face.

Geoffrey opened a narrow cupboard. "Look."

Inside were his vestments, several black suits, shirts, clerical collars, and several black hats. The Reverend Geoffrey Halsey was the most dapper cleric in the city. To him, appearing well presented was a personal responsibility very nearly biblical in its importance.

Removing a black suit on its hanger and smoothing the lapels, Geoffrey said, "Here, we're the same size, a couple of rugby types. Get undressed. We have to get you to Straithairn."

Henry began to undress.

"I'm going to hail a hansom out front," Geoffrey said. He gestured to a shelf of black ties arranged beside handkerchiefs, cufflinks, stays, and braces. "Everything else you need is in there. I'll check if your man's outside. Then I'll secure a cab and meet you in the rear alleyway near the coal scuttle." Henry nodded as he removed black trousers from a hanger. "Give me a few minutes."

Geoffrey walked down the long hall and told Thora that he would be out for several hours. Once outside he scanned the many pedestrians. But he did not see anyone suspicious in appearance—certainly no prototypical German. He flagged a hansom and glanced at the western sky. Heavy clouds were gathering.

The horse trotted down the alleyway, and Henry met the slowing hansom. He climbed in. Geoffrey called, "Victoria Station and hurry."

"Victoria Station? You mean St. Pancras."

"Henry, you can more easily lose the thug at Victoria, and we'll go on to St. Pancras afterward. You know Richard always plans several moves ahead." Geoffrey smiled, trying to lift Henry's spirits. "And by the way, you wear the cloth well."

The hansom rumbled through the streets, shaking and clattering over the bricks as Geoffrey removed his pocket Bible and tore out a blank end paper. He scribbled the address of the Straithairn cottage and drew a map.

"I can't thank you enough, old chap," Henry said, feeling more in control.

"I'll see Emma and Richard. They'll bend themselves to your case. If not, then Sherlock himself. Now listen, you shouldn't contact Mary. Talk to no one. You know they'll be questioning everyone... even the midwife in Wales who delivered you." Geoffrey smiled, but Henry's new-found sense of control evaporated.

It was Geoffrey who saw a trailing cab. "Is that the German?"

"I don't know."

Geoffrey sighted the cab line at Fortnam and Mason's ahead. "We'll find out. Driver. Stop." Henry knew the ploy. The two men alighted from the hansom and scrambled into the first one in queue. "Victoria Station, and fast." Both men twisted in their seats and watched the trailing hansom stop as theirs trotted away.

"Henry, we can't assume—"

"I know. I know."

Nothing more was said until the cab slowed at Victoria Station and the two big men jumped out and became part of the surroundings. They hurried to the south entrance and caught another cab to St. Pancras Station, arriving twenty minutes later.

"Go with God," Geoffrey said with a pat on the back.

Henry jumped out and shouted from the pavement, "Don't forget me." Then he ran into the station.

Geoffrey spent several minutes looking and waiting. Assured they were not followed, he called, "Elephant and Castle." The driver yelled to the chestnut, and she yanked the cab into traffic. "Don't forget me," he muttered under his breath. He thought he would never forget his friend's last words, so deeply were they seared into his brain.

When he returned to Metropolitan Tabernacle, Geoffrey went into his office and sat down to collect his thoughts. He poured himself a glass of water. The church secretary knocked on his door and half entered.

"Sorry to interrupt you, Reverend Halsey. The organist needs to know what hymns to practice for Sunday's service. You know how anxious Mr. Sloan can get."

"I know, Thora. I know. Tell him I'll get to it soon."

"One thing more."

"Yes."

"A man asked for Henry while you were out. He had an accent. I think German. Very thick, it was."

Geoffrey nodded. "Thank you, Thora." He stared at the closed door. *Not good. Not good at all.*

Mycroft Holmes spoke loud enough for people to hear beyond Chief Detective Inspector Gordon Lestrade's tiny office. "You will do what your father did many times with delicate matters I brought to him. As did Gregson. Stop the investigation."

"Unthinkable, Mycroft. You know very well I cannot. I'm duty bound to pursue Henry Davies. It'll be my neck if I fail to..."

"Lestrade, you are sticking your neck into a guillotine if you pursue this any further." Mycroft rubbed a thumb over his watch fob, its ornamentation worn smooth from years of nervous distraction.

Lestrade studied Mycroft's scorching eyes. "Why are you so interested in this formula?"

"Dr. Thornton's formula is a death weapon like no other ever conceived. It has become the highest concern of the State and strikes at the very stability of Europe."

"But—"

"Pay careful attention to me, Lestrade. You'll do well to listen."

Mycroft Holmes, the brother of Sherlock, was a brilliant man with an unparalleled memory, especially for minutiae that often proved vital in international matters. He alone had the freedom to visit the Crown and Whitehall without appointment. His involvement with the Admiralty and Ministry of Defence placed him in the middle of most issues of import facing the Empire.

"We are dealing with an organization completely devoid of compassion and thoroughly ruthless, Machiavellian, end justifies the means, what? The Crown has been watching them for a number of years."

Lestrade sat attentively, sun pouring on his back through his window overlooking the Thames.

"They call themselves *Nachtgeist*. Night Spirits."

"Nachtgeist. I've never—"

"They have dispatched several career assassins to London, and I suspect it has to do with Nigel Thornton's murder." Mycroft wiped dust from Lestrade's desk. "The most wicked of the lot goes by numerous aliases: Herr Stitt, Kreuger, Krajic, Rheinesdorfer, or Heinz. He's a pathological killer. Reviewing our growing dossier on him—all the horrors he's perpetrated—caused one of my men to retch. You recall the Dresden murders, do you not?"

"He was involved?"

"Yes, but I must tell you, Nachtgeist and their prime butcher, this Milos Krajic or whatever he is calling himself today, are instruments of violence. Diabolical. He is one with whom one must not play games. Krajic defected from the Black Hand Society in Serbia because their militancy was too weak for his taste."

"Black Hand Society?"

"They advocate a Greater Serbia. They're led by the head of Serbian military intelligence and seek to end Austria-Hungary's rule over Bosnia-Herzegovina. Mark my words, Lestrade. The Black Hand Society will cause enormous trouble, but even their brand of brutality could not satisfy this Milos Krajic. His devotion to anarchy is savage and tenacious. Krajic—or whatever his name—and his two soulless cohorts, Muellerschon and Hess, are in London at this very moment. They are here to implement a diabolical scheme, and I promise you that unless stopped, it will be executed with cold precision."

Lestrade stared, incredulous.

"Brutes like Krajic are either born or made, but that makes no difference to their victims. Nachtgeist sucks them dry of all humanity. I believe in Krajic's case he's never known guilt or remorse. He's the Son of Satan...just one of many sons. An evil progeny, Lestrade."

"Satanic!"

Mycroft tapped his fingers on the Chief Inspector's desk. "What I have been telling you is highly secret. Perhaps only four or five individuals in our government know what I am about to reveal. Even Number Ten doesn't know the whole of it. I shall tell you these things, not because you are a brilliant inspector, because you are not, but because I may possibly need your help to augment my own efforts at the appropriate time. Are we clear on this?"

Lestrade nodded.

Mycroft stood up, his limbs stiff.

"I've encountered them in Bergen, Norway, and Roosendaal, The Netherlands. Sherlock has connected Colonel Sebastian Moran to them, but without unimpeachable proof. If our agents hadn't been in Schweinemunde, Nachtgeist would have killed Nicholas II before his meeting with Wilhelm II. There are mounting reports that Nachtgeist's influence reaches into our current labor unrest."

Mycroft sat down again. "Their goal is worldwide anarchy. It is their religion. Satanic, most assuredly. They believe Satan will emerge from Hell and rule the world only when anarchy and political turmoil abound. Listen to me, Lestrade," Mycroft said firmly, as if Lestrade needed further inducement to listen. "Their agents are all trained in killing and maiming. They are ritualistic rapists and murderers, offering human sacrifices on our streets or on their cultic altars. And the level of their violence is escalating. Their ceremonies always end in agonizing death—dismemberment, symbolic of their anarchism. Tear apart social concord. Destroy the unity of nations. Fear and terror, perversion and death. These are their liturgy and faith."

"Good heavens, Mycroft—"

"Herr Krajic and others are snakes slithering among us, silent until they strike...unobserved. Nachtgeist...Night Spirits. But we must—" Lestrade's outer door rattled.

"Come in. Come in, I say," Lestrade called out.

Duty Officer Beatty swung the door open and entered the office. Inspector Swayne and Officer Muldowney strode in behind him. Lestrade sensed that Swayne was still smarting, jealous from being removed as primary detective-inspector on the Thornton case only hours earlier. But Lestrade outranked him, and Director Wallace had capitulated to Mycroft's earlier arm-twisting to have Lestrade assigned to the case. Lestrade knew Mycroft wanted someone he could intimidate. He entertained no illusions and was prepared for pressure.

"Yes, Beatty. What-what?"

"Sorry, sir. A woman 'n a child are gravely ill at St. Bart's."

"The place is full of the gravely ill," Lestrade said impatiently.

"We thought ya should know 'at blisters covered their hands or wrists. They got ill and faint. The woman found the nipper when she took out the waste. Called fur help. Then got infected 'n is at hospital, too."

Mycroft Holmes asked, "Pray, what caused it?"

Inspector Swayne shrugged his defiant shoulders.

"You don't know?" Lestrade said. "What's the report from St. Bart's?"

The officer glanced at his notepad. "The constable says a Dr. Hazeltine at hospital said it was some pois'nous ointment or the like. We're guessin' it's that pois'nous salve what blistered Dr. Thornton's arm, sir."

"How did the..." Lestrade stopped himself. "I'll talk with Dr. Hazeltine and the victims, if they survive."

Lestrade stood up and Officer Beatty handed him his notes. As the men walked from the office, Lestrade scanned the notes, then stopped the man in midstride. He thrust the notes under Beatty's nose and pointed. "What's this?"

Beatty pushed the paper away to better read his own scrawl. "Haas, sir. The woman's name, sir."

Mycroft and Lestrade looked at each other.

"Sounds German to me," Lestrade said. "And the little girl?"

"German, too, sir. Eh...Einbecker, sir."

"Mr. Holmes. I've heard what you said, all of it, and you can trust me to do my best. Do you wish to join us?"

Mycroft shook his head. "I have a meeting at the Admiralty."

CHAPTER 4

"Ten, eleven, ah, compartment twelve."

A feeling of security took Henry when he stepped into the unoccupied space. He hoped it would remain empty throughout his journey. He closed the door, took his seat, and gazed at the hubbub on the platform. Rain was pelting the window, scattering the travelers.

He searched for his German tormentor and police. "They can see me in here," he murmured. He unfolded a newspaper to conceal his face. He needed to stay calm. *Besides, the Hun's likely back at Victoria.*

Two police constables moved along the platform. He drew the newspaper to his face, then scanned the platform again. *Where the deuce did they go?* He had to calm himself, think of Mary.

He tented the newspaper over his head and thought about her. She must surely know about the murder by now. Must be out of her mind with grief, and he wasn't there to comfort her. Would his absence cause her to doubt his innocence? Would she actually believe he had killed Nigel? The questions pressed in on him, and he sank into the train seat. "Mary would never believe I murdered Nigel," he said out loud.

A chill shuddered through him. *Watch what you say.*

He was alone, and just the thought of it sent goose bumps welting across his flesh. Since he was left alone in London as a young boy, he deplored the word *alone,* but he fretted all the more over the reality. Eight years old then, now twenty years later, and still the hollowness deep inside had not changed but lain dormant, suppressed by a first happiness thanks to Mary and the Watsons. He felt the fearful word growing inside now, pushing aside all else. It was another tormentor, dark and menacing. Loneliness was what he feared most in life. More than pain. More than threats. More than a German killer.

When the compartment door jerked open, he jumped, crushing the newspaper he was using as a shield. A thick-chested, big man carrying a valise and a dripping umbrella, and dressed in Harris tweeds, entered the compartment. He had to tilt his head to enter. Henry watched him. He was not the one who had threatened him. Nevertheless, he remained guarded as the stranger stowed his bag on the shelf above the seat.

"Much rainink. I like ven it raints," the stranger said. Henry stared out the window.

"Yes, rain. Quite so."

The rain was battering the window so hard it sounded like tiny beads hitting the glass. The driving downpour slashed at the window glass. Lightning sparked in the distance, causing buildings, a steeple, and trees to sharply silhouette against the gray landscape. Thunder merged with the sound of carriage couplings. The train clanked forward.

"Priest? Vhat um, ah, religion? Vhat ah, church?"

Surprised, Henry shifted his hand to Geoffrey's clerical collar clamped around his neck. "Oh yes, of course. Metropolitan Tabernacle... at Elephant and Castle in London."

"Iz dat Protestant?"

Henry studied the man's rather brutal features, features seemingly borne of conflict, features that would be easily remembered—especially several scars on his chin, obvious relics from past struggles. There was a controlled savagery to the man. As Henry touched his collar, the word *evil* came to mind.

"Oh yes, Protestant. Yes, quite Protestant."

"Ah goot. Vhere are you goink?" He had an air of having a joke all to himself.

"Straithairn."

"Me, same."

How improbable that two people would be going to such a remote place on the same train, in the same carriage, occupying the same compartment. Henry might as well have handed him the map to Geoffrey's cottage. He was furious with himself. He groped in his pocket to verify the map was still there. *Richard and Emma would have been smarter.* He glanced at the stranger and found him staring back from under bushy brows.

"You feel goot?" He rose and pulled down his valise. Henry measured the man. He was muscular and tall, perhaps thirty-five years old. His eyes stayed on Henry's as his hand searched for something in the valise. Henry's muscles tightened around his vulnerability.

"You feel ah, vell? Healthy, ja?"

The stranger removed a book from his valise. Henry relaxed a fraction. "I'm very well, thank you. I've had a difficult morning." The stranger did not respond. He opened his book and began thumbing through its pages. Was it German? No. Polish or Hungarian. "Sir, what language are you reading?"

"Hunkarian. My um, parents at home spoke Hunkarian. I learnt from zem. I vas four vhen ve moofed to Germany...Bremen."

"Oh, I see," Henry said, forcing himself to smile into the unpleasant eyes.

Just then a man rapped on the compartment door glass. The stranger recognized him, and they disappeared into the passageway speaking German.

"My word, there's more than one German on this train." He wiped away a small patch in the window condensation. Black shapes in the distance were illuminated by lightning flashes. "Mary," he said.

The train conductor opened the compartment door.

"Sorry, Vicar. Your ticket."

Henry fumbled in his pockets and produced the ticket for the conductor, who punched it and left. After a few minutes Henry was thirsty. He walked towards the dining carriage and jumped when the conductor stepped into his path from another compartment.

"Is the dining carriage in this direction?" The conductor nodded and motioned with his ticket book. Henry drew in a deep breath and entered. He could see half of the occupants from where he stood in the narrow walkway near the kitchen. More of the room came into his view as he advanced. Then he heard boisterous laughter and a few German words he recognized. He saw the Hungarian with two other men enjoying conversation at the corner table.

"Good day, Vicar," a waiter said. "May I serve you?"

"Whittard's Earl Grey, please. I'll take it back to my compartment."

"Whittard's? This ain't the Ritz, Vicar. Plain black do ya?"

"Of course. Thank you."

Henry's attention drifted to a young couple having words, a frail red-haired Scot in a kilt, two men reading newspapers, and then to the three men looking at him—the Hungarian was half-turned in his chair, motioning for Henry to join them.

"Thank you, sir. I'll be taking my tea back to the compartment."

The stranger looked disappointed. "Dhese are mine friends, Herr Muellerschon unt Herr Hess. My name is Krajic. Your name?"

Henry's mind flailed wildly. "Henry Palmer. Henry Palmer of the Metropolitan Tabernacle." Immediately Henry noted too late how unprepared he was for subterfuge. He was sure his lie was completely transparent. The waiter rescued him with his hot tea.

"Vaiter. Add to our bill," Krajic insisted.

"Thank you, sir. You are too kind," Henry said, willing a smile.

"Referent Palmer. Iz room mit us," Krajic said, pushing a chair towards Henry.

"No, thank you. I must meditate. You will excuse me?"

"Of course, referent. You meditate." Krajic's mouth twisted into a half smile.

Henry returned through the passageway, hearing the men laughing behind him. *I'm an utter fool. Inexcusable. They saw through me like glass.* A woman passed, pressing her child to her side as he maneuvered around them with his tea sloshing.

In the compartment he tested his steaming tea and winced. He liked his tea warm, but this very nearly scalded his tongue. He put it on the tilt-up shelf below the window and closed his eyes. He thought of Mary. But holding her image was impossible; he could hardly frame a thought. Instead, Krajic's formidable bulk occupied the compartment space, crowding Henry to near suffocation. He hoped the Hungarian would join his two friends in their compartment or at least remain in the dining carriage and give him peace. He lifted the steaming tea to his mouth, blew, and then sipped again. In time, he drained his cup and leaned back, drowsy.

Shadows stretched like fingers across the parlor carpet, trailing over Dr. John's favorite chair and hassock. They moved over Mary as she lay on the settee. Emma and her father had checked on her periodically, and Mrs. MacIntosh had placed an afghan over her, one she had recently knitted for Emma.

The old housekeeper sat beside her, apron screwed up in her fingers. She was praying aloud for Mary and Henry when Emma entered the parlor. Her hands went to the housekeeper's shoulders.

"Your prayers availeth much," Emma said. "It's half five."

Mrs. MacIntosh got up, pressing at her knees. "Your prayers, too."

"God alone knows what we need, but I don't have a particle of knowledge yet. I'll wake her."

Mrs. Mac reached down and touched Mary's arm. "I'll be attendin' ta dinner. Do ye think yur Geoffrey'll be with us?"

Emma nodded, knowing that her suitor, Reverend Geoffrey Halsey, always dined with them when he could. "I'm afraid tonight's dinner won't be the usual happy affair."

She shifted her chair closer to the settee and sat for a quiet moment. Then Emma patted Mary's face and nudged her.

"Cooee, cooee, Mary. It's Emma. Wake up, Mary." Again Emma patted Mary's cheeks. Mary moaned.

"Mary, dear, it's me—Emma. Good. Yes, open your eyes. See, it's me."

Mary blinked. She recognized Emma and soon heard the china chinkling as Mrs. Mac approached with a cup of tea. Emma helped Mary sit up with her legs still stretched on the settee, reassuring her that she was at the Watsons'.

"Here, have a sip." Mary took some tea and smoothed the afghan on her lap. "Mum, may I trouble you for some tea?" Mrs. Mac made for the kitchen and returned with Emma's tea and honey, as she had liked it since childhood.

"Any news?" Mary asked, getting her senses about her.

"Nothing yet. I want you to relax, and then you can tell me everything."

The parlor door opened and the untidy figure of Richard Watson stepped into the room, dripping rain from his nose and goatee. He shook the rain off his macintosh like a great wet dog. Emma watched him.

"How many times must Mum and I tell you to dry in the vestibule? Take your mac and brolly out of here." Emma wiped rain droplets from her pince-nez.

"Mary, what a pleasant surprise," Richard said, ignoring his sister. "Beastly... a nor'easter, this one." He was nearly soaked to the skin, his goatee still dripping. He stared at the women. "Something's wrong. What?" Mary started to cry, pushing the tea cup aside, looking for her handkerchief.

"Dr. Thornton was found murdered in the lab, and Mary says Henry's suspected."

"Un-bloody-believable!" Richard exclaimed, swiping rain from his nose.

Mary began to weep in earnest. Richard dragged a second chair to the settee and slumped into it. The twins looked at each other, Richard shocked, Emma troubled.

As the door bell chimed, Richard said, "Murdered? How? And Henry's suspected? Impossible. What makes them think it was Henry?"

"Have you no eyes, Richard? Give Mary time."

"Reverend Halsey to see you, Emma," Mrs. Mac announced.

Richard waved his rugby chum into the room. "Geoffrey, we have a problem."

"Mary," Geoffrey said. "Thank God you're here. I saw Henry this morning."

Mary stared, her eyes red and swollen. "You've seen Henry! Where? How is he?"

"He was in my office this morning when I returned from my pastoral visits to St. Bart's. He wanted to talk over the morality of using his discovery to poison people."

"Poison," Mary exclaimed.

"Henry's innocent. I'm convinced of that."

"Well, I daresay, old man," Richard said. "You should know...you do guilt for a living."

"You're so artless, Richard," Emma said.

"After I had finished my visits, I walked across the Diagonal and saw the commotion in front of your building. I looked for you and Henry, then sought to help if anyone required counsel. Your people were huddled in a room waiting for interrogations. I talked with everyone, and Dr. Gregory said there was nothing for me to do. Then Evelyn Moxely claimed that Henry was the suspect. She was crying and very bitter about it. She waved me away. I left her wailing in a right state. I spoke with a constable and he confirmed Evelyn's news. I decided to return to church and rearrange my schedule before beginning my search for him. When I entered the church, Thora told me he was waiting in my office. Can you believe it? He told me everything. I believe he truly didn't know of the murder. I assume you know what he discovered."

"Yes, what else do you have?" Richard asked.

"Henry told me that Dr. Thornton had been hounding him to adapt his formula to poison people. That was what brought him to my office...the morality of it. Sometime yesterday, Thornton insisted he research poison." Geoffrey got up. "He told me that a few days ago a man and woman— Germans, representing a German chemical company—offered him fifty thousand pounds for the formula adapted to use poison. Another German threatened to kill him if he didn't accept their offer."

Mary's hands went to her mouth. "Dear God, Henry." Emma pulled Mary's legs off the settee and sat next to her, holding her in her arms. Mary felt Emma's hands on hers and clung to them. "Go on, Geoffrey," Emma said.

"Well, apparently last night, on the way to the dinner party, the German followed him. But Henry gave him the slip. Henry's classes were cancelled this morning, so he slept in."

Mary gasped, "I forgot."

"He discovered this on his table this morning," Geoffrey said, producing the crumpled scrap of paper. Richard grabbed it. "His door had been locked. He was quite certain of that. Goodness knows how someone got in."

After examining the note, Richard handed it to Emma. "Frightful. Bloody frightful, I say."

The two ladies read the note and were stunned. Mary got unsteadily to her feet. Emma guided her back to the settee.

"When Henry left his apartment to visit me at church, the German found him and threatened him again, and—"

Mrs. Mac entered the room. "Mycroft Holmes is here to see you."

Emma said, "Show him in, Mum." Everyone glanced at each other in surprise.

Mycroft Holmes strode into the parlor, brushing rain from his coat. He was quickly introduced to Mary Palmer.

"To the point, Miss Palmer. Do you know where Davies is? Does anyone know?"

"I'm sorry, Mr. Holmes, I don't know," Mary admitted, "but Reverend Halsey might."

"Well?"

"He's on a train to my parents' cottage in Straithairn."

"Straithairn!" Richard shouted. "Good God in heaven—"

Mycroft's hand came up, silencing him. "Davies is in trouble, and it probably involves a group of German cutthroats called Nachtgeist. Beyond that I will say nothing. When did he depart for Straithairn?"

"Late morning," Geoffrey said. "From St. Pancras."

"Is that all you can tell me?"

"He's wearing my black suit and clerical collar...a disguise."

"Disguise, my foot! You'll have to do better than that to slip past those fiends. Furthermore, I was with Lestrade a while ago, discussing the Thornton murder, when we learned that a child and a woman had been infected by a mysterious concoction this morning. They're at St. Bartholomew's. These monsters have already begun their reign of terror." His eyes drilled into Richard and Emma. "I do not want you two getting involved in this. For what it's worth, even my brother fears this lot. I should not have to say any more to you. Now, Miss Palmer, do you know of any reason why Davies might want to kill Dr. Thornton?"

Mary started to cry again. Mycroft tapped his foot impatiently and fiddled with his watch fob. Emma tried to help Mary compose herself. "No, she has no idea, Mycroft," Emma said.

"Reverend Halsey, what train did he take and where is he going exactly?"

"I don't know which train or the connections." Geoffrey searched for a pencil in his pocket, then scribbled the address of his parents' cottage in Straithairn. He did not see the flush of anger building under Richard's collar. "Here, Mr. Holmes."

Mycroft read the address. "I'll have a man board the train up-line to protect Davies. Whichever man finds him will bring him back. He thinks he is out of danger, but he's never seen such a loathsome tribe. You will excuse me." Mycroft withdrew to the vestibule. It was as he was leaving that he turned at the door and stabbed his finger at Richard and Emma. "You two stay out of this." The front door closed behind him.

As soon as the door closed, Richard jumped to his feet and grabbed Geoffrey by his well-pressed lapels and brought him out of his chair. "Richard!" Emma screamed.

"I have a mind to beat you senseless," Richard yelled, pushing Geoffrey back and against the wall, dislodging one of Richard's childhood paintings from its hook. Its glass shattered at their feet.

"You're a blithering idiot! You helped him escape!" he yelled into Geoffrey's face.

"Richard. Stop." Emma said, a hand on his arm.

Dr. John appeared in the parlor. "What on earth are you two fighting about?" He pulled the two men apart.

"Just boys, father. Go back to surgery."

Dr. John stood between them, looking from one to the other. "I'll have no truck with fighting in this house. Do you understand me?"

Richard went back to his seat.

Geoffrey straightened his coat and clerical collar. "Yes sir, I'm sorry. Very sorry, indeed."

"I have elder Mrs. Townsend in there," Dr. John went on, "and you know how excitable she is. She's working herself up to a stroke, thanks to you two." Dr. John left in disgust and went back to surgery.

Geoffrey looked at Richard. "What did I do?"

"You let him get away. You're a bloody fool, Geoff."

"Richard," Emma snapped. "Talk calmly."

"Henry's beyond our control now. Don't you see it?"

"He told me that if he turned himself over to the police, he was as good as dead."

"Geoff, you don't send the poor devil to a place like Straithairn alone. He doesn't know anything about it, nothing. And those Huns are up there looking for him most likely." Richard bit his lip. "You should've never allowed Henry out of your sight until we could get to the truth. If Mycroft's correct, you've led this Christian into the lion's den."

"I know the Germans were following him," Geoffrey admitted. "When I returned to church after St. Pancras, Thora told me a man with a German accent had been there looking for Henry just minutes after we left."

Richard stared incredulously.

"Enough," Emma demanded, nodding towards Mary, who trembled in her arms.

Richard excused himself and went to the kitchen. Several minutes later he returned carrying tea in a shimmering silver pot. "I'm sorry, Mary, we'll make things right. Don't fear."

Mary stared at the teapot.

"Is that all the information we have at the moment?" Emma asked, an arm around Mary.

"That's all," said Geoffrey.

Emma watched her brother, waiting for the next outburst.

"I shall go after him," Geoffrey said.

"No, you won't. Give me the address in Straithairn."

"I can't allow you to go, Richard. It's my fault."

"The address."

"Geoffrey, allow Richard to get Henry," Emma said. "He has more experience. Please."

"I know you did what you thought was best, Geoff. You knew he had to hide. You were right... absolutely correct. Your only mistake was helping him leave London for Straithairn. He doesn't know the place. He's at a complete disadvantage. Do you see it?" Richard extended his arm. "Now, the address."

"Geoffrey," Emma pleaded.

He relented and began writing.

"By the way, old man, I'm sorry. Henry's better than any brother, and if it were you in his stead, I'd be feeling the same." Richard stood up and playfully punched Geoffrey in the shoulder. It spoke volumes about Richard's apology. Geoffrey smiled and handed over the directions. "Henry'll need extra clothes. I better take my large valise."

"Richard," Mary said, her throat constricted. "Tell Henry I love him."

"Don't you worry." With that Richard hurried up the stairs to his studio and apartment.

"Mary," Emma said, "we should get you home and explain all this to your parents."

Mary was still unsteady and had to be aided with her coat. They walked to the vestibule and grabbed umbrellas while Geoffrey went outside to hail a cab. The rain was relentless. Far-off thunder rumbled as a cab appeared from the darkness. The horse clopped in the dung puddles and splashed Geoffrey's expensive trousers. The ladies hurried from the doorway. He handed each one into the cab and the three departed.

When Mrs. Mac entered the parlor to announce dinner, she found it empty. She heard the muffled hooves outside and hurried to the door in time to see Geoffrey and the ladies driving away. She looked out into the sheets of rain and saw the carriage disappear. When Richard thumped down the stairs carrying his valise, she jumped.

"Tell father I'm going to get Henry before Mycroft finds him… Straithairn, near Inverness." He pulled the door open and ducked out into the torrent.

"Straithairn." Mrs. Mac said. Several moments later, she thought she spied him at the crossing when lightning crackled in a single bright burst. Then all was darkness, and she stood for a moment, watching. "Those twins'll be the death o' me."

CHAPTER 5

Henry opened his eyes to a tapping on the compartment door and saw an anxious man gesturing. He sat up and nodded. The man closed the door behind him and timidly took the seat facing Henry. His thick white hair and walrus moustache reminded Henry of a caricature he had seen in *Punch*. Just as the man started to speak, Krajic stepped into the compartment.

"Excuse me, Vicar. Name is August Porter." He wiped his hand across his pink forehead, now damp with rain and perspiration.

"I am Reverend Henry Palmer," Henry said, ignoring Krajic. "How may I help you, Mr. Porter?"

Mr. Porter gave a concerned glance towards Krajic. "I saw you, a man of the cloth, and I said to myself, 'August, maybe this vicar can help you with your problems,' I said. I haven't been to church for many years and, well... oh, I'm sorry to bother you." He eyed Krajic again. "I would like to talk with you. Perhaps we could do so in the dining carriage. Have you eaten?"

"No, I haven't."

Mr. Porter found his pocket watch and asked, "Why not, say, around..."

"Iz fery bizzy," Krajic interrupted. "I vas yust dhere...an hour maybe goot."

"Yes, an hour, say eight o'clock, Reverend Palmer. It'll be my pleasure to treat you to dinner."

Henry was quick to accept. He was ravenous and didn't have enough money for dinner plus a cab to the Halseys' cottage. "Thank you, sir. I would be delighted."

Mr. Porter nodded, bid Mr. Krajic goodbye, and left the compartment.

"You should haf eat mit uz. Vee had goot time."

"I'm sorry. I wanted time to think and drink my tea."

"Uf course. You are referent. You t'ink big t'oughts. Heaven. Hell. Meditation. Ja?"

"I need to rest."

"I t'ink I'll take a valk. You rest unt t'ink," Krajic said, disappearing through the sliding door.

Henry was relieved to be alone once more. Krajic's sarcasm and the sharp edge to his voice unsettled him.

"Misery is worst at night," he said, to the gentle rocking of the train.

A terrible yearning swept over him, overlaying his loneliness. For an instant he could smell Mary's perfume. He could feel her close to him, her heart beating, their breath mingling—their oneness. The tender thoughts were like a balm on his frayed nerves, and soon he was asleep.

A quarter hour later a voice broke in upon him.

"Father. Please, Father," the voice implored.

Henry awoke with a start to find the train conductor standing beside him.

"Please, Father. Or is it Vicar?"

"Huh?" Henry pushed away sleep. "Sorry. I'm Reverend Palmer."

"Reverend, sir. There's been a most unfortunate...ah, incident," the man said, pressing his cap to his chest.

"Yes?"

"There's been an accident. Actually, there's been a murder. Please, would you follow me?"

"Murder! You said, murder?"

"Please lower your voice. Yes, two carriages down. The police will be meeting the train at the next stop. Must investigate, you know." He stepped back towards the open compartment door and saw confusion on Henry's face. "My boss is a religious man and wants you to perform the last rites or whatever you do before the body is removed."

Henry slowly stood up and wondered what he should do and say by way of ritual. Another murder unnerved him. He straightened his clothes, and the two men stepped into the passageway and walked grimly to the carriage. Several conductors stood guarding a center compartment as people peered down the passageway, quiet and sullen. Henry pondered what he should say and worried that his sham might be discovered. What would Geoffrey do? Then he remembered his brother's funeral service. But it was no use. His mind was black as slate.

When they reached the gathering of conductors, the man said, "This is Reverend...what?"

"Reverend Palmer," Henry said solemnly.

The senior conductor stepped forward. "I'm Catholic, but I figures, you'll do." He nodded towards the closed door. "A man's been murdered in 'ere. Shot. 'Tain't nice to look at. Blood all over. A right mess."

"Terrible," Henry murmured. "Who is he?"

"A Mr. Symonds. 'Twas on his way to Straithairn...boarded back a ways at Newton. Must be an official er somethin' fer us ta stop like 'at for 'im." The train shuddered to a halt. The men braced themselves against the wall. Pointing to the door, the senior conductor said, "Please, Reverend. Make 'im right with God." Sliding the door open, the conductor cautioned, "The blood...I'm afraid it's a sight, sir." Henry nodded.

He moved inside and the conductor closed the door. Henry was thankful the men had tacked a sheet across the door glass for privacy. He saw the splattered coagulating blood and bone fragments on the wall, seat, and a boggy puddle on the floor. He tried not to gag. Although he was accustomed to cadavers in medical college, this was very different. The corpse was a victim of hate—a fellow human being who had boarded the train alive. He was sprawled face down on the seat, one knee on the floor.

"God have mercy on Mr. Symonds." He nudged the man's shoulder. Henry suddenly stepped backward. "Mr. Porter!" he gasped. He had been shot in the neck at close range. *Was Porter his real name, or Symonds? What had been troubling this old soul?*

Henry checked the covered window, bowed his head, and prayed. He looked at the body for a few seconds more before he opened the door.

Bunched in the corridor were several constables and three conductors. Henry emerged, head bowed, and nodded.

"T'ank ye, Vicar," a ruddy-faced constable muttered as he inserted himself between Henry and the doorway, making the sign of the cross as he passed. "Charles? Here with ye," he called to the second constable who edged beside Henry.

"Sweet sufferin' Jesus," the constable gasped. He glanced at Henry and closed the door.

"Is there anything more I can do?" Henry asked, as he felt his knees weaken.

"I dun't think so," the head conductor said, looking around, not actually expecting anyone to speak.

"When will we be getting to Straithairn?"

"Depends. If'n we leave now, mebbe round midnight." The conductor pointed to the compartment and shrugged his shoulders. "Must wait for 'em coppers in 'ere, 'n' we gotta clean the mess."

On his trip back to his compartment, Henry answered inquiries from travelers poking into the passageway as he passed. "A man was murdered. Wretched business," he repeated as he edged past each inquiring face.

He stumbled into his compartment.

"Ah, Referent Palmer," greeted Krajic.

He sank into his seat. He felt a little sick.

"You lookink sick," Krajic said.

"The man who was in here earlier was murdered."

"Too bad," he said, scratching his scarred chin, as if it were an old tragedy, too commonplace to arouse emotion anymore.

Henry noticed the rain had stopped. His worries returned, plucking at him, frightening him. He didn't care if Krajic was staring at him.

An hour later, one of the constables appeared at the door, slid it open, and said, "There's been a murder on the train. I must ask ye some questions."

Krajic answered the questions calmly and asserted he was in the dining car with his two friends. Henry admired Krajic's composure all the more against his own nervousness. Ending a thorough interrogation of both of them, the constable snapped his notebook closed and departed. Henry wondered what could possibly happen next. They sat mute, Krajic reading, Henry staring into the darkness.

The carriage jolted forward some time later, and Krajic looked at his pocket watch. "Ah. Ve're movink. Goink ta be fery late."

Henry nodded, watching the black countryside moving past the wet window. The stress of his escape, the dead man, all closed in on him. A searing headache attacked him, and he massaged his temples. Visions of the Halseys' cottage and a bed, a sweet, comfortable bed, and a hot bath helped to lift his fragile spirits.

At twelve fifty-seven, the train chugged into Straithairn Station. Krajic and Henry walked down the passageway and joined a queue of people bunched at the exits.

The train shuddered and hissed to a stop. Porters and conductors jumped onto the platform. Henry stepped down and walked towards the station.

"Referent Palmer. I git bags unt take you to yur place."

Henry hesitated. "Thank you, sir. That will not be necessary. I must wait for a telegram," he lied, and was pleased with how quickly he conjured up an excuse.

"Are you sure?"

"Thank you, sir. Have a pleasant stay in Straithairn."

"I vill, danke. I vill," Krajic said.

Henry turned away, the station noise adding to his headache.

He walked into the station and took a position near a window, the better to observe Krajic and his two friends arrange for the last cab. He waited several minutes before he walked outside and found a driver and dogcart—or what passed as a dogcart—rather more like a child's wagon a Shetland once pulled for amusement a generation ago. He climbed in and sat down on a damp clapboard seat. He gave the address to the driver and was pleased the scruffy man knew of the Halseys' cottage.

After a quarter hour of rough road, then a rutted farm path, Henry spied two snug cottages silhouetted in moonlight. The three glowing windows of the smaller one sent him a warm invitation. It must be the Thompsons' place.

Geoffrey had explained that the Thompsons were old friends of the Halseys and they tended the grounds during their extended absences. Henry paid the driver and trudged towards the Thompsons' cottage, his feet discovering every muddy patch between the road and their welcoming front door.

Henry knocked. He filled his lungs with the bracing, unpolluted highland air, which contained just a hint of peat burning. Far from London, he relished the rightness about it. He rallied against his exhaustion and removed Geoffrey's tight clerical collar. As he looked over the stony façade, he heard the door creak open, and a red-cheeked old Scot in a kilt stood before him saying Henry's name. A robust woman appeared behind him. Their smiles were broad, and the man's face shone with a warm grace.

"Thompsons?"

"Aye. Ye must be tired 'n needin' a bed, professor," Mr. Thompson said kindly. He lifted his hand and jangled the keys he was holding.

"How did you know I was coming?"

"Got a wee telegram from Geoffrey. Told us ta make ye comfortable 'n look after ye," the old man said with a nod at his wife. "We're good at lookin' after the Halseys' friends." He threw on his coat that smelled of old sweat and peatsmoke and motioned towards the Halsey cottage. "This way."

Mrs. Thompson inquired, "What time'll ye be needin' breakfast?"

"I don't know, madam. I feel I could sleep for two days."

"Nary ye mind, then. Go on. Ye can have it any time."

The two men tromped through the muck to the cottage. Mr. Thompson fumbled with the keys, wiped his muddy shoes on the scraper, and opened the door. A fine fire was dancing in the hearth. The man groped for a match tin, and Henry waited. Soon the room was washed in a flickering glow from several spirit lamps and the crackling flames in the grate.

"Been stokin' the fire all night fur ye."

Henry looked around the room—very rustic, with heads of animals and preserved quail on the wing and other birds. Glass eyes caught the firelight. "I didn't know the Halseys were gamers."

"Aye. Every season they're 'ere. But not like 'em grandees that come with 'em. Halseys are good eggs." The man shuffled into the kitchen and pointed to the cast-iron grate with a glowing peat fire. "Ye'll have plenty o' hot water. Yer keys. Round 'ere folks don't lock doors. But ye Londoners fancy lockin' doors."

Henry walked him to the open door. "Thanks again, Mr. Thompson."

"Ye sleep good, lad," the old man said. "See ye in the marnin'."

Henry grasped the oak door, pleased with the strength of it. He noticed the thick walls, and after closer inspection, he picked at the exposed peat compacted between the stones. "Peat and earth—of course—double walls, solid." Henry swung the door and took pleasure in the firm thump of it closing and the metal clack-chick of its lock.

"Ye sleep good, lad," Mr. Thompson shouted from his threshold.

I will sleep very well. Very well indeed.

For the first time he began to relax, to feel safe. When an earthy sweetness touched his nostrils, he glanced up. "Ah, fresh thatching."

He went through the cottage and located the bedroom and a porcelain bathtub in a small room. He prepared his bath and later slid into bed, shivered, then curled up under the blankets. "Finally safe," he said into the darkness. He was asleep within moments.

CHAPTER 6

Early sunlight flooded through Emma's lace curtains. She sat in her chintz-covered chair praying, one of her daily rituals acquired from Mrs. MacIntosh. Her prayer time was especially long; she agonized over Henry and was thankful her father would take her patients for the day. It would be fatiguing for him, but she was determined to begin her investigation straightaway. Sherlock's instructions about delays came to her afresh as she closed her Bible and glanced at her clock. "The first forty-eight hours are singularly important," Emma quoted on her way to breakfast, "after which the difficulty of arriving at a solution will climb directly proportional to the interval of delay."

Sherlock had often been consulted after that vital initial period, after the police had tramped about the crime scene, often obliterating precious clues. Emma knew she must begin immediately and hoped the police had not had sufficient time to compromise the crime scene. Just one small piece overlooked could make the difference.

"Good marnin', dear," Mrs. Mac said. "My, but yer lookin' pretty. 'At's the blouse Geoffrey bought ya?" Emma studied her white-on-white embroidered bodice and ran her fingertips over the intricately sewn threads. It felt expensive and it was. She fussed with the high lace collar that accentuated her graceful neck.

"It's the one."

"Good morning, Emma," her father said over the top of his newspaper.

"Thank you for taking my patients today."

"Before ye two start a-talkin', we've got eggs, scones, ham, kidneys, and toast. Tea and coffee, a'course."

"I believe toast and tea will do quite nicely. Thank you, Mum."

Dr. John lowered the paper and peered over his spectacles. "Emma, you know I can't take all your patients for weeks like I did when you and your brother handled the Stimpson case."

"It's Henry, after all, and..."

"Yes, the dear boy. We must help, but don't dawdle."

"I am sure I..."

"I'm not getting younger."

"I'll make my rounds at St. Bart's. That'll give you a spot of relief. I shan't dawdle, Father." Her fingers traced over her embroidered bodice.

"Check on Mr. Walters. Consumption, you know. Then I'll be free to see our patients all day." He emphasized "our patients" and cracked a smile.

Mrs. Mac delivered Emma's breakfast and joined them at table.

"Oh my," Dr. John gasped. "Here's the item about Thornton's death. They're calling it murder."

Spreading orange marmalade onto her toast, Emma said, "Read it, Father."

"Found in the laboratory by a Miss Evelyn Moxely. Do you know this Evelyn Moxely?"

Emma pressed the serviette to her lips, preparing to reply, but her father had moved on.

"Says Albert Swayne was the investigator on the scene...Scotland Yard has put Lestrade—my word, Gordon Lestrade—on the case. Haven't seen him in months. Wonder how his father is getting on. Says here Thornton is thought to have died by the application of some type of purple, odiferous, poison salve applied to the underside of his wrist." He lowered the paper. "You don't suppose he applied it to himself as an experiment, do you?"

"Possibly. An experiment gone awry."

Mrs. Mac's mouth pressed into a crease. "This ain't fit talk for the table. I'm gettin' right sick."

"Says here that Henry Davies, Ph.D., of twenty-eight years, is the only suspect and has not been located. They believe he is a fugitive." He dropped the newspaper onto the table. "You and Richard must resolve this lamentable matter."

"Richard should be with Henry presently." Emma finished her toast and stood up. "I'll check Mr. Walters' file and be on my way."

Emma alighted from the hansom in front of the science building and entered the gloomy corridor. Her shoe heels clacked along the marble floor. She passed a series of doors: First was Professor Crane's. Next was Professor Davies'. Then Professor Thornton's office. A constable stood guard and nodded as she went to Dr. Gregory's office door. Inside she saw a pasty little woman dressed in black. For a moment, the woman's mourning attire surprised Emma, then she realized the appropriateness of it.

"Yes?" The woman spoke, as if Emma's presence was that of a child. Her eyes remained focused on the papers on her desk. "Dr. Gregory isn't seeing anyone this morning."

"I am Dr. Emma Watson and I—"

"Oh, gracious me! A doctor." The woman shot to her feet. "Would you be kind enough to wait here? I shall tell Dr. Gregory."

"Thank you, Miss...?"

"Please forgive me. I'm Miss Celia Norris. We're still very shaken by our tragedy."

"I can assuredly sympathize with you. It's appalling."

A few moments later the woman opened the door and ushered Emma inside the professor's book-lined office. Dr. Gregory rose and greeted her. She guessed the man had acquired four or five stone since she had last seen him. He was stooped over, as if his skeleton were buckling under the unaccustomed weight. His shoulders were bowed. Perhaps his chest pained him. His white hair was a tousled crest. As he extended his hand to greet her, she detected tremors of early-onset Parkinson's. She examined his pallid face and was troubled by what she saw. He appeared exhausted, alarmingly so. But his eyes were bright.

"My dear Dr. Watson. How long has it been?" He offered Emma a seat.

"No thanks, Dr. Gregory. I'm here to pay my respects. How is Mrs. Thornton?" Dr. Gregory appeared to falter. Emma considered sitting down more for the old man's benefit than her own.

"I may pay her a visit later today."

"You possibly remember Dr. Thornton taught several of my classes," Emma said, assaying the man's unsteadiness.

"We were very impressed with you around here. You were in my bacteriology class."

Emma smiled. "How kind. I learned much from you, sir."

Dr. Gregory hooked his thumbs in his vest pockets. "There was a time when we thought you might pursue a career in medical research, even teaching." Emma considered how alert and vigorous Dr. Gregory's mind was in contrast with his overall frail appearance. "But the medical profession gained at our loss," he said warmly, tapping his fingers against his large middle.

"I had heard somewhere that Dr. Thornton was involved in important work, special research," Emma said.

Dr. Gregory glanced at the closed door and leaned across his desk. "He made a breakthrough in your field, doctor."

"Medicine?" Emma feigned surprise.

"Nigel had been laboring tirelessly on his discovery. The poor man worked late at night and weekends, too. Wholly devoted except for one holiday... actually quite sudden it was. That was over a week ago." Dr. Gregory cleared his throat and reached for his Meerschaum pipe. "You don't mind, do you?"

"Please," Emma said.

He snapped a wooden match across a strike and sucked the flame into the bowl. The bright eyes focused on the glow.

"Wasn't that odd?" Emma asked, unsure where the question might lead.

"What?"

"He was on the brink of a breakthrough." Emma watched the wraiths of smoke curl and disperse. "If it were I, I can tell you, I'd want to keep pressing towards the end. Wouldn't you, sir?"

"My thoughts, precisely, Dr. Watson...and Germany—Bremen." He shook his head.

Emma noticed several pictures on a side table near his desk. The old man coughed and took some water from a beaker on his desk. Emma's interest returned to the pictures.

"Dr. Gregory, may I ask who these people are in the delightful pictures there? Of course, I recognize you in that one," she said, pointing.

"This is my wife, Jutta. We were on holiday visiting her brother in Germany several years ago. And this one is a photograph of Jutta and me with her famous brother. He's well known in Germany... high up on the Kaiser's general staff. Colonel Rainer Schmidt. He chauffeured us all over the country. In one of the Kaiser's motorcars, of all things. You see here? It's the Brandenburg Gate in the background."

"He looks impressive."

"No brother ever cares more for his sister than he does my Jutta. He's her only sibling."

"How she must miss him."

"She travels there each month...very active in the local German society here in London," Dr. Gregory said, shaking spittle from his pipe.

Emma extended her hand towards the old professor. "I best be going. I'm sincerely happy to have seen you again, Dr. Gregory, except for the dreadful circumstances, of course."

"Good day to you, Dr. Watson. I hope we meet again during pleasanter times."

"Indeed." Emma turned to walk away, then stopped. "If Dr. Thornton's discovery would affect the medical profession, as you say, then I do trust the research will continue."

"Of course. I can give you my personal assurance of that."

"Did Dr. Thornton use a research associate?"

"Oh, yes. But not on his discovery. I will be assigning Dr. Hugh Crane to carry on Nigel's work. He's a brilliant chap with no family or outside distractions. Thoroughly devoted to our efforts here. Of course, that's hush-hush for the moment... nothing official. But when the smoke clears from this mess—" Dr. Gregory fanned away a cloud of pipe smoke, and Emma suppressed a smile at the humor of it— "I plan on setting him to the task. I'll withhold no funds to assure the discovery's completion and commercialization." He sucked on the pipe and added, "Someday, Dr. Watson, you will be using Dr. Thornton's discovery."

"How very exciting. Come to think of it, doesn't Dr. Davies work here?"

He looked at the ceiling for a moment, clenching his pipe between his teeth. "Dr. Davies is no longer employed by the university." He reacted to Emma's confused look. "You are unaware that Dr. Davies is the chief suspect in this case? He has fled somewhere. Didn't report for work yesterday."

"Really?"

"Davies was Nigel's research assistant. He would've inherited the project but.... well, he was brilliant. I give him that. Actually the best professor I've ever seen. Gifted. A genius. Very bright future," he sighed and drank more water. "It is quite astounding that the man's darker side drove him to murder.

None of us sensed it. Never...not even once. He never got angry. He was passionate about his work. Must've had a very deep evil in him."

"You honestly believe Dr. Davies murdered Dr. Thornton?" Emma stepped back towards the doctor.

"It appears rather obvious, doesn't it?"

"Do the police have evidence, or is it all circumstantial?"

"If you put it that way, I suppose it must be circumstantial. But he fled. Is that not an admission of guilt?"

"We're all innocent until proven guilty, are we not?" Emma moved closer.

"I suppose you are right. Yes. A likable sort. The students loved him and learned much from him. His classes were always popular." The old professor pulled a handkerchief from his pocket and wiped his mouth. "When his students heard the news, they gathered outside my door and in the halls, the girls were all crying. Even a few boys."

"They must have been devastated over losing Dr. Thornton."

"No. Davies, actually. They somehow heard he was the suspect, and several of the girls fainted. The infirmary was overwhelmed with swooning girls with the vapors."

"Do you think Dr. Davies did it?"

"Everything points to him, doctor. As I say, he ran."

"Maybe he lay sick. Too ill to report in."

"Unlike him. Healthy. He never missed a day." Dr. Gregory pondered the ceiling. "I must say his absence alone is not the only reason he is the suspect."

"Oh?"

"The outer door to Davies' office and the door into the lab from his office were left unlocked. He alone had the key."

"Don't the doors automatically unlock from inside, like this one?" Emma pointed to Dr. Gregory's door.

"Yes. It's all quite confidential. The inspector found an incriminating note Davies had written to himself." Dr. Gregory quickly added, "The note said: 'Deal with Nigel's lie.' I saw it myself. On his calendar for yesterday." Dr. Gregory nodded over his words as if affirming truth.

"So it is the note that is the real clue?"

"Yes, Dr. Watson. 'Deal with Nigel's lie.' Preposterous! Outrageous! Dr. Thornton was an honorable man. Lie? In any case, a lie worthy of death? Absurd." He sucked on his pipe. "They were very close, I thought. Davies probably knew about the formula. If so, then the police say that he had the means. Davies is the only person beyond Nigel, you must understand, who could've known details of the formula."

"Odd, wouldn't you say?"

"What?" Dr. Gregory asked, his bright eyes on her.

"Odd that Dr. Davies intended to confront Dr. Thornton about the alleged lie and then murder him the night before."

The professor blinked and shrugged his shoulders. "It's all odd to me... horribly odd."

He tamped his pipe as Emma watched. "I had unwavering confidence in Davies. I'm as shocked as anyone. Perhaps I could say, more than anyone. But now..."

Emma said, "Dr. Gregory, you have my sympathy. I thank you for your time." She left him staring at his desk, his yellowed Meerschaum loose in his slack jaw.

Emma slipped from the smoky office, eager to breathe fresh air. Miss Celia Norris stood erect and Emma waved her to be seated. She interviewed the tiny woman, and afterward she concluded the woman knew less about the murder than she did. Emma also surmised that the woman knew marginally enough to perform the duties of her position as well. She clacked down the gloomy corridor and stopped in front of the constable.

"I'm Dr. Emma Watson. May I see Miss Palmer?"

The uniformed constable looked her up and down, confirming her early suspicions that he had enjoyed observing her when she had passed him on her way to Dr. Gregory's office.

"You're a fancy doctor," he said derisively, eyes roaming over her bodice. When his eyes were satisfied, he found Emma glaring at him.

"Miss Mary Palmer, if you do not mind, constable." He grasped the brass doorknob and leaned inward, expecting Emma to slide past him through the deliberately narrow opening. "Do you mind, constable?"

He backed away and gave her an acceptable space, which she quickly stepped through. Mary saw her and jumped to her feet. As Emma approached, she overheard the constable talking with his associate guarding the inner laboratory door.

"You figur'd this duty'd be bad. But look at 'em two birds," the one said.

Mary greeted her with a hug. Emma rolled her eyes towards the constables and sat down.

"I know," Mary whispered. "They watch every move I make. Next thing they'll be following me to the ladies'." The two friends commiserated, then Mary asked in a whisper, "Have you heard anything?"

Emma shook her head. "I talked with Dr. Gregory and Miss Norris. Dr. Crane is next on my list."

"His class is underway." Mary nervously traced the edge of her teacup with a finger. "Actually, he has classes for the rest of the day. He's taking most of Henry's and Nigel's classes, you know."

Emma glanced at the constable. "Shhh, we might be overheard."

"Let's have tea." Mary motioned for Emma to follow her to an old wooden storage cabinet in the corner. A makeshift shelf held china, tea, and coffee. A gas line snaked from a Bunsen burner on the shelf along the wall and under the door to the laboratory. They chatted about generalities and prepared tea, secure from the constable's eyes.

Mary said, "I talked with Evelyn Moxely this morning, and you won't believe what she told me. She was in love with Henry. Dr. Crane had been pursuing her, and when he wouldn't relent, she told him she and Henry were betrothed."

"Deplorable." Emma sipped her tea.

"It was all I could do to contain myself. Engaged to my Henry? Can you believe it? Evelyn said Crane was going to lodge a formal complaint about the engagement. He was livid when he left Evelyn's office the afternoon of the murder. You simply must talk to Dr. Crane. He might be the killer."

"I shall, Mary, in due course."

"And I don't mind telling you that Crane often complained about Henry getting new equipment and supplies. Nigel always approved Henry's requests. It rankled Dr. Crane. Everyone knows about his strong feelings."

"Why do you suppose Henry always got what he wanted?"

"I overheard Dr. Thornton telling Crane that Henry's research required the purchases. As if to say Crane's work was inconsequential. I pitied him once. But now..."

"Is Dr. Crane a violent man?"

"He's more like the child who gathers up his toys and marches home. He broods and whines like a spoiled child." Mary turned down the Bunsen flame.

"I expect Richard is with Henry at the moment."

"Oh dear God, may it be."

"He'll help Henry sort things out," Emma said, sipping her tea and hoping she was correct.

"Do you think they will return to London together?"

Emma hesitated. She knew that her brother wanted to bring Henry back and hide him until the killer was found. But Henry could be stubborn and he would probably resist—largely from fear.

"If Richard returns without him," Emma said at last, "then he will be satisfied Henry is absolutely safe. I'm certain of it." Relief flooded Mary's face. "You said Miss Moxely discovered the body. May I speak with her?"

Mary led her to Evelyn Moxely and made proper introductions, then drew back into the corridor. Within the hour, Emma rejoined Mary after leaving Moxely somewhat trembling over inconsistencies in her testimony.

Emma drank her now cold tea. "I shall be off to hospital. I must make my rounds and see a patient of Father's. While I'm there, I want to check on the child and woman Mycroft told us about. I'll be at home to lunch. If Richard sent us word, I'll make sure you know immediately. Chin up." Emma smiled. "Very well, then. I must prepare myself to run the gauntlet." She glanced at the constable at the laboratory door.

"Those two are vulgar, a disgrace to the force."

Emma straightened her skirt. "Dinner tonight. I insist."

She turned and walked towards the outer door, meeting the constable in the corridor. He stood rocking on the balls of his feet. He looked her up and down.

Emma said calmly, "I see your badge is two eighty-four. What's your name, constable?"

His look turned to surprise. "Your name, constable two eighty-four?"

"Ah, er...Graves. What's it to..."

"I think my friend, Chief Detective Inspector Gordon Lestrade, will be interested in your conduct, Constable Graves."

"Lestrade?"

"If I hear a single word from Mary Palmer about your vulgar conduct, and that of your friend inside, I will be compelled to report you to Gordon. And I can assure you, you'll be on the dole tomorrow," she said, snapping her finger for emphasis.

Emma turned on her heels and left by the main entrance. She had dealt with his kind before, and she knew he would not be her last, either. She thought this was yet another example of the abysmal quality of the local constabulary. She walked across the Quadrangle and hailed a cab to St. Bartholomew's Hospital.

CHAPTER 7

The antiseptic hospital smell was familiar to Emma. She no longer noticed it. It was her environment. She was in her element. She had been born at St. Bart's, eleven minutes before Richard, a fact she had lorded over him more than once. A smile crossed her face. Three days ago she had delivered her thirty-seventh baby there. A private dream was for at least one of her infants to enter the medical profession. She had known from a young age that she would be a doctor like her father. He had encouraged her despite the medical community's grudging admittance of females into their fraternity. Florence Nightingale's legacy was still chipping away at the solid walls that were confining nurses to little more than hospital orderlies, rather than a profession with a high calling. Had Emma not lived in London, the prospect of a career in medicine would have been improbable. She knew that had her father not been a physician and an alumnus of London University, and had he not intervened on her behalf with the school's officials, she could never have entered medicine. Nevertheless, Emma's close friends knew her determination was formidable. She would fight any barriers traditionalists might impose.

Emma visited her patients, including reviewing Mr. Walters' condition for her father. Walking towards the sisters' desk to inquire about the poisoned child and woman, she heard her name reverberating down the marble hall.

"Dr. Watson? Dr. Watson, a brief moment, please." Emma knew without turning that it was Dr. Hazeltine, chief of staff. She saw her friend and mentor with two female interns coming towards her.

"Dr. Hazeltine, good morning." She looked at the young interns and thought each could have been herself four or five years ago.

"Yes, good morning," Dr. Hazeltine said. "I wish to introduce you to my newest interns. This is Miss Carol Herbert, and this is Miss Greta Hoeksma. Ladies, please meet Dr. Emma Watson."

The two interns offered awkward curtsies.

"It's an honor to meet you, doctor," Miss Herbert said. "You're the first

female physician to graduate from the program. We owe you a great debt."
Before Emma could speak, the other intern chimed in.

"We have heard much about you, and that you are the finest diagnostician in all of England."

"You're embarrassing..."

"Please, Dr. Hazeltine, isn't that correct?" Miss Hoeksma said. "You have told us many times."

"I tell my interns if they could follow you on rounds for a week, they'd learn more about diagnostics than from any course of mine." His smile was surpringly shy. Emma had been his star intern, and he doubted he would ever see her equal in his lifetime. "Won't you please reconsider teaching in our program here?"

"Thank you, doctor, but I have equally important work with Father in our surgery. You do me a great honor, sir. Miss Hoeksma, you're from the Netherlands, aren't you?"

"Yes. Maastricht."

"And Miss Herbert, where is home for you? America?"

"Pittsburgh, Pennsylvania."

"Upon my word...Pittsburgh!" Emma allowed herself to consider the mother she never knew. She was from Pittsburgh. "You are a long way from home, aren't you?"

"You're very famous," Miss Herbert said. "I've been following your efforts with Emmeline Pankhurst. Women must have the right to vote."

Emma studied her. "Are you interested in the Women's Social and Political Union, Miss Herbert?"

Both interns nodded.

"I know you provided medical attention to the hunger strikers the other week. You also write the column on women's health in *The Suffragette*, and you had that row with that Irish member about the sex-relation boycott, and..."

"What sex boycott?" Miss Hoeksma inquired.

"She's an Irish woman, as you said," Emma began. "She pushed the notion of a sexual-relations boycott, to have the young members pledge to no engagements, no marriage, and no babies. Can you believe it? But I called it madness and fully supported Mrs. Pankhurst's view that it would only bring ridicule and not create sex-equality but sex-war."

"And right you are, I say," said Dr. Hazeltine.

Emma went on. "It's assumed here in England and in America, too, that married women fall under their husbands' representation and they don't need the freedom to vote."

Dr. Hazeltine cleared his throat. "But, ladies, Dr. Watson is famous for other achievements. She and her father were instrumental in getting the C.I.D. to experiment with a small forensic program."

"C.I.D.?" Intern Hoeksma asked.

"Criminal Investigation Division," said Dr. Hazeltine. "Our tradition of criminal and civil inquests, autopsies, and all has undergone a transition for the better in recent years. For centuries, cause of death was left to a judicial process, judge and, in most cases, a thoroughly uneducated jury. Very unscientific. If science had been applied, Jack the Ripper might've been caught. The police have resisted the notion of scientific detection. They're rather archaic... status quo and all that rot."

"Pigheaded," Miss Hoeksma interrupted, surprising the others. Everyone chuckled.

"Yes, pigheaded...stubborn. Dr. Watson, tell them the rest."

"You have heard of Sherlock Holmes, the consulting detective?"

The interns nodded.

Dr. Hazeltine broke in. "Her father is Dr. John H. Watson."

"There was a Chief Inspector Lestrade at Scotland Yard...retired last year. He eventually became a believer in Sherlock's scientific investigational methodologies. Before Lestrade retired, he cajoled Sherlock, my father, another physician, Dr. Mull, and me to argue the case for a forensic laboratory at Scotland Yard. They convinced the Board to experiment with it. After all," Emma turned to Miss Herbert, "your Bureau of Investigation has had one to great effect since nineteen-aught-eight. It's quite pioneering, you know. But the Board only permitted a woefully meager facility."

"Ladies, I have it on reliable authority that this fine doctor's apologetics won the day for the experiment."

Emma nodded politely. "I envision a day when forensics and scientific criminal detection will be a formalized course of study at university." Emma faced the interns. "Right then. A pleasure meeting you both. I've finished my rounds; otherwise, you three could join me. But doctor, may I have a private word?" Emma pointed to a vacant corner near a small window, and they withdrew. "What do you know about this mysterious poisoning of the little girl and woman yesterday?"

"How did you hear about this?"

"This morning's newspaper."

"Ah. It's a puzzling chemical. We haven't seen the like before. What's on your mind?"

"I'd like to examine the two victims, if I may."

Dr. Hazeltine led Emma and the interns to a special room with isolation warnings drawing-pinned to the white, newly painted door.

"The police wanted us to isolate them from the other patients for security reasons. It has nothing to do with infectious communicability."

"May I review their charts prior to talking with them?" Emma did not need to ask but did so as a matter of courtesy.

The two physicians walked to the foot of each bed, followed by the two interns, and acknowledged the families, but the child was asleep. After Emma examined the data and anecdotal comments, she approached the woman's bedside and pulled a yellow, stained divider screen for privacy.

"Mr. and Mrs. Haas, son Gunther, I would like you to meet Dr. Emma Watson."

The German woman groaned. Her husband and son shook Emma's hand and mustered smiles.

"Dr. Watson is one of the finest physicians in London. It's important for her to see you. You are in very capable hands. I must leave you now. We're a bit behind schedule. Dr. Watson, give me the benefit of your examination, please."

"Of course, doctor, and good day and best wishes to you, ladies. It was a pleasure meeting you." The two interns bid her goodbye.

Emma engaged in a few brief pleasantries that helped tune her ear to the family's German-accented English. She removed her notebook from her purse and began her interrogation. She scribbled details and learned that the woman had taken the family's refuse to the dustbin and had found the little girl, Hildegaard Einbecker, playing with a woman's greasy, black, right-hand glove and soiled handkerchief. The child had found the items near the dustbin and had been playing with them for only a few minutes. After Mrs. Haas emptied her refuse and swept the area, she found Hildy lying on the ground unconscious. She tried to revive the child. During the effort she inadvertently got the purple grease on her arm. She ran for a constable, and when they returned to the scene, Mrs. Haas suddenly fainted. When she awoke, she found herself in St. Bartholomew's, nauseous, with excruciating pain in her arm.

Emma cautiously examined Mrs. Haas' wounds. It appeared the epidermal and dermal layers would be permanently scarred, as surely as if nitric acid had been poured on the woman's skin and allowed to burn deep into the tissue. After applying fresh bandages, she walked around the divider and introduced herself to the Einbeckers. Emma questioned them and concluded that the girl could not have played with the glove and handkerchief for more than ten minutes. Both families had no idea who owned the soiled articles.

Emma carefully examined the little girl's injuries and guessed the child would be disfigured for life. She gazed at the apple-faced six-year-old, then smiled at her parents.

"I believe she will be all right. Her injury will be painful for several weeks. Perhaps an operation will be required. But Hildegaard will be playing with her friends before you realize it. I shall check on her daily." The Einbeckers smiled politely as Emma departed.

She left St. Bartholomew's fearing gangrene, even amputation, of Hildegaard's thumb. The poisonous burn was the deepest she had ever seen. She hailed a cab and was soon on her way to her home on Carlisle Street.

"How does such a formula function?" she mused, as the cab rattled over the cobblestones. "I must have Henry explain it to me." Other thoughts filled the ride home. *Who had discarded the poisoned items in the dustbin? And a right glove. What did that signify? It could not have been Henry... completely ridiculous. And how do the Germans figure in this mystery? Is there a connection between Thornton and Mrs. Haas and young Hildegaard?* Emma would need to inspect both crime scenes. And she would have to get past the guards at university. And she would have to report Mr. Walters' worsening condition to Father. Challenges assailed her. As the cab approached her home, she had one more thought: *Perhaps there's word from Richard.*

CHAPTER 8

Dew glistened on the laurel and thistle outside. Morning light spread across the fields and hedgerows. Henry stirred to insistent tapping on the window. He raised his head expecting to see Mr. Thompson's jolly face, probably inviting him to breakfast.

"Open the door. I'm cold," Richard snapped.

Henry tore off the down comforter and immediately felt the chill. He went to the door. Richard pushed inside, lugging his valise.

"Why are you here?"

"Where's the peat?" Richard said. "Get a fire going." He dropped his valise on the floor. Henry looked for fuel.

"Over here," Henry called from the kitchen. They grabbed up some peat, and within a short while small flames became a cheery blaze.

Henry asked, "What are you doing here?"

"You need clothes, don't you?" Richard said, looking at his friend standing in his drawers. "Get dressed."

"Geoffrey thought this would—"

"I know all that," Richard said as he watched a horse-drawn wagon pass the cottage and rattle towards town. "We have to talk."

"Have you seen Mary?"

"I saw her last evening. Sends you her love."

"Is she angry with me? What? Tell me," Henry said, plunging his arms into a shirt.

"She's fine, I tell you." Richard looked out the window. "I'm famished... been traveling while you've been sleeping like a baby. Let's breakfast." Richard took a Webley .45 army revolver from his coat pocket. "Maybe I should leave this here."

"Your father's. What are you doing..."

"I'll take it with me. Where shall we breakfast?"

"The Thompsons' next door, but why did you..."

"Henry. There's much to talk over, but not on an empty stomach. To the Thompsons'."

Out on the soggy path, the mushy earth sucked at their feet. They tapped on the door, and Mrs. Thompson greeted them warmly. She prepared a hearty Scottish breakfast, and the two men tucked in.

"Aye, ye lads be hungry this marnin', ain't ye," she said with a smile, putting another kettle on the grate.

"Where's Mr. Thompson?" Henry asked.

She waved her towel at the window. "Angus tuk the wagon ta town fur some harse feed and the like."

"Where does this road go, Mrs. Thompson?" Richard inquired.

"Well, she goes straight in ta town 'at way," she said with another towel wave. "Acourse ye know that. And she goes up 'ere ta MacDonalds' 'at way."

"How far is that?"

"Narly a mile 'n' it ends."

"Any turnoffs between here and the MacDonalds'?"

"Why are you so keen on local roads, old fellow?" Henry said, spooning porridge.

"None, 'ceptin' the dirt path 'ere."

Mrs. Thompson tried in vain to make them eat more, but they politely declined and praised her hospitality. Richard slipped several gold sovereigns under his plate and winked at Henry. He was always extravagant to a fault, in Henry's thinking.

"We must be going, Mrs. Thompson. We'll be at the cottage," Henry said.

Richard tugged Henry's coat sleeve. "Let's have a look." Outside, the fine smell of plowed earth enveloped them. They walked behind the Halsey cottage and viewed the hillside sloping down to a small lake. A wooden skiff was tied to a rotting post. Ducks paddled on placid water. Richard pointed to a herd of Scottish longhaired cows grazing on the far hill towards the MacDonald property, where thick hedges and brambles massed with great trees to the north.

"*But look, the morn in russet mantle clad, Walks o'er the dew of yon high eastward hill,*" Richard smiled. "Hamlet. Horatio to Marcellus."

"You should do a painting of this place, Richard."

They walked round the cottage and stepped inside. The fire in the hearth needed encouragement. They kicked off their shoes, pulled two chairs near the grate, and after adding more peat, they sat warming their feet. Richard poked and arranged the sweet fuel.

"Tell me everything. Start at the beginning and end at the end."

Henry did. He began with his scientific discovery, Thornton's stealing of it, and when he finished his exhaustive recounting, he said, "I'll put a kettle on."

"Jolly good."

Henry returned with a kettle of water and hung it on the iron hook in the hearth. Richard looked out the front window. "Anything interesting out there?"

Richard returned to his seat. "Beautiful country, this."

"God's country, Richard."

"God knows we've got to get back to the Big Smoke."

Henry eyes hardened. "London? I'm as good as dead back there. You know that."

"This isn't your country. You sure as blazes don't know your way around here if trouble strikes. And I'm bloody certain it will, old boy." Richard thrust the iron poker against the flaming peat. Henry was silent. "You told me your long story. I'll give you mine in a thimble."

Henry stiffened. "Go on."

"The stuff that probably killed Thornton also probably killed a girl and a woman yesterday. Emma's on the case. These Huns you talk about probably want the formula. They probably are connected to a radical group of Germans Mycroft knows about. And for what it's worth, Mycroft says Sherlock fears them. They'll stop at nothing. The Germans you met on the train might be part of this putrid business...maybe the murder on your train."

Henry started cracking his knuckles.

"And another thing. Mycroft said he was going to have one of his men board the train to protect you and bring you back to London. Did you meet the agent?"

"No. And I'm glad I didn't. I can't go back. You know Scotland Yard."

"Why do you think I'm here, to paint pictures? Don't worry. I'll smuggle you into my studio. You can stay there until—"

"Richard, think about it. Just think—"

"No, you think about it. You're a pigeon up here. I'm sure the Huns know where you are right now. Why do you think I brought the gun?"

"I won't be safe in your studio. Gordon and Mycroft know we're friends. They'll search every nook and cranny of your house. I won't go back. I'm dead hiding here, too. I'll give you that. Everywhere I turn, I'm stymied." Henry started pacing.

Richard listened. "A wagon. Is that your Mr. Thompson?"

"I don't know."

The men watched from the tiny window.

"Well?"

"I can't... wait." The wagon disappeared below the rise of the near hill.

"You simply can't stay here, Henry."

"I must."

The wagon finally appeared above the crest.

"Yes. It's Mr. Thompson. God Almighty. It's Krajic riding with him. Good Lord, Richard." Henry went putty grey, turned to his chum, and found him checking his revolver.

"Close all the shutters except the front window. They already can see it's open. And hurry!"

Henry was certain there would be violence. There had been a hidden violence to the man that had disquieted him from the moment of their meeting on the train. He slammed all the shutters closed and the rooms darkened. *We're surely going to die*, he thought. He joined Richard.

"If this Krajic comes to the door, Henry, then I want you in the hallway out of sight. I'll tell you what to say." Richard crouched beside a large rough-hewn breakfront. "He won't see me here."

Then they heard footsteps through the mud and a long pause, then knock-knock-knock. The door was solid; the sound was muffled by its massive bulk. Krajic was hitting the door with an object. Another long pause. Krajic tested the locked door.

"Referent Palmer, are you there? It's Herr Krajic."

Richard whispered, "Tell him you're taking a bath."

"I'm taking a bath."

"A bath."

"Tell him you can't come to the door right now."

"I can't come to the door right now, Herr Krajic."

They saw a shadow cast through the unshuttered front window.

"Stay back. I'll look." Richard peered around the breakfront. The shadow disappeared and Krajic was at the front door again.

"You haf somevun mit you, don't you referent, ja? I zee two chairs by zee fire."

"One's for drying my wet clothes. What do you want?"

"I vant to dine mit you. Tonight, ja? In town, maybe."

Richard whispered, "What time and where."

"What time and where, Herr Krajic?"

"Don't be embarrassed, Referent. I see nekkid man before."

"What time tonight and where?"

"I tink da Boar's Head. Vhy not at eight, ja?"

Richard shook his head, no. "Tell him you don't know the Boar's Head. Suggest the Loch Loman."

"I think the Loch Loman is good."

Henry looked at Richard and received a wink. Another long pause.

"Goot. Eight o'clock, ja?"

"Eight o'clock tonight, Herr Krajic."

"You can meet friends."

"Good-bye, Herr Krajic."

There was a pause, and the men could hear the mud squelch beneath Krajic's feet.

Richard looked at Henry. "Be quiet." They listened and heard more squishing.

"Start singing something. You're bathing, remember?"

Henry shrugged his shoulders and mouthed, "What?"

"Anything."

Henry began. "There'll always be an England..." Richard crept towards the window. Henry reached the end of the song, and Richard motioned with the revolver for him to continue singing.

Richard looked through the crack between the shutter and the window frame. He saw Krajic motion towards the road for someone to stay away. Richard kept watching as Henry sang and Krajic began to slog around the cottage, investigating. Richard followed him from room to room, listening to the muddy squelching of his boots outside, very aware that Krajic was thoroughly testing every window he could reach—pressing and softly pounding. After several minutes, Krajic left and made his way down the sludgy road towards the village. He disappeared behind the rise. Richard motioned for Henry to keep singing.

Richard thought if he were Krajic, he would know the rise would hide him from view of the cottage. He would use it as a blind and move from the road and into the woods to circle behind the cottage. Or maybe Krajic had his two friends hidden somewhere in the forest. In which case, he would continue walking down the road in plain view and have them circle behind the cottage to stand watch. On the other hand, the other two buggers might be close to the cottage right now, watching and waiting.

Richard transferred his heavy revolver to his left hand long enough for him to exercise his fingers. He made a fist several times and then gripped the revolver again. Henry was still singing. Then suddenly Richard motioned for Henry to stop and share the view from the window. They saw three figures walking down the road, away from the cottage.

"There's Krajic and his two friends you told me about," Richard said. "Are those the other two from the train?"

"I can't tell from here."

"If I were Krajic, I'd pay three locals to wait behind the rise and pretend to be the three Germans walking back to town, knowing they would be watched. Then we'd disperse through the woods, surround the cottage, and—"

"They're gone."

"He was testing you."

"Testing?"

"There's no Boar's Head."

"Oh."

"I took a cart throughout the village. I saw no Boar's Head. But there was a Loch Loman. They were testing your knowledge of Straithairn. If you knew this village well, then they would have to exercise more caution."

"Good Lord."

"I have a scheme. Walk over to the Thompsons' and bring the old man here. Make up any excuse. The Huns mustn't see me. I'll cover you from the side window. Lock the door. I don't want those swine sneaking in here behind me."

"You think they're out there?"

"I'll be aiming from the bedroom window. Go."

Henry unlocked the front door, stepped onto the muddy patch, relocked the door, and walked through the mud to the Thompsons'. Richard watched him enter, and seconds later Henry and Mr. Thompson were trudging to the Halsey cottage. Richard closed the shutter and returned to the front room, welcoming the men when they stepped inside.

Mr. Thompson grabbed Richard's hand. "Yer the one the missus said give us them sovereigns. Thank ye. 'Tweren't necess'ry. But thank ye." The old man released Richard's hand, and Henry gestured for him to sit down.

"We need your help," Richard said as he stood by the front window. The old man turned his chair towards Richard.

"I'm an agent of the Crown, and I need your help, Mr. Thompson. Henry's an important scientist with a significant discovery. The man you delivered to our doorstep a short while ago is one of three German agents trying to kidnap him."

"I knew he be a German way he spoke. I know'd right off."

"May we depend on you, Mr. Thompson?" Richard asked.

"Aye. Acourse ye kin. Me 'n the missus. Aye," the old man spoke without a flicker of fear.

"Did I see a road on the other side of the lake?"

"Aye, ye saw right, sir."

"Where does it go?" Richard asked, peering through a crack in the shutters.

"Starts at t'other side of MacDonalds' and runs to Dalnabridge."

"How far to Dalnabridge?"

The man rubbed his chin, his stubble rasping. "Guessin' better part o' five mile."

"Train station in Dalnabridge?"

"Aye. Folks on that side o' lake use it. Our'n on this side use Straithairn, acourse."

"Do you have any friends with horses on that road?"

"My brother. He's the gillie at Glenntavish's o'er yonder. Has harses 'n wag'ns, too."

Richard studied the old Scot. "How can you get a message to him?"

"Take ma wag'n o'er 'n talk to him."

"Have him livery two horses for us on his road opposite this cottage. We need to get to Dalnabridge."

The old man got up and tugged at his baggy trousers. "Aye. Be gone fur it'll take awhile... half hour. If he ain't there, I'll do it mesef—then mebbe 'n hour."

Richard smiled. "When you return," he said, peering through the window, "drive your wagon between the barn and our cottage so anyone watching from the road can't see the wagon. Understand?"

The old man nodded. "Aye, sir. I hurries back 'ere and go 'twixt Halseys' 'n the barn."

"Good, Mr. Thompson. Then you watch the back window. We'll toss you a bundle that you'll put in the back of your wagon. Understand?"

"Aye."

"When we give you the signal, you get your wagon to Straithairn station as fast as you can. Stop for no one. You'll divert the Huns' attention while Henry and I escape." Richard looked at Mr. Thompson for a reaction.

"Aye, to the station 'n nary a stop. Aye."

"I believe you'll be followed. So wait in the telegraph office. If you are followed, tell the Germans that you are fetching a telegram for Reverend Palmer."

Mr. Thompson rubbed his callused hands together. "Telegram. Reverend Palmer. Aye, sir."

Richard and Henry shook the man's hand and watched him make his way to his cottage.

Henry gripped Richard's shoulder. "Look, I'm not going back to London." There was no hope in Henry's face.

"Not to London, old man. I realize that now."

Relief gusted from him. "Then where?"

The two watched Mr. Thompson drive his wagon onto the road at full gallop—the horse's hooves spraying mud and sod and the wooden wheels flinging a fan of trailing muck. Steam came from the horse's nostrils as Mr. Thompson cracked his whip, bounced, shouted, and glanced back once to the cottage. They watched the wagon disappear over the rise where the road dipped, emerging on the straightaway a few seconds later.

Then Mr. Thompson disappeared around the bend leading to Straithairn.

"Where are we going, Richard?"

"Home." The two men looked at each other, Richard knowing, Henry wondering. "Why didn't I think of it before?"

"Home? Blaenllyn?" Henry's shoulders relaxed. Realization took some worry from his face.

Next to London, Henry knew Blaenllyn best. Even Richard knew Blaenllyn, Wales. Emma, too. During their adolescent years, the twins had joined Henry there and had made lasting friendships during summer holidays.

"Jolly good show, old man. Brilliant."

"Roll pillows into your bed spread. Make it look like a concealed body." Richard kept his vigil at the window, revolver drawn. Dazzling light slanted in.

"Pack the valise." Richard checked his pocket watch. "Aye, I hope the gillie of Glenntavish gits us harses," Richard said, imitating the old man's Scottish burr.

His calm eyes studied the road and the stands of evergreens. Purple heather blanketed the lush hills. Hedgerows budded with carmine berries along the dirt road. A footpath emerged from a mask of thick elder bushes. Richard watched birds flit among the spruces and heard distant squawks of ducks on the lake behind the cottage. It was a pity to be surrounded by such natural beauty, sullied by the German menace.

The two friends sat at the hearth in silence for an hour before Richard suddenly listened. "Sounds like our Mr. Thompson." The wagon passed them and left the muddy road. Richard handed Henry the revolver. "You stand guard," he said, going to the back room to heave the bundle into the wagon. Minutes later, Richard returned and took the revolver.

"Go outside and run to the back. I opened the rear window. Climb back into the cottage and instruct Mr. Thompson to rush into Straithairn. That's all you have to do."

Henry left the cottage running and moments later Richard heard him scrambling inside. He watched the horse and wagon appear from the far side of the cottage and head for the road. Richard smiled when he saw the man sized bundle in the wagon. The horse headed down the road as before, the old Scot huddled over its reins.

"Lock the door and follow me." Richard hefted the valise and they climbed through the rear window. "To the skiff."

They made their way down the slope towards the lake, where the wood thinned and lavender flowers grew down to the water. A few feet away the spring runoff gurgled into the lake. Richard tossed the valise into the old skiff; Henry untied the rope. They got into the swaying home-built boat and tugged on their oars. The lap and splash of clear lake water ran against the skiff. Reaching the other side, they dragged the boat ashore and clawed their way up the bank. The slope to the road above them required several attempts to scale. They ran along the muddy road to Dalnabridge with Henry in the lead, carrying the valise.

"Where are the horses?" Richard shouted.

At a bend in the road, they spotted a horse and wagon waiting with a man astride a highland pony. They ran for the wagon.

"Ma uncle sez yar' goin' ta Dalnabridge. Get in," the young man in a blue-green, Thompson-tartan kilt said from astride his mount.

Henry tossed the valise into the farm wagon and they clambered onto the seat. Richard grasped the reins as the young Scot slapped their horse and the wagon jolted forward.

"Ta," Richard yelled over his shoulder as he brought the horse to a full gallop.

The road was deeply rutted. It switched back and forth on itself as it snaked through the lush scenery. Once Ben Nevis loomed in the distance, then they were angling south toward Dalnabridge. A mountain rose up ahead, bristling with pines and birches, and the valley below offered its mosaic of pasturage and hamlets, hedgerows and brooks. From another overlook Henry spotted a train in the distance. Billows of black smoke flattened along its length. It gave the men a sense of comfort.

"I hope that's our train," Richard said over the noise of the careening wagon.

When they reached Dalnabridge, Mr. Thompson's nephew surged ahead and led the way to the small railway station. The men climbed down from the wagon. Henry went on ahead. When he looked back he saw Richard giving the lad a gratuity.

At the ticket window Henry inquired about the connection to Blaenllyn through Cardiff. He glanced at the station clock. They must wait for twenty-five, maybe thirty minutes. Richard arrived at Henry's side, hefting the valise, and handed him a handful of pounds. "Two tickets," Richard said.

Finally they heard the approaching train.

"Looks like she'll be on time."

The train belched and chugged into Dalnabridge Station, screeching and hissing to a stop. On board, Richard and Henry moved through every carriage, inspecting every compartment and water closet, looking for the Germans. They were satisfied that they had not boarded at Straithairn. Richard made a mental note of where the dining and baggage cars were located—a habit acquired from Sherlock. Next, they found their compartment and collapsed into their seats.

"Good Lord!" Richard exclaimed, pointing to the far road.

Three men on horseback were racing towards the station. One of them was Krajic. The train whistled, couplings clanked, and the carriage jolted. Krajic was in the lead and arrived first. He jumped off his horse and stumbled into a sprint towards the moving train.

"He'll be aboard. No doubt about it," Richard said. "Doubt if the other two'll make it."

"We're dead men."

"You're more important to them alive. I'm the one who should be worrying. They don't need me, but they need your brains. Let's wait." Richard moved to the seat next to the door and watched for Krajic in the passageway. "I'm guessing he made it but the other two didn't. We got up to speed rather quickly, wouldn't you say, old man?" He checked his revolver.

Henry was unresponsive. They waited.

"If I were Krajic, I'd try to locate you. Maybe not talk to you, but I'll wager he walks... Here he is." Richard closed his eyes, pretended to be asleep, his nerves taut.

The German opened the compartment door and gave Richard a long, estimating look. "Referent Palmer. Such brief fisit to Straithairn. Perhaps vee can dine together, ja."

Richard stole a look at the anarchist.

"Later," Henry said.

Krajic closed the compartment door and walked towards the dining and baggage carriages. Richard got to his feet. "Wait here." He stepped into the passageway and walked towards the dining carriage. He returned smiling.

"Jolly good. He's alone. We're twelve minutes from our next stop. I have a plan, so listen. Two minutes before we arrive at the station, we'll walk into the dining carriage. You'll be first. I'll follow a few paces behind you. When you draw even with Krajic, I want you to dash ahead to the baggage carriage. It's only two away. You keep the door open for me. I'll deal with Krajic. Don't worry."

"Don't worry?"

Richard went over his plan again and again in his mind. Then it was time to leave the compartment.

Richard checked his pocket watch. "Alright, then. You first."

Henry led the way through three carriages. They entered the dining carriage and saw Krajic facing them from a distant table, eyes alert, wary. Henry walked towards the German and as he neared his side, Krajic said, "Referent Palmer, please have a..."

Henry bolted ahead and through the door. Krajic slid his chair back and prepared to stand when Richard grabbed the metal kettle of steaming coffee and poured its contents onto the German's head and lap. Krajic screamed in pain, his big hands pawing at his thighs. With a powerful sweep of the kettle, Richard battered the German's face and his jaw. Krajic's head snapped backward, glancing off the wall. The kettle arced in a vicious chop to the anarchist's chin. Richard smashed the kettle down on top of Krajic's head, leaving him bloody. He thrust the kettle into the German's chest and ran towards the baggage carriage.

Henry watched from the open doorway and shouted, "He's coming!"

Krajic was stumbling and bleeding, gun drawn. Passengers were screaming and the waiter was motionless, pressing himself against the wall, like a hunted animal.

They slammed the baggage carriage door behind them.

Drawing his revolver, Richard said, "Over to the pile of baggage. When he comes in, shout into that corner: 'Hide, hide.' Do it now." Henry rushed to the jumble of luggage and both men watched the door. Richard stood behind it, revolver ready, a snake waiting at a rabbit's hole. Krajic tossed open the door, entered stumbling and bloody. He held a gun and looked this way and that. Henry yelled into the baggage corner. The train made its first of several braking stutters that tipped Krajic forward, eyes on Henry, arms fighting for balance. Richard slipped behind the unsuspecting German and smashed the revolver into the back of his head. Krajic collapsed in a heap. Richard closed the door and locked it. They dragged him to the baggage pile and tossed luggage and parcels onto him. They felt the train slowing for the station. They opened the side door and prepared to leap out.

"Our valise," Henry said.

Richard pointed to a waiting hire cart. "We're in luck. Tally-ho." He leaped from the train with Henry following. Their feet hit the gravel running and the men didn't stop until they reached the cart. "Straithairn, or you'll have the constabulary to answer to." The driver coaxed the horse into a trot. "Faster!" The driver snapped his whip, and the horse kicked into a full gallop.

"Straithairn?" Henry asked.

"This train'll be here for an hour while they search for us and investigate. The trains up line'll all be slowed or stopped on the tracks. We'll try another route. Maybe down to Glasgow and Manchester this time. Then Blaenllyn. Relax. We won't be followed."

"Where will we hide in Blaenllyn? Not with my parents. I don't want them involved in this."

"The collierymen's dormitory on the hill. The one I stayed in during our summer holidays."

"Excellent." Then Henry's face turned sour. "Word will get around. You know how it is there."

"Em and I'll solve this case. It'll be over before word circulates."

They watched the road behind them and then, satisfied they were not followed, relaxed. When Straithairn came into view, Henry nudged Richard's foot and pointed as the horse slowed to a trot nearing the station. There was a crowd of people and several uniformed constables gathered in the carriageway at the far end of the station, two more at the crossing.

"Look, police. And there's Mr. Thompson's wagon," Henry said.

Richard handed Henry a roll of pound notes. "I want to look around. Hold the cart. Rush to the cottage if there's any trouble." Henry watched Richard go into the station and within a few minutes he saw him waving tickets.

Their train to Manchester and Glasgow arrived as scheduled, they boarded it, and once underway, they made a check of all the passengers before falling asleep until Glasgow. They connected to Cardiff and later traveled to Aberystwyth, then on to Blaenllyn. During their long journey they managed to relax a little. Richard even found blank paper for sketching. They believed they were finally safe.

CHAPTER 9

"Richard and Henry are probably halfway to home," Emma said to Mrs. Mac, pressing her serviette to her lips and pushing her chair from the table. "Please tell Father I'll be here for dinner." She paused, deciding to drink the last of her tea. "Mary will join us."

She went out into the noise and hurry of Carlisle Street and hailed a passing hansom. "Queensway and Exeter."

When she arrived in front of the Thornton home, she noticed the obligatory black crepe over the door and the drawn curtains of mourning. The neighborhood seemed especially quiet, as if all the stately homes were paying proper respect to the grieving, unkempt three-story with its little frontage and even less decoration. Two men were busily scattering straw over the bricks on Exeter to soften the sound of horse hooves, this required by grieving rules. Looking at the grown-over brick footpath leading to the plain door, and the scraggly thatch that had once been one of a column of hedges she remembered, Emma was caught by the decline and its mean welcome from the street. It had been allowed to grow shabby, and the paint on the window ledges and doorframes was peeled. She pulled the bell and a young maid-of-all-work, dressed in a pressed but ill-fitted black blouse and skirt, answered and half-curtsied.

"Good 'ay, ma'am. May I help you?"

Emma placed her calling card into the young maid's hand. "I am Dr. Emma Watson. I wish to extend my sympathy to Mrs. Thornton and Elizabeth, if I may."

The maid curtsied and stepped backward, holding the door.

"I'll tell Mrs. Thornton yer 'ere." She left Emma standing in the dark hall, but returned within moments. "Right this way."

The girl swung open the door and Emma entered. The maid curtsied and withdrew. The curtains were drawn tight, and numerous candles flickered, shedding weak light on the dour mourning room. Black crepe hung from several photographs and across a sectional mirror. Chinese incense burned near a large portrait of Dr. Thornton. There was none of the usual flowers, paintings, vases, and curios. Only an ornately carved and lacquered Chinese screen guarded the hearth. It must be the right devil to clean, Emma thought to herself.

Mrs. Thornton sat on a chair beside a settee at the far end of the room. She was dressed in black. Her gloved hands held Emma's calling card. As a sudden afterthought, she lowered the black veil attached to her hat, hiding her pale face. Standing beside her was a lean, aristocratic gentleman with hair going grey, well bred in manner and perfectly dressed in black. He remained judiciously solemn as Emma approached.

"Mrs. Thornton, you have my deepest sympathy at this terrible time of loss." Emma waited for a response, which never came. The woman sat quiet and erect, eyes unreadable behind the veil. "Mrs. Thornton, your husband was one of my professors at the university a number of years ago. I dined with you and Elizabeth here at the end of term."

The woman remained remote. Emma's words might as well have been reflections on water, leaving no imprint on her mind. Then Mrs. Thornton looked at Emma again and either pretended to remember, or she lacked the energy to respond except with a quiet, "Be seated."

The gentleman adjusted a chair for Emma and introduced himself in a well-modulated voice as smooth as heavy cream.

"Dr. Watson, I am Charles Steele, Mrs. Thornton's brother. Please, be comfortable, and thank you for your kind words of condolence."

Mr. Steele's starched winged-collar pinched his pink neck. To Emma, his silk tie was worth a day of patients, maybe more, and his impeccable suit was clearly upmarket—Saville Row, no doubt. Its style declared an understated wealth.

"How is Elizabeth, Mrs. Thornton?" She watched Mr. Steele glance at his sister.

"Good," Mrs. Thornton said. "She is in the house. I should think you will meet her while you are here." She hesitated, still holding Emma's card in her gloved hand. "Yes, you dined here a few years ago. I remember now. There was another student with you, I believe."

Emma caught herself before she blurted Henry Davies' name.

"I am sure Elizabeth is quite devastated by this tragedy," Emma said as she looked from Mrs. Thornton to her brother, sensing a private matter between them. "May I ask when the funeral service will be?"

Mr. Steele paused to give his bereaved sister an opportunity to respond. When she didn't, he said, "We don't know, Dr. Watson. The inquest and the...shall I say, the unparalleled nature of his passing, is introducing an abnormal and indeterminate delay."

"Upon my word," Emma pretended. "How unfortunate...may I inquire what happened?" Mr. Steele stood and politely motioned for Emma to follow him across the room to a desk.

In a hushed voice Mr. Steele said, "Dr. Watson, I am sure you can understand how my sister feels about the ugly details."

"What happened?"

"My brother-in-law recently made a significant discovery. Somehow, a chemical, or whatever you may call it, was employed in his murder."

"Murder?" Emma lifted her eyebrows.

"I'm afraid it is true, doctor. The investigators are understandably cautious as they probe this complicated matter."

"My word, how frightfully appalling." Her eyes shifted to Mrs. Thornton. "The poor woman...the autopsy, the inquest...how terrible."

"It is a terrible thing, doctor," he said, easing his collar.

After hearing Mr. Steele's exhaustive recounting of the tragedy, Emma asked, "I should imagine Dr. Thornton is reasonably insured. I would not wish your sister and Elizabeth to suffer more than they are presently."

"I will be helping her with such things, doctor. I am a barrister and I have looked after their affairs for years." His hand went to his barrister's case. "My sister need not worry."

Emma glanced at the black leather case on the desk. "This is very handsome." Her fingertips caressed the finely tooled surface.

"It is only a week old. No scuffs yet."

"Would this be gold?"

"It had better be gold. Expensive enough, I can tell you."

"CSS," said Emma admiringly, her fingers sliding over the golden letters.

"Charles Samuel Steele. It is handmade by a craftsman on Regent. Would you like the name?"

"Oh, I would. Indeed, I would, sir," Emma said with the idea of buying something like it for Geoffrey.

Mr. Steele opened the case to the creak of fine leather and withdrew his calling card. As he scribbled on the back of it with his well-manicured hand, the maid opened the doors and announced, "Mr. Trevor Clark to see Mrs. Thornton." Not waiting, the man rushed past her. Mrs. Thornton leaped to her feet and raised her veil to kiss him. Her plain face glowed, and they hugged well past the point of politeness. Emma noticed the barrister's sudden agitation when Mr. Clark arrived. He winced, his eyes sullen.

"Here, Dr. Watson. They do the finest work in London."

She accepted the card and held it by the edges like Sherlock had taught her. She could hear him saying, "It is more elegant for a woman to allow a business card to be placed in her dainty hand. But, of greater significance is by doing thus, one retains the owner's prints." Since then, it had become an unconscious act for her.

"I'm sorry to have engaged you with such materiality, Mr. Steele. You have another visitor, I best be on my way."

"Nonsense, doctor," he said, a strain in his voice, his eyes on his sister. "Several months ago Dr. Thornton took an apartment near the university to be closer to his work. Meanwhile this..." He shook his head and glanced disapprovingly at his sister and Mr. Clark. "I am sorry about this, Dr. Watson."

Emma waved her hand discreetly. "Not at all."

"May I introduce you to Mr. Trevor Clark of Clark's Merchant Bank? He is a..." Mr. Steele halted briefly, "...a friend of the family." Then, to Mr. Clark: "This is Dr. Emma Watson, a former student of Nigel's."

"Doctor Watson," Mr. Clark said, weighing her at a glance and dismissing her.

Emma responded with equal brevity, her own condescension in her voice. "Mr. Clark." But she regretted her temper. Pomposity always burrowed under her skin rather quickly.

Emma was expert at reading people. It was what made her an excellent physician and gave her confidence in her own diagnoses. To her, Clark's tone and manner declared that it was an effort for him to include a young, professional woman into his sophisticated and privileged personal sphere; she was clearly his social inferior. The banker's affectation stemmed from the power and privilege to which he was born—the preeminent merchant banking family of England. Wealth gave him invulnerability. Emma's eyes rested on his aggressive red tie and regarded the attractiveness some women would find in such power and influence...but not Emma. She found him self-important and shallow.

"You have my sympathy, Mr. Clark. I must take my leave. Mrs. Thornton, I am so very sorry. Please communicate my condolences to Elizabeth." Mr. Steele walked her to the door.

When the door swung open, a couple stood kissing rather passionately in the entrance.

"Elizabeth, have you no respect?" Mr. Steele hurriedly closed the door behind him. Her eyes challenged her uncle in a manner unique to adolescent girls.

Elizabeth hung defiantly onto a man of military bearing.

"I'm frightfully sorry, Uncle Charles," Elizabeth said, her voice acid.

The girl was eighteen or nineteen, clothed in an appropriate black dress, and her copper hair was pulled back in a tight chignon, making her plain face harsh. Emma instantly recognized her, not by her face that was more her father's than her mother's, but rather by her deformed, inward-pointing right foot. Emma was surprised by the sourness Elizabeth exuded towards her uncle. Years ago at the end-of-term party, the young girl had been delightfully warm and polite. Elizabeth's eyes flickered with an inner passion or a contained rage. Emma decided it was venom.

"Elizabeth, this is Dr. Watson. She was a student of your father's." Mr. Steele's voice barely governed anger.

"Elizabeth, you have my deepest sympathy. I am very sorry."

"Thank you, Dr. Watson," she said with a forced courtesy.

"And this is Mr. Burton Howell, Mr. Clark's personal chauffeur."

"Pleased to meet you, Dr. Watson," the man said. Emma judged the man to be in his middle thirties and wondered about the large age difference. He was in fact closer to his late thirties. He tugged Elizabeth against him, and the girl relished the obvious message the action sent to her uncle.

"And I am pleased to meet you, too, Mr. Howell." Emma nodded. "The last time I saw you, Elizabeth, was about seven years ago. You were probably twelve then."

"I'm eighteen, doctor."

"If there is anything I can do for you or your mother," Emma said, offering her card to Elizabeth, "I should be only too happy to help."

"You are most kind, Dr. Watson," Mr. Steele said as Elizabeth accepted the calling card.

"I must be on my way, Elizabeth. Again, I am very sorry about your loss. We should have tea sometime once your mourning is over."

Emma was concerned how Elizabeth's deformity had become more severe since she had last seen her. Knowing that an orthopedic specialist from Boston was planning to teach a new procedure at the university gave her hope that Elizabeth could be helped.

"Thank you, doctor," Elizabeth said quietly, adopting a façade of sorrow.

Mr. Steele extended his arm towards the front door. "It was very thoughtful of you to call. Allow me to see you out."

"Permit me, Mr. Steele," Howell said, releasing Elizabeth.

"Very well, then. But Elizabeth, you should remain inside, mourning. What will the neighbors think?"

"Go back to the Old Bailey and your money," she said.

Resigned, Mr. Steele reached for the mourning room door. "My sister and I thank you. Have a good day, Dr. Watson."

"Goodbye to you, Mr. Steele. My offer of help extends to you, of course."

"Be assured that when the date of Dr. Thornton's funeral becomes certain, I shall notify you. I know you would wish to be present."

"Indeed, I would." Mr. Steele bowed and withdrew.

Howell opened the front door with a panache designed to impress. Emma squinted, adjusting her eyes to the drenching sunlight bathing Exeter and a breathtaking motorcar at the curb. The reflections from the gleaming burgundy paint in the sun were stunning.

They passed two men tossing the last of the straw onto the carriageway, and Emma overheard them mumble curses about the contraption and Mr. Howell.

"My new Alpine Eagle," Howell said proudly, then, "It's Mr. Clark's."

"However does one drive this thing?"

"I've driven it," Elizabeth declared, her smile small but sincere.

"Don't tell Mr. Clark, please," Howell said as he secured Elizabeth to his side. Emma admired the dark beige leather seats. "It's rather simple to drive, and no dirty horses to deal with, you know."

"My Burton knows all about engines and motorcars. He worked on ship engines. He was a merchant seaman for a few years and he knows all about such things." Elizabeth was proud of her lover and seemed eager to parade his accomplishments. "He's been all over the world. He's worked on every ship engine there is."

"I've been away from the sea over four years now. Mr. Clark hired me because I'm completely familiar with engines, even this petrol type." Howell pointed to the expansive bonnet.

"Do you miss the sea, Mr. Howell?" Emma traced her fingers against the spare tire mounted to the running board.

"He's been to the Americas, the Orient, Africa. Where else, dear?"

Howell shrugged. "Scandinavia and Australia. I drive Mr. Clark exclusively. He has two other drivers, but they prefer the carriages, broughams, and phaetons. I taught them to drive his motorcars. Of course, they're all Rolls Royces. But this Alpine Eagle is the grandest."

Stepping back to better gather in the motorcar, Emma said, "It must be very exciting to drive such a machine." She glanced at the lovers. "It is beautiful. But I must be on my way." Emma dragged her hand across her skirt and brushed away straw.

"We could give you a ride, but I must remain here. Mr. Clark, you know."

"That would be very exciting. Perhaps some other time."

"Goodbye, Dr. Watson." Elizabeth fastened herself to Howell's arm.

Emma stepped into her waiting hansom behind the Alpine Eagle. It moved into the carriageway, and she waved to the couple. She surveyed the Thornton home and noticed the maid standing at an upstairs window, barely visible from the carriageway, watching the lovers kiss.

She carefully slipped Mr. Steele's card from her purse and considered Geoffrey's birthday. The barrister's case, or something similar, would be perfect for him. She was certain it would be expensive, but she cataloged all of the gifts he had lavished on her and was determined to give him something rather extraordinary.

She mulled over the enthusiastic welcome Mrs. Thornton had given banker Trevor Clark and how suggestive it was. Were they having an affair? Even so, it was intolerably gauche behavior given the circumstances. She certainly expected better from Mr. Clark. Perhaps money infected and numbed one's social sensibilities. Geoffrey, too, had been born into privilege—actually titled—but manifested no such affectation or snobbery. His conduct, like his father's and mother's, was always warm and mindful of polite society. Their wealth notwithstanding, Emma thought Geoffrey had inherited the better part from his parents, a singular aplomb tempered with kindness in dealing with people from all social classes.

"Here we are, madam," the driver shouted. She paid him through the trapdoor above, alighted, and referred to a folded pink paper with scrawled addresses.

She walked down the pavement past several well-maintained townhouses, all with neat window boxes with freshly planted flowers that in a month or so would be bursting in vivid color. She checked her paper again—the Haas and Einbecker addresses. She slipped between the buildings and found the dustbin. Everything had been scrubbed clean. She scoured the area for stains, clues, something seemingly innocent, yet indicative. After a ten-minute search, she walked to the front entrance and, had she not grabbed the door handle securely, she would have been knocked down the stone steps to the pavement. The man didn't utter so much as an apology as he burst from the building and dashed across the carriageway to the telegraph office.

Emma collected herself and entered the apartment building. She interviewed the ground floor neighbors, who were all Germans, but no significant leads were discovered. She climbed the stairs to the first floor and found workmen attempting to clean a patch of carpet in front of a flat across the hallway. She knocked on the door opposite the workmen, and a small German woman with uncombed white hair appeared.

Emma was invited in and breathed the sour smell of boiled cabbage coming in waves from the kitchen. She gave Mrs. Haas' close friend a good report on her condition and prognosis. The woman was pleased to hear the news.

"Can you think of anything unusual, disturbing or worrisome that has happened in or around this building prior to Mrs. Haas' unfortunate infection?"

As they sat at a table near the front window, the woman weighed Emma's question. "Herr Krauss, he fery loud 'n angry all da time...'specially da night before. Zorry, dats all I kin tink of." Then she glanced out the window, pointed across the street, and said, "Dat's him."

Emma looked. It was the man who had nearly knocked her down at the entrance. He looked like the kind of man one saw ducking in and out of alleyways. Krauss was talking, gesturing, and appearing very enraged at two women in front of the telegraph office. She leaned closer towards the window. One of the women resembled the German woman she had seen in Dr. Gregory's photographs—Mrs. Gregory.

"Do you know those women?"

"No. I zee dem 'round here," the woman replied, brushing a few stray wisps of hair from her face.

Emma excused herself and said, "Danke." Then she dashed down the stairs to the pavement. The women were getting into a hansom, and Herr Krauss was nowhere in sight. She walked across the carriageway and flagged a hansom, telling the driver to follow the cab ahead but to keep a safe distance.

Her hansom rattled over the cobbles, and Emma hoped the pursuit would not be a waste of her precious time. Despite her devotion to science and logic, she often followed her intuition. Sherlock and her father had sharpened her instincts in her investigations. Especially useful were the times Richard spent with her, retelling their cases and dissecting events in instructive detail. The twins called them postmortems. It was this analytical rehashing and their experience with Sherlock that gave her confidence to follow her hunches, aware that there was a powerful process at work beneath her consciousness. Richard called it female intuition.

"They're stopping," shouted the driver, and reined the horse to a stop.

Emma observed the blonde woman alight from the cab and move quickly towards a grey apartment building. She paused before entering, turned, yelled at her companion in German, shook her fist, then disappeared inside. Emma noted the address, and her body pitched backward against her seat as the hansom lurched into traffic, shadowing the other woman along Benton and Turlingham streets.

The hansom jostled for several blocks. In time the crowded streets gave way to leafy, shaded boulevards lined with grand homes. The cab slowed to a stop near a row of split timber dwellings set back from Warden Street.

She observed the Mrs. Gregory look-alike step from the hansom and walk along a brick and grass approach towards a stately private residence. A large oak offered its shadow along the walkway. When she saw the woman use a key for entry, Emma noted the address and concluded it was the woman's residence.

"St. Bartholomew's, please."

Emma's concern for young Hildy and many new questions searching for answers impelled her to return to the hospital. Hopefully the Einbecker and Haas families could satisfy her curiosity. *Who is this Herr Krauss? How long has he occupied his apartment? Where does he work? Who are his friends? Especially, who are his female friends? Is the woman actually Mrs. Gregory? Why is Krauss angry?* Emma feared the Krauss lead might be fruitless, but she would pursue it to the end.

She visited the two German families at St. Bartholomew's and was disappointed with their guarded comments. She had the strong conviction that they were lying about Krauss, even fearful. Mrs. Haas's son, Gunther, defended Krauss and stomped to the hospital window, withdrawing himself from any further contact. Emma comforted the families, checked the patients' vital signs, and amended their records. She left for home, eager to see Henry and Richard.

When she arrived, Mrs. Mac suggested she talk with her father. She entered his consulting room, and when he saw her, he excused himself to his patient.

"I have a full waiting room here. Can you help? If not, I'll be here until midnight and some of them have been waiting for hours."

"I'll wash up. Where's Richard and Henry?"

"Haven't seen hide nor hair."

Emma served the overflow of patients, and they completed their work for the day nearly on time. Afterward they walked from surgery into the dining room and found Geoffrey, Mary, and Mrs. Mac at table talking. At first Emma did not notice the concern on Mary's face.

Emma explained Hildy's condition to her father. He shook his head bleakly.

The door chimes jangled, drawing Mrs. Mac from the room; she returned with a telegram for Emma. "It's from Richard."

"Read it. Hurry," Mary said.

Emma read aloud:

```
EMMA
IN BLAENLLYN.  ALL IS WELL.  HENRY
SENDS LOVE TO MARY.  MUCH HAS HAPPENED.
COMING HOME.  HENRY STAYING HERE.
RICHARD
```

"Thank God, they're safe! Why didn't he bring Henry back?" Mary asked, concern not yet in her voice. "I'd prefer Henry at this table."

"Wouldn't we all," Mrs. Mac added.

"He says that much happened," Emma said, looking at a glum Geoffrey. "What's wrong?"

Everyone exchanged glances. Mary's smile faded. Geoffrey reached in his pocket.

"I received this telegram an hour ago. It's from my parents. You remember the Thompsons in Straithairn?" He swallowed painfully around his news.

"Go on." Emma felt tension rise in her.

"Mr. Thompson was murdered today at Straithairn station. The killers escaped. Father says rumors tell they were Germans."

"Richard doesn't know about the poor man," Emma said, shaking her head. "I'm sure of it. He would've told us if he knew...for your sake, Geoffrey, if for no other purpose."

"Maybe that's what he meant by 'much happened'?"

Emma wondered but said, "Perhaps."

She brought her notepad to the table and asked Mary for Dr. Gregory's address.

"He lives on Warden Street...middle of the block—an old home. I've delivered parcels there a few times for him."

"Is this address familiar to you?" She pushed the notepad across the table.

"My birth date...one-sixteen. How could I forget the address of my department head and his German wife? It's the Gregorys.'"

CHAPTER 10

"Looks like a fine day," Richard said as the spring wind coaxed the fog up the valleys. "You'll need these." He handed Henry a roll of pound notes.

"I can't. I won't."

"Don't start that again, Henry." Richard stuffed the roll into Henry's pocket. He slapped his chum's back and walked outside. "Stay hidden. Hear me now. Keep your eyes skinned for the Huns. Don't leave this dormitory. Remember, Lucas will be arranging your meals."

The colliers were leaving for work as Henry stared at the wad of money. He pushed it deep into his pocket and looked up to see Richard, but he had joined the exodus of miners from the colliery men's dormitory, where they had spent the night.

He hurried to the door. "Richard, tell Mary I love her. Solve this business."

"I will. Don't worry, old chap. We'll set everything to rights. *Truth will come to light...in the end truth will out.* Merchant of Venice. Stay low, old chap." Richard ambled down the dirt road until he disappeared behind rows of sooty, slate-roofed houses.

Henry stood in the open doorway of the dormitory and admired his old church bathed in morning light. The stained glass glowed as a steady trail of colliers trudged past her for their sunless work deep underground. He was drawn outside and decided to walk the gravel and cinder slope used for haulage to the top of a slag pile next to the Number Ten shaft—a new anthracite dig. He sat down and dangled his legs over the edge of the slag. He hadn't seen the panorama of his valley for many years. From a vast distance Henry watched the slow parade of men treading up the hill for their black duty. These were Henry's people more than the university pedants and the snooty elite of London. The colliers were genuine, possessing unstinting loyalty to each other, to their valley, and to the black gold they mined. As they went past him, he recognized many. Those he knew by name returned his call and rapped their knuckles on their helmets or tin lunch pails filled with pasties.

"Henry," his old friend Lucas Griffin called out. "Tonight at seven. Margaret and the children wanna see ya at dinner."

"Be careful down there, Lucas."

He sat on the slag and reflected on the pivotal night his father had returned from work covered in coal dust, his eyes and teeth the only part of him unblackened. Henry was seven years old then, and his teacher had informed his mother that Henry was gifted. He remembered how his father's eyes blinked at the news that Bramwell Rhys, patriarch of the Rhys family, had learned of Henry's unusual scholastic promise and would fund his enrollment at a prestigious academy. Bramwell Rhys had offered to move the Davies family to London so Henry could attend the elite Penrose Academy for Boys and Girls. Henry's parents were to work in Rhys' London office while Henry boarded at Penrose. Within a month of their arrival in London, an incident happened at colliery Number Eighteen that caused Henry's family to return to Wales, leaving him at Penrose profoundly alone for the first time in his young life.

Young Henry's aching loneliness had slowly dissipated more because of the Watsons and less because of his grit. Henry chuckled as he sat on the slag. He remembered the moment when his loneliness had broken like a high fever. He sat there smiling, his heels digging into the slag, sending fragments rolling down to the bottom.

It was the day Mr. Campbell had introduced the Watson twins to his Penrose class. The headmaster had opened the classroom door, and Richard and Emma self-consciously tiptoed towards the man's desk at the front of the classroom. Mr. Campbell said ceremoniously, "Young ladies and gentlemen, please welcome Miss Emma Ann Watson and her twin brother, Master Richard Sherlock Watson."

It had been only four months prior to then that Henry had stood in the same place for the same reason and had seen the same clean-faced, grey-jacketed boys and pinafored girls. Perched on the slag, Henry heard the voices of his classmates reciting the class welcome to Richard and Emma. Then the exuberant headmaster swung his hickory pointer across his desk and accidentally launched the open bottle of India ink into the air and onto Emma, Richard, and four children in the front row. The twins danced and jumped, swiping at the ink. Ink went everywhere, and in the confusion, Mr.

Campbell tripped backwards and fell to the wood floor, knocking over a rack of maps and a pitcher of water. When he got to his feet, he slipped on the wet floorboards and shouldered the front wall, bringing Queen Victoria's solemn portrait shattering down on his head. Most of the children were giggling and squealing. Others sat mute, frightened, while the two ink-stained children he would soon regard as brother and sister were hopping around. That was the moment Henry sensed his time at Penrose would never be the same. He did not know then that Richard and Emma's friendship would become a vital part of his life forever.

Abruptly, shrill whistles sounded and echoed throughout the valley. They signaled the shift change at the collieries, quarries, and carriage shops. Valley people claimed they could discern the subtle differences among signals at various shafts. Henry played the game atop the slag. *That's Number Seven. Number Eighteen.* Their pitch and warble had not changed since he had lived there as a child. *That's Number Six*, and he glanced sadly in its direction to the south. His eyes fixed on Number Six for a long moment.

"James. Good old Jamezee."

He bit his lip and thought of his only brother. How they had played and enjoyed each other during his summer visits to Blaenllyn. James had been killed in an explosion at Number Six. Twelve other men perished with him. Coal gas—methane, odorless and highly flammable. It or its evil companion, structural collapse, had affected every family in the valley.

The whistling stopped, their last reverberations fading across the valley. An unexpected horn blared. Speeding up the cindered road towards him was a red motorcar with a woman at the wheel. She honked and waved all the way, coal and cinders pluming from the spinning wheels.

"Henry! Henry!"

The car pulled around several coal-laden lorries, causing the hauliers to swerve and brake. The motorcar shot to the top and chattered to a sliding stop. A woman with a torrent of redwood-colored hair jumped out. She deliberately stopped for him to view her from head to toe. She pirouetted; she was dressed like an Argentinean gaucho with high leather boots, a brown split skirt with fringe, white blouse, and a fringed, orange leather vest spangled with silver.

She placed her hands on her hips. "It's me. Fiona! Fiona Rhys."

Henry climbed to his feet, slag sliding underfoot.

"Be careful, Henry."

They faced each other.

"Fiona?"

Fiona Rhys was the only child of Bramwell Rhys. She was a free-spirited, adventurous woman who took a train to Edinburgh without permission when she was six years old. That launched a three-day, frantic search across the whole of England. Fiona was born three days after Henry, and their mothers, while in hospital together, made a pact—Henry would marry Fiona.

Henry considered it an impossible match. During four consecutive summers, Fiona carried on a regular flirtation with Richard when he and his sister visited the valley with Henry. Fiona's father and mother tolerated Richard's unorthodox style, but reserved their adulation for Henry. After all, Richard would be a starving artist in some God-forsaken garret far away. Fiona could never be happy with him. But Henry was solid, dependable, and brilliant. The Rhyses kept fanning the flames for Henry in spite of Fiona's many capricious affairs and boisterous adventures across the Continent and beyond.

"Fiona, will you never change?" But she had, he realized. She was beautiful.

She whirled around. "Do you like it? I got it in South America last year. Should I wear a hat?"

"No. It would hide that spectacular hair."

Henry extended his hand, but Fiona Rhys went into his arms and pressed herself against him. He had to hold her tight to keep them from tumbling down the slag.

"Henry. They said you were here. I can't believe it!"

"Fiona, you look...wonderful."

"Is that all you can say?"

"I...I think of you often," Henry replied, not knowing why he said it.

"You're always on my mind, too."

Perhaps beautiful was not the word. She had matured into a sultry woman of twenty-eight, wise to the world, and bent on seeing and experiencing life on her terms. Since Henry could remember, Fiona was rarely still. Even in a photograph, she appeared to be poised for flight, hair whipping in all directions, dark eyes challenging, and a full-lipped mouth pouting coquettishly. She grew up playing with boys and had no interest in female friendships, although she was fond of Emma, who was the only female with whom she exchanged regular correspondence.

"How are Richard and Em?"

"Well. Quite well, I should say. Is this your motorcar?"

Fiona grabbed Henry's hand and tugged him towards the machine. It was gleaming, shiny red with painted gold trim. "It's a Fiat Zero. Made in Italy only a few months ago. A roadster! I've had it up to seventy kilometers per hour. Can you think of it? Seventy."

Henry circled the motorcar with Fiona at his side. He touched its brightwork, paint, and white canvas top.

"Let's have a ride." She scrambled inside to unfasten the canvas. "Help me." Henry didn't move. "Henry, now." Fiona Rhys, like her father, was the type to whom one had difficulty saying no. After the canvas was removed and stowed, she cranked the engine, climbed behind the steering wheel, and bounced up and down on her seat. "Get in. Get in."

Henry slipped onto the supple black leather seats. He closed his door and Fiona spun the motorcar and shot down the cinder path, soon speeding through the small village of Blaenllyn. Henry's one hand was on the door, and the other was braced against the dashboard. The windows were down, and her hair caught the wind. "Let's go to Aberystwyth."

"Aberystwyth! You're mad, Fiona."

She laughed, hair strands caught in her mouth.

"It'll take all day, Fiona," Henry said, gently freeing the hair, tracing his finger across her soft cheek.

"I know. I know."

"And slow down. We aren't in London."

"Let's see how fast we can go." Fiona glanced at Henry. "I'm a great driver. Don't look so terrified."

"Mind the big rock." Henry stiff-armed the dashboard as Fiona veered left and right.

"All day together."

"I'm having dinner with Lucas and his family tonight," Henry shouted as the machine sped up.

Fiona glanced across at him. "We might be back in time."

"Strange," Dr. John said. "I've scoured the paper. There's no mention of the murder investigation. The police are being tight-lipped on this one."

"I found a thread to follow," Emma said. "I'll see Gordon this morning. Hopefully the crime scene, too."

"My regards to Lestrade. Ask about his father for me." He folded the newspaper and tossed it across the table to Emma. "The article there. That's good for Henry."

"A new science building?" Emma adjusted her pince-nez. "Says the contracts were signed yesterday at a ceremony attended by Chancellor McWilliams, Dr. Gregory, Trevor Clark, who gifted the funds, and Ian Mansfield of Mansfield Builders." She looked at her father. "Good for Henry? Father, Henry's no longer employed by the university."

"The university will welcome Henry back if for no other reason than because of his discovery. Money...prestige...you know academia. You and Richard will get to the truth. Hurry home. I'll be needing your help if today is like yesterday."

Leaving her scone half-eaten, Emma collected her purse and checked herself in the mirror.

"You've given up corsets, have ya?" Mrs. Mac asked.

"Never again...terrible things," Emma said, smoothing her skirts. "Rearranges a woman's internal organs. It's a tyranny...a whalebone tyranny. I've treated many women for dislocated shoulders and elbows as a result of hanging from the lacing bars...all for the hourglass. It's torture. Too confining, like not having the right to vote."

"Yer waist is tiny 'nough as 'tis. Yer the very image of your beautiful mother." Mrs. Mac's loving eyes watched her. "No split skirt. No bicycle today?"

"I'm giving Freedom a spot of rest. I'll try to be home for lunch."

Emma hurried outside, hailed a hansom, and headed for St. Bartholomew's. When she entered the women's wardroom, she discovered Mrs. Haas sitting up and eating breakfast with her husband at her side.

"I see Dr. Hazeltine examined you this morning."

"Ja, today I go home."

"That's welcome news. Where's Gunther?"

Frowns crossed their faces.

"Gunther, vell...Gunther..." Mr. Haas stammered, "he had accident. At home."

"I trust nothing serious."

"Nein. No. Not serious."

"Please give him my regards. Now, about Herr Krauss, your neighbor." Mrs. Haas stopped eating.

"He yust comes unt goes," Mr. Haas replied.

"Where does he work?"

"Fur da Deutsch...zorry, da German guferment."

"I'm told he is an angry man. He almost knocked me down the steps of your apartment building."

The Haases tried to mask their growing unease. Emma waited, her eyes darting from husband to wife and back. She had touched on a sensitive spot. The woman glanced at the divider screen separating the Einbecker bed from her own. She gestured for Emma to move closer. Mr. Haas edged closer, too, more for inclusion than for information.

Mrs. Haas whispered with a watchful eye on the divider. "Herr Krauss is not...goot man. Vell, heez noisy unt loud, ja? Alvays yellink. I don't know vhat say."

"What do you know about the women who visit him?"

"Not'ink. Dhey sometime yellink, too. Ja, dhey meet in German...vhat shoult I say...German Club, I t'ink."

"You mean the German Society Hall down the carriageway a piece?" Emma asked, remaining close to Mrs. Haas.

"Ja, dat, too. Dhey members."

"Herr Krauss belongs to the German Society and another club?"

"Ja, doctor. I dun know 'bout da utter club."

"Do the women belong to those clubs?"

"Da vemen go to both clubs, ja," whispered Mr. Haas with his hand to his lips.

Emma was getting close to something.

"Have the police asked you these questions?"

"Dhey yoost ask if vee knew vhere da gluff and hank-vhatefer came from. Ja, dhat's all."

"The glove and handerkerchief?"

"Ja."

"What did you tell the police?"

"Nefer seen dhem tinks."

Emma smiled and patted Mrs. Haas' arm. "Thank you. Now, get some rest."

"Ja, rest," Mrs. Haas said.

"I will visit you at home to check your progress."

Mrs. Haas became noticeably fearful. "Oh, dat von't be needed. Tank you anyvay."

"I care about your progress."

"Vee are zimple people," Mr. Haas added. "You don't need care for us."

"Your case is very unusual. I'm required to watch your progress." Emma observed the couple attempt to hide something very deep. "Don't worry. I merely want to examine your injury and make certain it is healing properly and change the bandage. That's important, you know." Emma withdrew to the other side of the divider.

Hildegaard's mother was brushing the girl's silky hair.

"Hildy, dhis iz Dr. Vatson."

"Pleased to meet you," Hildy said in perfect English.

"You speak wonderful English." Hildy blushed, bringing a wash of pink to her plump cheeks. "I want to check your chart for a moment," Emma said, and lifted it from the hook. There was no sign of further infection, and her vital signs were improving.

Emma sat on the side of the girl's bed, chatted, and had the girl smiling and giggling within moments. But Hildy winced and screwed her face when she moved her injured hand. Emma placed her own gently on the girl's knee and patted and stroked her as they talked.

"You might be going home in a few days if you keep up this progress," Emma said. "I will visit you at home, and I promise to bring a lovely surprise." Hildy's eyes brightened. "Do you remember the smelly purple cream that was on the glove and handkerchief you touched that made you sick?"

Hildy nodded, anxiety shadowing her face.

"It's the same bad substance that hurt Mrs. Haas next to you." Hildy pointed towards the divider. "Have you ever seen the glove or handkerchief before?"

"No."

"Do you know to whom they belong, dear?"

She shook her head.

"Have you ever seen or smelled that bad purple substance before?"

"Yes." The word tripped out, spontaneous and without guile.

"You have?" Emma looked at the girl's parents, who were wide-eyed. "Where? When?"

"The night before I got sick," Hildy said. Her eyes searched Emma's.

"Where did you see it?"

"I smelled it."

"You smelled it at night? Where?"

"In front of our building. A mean lady," she said and mumbled a sentence in German to her parents. To Emma's ear, it appeared to include the name Herr Krauss. Her parents gave knowing looks to each other and made no effort to hide it.

"A mean lady? Have you seen her before?"

"Oh yes, doctor. She visits Mr. Krauss every day." Hildy glanced at her parents, and they nodded agreement.

"What was this mean lady doing when you smelled the substance?"

Hildy's gaze went to her parents.

"Go on. Tell goot doctor," her father said.

Emma displayed her warmest expression, hoping Hildy would feel free to continue.

"I was a bad girl. It was past my bedtime and I was bad. I went outside to play with Gertie. She pushed me away and made me fall. That's when I smelled it."

"Gertie pushed you and she had the stinky substance?"

Hildy giggled. "No, doctor. The mean lady pushed me away from her. She was in a hurry. She pushed me down."

Hildy's father spoke up in halting English. "Ja. Vee heard Hildy cryink and ...vee caught her out vhen she suppos-ed ta be in. Vee spank-ed her.

Didn't vee?" Hildy was embarrassed. She rested her head on the pillow and closed her eyes.

"You've seen this woman before? Do you know her name?"

"Seen before many time," Mrs. Einbecker said. "No name."

"Would you recognize her if you saw her again?"

They nodded and Hildy said, "Ah-huh."

"Have you told any of this to the police?"

Hildy shook her head. Her father added, "She only yust voke. Vee hafen't zeen da police today. Yesterday, ja."

"What did they ask you?"

"Just about da poison unt da gluff."

Emma kissed Hildy's forehead. She removed the girl's bandage and examined her injury. Emma was thrilled at what she saw and applied a fresh, sterile wrap with a splint to minimize Hildy's painful hand movements.

"After you're home I'll visit you and I'll have a wonderful gift."

"What will it be?"

"A surprise, Hildy."

After disposing of the old bandage, tidying the instruments, and adding notations to the chart, Emma left the wardroom on her way to visit her childhood friend, Chief Detective Inspector Gordon Lestrade.

CHAPTER 11

"Emma."

Lestrade hurried to the front of his small office desk, delighted by her arrival. He led her to a chair and offered tea.

"Still in your father's old office. Could do with some paint."

Brushing her dress and blouse while his back was turned, she surveyed the office and considered the similarity of their lives. She had not realized until then that they both occupied their fathers' old offices. The room had not changed one whit since they were children.

"And the old desk. Wonderful." She wondered if the mark was still here. She sighted along the desk's front edge and found the deep groove Richard had gouged with his jackknife when their father had dragged the twins along to see Gordon's father on a case with Sherlock. "Father gave Richard a perfect hiding for this." Her finger crossed the long, defacing groove in the wood.

"A great artist did that." Lestrade laughed. He handed Emma a beaker of tea, taking a furtive glance at her ring finger. He sat beside her, not behind his desk—the custom drummed into him by his father. Lestrade's eyes danced over her familiar features, and when her eyes met his, he felt an inner thrill only Emma could arouse.

"I haven't seen you for a month or more," Emma said, sipping her tea. "Father sends his best and asked about your parents."

"Father is well, all things considered. But Mother is unwell. She's using a cane now. Progressive, you know. You should visit them sometime. It would lift their spirits."

"I shall do that, Gordon." Emma sipped more hot tea, rather pleased at Gordon's attention to her. She had applied a light touch of lip rouge, and his attentive eyes fastened on her mouth and lingered. Emma blushed. "I heard you are on the Nigel Thornton case," she said quickly.

"I knew you or Richard would be coming to me." Lestrade looked at his childhood love. "We'll find Henry."

Emma disliked not being able to tell him as much as she knew. Lightly she asked, "Do you honestly believe Henry committed the murder? You know Henry almost as well as Richard and I—in some ways, perhaps better."

"The facts, Emma. I must allow the facts to direct the investigation. You know that." He knew that she did, but he was compelled to say it anyway. They shared an interest in logic and a thoroughgoing pursuit of evidence, whether in medicine or criminal detection.

"Gordon, we both want to get to the core of this awful murder, don't we? Two heads are better than one, so—"

"This case is highly confidential, Emma," Lestrade interrupted her. "It's sealed. The Crown is giving it the highest attention. Mycroft is involved, and you know what that means." Lestrade stared at his cup. "He tried to arm-twist me into backing away from this case. He and the Admiralty want carte blanche, no interference. Mycroft believes there are international implications to Thornton's death."

"But you will not accede to his wishes, surely."

"I have responsibilities. Mycroft knows I'll share my information with him, as I have done before and like my father before me. We're all seeking Henry."

"You see, Gordon? Two heads are better than one...you and Mycroft. Like the Bible says, 'A wise man profits from many counselors.' You must continue. If this case has international ramifications, think how its successful conclusion will bring glory to the Yard. You'll be given your due. And I want to help you on this vital case, secretly, of course. You know I must find the truth, even if it hurts Henry. This case has struck too close to us to be ignored. I can't turn my back on it. We must work together regardless of Mycroft's bluster."

"Emma, please."

"You will agree that people will confide in me because I'm a physician?"

"I've skirted the rules and turned a blind eye in the past, but Emma, this is—"

"And you'll agree that our past collaborations have been fruitful?" She glanced around his office with its appointments and awards. They were a clear acknowledgement of his rapid ascension to his position as Chief Detective Inspector, the youngest in the history of Scotland Yard. She never doubted Gordon's awareness of the significant role she and Richard had played in his rapid rise. The cases they had helped him solve—the truth would never be known that they had cracked several famous cases for him, not so much with him; nevertheless he garnered all praise, propelling his advancement. But she had to remind him. "All your awards and progress at the Yard were achieved by you acting alone...in a vacuum? Think about it, Gordon."

"But this case has monumental implications," Lestrade protested, gripping the arms of his chair. Emma placed her hand on his.

"You must not ignore my eyes and ears and brain. Unless you think I'm an ignoramus and impotent to help," Emma said, an eyebrow arching. She knew he was fond of her. She was the first girl he had ever kissed. It was in Beeton Park. She detested asserting her femininity, but it had always worked with Gordon. She desperately hoped it worked now for Henry's sake.

Lestrade heaved a sigh. "Emma, you know that's not true. I respect you and I—"

"Then let me help you. You know in your heart I'm better than any man you have on the force." Emma watched her words sink in. She stroked his forearm as if massaging the truth into him. "I can assume every man Jack you have involved in Henry's case is the best the Yard has to offer."

"Yes, I've assigned our best. Muldowney and Swayne."

"And I'm sure you have your top men guarding the crime scene at university."

"Of course, Emma. Reliable chaps, all." Lestrade sipped his tea.

"Gordon, if your men at university are, as you say, reliable, then you are going to need all the help you can get," Emma declared as she delivered a scathing report on Constable Graves's behavior. She explained the story of her harassment in graphic detail and Lestrade's jaw tightened.

"Emma, please accept my apology. I'll see to this matter personally."

"Of greater importance is getting to the truth," Emma said, exploiting her advantage. "That's what we both want. Gordon, I want to see the crime scene. Take me there. Now."

"I can't—"

"I'm a scientist. It's a laboratory. We can view the scene together. Maybe we can see it from a fresh viewpoint...together. Like old times." Emma didn't wait for his reply. She stood up and straightened her skirt. "Let's be on our way."

"Emma." Lestrade slowly pushed his chair away. "Very well...a ten-minute look. That's all I can give you."

"Ten minutes or perhaps less." Emma pulled him towards the door.

When they arrived outside, he commandeered a Scotland Yard carriage going to the livery. He handed Emma into the carriage, and they arrived at university far too soon for Lestrade's taste. They strode down the school's corridor towards Mary Palmer's office, where Constable Graves snapped to attention and turned white as the walls when he saw Emma approaching with his Chief Inspector. He greeted Lestrade with military stiffness, and he received an unrelenting and crushing censure. Lestrade was red-faced and strident. Then he finally realized his voice was resounding in the marble hall. He stopped mid-sentence. Lestrade opened the door and allowed Emma to visit with Mary; then he took Constable Graves outside for a final dressing down loud enough that the ladies could hear him from inside the building. They laughed at first, but it continued.

Emma was surprised at Gordon's vehemence. As if he were punishing the man for complete dereliction of duty or, in Lestrade's view, something far worse—dishonoring a woman. She knew one of Gordon's undeniable qualities was his moral rectitude. She did not realize Gordon could become so incensed—not the normally placid Gordon she had known since childhood. She expected volatility from Richard; he was explosively passionate—but Gordon? Emma nudged her chief inspector friend a bit higher in her esteem.

Minutes later when Lestrade arrived composed, he found Emma standing with Mary. He pointed to Constable Miller guarding the inner laboratory door and asked, "What about Miller here?" Emma and Mary reluctantly nodded in the constable's direction—feeling uneasy, not wanting the same fury to be visited upon the man. Lestrade settled on a solemn warning that caused the constable to stand like a statue. He gave him a final warning, then opened the door to the lab. There he found Constable Stratton looking out the window. He was aghast to see Lestrade striding towards him.

While Lestrade was busy dressing down the third constable, Emma began her inspection. She entered Henry's office and surveyed his desk. She noticed a scribbled note on his calendar. It was the one considered very incriminating. "Deal with Nigel's lie." She made a note of it and glanced around for anything else that would catch her interest. Nothing did, and she entered Dr. Thornton's lab, where Lestrade was watching Constable Stratton return to his post inside the laboratory near the door. The constable walked past her with his eyes straight ahead.

"Emma, you and Miss Palmer won't be troubled by them again. And if you are," Lestrade spoke loudly in Stratton's direction, aware the other two beyond the wall would hear also, "I'll personally give them the sack."

Emma squeezed Lestrade's forearm. "Thanks, Gordon. Now, about Henry's note." She motioned for him to follow her to Henry's office. "Have you fingerprinted it?"

"Why?"

"If I wanted to falsely implicate someone, I'd write a note like this one. Wouldn't you?"

"I never thought of that. Do you really think—"

"It's a possibility, and it's easy enough to check, is it not? I'd have your people compare the handwriting and fingerprints."

Emma kept her hand on his arm with complete knowledge of its effect. Richard had told her many times that she knew how to steer Gordon as if he were a ship and she the rudder. He wrote himself a note, eyebrows knitted, fascinated by a new idea.

"What's the estimate of time of death?"

"Dr. Mull says between ten and midnight."

"Would you be a dear and explain the crime scene to me?"

Lestrade wasted no time to showcase his knowledge of the investigation. He showed her where Dr. Thornton was found, where his body was positioned when discovered, and he described the condition of the corpse. Emma hung on his words as if they were coming from King Solomon himself. He showed her where two cups with saucers, tongs, and a tea pot were found on the laboratory counter, along with rolled floor plans for the new science building. And he led Emma into Henry's area of the lab and pointed to where a distillation apparatus was found broken. He pointed in a wide arc, indicating the area where pieces of its glass were found. "There had been a struggle, knocking that contrivance to the floor. See all the shards in the rubbish bin here?" Emma oohed and aahed. "The killer had hurriedly cleaned up the mess, you see," he finished.

"Splendid. Let's have a look in Dr. Thornton's laboratory again." She took his hand. "Where are the cups and teapot and tongs?"

"Over there in the sink."

"How did they get there?"

"I...well, I assume one of the detectives."

Emma read his hesitancy. "You assume, but..." she prompted

"Maybe, what's her name, Evelyn Moxely, put them there. She found the body. Works in the next room." He looked at Emma and could see she considered it curious. He ordered Constable Stratton, "Ask Miss Moxely if she placed the pot and teacups in the sink. Now."

"Where are the tongs?" Emma asked.

"At the Yard. They were dripping with poison."

"Really! Was the china fingerprinted and analyzed?" Emma kept her query soft. Lestrade shook his head. "Probably it's of little consequence, but if Henry's fingerprints are on one of the cups, well, I was just thinking. And I notice that the can here contains green tea. You surely know Henry detests green tea, for some reason."

"Give me good old black or Darjeeling...orange pekoe."

Emma frowned. "I'd have that tea analyzed and the china, too. It's surely a minor thing, but I imagine you need to collect as many clues as you can, don't you? Did you discover anything from the surfaces of the laboratory?"

"The poison was smeared on the counter and floor. Terrible. Vile. Lethal."

"Was it widespread or concentrated?"

Using his pencil, Lestrade outlined an area at the corner of the granite countertop.

"Less than a square foot, then. And the floor?"

Lestrade squatted down and outlined a discolored patch on the stained wood floor. Emma had already noted it.

"See the faint purple, or is it violet?" Lestrade asked.

"Upon my word. It looks like a smear left by the heel of a hand...the wrist and probably the palm, here and there," Emma said, pointing with the toe of her high-buttoned shoe. "Any blood?"

"None."

"None? Not from the invasive poison or from his fall to the floor or the broken distillation apparatus?"

"None."

A large, locked storage cabinet caught Emma's attention. "What's inside this cabinet?"

"Chemicals and laboratory notebooks."

"You fingerprinted this cabinet, of course?"

Lestrade bit his lip.

"Let's have a look," she said, smiling. "How ever shall we open it without disturbing the prints?" She waited for Lestrade to rescue her.

"Ah!" Removing his wooden pencil from his pocket, he wedged it between the doors and pried them apart. He pushed them open with the pencil tip, and Emma nodded. "Gordon... very clever. Was this cabinet unlocked when you found it?"

"Yes."

Emma scanned the contents.

"The left side is Dr. Thornton's. The right side is Henry's," Lestrade said.

Officer Stratton interrupted and reported that Miss Moxely did not touch the china and did not know who did.

"It took you long enough," Lestrade said. "You weren't in there chatting her up, were you?" The constable shook his head and resumed guarding the laboratory door.

"Look how fastidious Henry and Dr. Thornton were with their labels," said Emma. "See the printing and information? And notice how neat the lab notebooks are. You should've seen mine when I was in school. I'm impressed with this." Emma gave it all a sweep of her hand.

"Aw, go on, Emma...your notebooks were probably perfect. But you're right, it is impressive."

She studied the boxes and bottles and jars of chemicals, then found an empty cubbyhole. She fished in her purse and removed a brass jeweler's loupe. Emma's eye studied the cubbyhole's surfaces.

"Gordon, here's the same violet stain. Here and here and there," she said, handing the loupe to him. "Have a look."

Lestrade examined the stains. "By Jove. Violet, indeed."

"Any indication of it elsewhere?"

Lestrade studied the other cubbyhole partitions and after several moments said, "None."

"What do you make of that?"

Lestrade shrugged his shoulders and reexamined the surfaces.

"There was a container of poison in the empty slot," Emma said.

Lestrade looked at her, his face blank. "Here's your loupe," he said.

Emma said carefully, "Someone nicked the poison, and if it's the Germans," she hesitated, "if they decide to use it, good heavens! Perish the thought."

Lestrade stood loose-jawed. After a long pause, he said, "Quite. You could be correct. On the other hand, Henry probably took it with him when he fled."

Emma gave him a look.

"Why not, Emma?"

She refused further comment and glanced around the cabinet as if trying to find something. Suddenly she reached back and grasped Lestrade's arm.

"Hello. Look at this."

Lestrade didn't know what to look at; his eyes roamed everywhere inside the cabinet.

"Here." Emma pointed. "Two lab books with the same number. They're on Dr. Thornton's side. And look at all his notebooks. Dr. Thornton has eighty...let me see, yes, eighty-six. Henry only has fifteen." She looked at Lestrade again and saw a complete lack of comprehension.

"Gordon, observe the condition of Dr. Thornton's number sixteen. Compare it with the newer styles. Why is a new number sixteen on Dr. Thornton's side of the cabinet beside his old number sixteen? And please study the labeling on the newer one. It matches Henry's labels. Then why is it on Dr. Thornton's side?" She stared at the notebooks. "Maybe fingerprinting might suggest something. You surely must agree, Gordon." Lestrade grunted. "Someone unaccustomed to the scientists' scheme misplaced the newer number sixteen, and quite likely he did so in great haste."

"Curious."

"Which way to the deceased's office?" Emma asked.

He led her to the dangerously overfilled room crammed with stacked books and charts and teetering piles of chemical catalogs. It was difficult to move about. Emma stepped over two low heaps, already on the floor near the entrance. The office was dark and smelled of old, yellowing paper and chemicals—sour, like a closet filled with old linen.

"Looks a bit dodgy to me," said Emma.

"I asked Mary Palmer if this place had been ransacked. She said that it's always like this. But who would know?"

"Gordon, light the gas mantle, will you?"

He found a match in his coat pocket and snapped it with his fingernail. Before long a warm light revealed the full extent of the disarray. Emma studied Dr. Thornton's desk. All the drawers were pulled out at varying distances.

"What higgledly-piggledly," she said. "Richard would be at home in this jumble."

"I should have this desk dusted for prints. It does look like someone rifled it. That idiot Swayne should've seen to it."

Emma encouraged him, determined to make certain all avenues of inquiry led away from Henry. She scanned the top of Dr. Thornton's desk, reading addressed envelopes, notes, and scribblings.

"My word, Gordon, look. What do you make of this?"

Lestrade stepped over and around the stacks and stood as close to Emma as he dared, but not as close as he desired. She pointed to a square sheet of costly writing parchment.

Lestrade read it aloud. "Nigel. You know why I'm here. Time to settle your debts. CS." Lestrade reread it, looked at Emma, and knew what she was about to say. "This must be fingerprinted, too. Rather interesting."

In such disorganized, close confines, Lestrade became uncomfortable next to Emma. His hand was hesitant as he took hers and helped her step over several awkward stacks. They walked through the laboratory, and she stopped where Dr. Thornton had been discovered. She eyed the doors, pointed, and asked, "Have you fingerprinted—"

"We printed Henry's door and the communicating door leading into the lab. They were found ajar and unlocked, and that's very incriminating. You must agree with that."

"No one forced their way in?"

"Only Henry had the keys."

"Unless they were picked. That is a possibility. Were Dr. Thornton's doors unlocked?" He nodded. "Gordon, you mentioned the plans for the new science building. Where are they? Were they fingerprinted?"

"Maybe we should print them. I believe they are in Dr. Gregory's possession. I must check."

They walked out of the lab, and Lestrade glared at each constable. Emma said, "I would like to ask a question of Miss Moxely." He led her down the hall and into the office.

"Miss Moxely," Emma said, "how is the lab storage cabinet maintained so neat and well arranged?"

"Dr. Thornton and Dr. Davies are fanatical about it. Nobody is permitted to touch anything."

"You don't file their laboratory notebooks, or place specimens or chemicals in the storage cubbyholes?"

"No, madam. Only Thornton and Davies. If a shipment arrives, Mary or I put it in their office. That's all."

"How did the tea service get moved to the laboratory sink?"

"I really have no idea," Miss Moxely said.

They thanked her and left. When they arrived at Constable Graves, Lestrade stopped. "Well, Graves?" The constable apologized profusely to Emma. It had become a confession, not simply to be endured but for Emma's entertainment. The situation was becoming humorous, and she feared her eyes gave her away. When Graves finished, Lestrade and Emma boarded the waiting Scotland Yard carriage and headed for Emma's home and surgery on Carlisle Street. On the way the two old friends shared a few memories and compared theories on the case. Still, Gordon Lestrade defended his pursuit of Henry as the only viable suspect with a motive, method, and opportunity.

"Please give my regards to your father and Richard," Gordon said as he handed her down from the carriage.

"And my best to your parents, too."

She waved as he drove off.

"For Henry's sake," she admonished herself, "stay on Gordon's good side."

CHAPTER 12

Richard emerged from Paddington Station and made for Carlisle Street, eager to learn of Emma's progress. A curiosity suddenly drew him to Henry's flat. He stood outside the grey stone building and surveyed the busy street for any sign of police surveillance and found only the usual fuss and clatter. He quickly went to Henry's flat and examined the locked door, but found no sign of forced entry. He went to the ground floor and knocked on the landlady's door. He turned around to face her as she grumbled in through the entrance behind him.

"Richard. Ain't seen yer fur awhile. Ya look a right sight like ya slept in 'em clothes."

"I did, madam."

Much of her grey hair was free of pins. She blew stray hair from her eyes and lowered her grocery bags. "'Ave yer 'eard 'bout 'enry? Pityful. I thought 'e were a fine Chrishun boy. 'E knew 'is Bible. I kin say 'at fur 'im."

"Madam, Henry's innocent."

"'At ain't what people are sayin'," she said, opening the door to her flat. "'Ere, kin yer give an old lady 'elp?" She pointed to the two overfilled cloth bags from the greengrocer. Richard toted them inside for her.

Helping her arrange the vegetables on the drain board in the scullery, Richard asked, "Madam, have there been investigators or anyone asking about Henry?"

"That one goes o'er 'ere with 'em," she said, scrubbing potatoes. "And these go, too."

"Madam, have people been round asking questions?"

"Coppers. All kind of 'em."

"Any other people?"

"Ain't been t'others 'ceptin' that one 'cross the way. Yer'll see 'im out the window." Richard accompanied her to the living room.

"The one with the sling?"

"Aye, 'at's 'im. Olduns come at night. Watchin'. Lookin'. Do yer think they be coppers?"

"Absolutely not. Look at his clothes. They aren't British."

"N'er noticed. Acourse yer right. 'N there were a gil askin' fur 'im. Purdy l'l thing she were. She as like she been cryin', I'd say. Fussin' 'n goin' on, she were."

Richard thought it might be Emma. "Short brown hair, brown eyes, pince-nez, dimples here and here, about this tall," Richard said, raising his hand, "carrying a physician's bag?"

"Nah, 'tweren't 'er."

"Of course," Richard mused to himself. The woman said the girl was asking for Henry. Emma knew he wouldn't be here. Then it must have been Mary.

"Did she have angel eyes, fair, light long hair to her shoulders, a tiny mole here at her lip?" Richard asked, pointing to the corner of his mouth.

"Aye, the mole. Aye, 'at t'were the gil. She were polite, but she were wound up like a clock. Left 'im a note."

"Where?"

"'Pigeon'ole out 'ere," she said with a wave towards the entrance.

"Thank you, madam. I'd like to see it," Richard said, walking away.

"Don't bother yersef. I saw a man walk in, plainer 'n dirt 'n take it. I yelled I did, 'n he yelled at me. Coont make out a word."

"A foreigner, madam?"

"'E were angry. I knew 'at much. Don't want me eyes ta see 'im again."

"I shall take my leave now. Good seeing you."

"I pray yer right," she said, adjusting her apron.

"About what?"

"'Enry, 'at's what. 'E's a good lad. Pays rent on time. Reg'lar, not like 'em t'others."

Richard returned to his waiting hansom. As the cab jockeyed in the carriageway, he assessed the young thug with the sling and fighter's nose watching Henry's flat. He was shuffling his feet and looked unhappy to be there. Richard wondered about the surveillance. *Who is he? He's no Yarder. Probably a German... perhaps the German crowd Mycroft spoke of. He should be interrogated. Who is the man who took Mary's note? What did the note say? Mary will remember what she wrote.* He hoped it didn't contain information the Germans could use against Henry.

Arriving at university, he asked the cab driver to wait again and he proceeded into the science building and down the corridor. He approached Constable Graves, and as he reached for the door, the officer stopped him with a stiff arm.

"Where do ya think yar goin'?"

"Mary Palmer. I'm Richard Watson. Tell her I'm waiting to talk with her."

"Watson. You wouldn't be... Do ya 'ave a missus?"

"No. Why?"

"There was another Watson come bargin' in 'ere like she owned a place. Friend o' me inspector."

"Ah, yes...right. Dr. Emma Watson, sir."

"Ya know that un?"

"My sister."

The constable stepped back. "Go right ahead, sir."

Richard opened the door.

"Richard? Over here," Mary called out, coming to him. "I didn't expect to see you here. How is...?"

Richard pulled her to him and kissed her lips to shut her up. Mary gasped and stepped backward—blushing, horrified.

"Be quiet, Mary. You almost said his name. They mustn't know." Mary's face was hot with shock.

"Richard."

"Whisper."

He sat down, and she motioned for him to wipe her rouge from his lips.

"Henry's fine. He's staying at the men's dormitory, and Lucas Griffin is supplying his food. Margaret's a fine cook, so he's well cared for." He leaned over her desk. "I talked with his landlady. She said you left Henry a note. When?"

"That awful morning. Why?"

"What did you say in the note?"

"I don't know, Richard. I forget."

"Think. You were probably frantic, weren't you?"

She tapped the desk as she tried to recollect.

"Did you sign your name?"

"I don't know. Probably just Mary."

"Think."

"I'm thinking. I'm thinking."

"Did you mention the university or the murder?"

"I don't think so. I think I told him I was at your home," she said with growing fright in her eyes. "You have me shaking. It must be important," Mary whispered as she glanced at the constable, then back to Richard.

"That's alright, Mary. It probably is of little import," Richard said for her benefit, but he was troubled.

"My word, Richard, you're worried," she said. "Have you been home?"

"Went straight to his apartment from Paddington, then here." Richard looked at the constable. "I want to see the crime scene."

"They won't let you in. Emma and Gordon were in there before lunch. He put the fear of God into those constables. He straightened them out straighter than this ruler."

"It's the end of your day, Mary. After I'm finished in the lab, I'll take you to Carlisle and we can talk with Emma."

"They won't let you in. Mark my words."

Richard walked over to the constable, and they talked for a few moments. The constable opened the door, and Richard stepped into the lab. He returned within ten minutes and found Mary tidying up.

"Let's be on our way. My hansom is waiting."

The two left the building and headed for Carlisle Street.

"What in the world did you say to that constable?"

"He wanted to know who I was, and I told him I was Dr. Emma Watson's brother, Richard. And Chief Inspector Gordon Lestrade is about to become my brother-in-law, and he wanted me to check on a few things in the laboratory while I was in the neighborhood."

Mary erupted in laughter, and Richard joined her. They needed the release, and they chuckled longer than the matter deserved.

When Mary had composed herself, she said, "Richard, you're a perfect devil."

He pulled at his goatee. "On occasion, Mary, on occasion."

"I'm delighted that Henry is finally safe," Dr. John said to everyone at the dinner table. "But I'll have no truck with discussions involving this case while we eat. I spent too many meals with Sherlock's palaver and always got indigestion and dyspepsia. Tension at the table affects proper mastication and digestion and leads to intestinal discomfort and, if you ask me, sleeplessness. After dinner, when I repair to the parlor with my port, you can talk about it all you want."

"Stop, Father, you're giving me a headache," Richard said, his eyes dancing. Everyone concealed a smile, then Emma burst into laughter.

Afterward Mary and Emma helped Mrs. Mac clear the table and sideboard. Eventually the four friends took their place at the dining table and listened to Richard begin his narrative. Everyone could sense he was eager to tell a story, and they were excited to hear it. When he described how he and Henry had fled Scotland and Mr. Thompson's decoy role, Geoffrey interrupted.

"Richard, I'm dreadfully sorry, but Mr. Thompson was murdered at Straithairn Station."

Richard stared in shock. They remained silent as he looked first at Geoffrey, then Emma, and finally Mary.

"It was those filthy Huns," he said finally. "They did it. I'm sure of it." He looked at Geoffrey. "If they'd murder a man for simply driving a wagon to the train station, then there is nothing beyond their limits. Nothing."

Richard collected himself and returned to his story. When he came to his attack with the pitcher of coffee against Krajic's face, Richard grabbed a digestive biscuit, crumbling it with his fist, dramatizing the sound of his opponent's cartilage rasping. Mary gasped and turned away.

When he finished his account his audience sat drained, and Mary, unaccustomed to such a dramatic delivery, said, "I feel like I was right there with you and Henry."

"Let's discuss the facts at hand," Emma said, wisely moving on.

"My studio or down here?"

Mary appeared confused. "Emma?"

"It's our custom to outline the facts and diagram theories on large easel paper," Emma said. "I think down here is better. His studio's a pigsty. A veritable refuse heap."

Richard went to his studio and returned with a wooden easel, sketching newsprint, and a black wax pencil. He waved the pencil at Emma. "Wax, no charcoal dust, Miss Neat."

While Richard assembled the easel and attached the pad of blank newsprint, the ladies and Geoffrey took advantage of the moment to stretch and brew more tea. Mrs. Mac brought several plates filled with biscuits, staring at the pile of digestive crumbs on Richard's plate. When everyone settled and looked at the easel, they watched Richard print in large, black letters:

Nachtgeist!

CHAPTER 13

"Here's what we have so far," Richard declared, standing beside his easel, pointing to the key facts and theories they had advanced. "First, the Germans. Second, a person with the initials C and S. Third. Dr. and Mrs. Gregory. And fourth, Dr. Hugh Crane. Are there any others?"

"Gordon says the time of death is between ten and midnight."

Recording the time of death, Richard then pointed to the next item on the pad. "Now, this teapot and cups you mentioned. Henry hates green tea, so the prints'll be Nigel's and someone else's on the cups, presumably the murderer, although we can't be certain." He waited for disagreement. None was offered. "And next, the broken distillation apparatus."

"Gordon failed to have the larger shards fingerprinted initially," Emma said, munching on a biscuit. "But on my suggestion, he did. We should have the results tomorrow."

"But why does he think there's a connection between the apparatus and the murder?" Richard asked.

"Only because it was Henry's equipment. He thinks there was a fight when he confronted Nigel about the lie."

"If that apparatus was broken during the course of Henry's work, wouldn't he have ordered a replacement? We must investigate."

"I'll check on that tomorrow," Mary said.

Emma said, "What would explain the two number sixteen laboratory notebooks in Nigel's side of the cabinet?"

Mary waved her hand. "I can't imagine either of them misplacing their materials."

"My theory," Richard said, dunking a biscuit in his tea, "is that the person who murdered Nigel knows about laboratory work. He also knew about the formula. So he stole Henry's notebook, reviewed its contents, perhaps copied parts of it, and misplaced it—probably acted in haste. How else would a new style of book, numbered sixteen, be in sequence on Nigel's shelf?"

"Then I'll wager the prints on the book and the prints on the cabinet will match," Geoffrey said.

"And perhaps the apparatus as well," Emma added.

"The teacups, too," said Mary.

"If he took the book somewhere to copy, then this means he returned to the laboratory a second time," Richard exclaimed. "What about Henry's message on his calendar? You said you were having Gordon fingerprint it. Why? Henry told me he wrote the note."

"Simply to put doubt in Gordon's mind and to keep him busy. Every minute Gordon devotes to pursuing evidence is one more minute of freedom for Henry and one minute closer we are to the truth."

"Em, what about the condition of the body?" Richard fingered his goatee.

"The poison was applied to the inside of his right forearm, and there was no evidence of the poison on his left hand or under his fingernails either. The poison was on the palm of his right hand and not his left. That's why I tend to agree with Gordon that it was not self-inflicted."

"I should think that, too," Richard said. "But he might've opened the jar with his left hand, removed the poison, and applied it using the woman's glove. And it might have been a human experiment gone amiss."

"Wrong," Emma said emphatically. "They use rubber gloves in the laboratory. The same type we use in surgery. I saw a supply in their storage cabinet."

Richard began pacing. "If someone suddenly applied poison to my right arm, you can be sure I'd be removing it as fast as I could with my left hand. Even if I used a teaspoon to scoop away the poison from my arm, the chemical would be on my left hand somewhere. Thornton's clean left hand makes no sense, does it?"

"Baffling," Emma said. "I agree."

"Why were Henry's doors unlocked?" Geoffrey asked.

"Henry's door to the hall is closer to the main entrance than Nigel's," Mary said. "The killer could escape quicker that way."

"And we know the doors require a key from the outside," Richard said, "but open without a key from the inside. Right? Someone fleeing would leave the doors open in haste. A professional would've closed them. It's an amateur we're dealing with."

Emma added, "There was no sign of forced entry, remember. Unless Henry's locks were picked."

"We know one lock was picked," Richard said. Everyone looked surprised. "Henry's apartment door, of course."

"That's true," Mary said.

"The way I see it, the murderer knew Nigel and was welcomed into the lab through Nigel's office, then he fled through Henry's office doors, leaving them ajar," Geoffrey said. "That means the killer knew the building rather well, I'd say."

"Drat it all!" Richard said. "If the murderer wore gloves, there won't be prints on the cabinet or on Henry's doorknobs. Maybe not on the china either."

"I forgot. Tongs were found dripping with poison," Emma said. "The killer could have used the tongs to remove his gloves. He's a smart one."

"Evidently just one glove. You said only one glove was discovered at the German apartment building, correct?" Richard asked. "That means he left prints with his ungloved hand somewhere."

"Maybe he wore both gloves to the apartment and only one was found. Mrs. Haas said the dustmen would have arrived soon after the accident," Emma said. "Remember, the constables at the crime scene made no connection to Nigel's murder at first. Gordon told me they didn't secure the scene until they had received the report from the hospital."

Geoffrey asked as he stood up and stretched, "What about the mystery note on Nigel's desk?"

"I think the CS is Charles Steele and fingerprints will prove that," Emma said. "Steele told me he handled all of the Thorntons' business... insurance and what not. Nigel apparently owed him money." Emma sighed. "Who knows? But I'm guessing the prints will prove Charles Steele wrote that note."

"Would he have known about the formula?" Mary asked. "I doubt it."

"I wouldn't dismiss him that easily," Richard said. "If he'd talked to his brother-in-law about money and if Nigel had painted a rosy picture of the income he would receive from this discovery..."

"But," Mary inserted, "do you think he would tell his brother-in-law it was lethal poison he was developing? Seems unlikely to me."

"You're wrong," Richard said. "Nigel would've told Steele everything, anything to gain his support and to buy time, wouldn't he? But why was Thornton so interested in poison?"

"The Germans," Emma said. "They possibly contacted him about the formula as well as Henry. And the woman's glove...perhaps Mrs. Thornton was there with her brother. Maybe she actually did the deed while Steele manhandled Nigel. That's how the apparatus got shattered...in the scuffle. Perhaps Steele restrained Thornton's left arm...thus, no poison on it."

Richard drew a star beside *CS*. "He knew the value of the formula or could imagine its importance to groups like the Germans. He copied the formula from Henry's lab book or maybe from several books. Steele's prints will be on the book and maybe on the shards of the distiller."

Removing her pince-nez, Emma shook her head. "Steele is smart. But he wouldn't possess the knowledge to read the laboratory books. No, utterly impossible."

"But what's the connection between the German apartment building and Steele and his sister?" Geoffrey asked. "Wait! I can answer my own question. The Germans want the formula and that's where the Germans live...in the apartment building. Maybe they're all Nachtgeist."

"Steele or Mrs. Thornton or both wanted the Germans' money for the formula," Emma said.

Richard clapped his hands. "There you have it!"

Emma shook her head again. "But what is vexing in all this repugnance is, why do the Germans continue pursuing poor Henry?"

"Very well," said Richard. "The fact that they are pursuing Henry means they don't have the formula. I'll bet they found nothing helpful in that lab book."

Everyone watched Richard add "Germans want Henry's brain" to the list.

Richard rubbed his head vigorously with both hands and stared at the easel. "Somehow, the Huns learned that Henry was the key. Steele and Mrs. Thornton discovered the German contacts and approached them with the jar of poison and Henry's lab book. The Huns ejected them from the apartment and they hastily disposed of the gloves—"

"And handkerchief," Emma added.

"And the handkerchief in the nearest dustbin. Voila! They left empty-handed," Richard said.

"What about the lab notebook?" Emma asked.

"They returned it to the laboratory later that night but accidentally placed it in the wrong section...Nigel's section."

"Why wouldn't the Germans kill the pair because they knew too much?" Geoffrey asked.

"Simple," Richard said. "Mrs. Thornton and her brother are Nachtgeist. They wouldn't kill their own, would they? About Krauss. Who said he works for the German consulate?"

"Mrs. Haas."

Richard tore a piece from the easel paper and scribbled a note. "Must have Mycroft check on that. He'll know...probably carries it in his head."

"Mycroft then. Tomorrow," Emma said, then suddenly gasped and everyone looked at her. "Upon my word, I forgot to give Steele's card to Gordon for fingerprinting. I must do that."

"Geoffrey," Richard said, "we should have Gordon fingerprint the threatening note Henry found on his table. Let's have it. Emma and I'll—"

"Blast, I left it in the shirt I took to the laundry."

"A fat lot of good you are. Now what about Dr. Gregory?"

Emma removed her pince-nez. "I'd hate to think he's involved. But if his wife's part of the German crowd, then he might be in this as well."

"You said he has the plans to the new science building, didn't you? He could've been talking to Nigel about them, reviewing them, and occupying Thornton's attention while he or someone else gathered the poison."

"Maybe he is more familiar with the formulation than we suspect," Emma said. "Ah, but he would've been sure to replace the lab notebook correctly. And there's Dr. Hugh Crane, the last person on your list."

"From what Evelyn told me," said Mary, "he was angry with Nigel and Henry. But angry enough to kill?"

"I wonder," Emma said, squeezing Geoffrey's hand for a moment. "I hope to interview him tomorrow."

"All that we've covered tonight," Richard said, with rising optimism, "all of the possibilities, even the most unlikely one, are more probable when measured against the absurdity of Henry's guilt. All this will be sorted out. I'm sure of it."

Everyone agreed, but Emma wished she could share her brother's enthusiasm. There were too many possibilities and too little time. She forced a smile for Mary's benefit and hoped her friend would not sense the insincerity behind it.

"I'm sorry, but I must go home," Mary said. "My parents are worried for me, and what with police watching us, Mother's got herself in a right state. And we were so looking forward to shopping for my wedding dress."

"Let's all see Mary home," Richard said.

They engaged a carriage, dropped Mary at her front door, and delivered Geoffrey to his flat. He kissed Emma goodnight and stepped from the carriage, berating himself for losing Henry's note. Emma waved as the horses trotted away.

When she sat back into her seat and looked across at Richard, he asked, "How long is he going to keep you waiting?" Emma did not answer. She looked out at the gas lit street. "Do you talk about marriage?"

"Some day, perhaps. I'm happy Mary is doing well under the circumstances. She's still keeping her engagement a secret. It's best that way."

"The subject of marriage has never come up?" Richard asked. Emma saw understanding in her brother's eyes. He had a gift for peeling her thoughts away.

Her voice became brittle, and for an instant her pain within her was exposed. "We are quite busy...it's our professions. I don't have time to dwell on marriage like other women my age," Emma rationalized, but in her heart she was beginning to doubt Geoffrey would ever propose. He was so settled, so stable, that she thought he had been born an adult, never a child or adolescent—at least not like Richard, born a child and remaining a child at heart. She looked at her brother, at his rumpled clothes, his straggly goatee and moppy brown hair and thought that he looked like a youngster who had been playing outdoors all day and needed a good scrubbing...so unlike Geoffrey.

"Richard, describe me."

"What?"

"Not physically... my nature... my character."

"Be serious, Em."

"I'm serious."

Without hesitating, as if his lines were well rehearsed and this was his cue, he said, "Bossy, stubborn, and impertinent." Richard watched her quick anger. Her chest swelled, taking in air for a proper Emma Watson retort. Then he added, smiling, "Intelligent, loving to a fault, loyal, God-fearing, the best sister on earth. You'd be perfect if you realized I was wise in all things." He laughed. He knew what she had been thinking, not in detail but in the overall. "Geoffrey loves you the way you are."

"Even my suffrage involvement?"

"Of course, even your arrests. He supplied your bail the last time you handcuffed yourself to the Parliament railing, didn't he?"

Emma looked out the window as they went by their old childhood haunt. "Look Richard, Beeton Park. There's the old shed. Remember when Sherlock tricked Baron Croydon into slipping the memoirs under the door of the shed, and how Henry took off running with them all the way to Baker Street?"

"That was in the dim and distant."

"You and I hid in the dark and watched Croydon give chase. You and Henry couldn't run like that today." She reached over and gently punched her brother's middle.

"Don't you bet on that."

Richard leaned forward to the carriage window. "Look. It's Henry's apartment. Sad, no lights are on." He pointed across the carriageway. "There he is! That's the same bugger I saw watching Henry's apartment this afternoon."

Emma scrambled down to the carriage floor, exclaiming, "Be quiet." After a few moments, she returned to her seat. "I hope he didn't see me."

"The man watching Henry's apartment?"

Emma exclaimed in a whisper, "Gunther Haas!"

CHAPTER 14

Dr. John tapped his finger on the newspaper and tossed it to Richard, accidentally brushing the butter.

"Dreadfully sorry. What do you think?"

Putting down his forkful of Scotch eggs and scraping butter from the newspaper, Richard read the brief piece. "What new incriminating evidence?"

Dr. John shrugged. "I must prepare for the day."

Richard went to the easel and printed "Gunther Haas" on the easel paper.

Emma breezed into the room well rested. "Yes, Gunther. Quite interesting."

"Marnin', Emma," Mrs. Mac said, offering a plate full of hot sausages still spitting grease from the plate.

"No thank you, Mum. I believe I'll have tea at the Yard. Richard and I must talk to Gordon immediately."

"Who's gonna eat all these?"

"Save them, Mum," Richard said and received a look. He poured Worcestershire sauce on one, forked it into his mouth and gasped, waving his hand at his mouth.

"Hot?" Emma asked, her face showing mock concern.

Richard got up, still chewing. The twins headed out of their home and stepped onto the pavement.

"Richard, Emma, wait!"

Mary ran up to them. "Here, read this. It's from Henry." Mary handed the telegram to Richard. "I miss him terribly. It pains me to think of him hiding in Wales and being so alone and worried. He hates being alone."

Richard gave the telegram to Emma. "Henry isn't hiding like I insisted. He's probably not doing anything I told him to do. He had to appear at the train station's telegraph office to send this. Or he had to contact someone to deliver the telegram for him. Damn the man! All of our effort, the very least he can do is to remain concealed." He stepped aside as the first patient of the day arrived, giving Richard an angry glare. "Let's arrange a carriage. Follow me."

He walked the ladies a half block to the livery. When they were comfortably seated in the carriage, Richard restlessly thumbed through his sketchbook. His eyes roamed everywhere except at Emma and Mary, who remained silent, knowing from experience that his anger would soon pass.

Mary broke the thick silence. "What should I tell Henry?"

Richard shrugged. "He misses you. Tell him you miss him also. It's a private matter between the two of you." Exasperation colored each word. "Do not, I repeat, do not tell him anything about what we are doing, thinking, or suspecting. Understand?"

Mary nodded and glanced at Emma, who agreed.

"Do not include names or addresses of anyone," Emma added. "You must assume the Germans will read it before Henry does."

Mary's lip quivered. "I was happy. Now I don't know what..."

"Mary, it was grand that he told you of his love and that he's lonely for you," Richard soothed, leaning towards her, touching her hand. "But we are just beginning this investigation. You must be patient. I'm less worried about you than Henry. Here's paper. You must tell him to forbear during these lonely days, perhaps weeks. You have Emma and me if you lose heart. Henry doesn't. Assure him of your faith and that you stand resolutely behind him. Look at me, Mary." She looked at him. "Tell him he must remain hidden and not to send another telegram. Tell him R said so."

"I'll send it for you in case you are being followed," Emma said. "We don't want your message falling into German hands here. We cannot be certain of it in Wales."

Mary wrote while the twins were quiet, deep in thought. They arrived at university and Mary handed the composed telegram to Emma.

"I'll send it this morning," Emma said. "I promise."

The twins discussed their plans for the day while their carriage hurried to Queens Embankment and Scotland Yard.

Richard paused before alighting. "Gordon's the key. No Gordon... no forensics laboratory."

"Gordon can be stubborn."

"Give him your lost-little-girl look."

The twins arrived at the duty officer's desk, and he escorted them to Lestrade's office.

"Good to see you, Richard," Lestrade said, though he was gazing at Emma. "Missed you at rugby club. Where have you been, old chap?"

"Paris. Returned a few days ago."

"More time with those artistes, I take it?"

"Gordy, Em's found something interesting."

"Oh? Well, thanks to you, Emma, I believe we have an important jigsaw piece for the puzzle."

"Do tell us, Gordon."

"Henry's note. Remember you thought someone else might have written it to incriminate Henry? It's Henry's writing, our expert verified it, and Henry's prints and his alone are all over the calendar. Even the pen he used establishes the connection." Lestrade swelled with pride. "Not the way any of us would've liked for Henry's sake, you understand."

"It was right that you investigated so thoroughly as you always do, Gordon," Emma said. "Before I show you something we found, there was a variety of issues I raised when the two of us were in the laboratory together. Did you find any fingerprints on the shards of glass?"

"Simply fragmentary prints. My man says there are print portions with characteristics of Henry and Dr. Thornton. But they're inconclusive," Lestrade said, leaning back in his old wooden desk chair. "Nevertheless, it supports my strong contention that the deceased and Henry struggled, causing the apparatus to fall to the floor. I'm sorry to say, Henry committed the murder."

"What makes you think there isn't another story to be told?" Richard said.

Lestrade watched him.

"It's Henry's apparatus, for God's sake," Richard said, anger rising. "It's logical that his prints would be found on the glass. Perhaps Thornton struggled with someone who knocked it over without touching it with his hands. Then Thornton cleaned up the aftermath. Perhaps Thornton or Henry broke the apparatus and cleaned it up long before his murder.

Maybe even a student. The apparatus has no bearing on the matter."

"I would like to see other, more convincing proofs to the contrary."

"Why are you so fascinated with Henry when the real murderer is skipping around London at this very moment?" Richard struck his fist on Lestrade's desktop. "You refuse to believe that Henry's innocent and you structure the investigation accordingly, don't you?"

Emma spoke as Lestrade got half out of his chair. "Gordon, please forgive him. You know how close he and Henry are. We're terribly frustrated about this matter, as you are, and he desperately wants to interrogate him himself, if he only could. Forgive us, please."

Lestrade relaxed somewhat.

"My apologies, Gordy. One of my best friends is missing, accused of murder. My other best friend is doing the accusing."

"And you understand my position. I must allow the evidence to point to the murderer."

"I agree, Gordon. And I heard there was a teapot and cups. Your analysis?"

Lestrade cleared his throat.

"We found Nigel's prints on the pot, one saucer, and one cup. An unknown set of fingerprints is on the lid, the other saucer and cup...not Henry's."

"And its contents?" Emma asked.

Lestrade heard the question he feared. "Dr. Mull is conducting more analysis."

Emma arched her brows. "More analysis? It would've taken me two ticks of a clock to verify it contained green tea, assam, or Earl Grey."

"Why are you so interested in the contents?"

Emma stared intently at Lestrade. "Gordon, something's amiss." She waited. "Gordon?"

Richard considered speaking but thought the better of it. If anyone could draw out Lestrade, it would be Emma. He waited as his friend sipped his tea. Gordon knew if he revealed the answer, it would satisfy Emma but leave the case more confused and Henry's guilt less certain, sending the investigation spiraling back into darkness. But he owed Emma the answer. After all, she had suggested the analysis that had produced the shocking results.

"It was green tea, as we suspected. However, Dr. Mull has concluded that there was curare in Nigel's cup."

"Curare!" Emma exclaimed.

"The murderer," Lestrade said, "wanted to make certain Thornton died. If the formula poison didn't do the job, curare would finish it."

"Curare in Thornton's cup. What about the teapot?" Emma asked.

"That, too. But no trace in the other cup with unknown fingerprints."

"Was the cup empty?"

"No. Just untainted green tea."

"Well," Richard smiled, "There it is, then. Henry's innocent. Someone tell me how he's implicated?"

"Henry might've laced the tea with the curare after some innocent visitor joined Thornton and drank from the untainted cup...the one with the unknown fingerprints. A lucky chap, I'd say. In any case, Henry would not have cared about one more murder," Lestrade said tentatively, unsure of his own convictions.

Emma waited until Lestrade was looking at her. "Now let's think this through together. If Henry mixed curare with the tea, then his fingerprints should be somewhere on that tea pot...most probably the lid by my reckoning, but his prints were not on the china. So why Henry?"

"I think I agree with you, Emma." Lestrade stood up. "How could Henry taint the tea with curare without touching the teapot?"

"Did Dr. Mull test the canister of tea?" Richard asked.

"Yes. Nothing. Just a tin of good green tea," Lestrade said. He began pacing. "How could you do it without touching the pot?"

Emma gasped, remembering. "I'm thoroughly ashamed of myself. Curare is not fatal if ingested. It must be introduced to the bloodstream directly, usually through injection or puncture."

"Henry would know that type of detail, wouldn't he, Em?" Richard asked.

"Of course he would. Any of those Ph.D.'s in the department would. Only a fool would administer curare in tea...a rank amateur, really."

"Puncture?" Lestrade asked. "Drinking it would not kill a person?"

Emma nodded. "Curare could not have killed Thornton...at least not by ingestion. Let's talk with Dr. Mull."

"No. I'll cover this with him," Lestrade said, writing a note. "How quickly does curare kill?"

"Very rapidly. Minutes, but probably within an hour," Emma answered. "I'd have Dr. Mull examine Dr. Thornton's oral cavity for a break in the dermal integrity," Emma said. "If Thornton had a bleeding gum...even a bleeding stomach ulcer, esophogial lesions, the curare would rather surely have gotten into his blood by that entrance as well as if he had been injected. Yes, at Thornton's age, maybe stomach ulcers."

"This is getting more confusing, isn't it?"

Richard could not resist. "It's getting more confusing because we must accept the possibility that some unknown person committed this crime—not Henry."

Lestrade said, "Anything more?"

"Those laboratory notebooks," Emma said.

"Thornton's prints, and his alone, are on his books. However, on Henry's book number sixteen, we found two other sets of prints in addition to Henry's. It's the only book of his, or Thornton's for that matter, that contains any prints other than the owner's. Dr. Mull examined the contents of several of Henry's books. I think they were fourteen, fifteen and sixteen. I asked him to find Henry's special formula. I guessed that Henry might've given or sold his formula to the anarchists. In that case, I surmised, the important volume would be the one with the basic formula."

"And?"

"According to Mull, and I must say he admits Henry's discovery is not easily understood, the vital information is in book fifteen. Book sixteen contains only records of experiments. Just experiments and results. That's all. And there's more. The sets of alien prints on it don't match any other unknown prints so far collected."

"How did you know it was Henry's discovery and not Thornton's?" asked Richard.

"Mull has been awake all night on this. He worked backward through their notebooks. He's one curious man. He found that Henry made the discovery and Thornton was working to make poison compatible with it."

"The deeper we probe, the more confusing the case becomes, doesn't it, Gordon?" Emma said and received a reluctant nod from Lestrade. "If we cannot completely disqualify Henry, we must include at least three other individuals in the investigation because of the number of unknown prints and the killer's ignorant use of curare.

"Gordon," she said while fishing in her purse. "Handle this card with care." She placed it on his desk and slid it to him using her fingernail.

"Charles Samuel Steele, Esquire. So?"

"Did you get the note fingerprinted...the one signed CS?" Emma asked.

"CS. Are you saying this barrister wrote that note?"

"He's Thornton's brother-in-law," Emma said. "The Thorntons were separated. I strongly believe Mrs. Thornton's having an affair, the details of which are too insubstantial at the moment. Thornton owed Steele money, according to the note. And Evelyn Moxely claims Charles Steele paid a visit to Dr. Thornton the very night of his murder. The prints on that card will match those found on the note. This man must be investigated."

Lestrade carefully slipped the card into an envelope. "Wait here. I'll get this printed now."

"Be gentle with Gordon," Emma said, after Lestrade had gone.

"He always—"

"I know, but he's better than the rest of this lot around here. He doesn't have the advantage of questioning Henry like you. Be patient."

"Longsuffering, you mean."

"He's becoming malleable. I hope we can see the evidence collected from the German apartment building."

Richard walked to the window behind Lestrade's desk and gazed at the Thames.

Lestrade returned. "We'll have the results in a short while."

"Who did you fingerprint for this case?" Emma asked.

He opened a folder. "A total of twelve. And, of course, Henry's prints from his books and office items make thirteen."

"Anything unusual when you fingerprinted the doors?"

"We expected to find Henry's prints on his doors, Dr. Thornton's on his, and we did. But we also found on the deceased's door the same unidentified prints that are on the second cup and saucer." He waved his hand at Richard to discourage any interruption. "We theorize that Henry had an accomplice, someone who entered or departed through Nigel's office. We also found two different sets of prints on the number sixteen notebook and on Henry's doors...also the storage cabinet, too. This we find puzzling."

Richard waited until his friend appeared to have nothing more to add. "It is puzzling. Now I suppose you would have us believe that Henry had three accomplices. The more information you collect, the more difficult it is for me to believe that Henry did it. Mycroft told us that there are German anarchists afoot in London. Who better to orchestrate such mayhem? Gordy, you're approaching this case from the wrong direction."

"And what's your theory?"

"I believe this is a case of murder and abduction. Why do you suppose none of us can find Henry? Because he has been kidnapped...not for ransom but for his brains. Somehow they learned that it was Henry's formula. The Germans killed Dr. Thornton. Henry returned unexpectedly to the laboratory that night. You know how often he has missed our rugby club meetings because of his late night research. He found the killers and was kidnapped. God only knows where they have him. Maybe they smuggled him to Germany."

Lestrade scribbled a note. Emma happily nudged Richard's foot.

"Brilliant. I shall inform our offices at Dover and Southampton. Don't you think Mycroft is working this angle?"

"Possibly," Emma said, "but we can't be certain. He might be still laboring like you under the flawed assumption that Henry did it and is hiding somewhere here in Britain."

Resigned to off-hours work on the possible abduction theory, Lestrade said, "Your kidnapping theory is one we haven't explored. And we must. I'm very much obliged to both of you."

"We haven't seen the evidence found at the Haas' building," Emma said. "You'll be kind enough to show us, won't you?"

Gordon checked his pocket watch. "Follow me."

They moved to the evidence room along narrow corridors, past a gloomy warren of rooms—rooms in name only, more like niches crammed with files. They arrived at a large wall of grey metal drawers. Lestrade's eyes scanned the immaculate drawer fronts until he located the one he wanted. Lestrade opened a drawer, removed a sealed glass case, and placed it on a wooden tabletop.

"A woman's glove, definitely," Emma observed. "And laboratory tongs... not the kitchen variety."

"Hello," Richard exclaimed. "This handkerchief has a monogram."

Lestrade stepped back to allow his friends a better view. "We've talked with everyone in the apartment building and neighboring apartments. No one with those initials resides there."

"Very thorough, Gordon," Emma said, adjusting her pince-nez without looking up. "J-S-G. J-S-G," Emma repeated for her brother's benefit, hiding a wink at Richard. "What can you tell us about the poison?"

"Nightshade."

"Ah, belladonna."

"It's purple as you can see, and foul smelling. That's why Dr. Mull sealed the evidence in this glass container. One of the clerks smelled it before we sealed it. She vomited and we had to send her home for the day." Lestrade nodded in the direction of a young woman seated at a desk in the corner, sorting papers into several stacks.

"No possibility of prints here," Emma said.

"That vile formula covered every surface. If you're finished, then let's visit the lab. Maybe the fingerprint analysis is complete by now."

While Lestrade secured the evidence in the locked drawer, Richard opened his sketchbook and he scrawled a note. "J? S? G?" Emma took his pencil and wrote "Jutta Schmidt Gregory." Richard nodded.

Lestrade turned the key in the cabinet's lock. "This way."

As he led them through another maze, Richard observed Lestrade's hand solicitously near Emma. Gordon had set his cap for her when they were adolescents. Richard thought that if Geoffrey didn't propose marriage soon, Emma might settle for Lestrade, which would not be bad at all. Considering everything, he was a good rugby man.

As Lestrade opened a door, he finally placed his hand on Emma's back to guide her through the entrance.

When they entered, the laboratory assistant said, "Excuse me, sir. Simon just went to your office."

"Any matches?"

"Yes indeed, sir."

"Maybe you've uncovered something vital," Lestrade said.

Simon emerged from Lestrade's office.

"What did you find?" Lestrade asked eagerly.

"The prints perfectly match those on the note found in the victim's office, sir."

"Good. Very good indeed," Lestrade said, dismissing Simon. "This man Steele will be questioned. You realize, of course, this doesn't mean we'll stop searching for Henry. If found, he'll have some explaining to do."

"Quite right," Emma agreed and hated saying it.

"But we'll explore the abduction theory and this Charles Steele."

After the Watsons withdrew from his stuffy office, Lestrade peered at the Thames from his window, enjoying Emma's lingering fragrance as he pondered.

He murmured, "Hmm. Charles Steele."

CHAPTER 15

"Em, you really know how to charm ol' Gordy."

They walked hurriedly along Victoria Embankment towards Westminster Bridge. Two straight-backed and very prim nannies pushing prams came toward them. Emma glanced at the babies.

"I hate doing that," Emma admitted.

"Gordy still wishes you hadn't broken off the relationship when you went to medical college."

"Do you think so?"

"He always asks about you at rugby club."

"He knows about Geoffrey, surely."

"Of course he knows. Does Geoffrey know about Gordon?"

"He doesn't like me visiting Scotland Yard for that reason. But he can't control me."

"Ha! Who can?"

Emma tapped Richard's leg with her umbrella. "Enough. Very interesting information back there. This curare and monogrammed handkerchief..."

"Mrs. Whatever-Schmidt Gregory. How did you know?"

"Her husband told me. He called her Jutta and told me her German brother's name is Rainer Schmidt. Jutta Schmidt Gregory. Simple. And I'll wager the glove is hers and her fingerprints match one of the sets of unknown prints in Thornton's laboratory. The handkerchief and glove must be hers because of the initials, and we know she keeps company with Krauss."

They crossed the carriageway and stopped on the other side. Big Ben's deep bong sounded ten times. Richard opened his sketchbook to refer to his notes. "I'm going to see Mycroft; I trust he's in his apartment or at Whitehall. I'll have him check on Krauss. But first I'll get the Baker Street Irregulars to tail Mrs. Gregory and the blonde one...Krauss, too. Are these addresses and descriptions correct?"

She reviewed her brother's notes. "Correct. Try to get Petey. I'm on my way to hospital."

Richard hailed a hansom and handed his sister inside. "Good luck, Em."

He signaled another cab and headed to Lambeth, to its grinding riverside dereliction, and to Petey's ramshackle home. Each visit to the place never failed to touch him with its utter wretchedness. To him, all the miseries of mankind seemed gathered there. The bleak and dilapidated wooden hovels, many perched upon rotting pilings in the Thames, were symbols of the crushing human pain within. Congestion, malnutrition, and nearly non-existent sanitation inevitably led to disease throughout its slums. Most children in such rookeries died before the age of five. But Petey and his Baker Street Irregulars were among the fortunate few.

The hansom's arrival drew the usual excited attention from the urchins in the alleyways. Richard stepped down from the cab and asked the driver to wait—knowing that finding another one in this troubled place would be impossible. When he turned towards Petey's home, he discovered the boy's five-year-old sister, Lizzie, standing at his feet looking up, runny nose, matted hair, and trying to beam through cloudy eyes. They were quickly surrounded by ragged boys, knowing that Richard always slipped them a few pence or even a shilling. But little Lizzie didn't speak. It was not that she couldn't. It was her nature, and to him her silence seemed to underscore the hopelessness he saw in her sad eyes. He swept her into his arms and kissed her.

"Lizzie, dear. Where's your brother?" He gave her a needed hug.

She pointed to her house, and tugged at Richard's neck.

He carried her towards her home, bouncing her as he walked. His hand fumbled in his bulging pockets, searching among pencils, erasers, charcoal sticks, and blending stumps used for sketching. He handed a mint humbug to Lizzie that brought a thin smile.

Inside, there were seven men, three women and eight boys, including Petey, sitting on the dirty floor, sweating and working among awkward stacks of cardboard, bundles of shoe leather, and heaps of miscellaneous leather parts. A shaft of sunlight hardly dispelled the darkness of their den. Richard wondered how they could labor in such dim conditions.

Standing in the doorway unnoticed, Richard held Lizzie and watched for a moment.

Lizzie grunted, "Uh-uh."

Petey and his mother glanced up.

"Mr. Watson, sir." Petey shouted, clambering to his feet.

He jumped towards Richard and his mother smiled, showing missing teeth. The woman said nothing, but gratitude was in her face. She knew what Richard probably wanted and was delighted, happy her son would return from his assignment with a year's wages in his pockets.

"Petey," Richard said, lowering the girl to the floor. "Where's Taddy and Ollie? I need you blokes immediately."

"This way, guv," Petey said, heading for the door.

Richard bowed to Petey's mother, and they hurried into the alleyway to find the other Irregulars. They descended a rickety wooden ladder to the tumbledown quay and found the two boys helping men patch and cobble delivery boats. Black smoke from two drumfires joined wraiths of steam and fog retreating across the water. A ship's foghorn echoed up the Thames, and the waves from passing barges sloshed beneath the timbers under their feet. Two boys scrambled when Petey called. A trawler moored as seagulls squawked. Richard tore two sheets of paper from his sketchbook and gave the Irregulars addresses, descriptions, and careful instructions concerning their surveillance assignment. He slipped Petey five shillings for transportation and incidentals.

"You're the sergeant, Petey. Spend the money wisely. You'll probably need to engage a few hansoms on this assignment."

Petey Broom had been handpicked and trained by Sherlock Holmes and was completely trustworthy. The boy was bright, evident in his inquiring eyes. He was dependable, and he always applied his intelligence to report more than the facts alone, delivering insights and observations that would escape many professionals.

"Gather as much information as you can."

"We'll foller 'em like shadows, guv," Petey said, saluting. "Don't fret none."

Richard hustled the three Irregulars up the shaky ladder and into the waiting hansom, cramming them onto the narrow seat. He explained their mission, tore additional paper from his sketchbook, handed them pencils for note taking, and deposited them near their three posts, where they joined the street hubbub. He was confident that the boys' thoroughness would be the equal of anyone at the Yard.

As the hansom bounced towards Mycroft Holmes' apartment near Pall Mall, Richard withdrew inside himself, gravely concerned over the need for urgency. He knew he must discover something soon; otherwise, Lestrade or Mycroft might find Henry, or worse, Nachtgeist would find him. Nachtgeist's fascination over Henry's discovery was obvious. Anarchists would attach a high value to a poison that could be secretly slathered on public surfaces, causing rapid and mysterious death or illness to all who touched it. The public fear and outrage over such colossal threat would spread like a raging fire. Scotland Yard and the authorities would be helpless, both in numbers and ability, to extinguish the menace. Such an unseen enemy could propagate its terror anywhere and any time. Even the Continent would be ravaged. The hansom slowed near St. James's and Pall Mall.

Richard alighted and tramped towards Mycroft's residence, trying to digest all of the implications of this case. He stepped inside the apartment building and pulled the chain. The big man soon appeared at the door.

"Richard," Mycroft said. Richard caught an unfamiliar temper in his large face, but it softened before he turned away from him and moved towards his library: "Ah... yes. Sit. Fancy tea? Rather occupied at the moment. Now then..." Mycroft leafed through correspondence and a stack of files on his desk. Richard walked across the hardwood floor. "How was Italy? Or France?"

"France."

"Ah, Matisse or Rodin or...who this time?"

"Rodin sends his regards."

"And the Burghers of Calais?" Mycroft asked without looking up.

"The sculpture will be ready on time, but will Westminster Court be ready for the Burghers? Rodin thinks..." Richard hesitated, measuring Mycroft's distraction.

Mycroft opened an official file having German lettering and a State seal. He mumbled something unintelligible, then asked, "What, Richard?" He thumbed a few pages, squinting at something.

Mycroft clicked his tongue and his agitation grew. He had the usual pressing affairs of state engaging him, and his tolerance of Richard's presence was wearing thin as Bible paper.

"Thank you again for appointing me as the government's liaison with Rodin on the Westminster Court project."

Mycroft threw the German file against the wall and shuffled more documents, searching and frustrated that he could not find what he required. He moved to the open window behind his desk. He slammed it closed on the distracting noise from Pall Mall.

"What do you want?" Mycroft asked. "You and I are busy. I must be leaving for a meeting, and I do not want to talk about Henry Davies... unless you know where he is."

Richard forged ahead. "This business involving Henry...we think a German named Krauss is involved and we think he works for the German government... can you corroborate this?" Richard watched Mycroft's tensing face.

"Who's this...we? For the sake of Almighty God, not you and Emma?"

"Do you know this Krauss?"

Mycroft loomed across his desk and propped up his considerable weight by his fingertips.

"Who's this...we?"

"Sir, who is Krauss?"

"I know Krauss...a minor in Nachtgeist. They murdered the one man we got onto Henry's train to Straithairn. The revolutionaries who killed him eluded us. The killer is Nachtgeist's top assassin. They kill innocents and rape and torture women who cross them. And the whole repugnant horde reports to a General Rainer Schmidt. At present he has the Kaiser's ear but is altogether disloyal to the Reich. They have wormed into government agencies here and on the Continent. I'm concerned about international conflict building on the Continent, and I tell you Nachtgeist and this Schmidt might well be the flame to the gunpowder."

"What's the assassin's name?"

Mycroft straightened, gathering his papers. "Today, who knows? On Henry's train he went by Krajic. Today he is someone else. Tomorrow, different again. He is the worst of the foulest, beastly lot I have ever encountered." His face twisted. "You and Emma will withdraw from this evil. You are out of your depth."

"But Mycroft, we must clear Henry's good name and—"

"Listen to me, boy." Moving around his desk, he grabbed Richard's lapels. "For the final time. Stay out of it. I can assure you these people are inhuman." He gripped the lapels even tighter. "They are from the very bowels of hell. These fiends have only begun their work, and the fools at the Yard have not the slightest idea about Nachtgeist's power, especially Krajic's. Now he is here!" Mycroft pulled Richard's coat until he heard the snap of a seam. "Stay away from this. Far away and..."

Richard twisted free of Mycroft's grip. "Henry's my best friend. What is friendship or...or loyalty for, if not for times like this?"

Mycroft stepped away. "Do what you must, but mind me, keep your sister out of it. It is ugly what they do to women...completely beyond the pale. Is that what you want for Emma? Answer me...no shilly-shallying. Answer me!"

"Of course not."

Mycroft brushed his finger against the artists' pencils visible in Richard's breast pocket. He removed a pencil and was about to break it in front of Richard's nose. "They will snap you like one of these. They broke our man's neck on Henry's train before they shot him." Then he snapped the pencil and tossed the pieces aside.

"I know you will not disengage from this matter. I will not compromise my oath to the Crown and my work with the Admiralty. You have been warned, Richard, international implications...the King. Carry on at your own risk. But I insist that you keep your sister out of it!" At the door he wagged a meaty finger. "I speak for the Crown on this matter. And do not get in my way."

Mycroft left without another word, settled into his government brougham, and headed for Whitehall. Richard stood on the pavement shaking as three ladies of high fashion swirled their dresses past him, laughing and swishing along. Sunlight could not overcome the chill he felt. Mycroft had thrown him off balance. He needed time to think, or did he need time to steel his resolve and overcome the new fear Mycroft had implanted...a fear for his sister's safety? He walked along Pall Mall, hoping the exercise would be refreshing, but in time he concluded it was pointless.

He stepped onto a horse-drawn tram. He needed to visit Beeton Park.

Emma arrived at St. Bartholomew's. After interviewing Dr. Beecham, chief of toxicology, about curare and belladonna interactions, she visited Hildy Einbecker, examining her wounds before making her patient rounds. After an hour or so, she found a hansom at the Dennison Street crossing. She noticed a man watching her every move and dismissed him as a roué who roamed the streets, inebriated or hungry for companionship. But usually their kind slithered into the open at night, and certainly not in this area of London. She told the driver to take her to Rundell's Toy Shoppe. She began going over Dr. Beecham's information.

The fact that there's no known interaction between belladonna and curare doesn't mean that there is none. The data is sparse and in every case, curare was injected, entering the blood stream in such a significant quantity that rapid expiration resulted.

Dr. Mull's examination of Thornton's oral cavity or stomach will be important if no puncture or injection site is found. Furthermore, if curare was administered orally, then the perpetrator was ignorant of the proper delivery method, presumably disqualifying Dr. Gregory's knowledgeable staff at university—including Henry. "Yes, indeed, Dr. Mull," Emma murmured.

Arriving at Rundell's, Emma realized that she had not been shopping for toys since she was a child. She alighted from the hansom, paid the driver, and paused to look into the cheery window display. *Perhaps a doll with a fine dress. Hildy would enjoy that. Then there is the children's tea set.* As a child she had loved to play house, but Richard never wanted to join her. A smile flickered in her face at the remembrance of him disagreeably pretending to sip make-believe tea. Her eyes followed one of the new electrical toy trains around its circuit through a miniature village and tunnel.

"If I ever have a son, I'd want him to have one of those trains... even if I had a daughter." She allowed a thought of Geoffrey to come and go.

Emma stepped into Rundell's and looked at the window display from inside. She touched the doll, and suddenly her eyes caught the image of the man she had noticed earlier, stepping down from a hansom outside. She slipped behind a display in the center of the store. She watched the man take up a position by the gaslight in front of the store.

She began to browse, hoping the man would lose interest. She found a charming display of stuffed animals. There were giraffes, American bison, a lion, a fawn, cows, and an adorable Paddington bear completely outfitted with a bright yellow macintosh, wellies, and matching rain hat. Emma hugged it and carried it under her arm to the counter. She paid the counter attendant and glanced towards the front door. The man outside was watching her.

While she waited for the gift to be boxed and wrapped, she pretended to browse but searched for a rear exit. She asked a clerk, who was restocking a shelf, if there was a back door she could use.

The young clerk curtseyed. "Oh no, madam. I mean there ain't one for customers. Back 'ere is deliv'ries only."

"Do you see that man out there, standing and waiting?" Emma pointed. The clerk nodded. "He's following me. I need to escape."

"I sees, madam. I'll fetch Mr. Rundell." Then she hurried up a wooden staircase to the loft.

Emma returned to the counter and received her beautifully wrapped package with its pink ribbon. She turned towards the stairs as the girl was descending. She met her at the display of clockwork animals.

"Proprietor'll be down for ya, madam," the girl said.

Emma waited at the bottom of the stairs, and soon Mr. Rundell appeared.

"A man is following you, madam? Where?"

Emma turned and pointed. He was not there.

"I don't see anyone," Mr. Rundell said.

"He was, sir. Most assuredly he was," Emma said, suddenly anxious. "Would you be kind enough to escort me to a cab?"

The proprietor walked Emma onto the front pavement. She saw the man standing on the corner.

"There he is," Emma said under her breath.

She snapped up a cab, and the proprietor helped her inside, thanked her for her purchase, and she was on her way. She glanced behind her and observed the man looking for another cab. She sat back and exhaled, keen to see Richard and hear news from Mycroft.

The hansom slowed to a stop at her home. Patients were overflowing into the vestibule. They pleaded to see her. She agreed to conduct several consultations before luncheon. She went up the stairs to Richard's room overlooking Carlisle. There she peered through the dirty lace curtains, watching for the man, but he was nowhere in view. Back in her office she conducted a routine examination of an infant, treated a man afflicted with gout, two children with influenza, and a seven-year-old boy with mumps—all before luncheon.

The late morning sunlight cast bright dappled patches throughout Beeton Park. There was no breeze to stir the lake; it lay still, mirroring St. Mark's dome and its golden, radiant cross. Richard stood on the slope in front of the old shed and gazed at the reflections in Beeton Lake. They called it a lake, but it was small and should have been called a pond. Nevertheless, as children, Emma and Richard had considered the lake enormous and had often pretended it was the Atlantic Ocean. On the far side was America, where the story book Chiricahuas and Iroquois hid behind the trees.

He stood in his favorite sanctum, watching a bumblebee buzzing lazily from the wild irises to the honeysuckle.

Richard walked up to the shed. The earth and grass were spongy, offering smells of leaf mold. He watched willow branches bend across the lake water. Closing his eyes, he melted into Beeton, utterly indifferent to time.

Refreshed, he began considering Henry's case.

"So Krauss is Nachtgeist. Mrs. Gregory, Gunther Haas, and the unknown blonde woman are probably Nachtgeist predators, too. Drat it, I should've asked Mycroft about them. So, Mrs. Gregory's brother is head of Nachtgeist. They used a combination of curare and Nigel's poison formula to commit the murder. Perhaps Charles Steele has nothing to do with the murder. Maybe he has everything to do with it."

Mycroft's words thumped in the back of his head. And more than his words, it was the fire in his eyes, the vehemence in his voice. Or was it Mycroft's profound dread that was infecting Richard? All of it bore upon him. He had never known Mycroft to be capable of such emotion as he had exhibited in his library.

"What'll I do?" He picked up a twig and scraped at a patch of soil.

As in no other case, Richard knew it would involve personal risk as surely as Big Ben's hourly toll. He felt fear as he scraped and prodded. The twig snapped.

When it came it was a mere glimmer. It came in, gossamer soft, slowly forming. It was audacious and it excited him. He had a goal, and more than that, a grand goal.

He opened his sketchbook to a blank page and furiously drew a snake. "I must sever the head!"

He attacked the drawing of the serpent with his pencil, slicing and cutting the paper and breaking the pencil point. He tore the page from the book and crumpled it but stopped abruptly, hardly noticing a Monarch butterfly drifting past. Richard smoothed out the paper's wrinkles with his hands and slipped it into the back of the book. It would serve as a reminder of the new transcending purpose of the case. It would pit him against Nachtgeist.

Richard rested against the chalky wall of the shed. No plan came to him. Not a flicker giving him a means to kill the serpent.

"Attempt something daring and Powerful Forces will come to your aid," he muttered, quoting his favorite dictum. "I must confront this Colonel Rainer Schmidt."

Still, he wondered how. Ducks quacked and traffic hummed.

How?

CHAPTER 16

Emma was delayed in surgery with an irksome old woman suffering from hypochondria. The patient would listen only to Dr. John and certainly not to Dr. Emma, steadfastly believing a woman's calling was in the home and definitely not in medicine.

"Any self-respecting Christian woman your age should be married with a family. Women's brains and nature are ill fitted for a man's world. And you, Dr. John, are to blame for encouraging this flibbertigibbet daughter of yours towards unnatural pursuits."

The woman straightened her dress and hair while she attributed all of the ills of society to modern women like Emma and the decadent socialist ideas infecting the country. She roundly criticized the woman's suffrage movement, knowing fully of Emma's involvement and recent incarceration. Dr. John winked furtively at his daughter and gave the woman an envelope of placeboes. She departed delighted, thankful, and calmed.

"Take luncheon, Emma, and I will carry on awhile longer."

Emma and Richard enjoyed Mrs. Mac's pea soup and homemade bread and shared all that had happened after their meeting with Lestrade. As his sister described the incident at Rundell's Toy Shoppe, alarm coursed through Richard afresh. Mycroft's warnings loomed once more.

"Mycroft confirmed Krauss's connection with Nachtgeist... Rainer Schmidt's, too. Em, the man who was murdered on Henry's train was Mycroft's agent."

"Good heavens."

"And Krajic is Nachtgeist."

"You two look white as sheets," Mrs. Mac said as she entered with Mary trailing after her. "Sit down over here and give 'em some cheer. I'll bring pea soup 'n bread."

"Mary, I need you to nick Mrs. Gregory's picture from Dr. Gregory's desk," Emma said, tearing a piece of bread and sopping a little soup.

"Her picture? What in heaven's..."

"Just for a day. He won't miss it…"

"Mrs. Gregory's picture? Have you taken leave of your senses?" Mary turned to Richard for support, but he was occupied with swabbing the inside of his soup bowl with a tuft of bread.

"Please, Mary. I've found someone who can place Mrs. Gregory at Krauss's apartment. Hildy Einbecker. Here." Emma pushed the bread loaf towards her. "We can possibly connect her with the poison formula. We need that photograph. Henry's case can hinge on such a thing as this, you know."

Mrs. Mac entered from the kitchen with Petey Broom fidgeting behind her.

"Petey, come here and eat," Richard said, patting the chair seat beside him. Petey's kneebreeches were threadbare and several sizes too large. He removed his cap and nodded shyly to the ladies, uncomfortable in his surroundings.

"Petey, this is Miss Palmer. Mary, this is Petey Broom," Emma said proudly. "Father and I delivered him before I was in medical college. Isn't that correct, Petey?"

"So's um told, madam. Pleezed ta meetcha, Miss Palmer." He groped in his too-deep pockets and removed a scrap of paper. "'Ere, guv, I sez to mesef that yer'd be pow'rful keen ta see this, so I nicked it. Taddy 'n Ollie follered 'em women all a way ta nearly the univers'ty. 'Twas a 'partmint of a Thornton. The Greg'ry woman went ta the 'partmint ya tollus about. All Krauts in…ah…er, excuse me…all Germans in 'ere. Her un a man ran like blazes ta send 'at telegram yer holdin'. Mad as a bag a frogs they was. I sez to mesef ya need ta see 'at telegram. Dun't worry none. Taddy 'n Ollie'r spyin' 'em good. Trouble is 'em women tuk cabs 'n we had ta do the same so we cud stay on 'em. We be needin' a few quid."

"Here. Sit and eat, my boy."

"Dun't mind if I do."

Richard waved the telegram. "This is all in German."

Mrs. Mac gave the boy a large bowl of soup and patted his head.

Petey tore a handful of bread from the loaf and began to eat ravenously.

"Em, what do you make of this? To Schmidt from Krauss."

Emma flattened the paper against the table, adjusted her gold pince-nez, and scanned the German printing, penning her translation in the margin.

Mary watched Petey slurping his soup.

Richard took the boy's bowl to the kitchen and returned with more.

"Ta, guv. Ya be too gud ta the likes a me."

"Not at all, my boy," Richard said, smiling at Mary, who was staring at Petey, mildly baffled.

Emma waved the telegram. "Richard, a brief word in my office. We'll only be a moment."

Mary nodded, now smiling at Petey's entertainment.

Before Richard closed the surgery door, Emma whispered, "We must not reveal the contents of this to Mary. She's doing well, considering everything. She mustn't know about this."

Richard read her translation: "Rainer Schmidt. Bird in sight. Can kill, capture or observe. Decision? Krauss."

Richard bit his lip. "Bird. That's Henry, of course. The Huns are in Blaenllyn." He rubbed his beard, frustrated. "We'll tell Mary it was irrelevant...government business... a government communiqué. I'll station Petey at the telegraph office to intercept anything more involving Krauss. I hope Henry stays out of sight."

"Gordon should see this, Richard. I know it's inconclusive, but Gordon's eyes should open a trifle more. I'll go to the Yard after I deliver Mary to university."

Richard grabbed her wrist. "We must not tell Gordon how we obtained the telegram."

"Agreed. We should leave straightaway."

Returning to the dining room, Emma stopped at Petey's side and stroked his shoulder. "If you're finished, please run to the livery and ask for Lloyd. Tell him we need a carriage for the four of us immediately."

"Acourse, Dr. Watson." He reached for a lone scrap of bread and paused, looking at Emma. She nodded, and the boy started for the back door, cramming a fistful of bread into his mouth.

Minutes later, Petey arrived with the carriage and they rushed to the University of London. After conveying Mary to the science building and Petey near the German apartment, Richard and Emma arrived at the official entrance to Scotland Yard.

"Richard. Emma." A young, fresh-faced, uniformed man called out from half a block away. He hurried towards them on rather spindly legs.

"Harry! Very good to see you," Richard said as the man pumped his hand and bowed to Emma.

"Let us look at you," Emma said. The twins stepped back and rather ceremoniously examined Harry Coyle up and down. He was wearing his new constable's uniform that tried its best to disguise the man's natural awkwardness.

"I started at th' Yard o'r three weeks ago," Harry said, brushing his lapels proudly. "Thanks ta you two 'n Sherlock Holmes givin' Director Wallace a good word fer me." Harry grasped Richard's hand and shook it again enthusiastically.

"We're here to see Lestrade." Richard motioned for their friend to accompany them inside.

"All your work as an Irregular has finally paid off," Emma said as Harry opened the large double doors for them.

"Am on watch detail. Hubbard's, the greengrocer. Gettin' vegetables scotched every day, he sez. Borin'. Not complainin' none. An' am gettin' married in a month. I got a desk all me own. Come see."

Handing the German telegram to his sister, Richard said, "You talk to Gordon. I'll spend a few minutes with Harry." He followed the excited ex-Irregular who was waving him on down the corridor.

Emma was happy that she would be with Gordon alone. She wanted to avoid any confrontation between Gordon and Richard. This was not the time or place for argument. She pressed her hand to her hair, looked down at her blouse and skirt, and stopped in front of his office door. As she reached for the door pull, the door swung open.

"Emma. My word. Twice in a day. Come in. Where's Richard?"

"I've something you must see." He closed the door and adjusted a chair for her. He sat beside her, and she was aware of his eyes on her. She could feel their warmth like sunlight on her cheek. To forestall a blush, she thrust the telegram in front of his nose.

"You must see this." So long was his gaze on her that she became uncomfortable.

"What's this...?" The night Emma had told him she needed time to devote herself completely to her medical studies could have been only last evening, so fresh was his hurt. He thought he could still taste the shepherd's pie Mrs. MacIntosh had served the evening their romance ended.

Emma pointed to the German words on the paper. "Gordon, please read it."

"Yes. Of course." He scanned the telegram. "German?" His eyebrows rose.

"Mycroft has confirmed that Herr Krauss, the one who sent this telegram, is a German anarchist and Rainer Schmidt is the head of Nachtgeist. Schmidt is on the Kaiser's personal staff. Evidently that's the reason for the Crown's keen interest. I printed the English translation. See? Krauss lives in the same building where the two poisonings occurred. It's much more than mere coincidence, Gordon."

He reread the telegram and finally looked at Emma. She jumped when a sharp knock at the door startled them. Dr. Mull entered and nodded to Lestrade.

"Yes, what is it, Mull?"

"We have reconfirmed the curare. It was definitely in the teapot and the cup with the deceased's fingerprints...mixed with green tea." He fumbled in his white lab coat for his spectacles. He hooked the wires over his ears and handed Lestrade several papers. He pointed to the first page. "There. The other cup had only green tea."

"May I pose a question?" Emma said.

"Certainly, Doctor Watson." Dr. Mull's eyes were large behind his lenses.

"Are you aware of any interaction between belladonna and curare?"

"There is none, doctor. I am convinced that curare alone was responsible for Dr. Thornton's death. I thoroughly reexamined the corpus delicti for puncture wounds."

"And?" Lestrade asked.

"I found none. No punctures...anywhere. I can unequivocally state that Dr. Thornton's murderer did not use a needle to deliver the poison into the deceased's circulatory system. However," Dr. Mull said, clearing his throat. "Dr. Thornton had a tooth extracted the day of his death."

Emma gasped, thrusting herself against the back of her chair. "Pray continue, Dr. Mull."

"I attached no particular significance to it when I first examined the corpus. One is not thinking of curare when the belladonna appeared to be so uniquely and prominently suggestive. But now, after analyzing the oral tissues, I am convinced the poison entered his system at the point of a bicuspid extraction...upper right quadrant."

"If Dr. Thornton had only delayed the extraction, he might be alive now," Lestrade said, shaking his head.

"Will that be all, Inspector?"

"Thank you, Dr. Mull," Lestrade replied.

Dr. Mull nodded to Emma before withdrawing from the office.

"Gordon, they wanted Dr. Thornton dead very badly," Emma said excitedly. "Belladonna and curare. Whoever killed him is a beast."

"Quite right."

The office door swung open. "Gordy," said Richard, "I just saw Coyle. He thanks you for giving him work. Em, did you tell him about the man who followed you to Rundell's?" Lestrade's eyes went to Emma.

"From St. Bartholomew's to Rundell's Toy Shoppe. He waited outside Rundell's. Fortunately, I got the only hansom in sight. But had there been another, he would have followed me home, I'm quite sure of it."

"The swine!"

Richard sat down. "It was a man Em had never seen before. This has to do with Thornton's murder. I'm certain of it."

"Emma, describe him," Gordon said, poised for notetaking.

"Richard's height and build—tall, stocky, black hair, and clean-shaven but bushy muttonchops. Perhaps forty. Brown tweed suit. He kept his hands in his coat pockets. No other distinguishing features, I'm sorry to say. Had Sherlock seen him, he would've discerned the stalker's life story."

"Gordy, this means that whoever murdered Thornton knows Em's poking around."

Lestrade opened a file and scanned a list. "Harry Coyle's available. I'll have him escort you home."

"Splendid," Richard said.

"Gordon, I'll be fine." Emma tapped her brother's shoulder. "Dr. Mull says that the curare entered Thornton's bloodstream through his gum...a tooth extraction. He confirmed my suspicions. Curare in only Nigel's cup and teapot but unknown prints on the lid match the second cup." She poked him for emphasis. "The person who drank from that cup put the poison in the teapot."

Lestrade excused himself for a few minutes and returned with Harry Coyle.

"Harry will escort you home," Lestrade announced.

"That's most kind of you, Gordon, but I do not need..."

"That's the end of the matter. I insist. Now, old chum, you and I must talk with Mycroft. I must hear him officially confirm what Emma has reported about Nachtgeist." Gordon took Emma's hand as she rose. "Richard, it's not that I don't believe you. Of course I do. But I must..."

"Say nothing more, Gordon. We understand," Emma said softly.

He pressed her delicate hand, then glanced at her ring finger. Lestrade pictured the engagement ring, which he still kept hidden at home, reserved exclusively for that graceful finger.

After handing her into the official carriage, followed by Harry Coyle, Gordon waved goodbye and threw her a kiss, surprising himself with his boldness. It was entirely reflexive and expressed his inner feelings. Emma nodded demurely as the carriage turned onto Embankment.

Richard and Lestrade arrived at Mycroft's apartment and received a stinging rebuke for pursuing the case, and another enumeration of Nachtgeist's shocking cruelties. Even more alarming was Mycroft's accounting of Krajic's depravity across the Continent—his torture, his murders, his sacrificial rapes, and the savagery of his other crimes. Mycroft inventoried what he knew of their anarchist aims: to create economic and social mayhem; to topple governments, and to tear apart the fabric of decency. Surprisingly, there was no evidence that Nachtgeist had ever used poison. They employed instead deadly, physical brutality to advance their cause. And it was a cause they pursued with the terrifying religious zeal of new converts. Richard and Lestrade left the apartment quiet and somber.

They stood silently at the carriage, Lestrade's hand on the door. Each man knew that England and decent people everywhere would soon face an evil of unparalleled wickedness unless a miracle happened. Lestrade finally opened the carriage door, and both men took their seats. The black, matched pair lurched into a gallop towards Carlisle Street. The two friends sat silent and reflective. Richard held his sketchbook firmly on his lap, uncharacteristically closed shut. As the carriage neared its destination, Lestrade referred to his pocket watch. "It's getting late. I want to interrogate this Charles Samuel Steele, Esquire."

CHAPTER 17

In Wales, Henry watched the cloud trailing Fiona's speeding red motorcar. His hands tapped the railing outside the men's dormitory. He took a jealous nudge and an envious smile from a colliery friend. The motorcar disappeared behind a pile of slag, and he heard the sound of her blaring horn seconds before the car roared into view. A small crowd of colliers joined Henry, waiting for the wild Rhys woman to arrive. Henry walked down the slate steps and onto the gravel path. Fiona sped up the road and chattered to a stop. Henry stepped back. She was laughing.

"Hurry," Fiona said.

He got into the car, and before he could close the door, Fiona wrapped her arm around his neck and kissed his cheek. They sped away through the dusty air. Henry swiped his fingers across his cheek and saw the bright red lip rouge on them. He wiped them again as the motorcar bounced along the road.

"Father's eager to see you. Never saw him so thrilled," Fiona shouted over the wind and engine roar. Her hair was streaming back as she gripped the steering wheel with one hand and groped to find Henry's hand with the other. He took her hand for a moment and then placed it on the steering wheel.

"How was your time with Lucas and the family last night?"

"Thirty minutes late from Aberystwyth. They'd all but given up on me."

"Grouse. Grouse. We enjoyed our day out, didn't we? Will Lucas and Margaret meet us at the pub tonight?"

"I hope so. She's a fine cook. I'm concerned about young William. Tuberculosis, you know."

Fiona turned. "Oh, dear me, I hadn't heard. How long has he been afflicted?"

"Too long...over three months. Lucas should've written me about it."

"And baby Edgar?"

"Ha, ten months old and a ton. Held my fingers like a vise. He'll be like his father. But they're struggling and want to leave the valley. Margaret's rather desperate for Lucas' safety. He barely escaped the last collapse, didn't he? And now William. She's at her wits end."

"I had no idea they were having such difficulty."

"Since childhood, it was Lucas and Margaret. A dead cert. They were made for each other. I've never seen two people more in love."

Fiona nodded.

"I wish there was better medicine in our valley, Fiona. Young William needs a specialist. I examined him. Labored breathing. Pulmonary edema. Dropsy. I insisted they take him to Emma. They can't afford the trip. I know she wouldn't charge them. The boy won't be long with us, I'm afraid."

"I must tell Father. He'll supply the funds. Did you know he wants to build a clinic here?"

"That won't help William, will it?"

"There are only two physicians for all these valleys. Dinosaurs. Fossils. You remember old Dr. Thomas. He was ancient when we were children. He still uses leeches...even spring blood-lettings. For the old people who still believe in it, like him."

"Venesection—evacuate the accumulated bad blood from winter? Surely, Fiona, he doesn't—"

"Both doctors do...even cuppings. Remember cupping? Scared me half to death. The heated glass cups on the flesh? The blood. Can you imagine that and blood-letting and leeches nowadays? We need modern medicine like you teach and Emma practices."

The Fiat roared onto the private road winding up to the Rhys estate.

"The last time I was at your home was over five years ago, when your parents hosted my Ph.D. party."

"I wish I had taken a few days' leave from the Sorbonne."

"Your curatorial studies were demanding. Your parents were far too extravagant on my behalf."

"Over there. Remember?" Fiona pointed to an old crumbling stone wall behind the stableyard. He looked at the wall and when he saw her smile, he understood her meaning. "Don't tell me you forgot."

"You kissed me."

"Rather, you kissed me."

Henry remembered it differently. It had been his first kiss, and he knew Fiona had been well practiced in the art by the time she had introduced him to such delights. She had tugged and teased him until he joined her behind the wall, where she threw him down and kissed him—typical Fiona Rhys. He also knew the place held a romantic memory of Fiona with Richard, during his visits to Blaenllyn with Emma. She had given him his first kiss there, too.

Fiona slowed her car in view of the Rhys mansion. It was framed by green slopes and dotted with wildflowers. Poplars and sycamores lined the approach. Sunlight dappled Fiona's face as she brought the motorcar to a stop in front of the steps leading to the imposing entrance.

"Father gets angry when I drive too fast."

The footman opened the door and they entered the house.

"Father. Mother," she called, entering the drawing room. Her parents rose and greeted Henry with genuine delight.

"Please, have a seat," Bramwell Rhys said, motioning him into a chair next to his own favorite wingback.

The Rhyses listened as Henry explained his work. He felt a comfort in the room. Each time he glanced at Fiona he found her eyes on him, and he fought to give her parents equal attention. Bramwell's questions were thoughtful and engaging, and Henry offered more technical subjects he had been pursuing in his laboratory. But he stopped short of his discovery.

The butler knocked, then entered. "Dinner is served."

The table was laid for four with a brace of glowing candles, cut crystal, polished silver, and a large floral centerpiece. He and Fiona sat together on one side with Bramwell and Glyn Rhys at opposite ends. There followed a procession of edible delights over the two hours that followed. After they desserted on elderberry fool, Bramwell Rhys pushed his chair away. "Let's retire to my den for a good cigar and port, shall we, my boy?"

Henry tried to stand, but Fiona pulled him to his seat and kissed his cheek. "Be careful of Father. He wants to smoke and drink all evening. Remember, we want to meet Lucas and Margaret at the pub, don't we? Evan and Kynan will be there, most likely."

Bramwell was waving his hand at Henry and smiling. "Fiona. You give me only minutes with Henry and you have him for hours... days."

"Father, I do hope I have Henry much longer than hours or days." She added loudly, "Infinitely longer."

Her inference was not lost on Henry. Mary had probably all but given up on him. After all, she had not replied to his telegram. If she had, surely Lucas would have delivered it straightaway. Henry knew the murder, the shock of his flight, and the corroding acid of suspicion would etch a gulf between them. He brought his mind back to Bramwell offering port.

Inside the den, Henry glanced out the big mullioned window from which he had helped Fiona escape one day to go fishing with the lads. For a brief moment Henry believed he saw a dark figure move from the window towards a stand of eucalyptus. He blinked once and dismissed it as nothing more than his fearful imagination.

"My son, your family is important to us. Will always be. This is the first time since your brother's funeral that I've seen you. Please, Henry, accept my sincerest condolences again. I know how close you and James were."

"Thank you, sir."

"Over here, son." Bramwell moved toward the large window. Henry joined him and scanned the darkened stand of eucalyptus for the lurking figure. Nothing moved. The trees were still and silent. The sound of the church bell carried over the hills to reach deep into the valleys.

"I enjoy seeing the village from here. My father did, too. There, the third gaslight...your parents' house, I believe."

Henry got his bearings. "Yes...my home."

Bramwell draped his arm over Henry's shoulder. "Our families go back a few generations, do they not? Rhys Collieries and Quarries have been a part of this valley for a long time. Well, of course, you know that." Bramwell faced Henry. "I inherited this wealth, and I'd like to believe I honored my father and grandfather by expanding our enterprise."

"You have certainly done that, sir."

"May I be honest with you, Henry? Of course, I can."

Henry smiled, remembering how Bramwell often answered his own questions.

Bramwell led Henry to the leather chairs, and they sat facing each other with their port and cigars.

"What will happen to Rhys Collieries when I pass on? Fiona is our only child. And you know Fiona." He shrugged. "Many collieries, quarries, too, are being sold to wealthy, know-nothing, bloodsucking Londoners who wouldn't know a piece of coal if they sat on it. They're bleeding the valleys. Bleeding, I tell you. They want a quick kill. Fast money...no commitment to the valley. Especially not to the people." Bramwell's face flushed. "You probably don't know this, Henry, but Deeside Slab Quarry in Llangollen is gone. It only took them two years to rape Deeside. I just hired nine of their best hewers. Put them down in the Caerphilly quarry operation. You know... you worked there for two summers, eh? All of them can handle a twabill pick like it was their own hand. I think the Portland blocks see those fellows a-coming and start asplittin' before the twabills hit and the wedges are struck. Glanadyn, Llyswen, Disserth, Clunbury... all of them are being sucked dry right now..." he clenched his fist, "...by those greedy leeches."

Bramwell stared at his port, ruby in the light. "Trgynon, Brettswygan, and Aylton will be next, I'll wager."

Henry said, "I had heard about Llyswen."

"What? Oh yes, of course you would've heard. Llyswen. Your good mother is from there. Listen to me, Henry." He leaned forward. "If your father were only twenty years younger, this operation would be his...the whole thing. Please understand me, dear boy. I have many fine men working for me. None like your pap...or you. We're coal men. Those London pantywaists are not valley people. They aren't coal, Henry. Not like your father. I look at my men. None of them are like you or your pap. Of course James, too, you understand." Bramwell gripped Henry's knee. "And you're educated. You know how to plan and figure. You care about people. You know the valley. You were born here. You know coal. You are coal, Henry. Come back home, my son."

Shocked, Henry stammered, "Sir, I..."

"Let me finish. You know the Vaughns. They want to sell...sell, mind you! Talked to Arthwyr Vaughn after church two Sundays last. Pulled me aside and told me. All hush-hush, you know. Good Lord, someone must put a stop to this madness. If I knew you'd move back, I'd buy out old man Vaughn tomorrow." Bramwell snapped his fingers. "This is where you belong. All this can be yours. I know you'd be forsaking your teaching and research, but consider the families you'd be helping here. You could establish a medical clinic. The valleys need it." Bramwell leaned closer. "You know Fiona has been carrying a torch for you since...well, ten years, maybe longer. You both are at a loose end. I can see you two getting married and living here in Blaenllyn. We'll make Rhys & Davies Collieries and Quarries even grander than it is now. We'll own these valleys. Think of it."

"Sir, you have—"

"Think of how happy your dear father and mother would be if you returned to run the operations. You're their only son now." Bramwell drew deep on his cigar. "You and I are from the same vein of coal, aren't we? The eldest son takes care of his parents. I did for mine. You must, too. What will you do? Move them to London? Rip their roots from the valley? Think of your dear mother. These are times that demand pragmatism. This estate will be yours. When the missus and I cross the river, you bring your parents to live here with Fiona and your children. I'd insist upon that. I love your father like he was the brother I never had. I can do no less. We are the valley, remember. Coal. Not those London dandies."

Bramwell sank into his chair. Henry's mind reeled.

"Well, my boy?"

He nervously sipped his port. The silence was as dense as the cigar smoke. Henry had grown up surrounded by Rhys money. Their fortune held no particular appeal to him. But the idea of a medical clinic! He could manage the collieries and advance his discovery, too, while providing medical care for the valley. But he would be giving up teaching. The irony touched him: grand thoughts for a man on the run.

"Henry, you and Fiona must settle down. She's always gadding about all over. She wants to go on a safari next. Imagine...a woman on a safari in the desert and jungle. She wants to research aboriginal art and antiquities. Pish tosh." Bramwell leaned towards Henry again. "I realize I have surprised you. I've been giving it a lot of thought over the past months. Then you arrived here unexpectedly. Here you are." Bramwell gestured with his cigar, spilling white ash. "It all seems foreordained, would you not say? Give it serious..."

The door to Bramwell's den opened, and Fiona entered. "Father, you've had Henry long enough." Her eyes found Henry, and she grabbed his hand. "Goodness. Your hand is ice! I'll make it warm."

"Will you promise to give our discussion serious consideration?"

"I shall, sir. Indeed I shall." Henry shook Bramwell's hand.

"Good, good."

Fiona and Henry returned to her Fiat Zero and waved goodbye as they rumbled around the circular drive and down towards the village.

Glyn Rhys turned to Bramwell. "Fiona is serious this time. She's always loved him, hasn't she, Bram?"

CHAPTER 18

Mary Palmer fished in her shopping bag as Emma and Geoffrey pointed to Dr. John, sprawled on his favorite chair dozing contentedly, after Mrs. MacIntosh's hearty dinner and a taste of port.

"There he goes," Emma said. "He doesn't believe he snores."

"I must have this back very soon," Mary said, handing Emma a framed photograph. "I thought I'd die when I was in Dr. Gregory's office. And to think I have to sneak in and return it."

"See, Richard? This is Mrs. Gregory and her brother, Rainer Schmidt."

"When can I have it back?"

"Tomorrow...if my hunch works. Perhaps the afternoon."

"He has a weekly meeting in his office all afternoon. What shall I do?"

Emma removed her pince-nez and breathed on the lenses. She opened her reticule for her handkerchief, and as she did, something she saw inside made her slump backward in the settee, disgusted with herself.

"What was I thinking?" Emma said, removing her handkerchief and the telegram she had promised to send to Henry. Flushed with embarrassment, she looked at Mary. "I am very sorry."

"My word, Emma," Mary said.

"Give it here." Richard grabbed the paper and slipped it into his coat pocket. "I'll send it tonight. I must check Petey at the telegraph office anyway."

"I'm terribly sorry. Forgive me."

The door chimes suddenly jangled, and they heard Mrs. Mac scurrying down the hall. Seconds later, she opened the parlor door and announced, "A Charles Steele, Esquire, is here to see Richard and Emma."

The twins looked at each other and Emma said, "Please show him into my office. It's dark in there."

"I'll take care of the gaslights," Richard said.

"Why would Steele be visiting us? Perhaps the date of Thornton's funeral has been settled. I should think we shan't be very long. Geoffrey, keep Mary company."

When she arrived in surgery, Mrs. Mac was introducing Richard to Mr. Steele, who looked aggravated, every muscle wound way too tight and the very opposite of the polished man she had met at the Thorntons'.

"May I offer you some tea or perhaps some port, Mr. Steele?" Mrs. Mac inquired.

"You are very kind, madam. No, thank you." Then he saw Emma enter the room. "I offer my sincerest apologies for this intrusion at such a late hour. I—"

"Please, Mr. Steele." Emma motioned to a side chair. "Do sit down, sir. I see you have met my brother, Richard."

"It's a pleasure to meet such a famous artist."

Richard waved down the accolade and found a chair. "How may we assist you, Mr. Steele?"

The barrister sat rigid.

"You appear somewhat overwrought," Emma said, finding her pencil for note taking.

"I'm in frightful trouble and I'm quite desperate. I fear Scotland Yard shall charge me with my brother-in-law's murder. I-I am—"

Richard touched the man's arm. "Start at the beginning, sir."

"Well, yes. I suppose. I'm a barrister, an expert at interrogatory and verbal fisticuffs, and look at me." He extended his hands for the twins to observe his shaking.

"Mr. Steele, we are very well acquainted with your victories at the Old Bailey," Richard smiled. "Your work before the bar is ranked among the best. I should think you'll soon be taking the silk for Queen's Counsel. Please begin."

"I had an appointment this afternoon with a Chief Detective Inspector Lestrade of Scotland Yard. He questioned me mercilessly concerning my brother-in-law's murder. He claimed he had my fingerprints and they matched a note I had written. His sergeant fingerprinted me right there in my office. I told him about the note I had written to Nigel. I confessed to writing it. He said I was on extremely thin ice, and if the prints on the note matched the official ones, I would be charged with Nigel's death." He paused for a second to catch his breath. "Afterward, I knew I would need the services of my solicitor. Hearing my case, he advised I seek a consulting detective. The very best, you understand. I left my office and rushed to Baker Street and Sherlock Holmes. He would not hear me out and sent me to you. He said you solve the cases that confound the police. Such a glowing recommendation. I was unaware that you two were—"

"My brother and I are only amateurs, sir. We only take cases when a crime reaches into our personal sphere. Tell us about the note, Mr. Steele."

He swallowed hard. "It pains me to reveal all this to you. Especially to you, Dr. Watson, since you were Nigel's student and you hold him in such high regard."

"Yes?" Emma prompted.

"Over the past several years, my sister and Dr. Thornton had not been, shall I say, amicable. Their marriage had begun as a rather impetuous affair. Then Elizabeth came along...have you met Elizabeth, doctor?" He immediately caught himself. "Yes, I should have remembered that you know her."

"You must surely know, sir, that her foot needs medical attention."

Warmth briefly replaced fear in his face. "Well, as you know, such an operation is very expensive, and Dr. Thornton's teaching position would not produce the level of income my sister normally requires. Then the additional cost of the medical procedure, traveling to Boston for the surgery...you can understand, it was far beyond Dr. Thornton's wherewithal. He approached me about underwriting the medical expenses, and he promised to repay me over time. Then, several months ago, he moved out of his home and took up residence at a flat near the university. He promised to provide regular support and living expenses, but never did. I found myself supporting Elizabeth and my sister while she carried on an embarrassing flirtation with Mr. Clark. You might recall meeting him when you paid us a bereavement visit."

"Yes, of Clark's Banks."

"Nigel had signed a child support document, which he never fulfilled. Furthermore, my sister was about to prepare divorce proceedings, and lately Nigel bragged about an important discovery of some kind, rather significant he said, and was excited about the enormous financial proceeds he would share with the university and his family. It was all simply so much talk from a dreamer. When he returned from his brief holiday in Germany, he was highly excited over imminent monetary gain."

The barrister looked at Richard and Emma, checking if he was going too quickly.

"I made an appointment with him for early evening...the night of his death...or I should say, murder. I arrived on time, but a secretary informed me he had a toothache and had left early. An unlikely story, of course. I can assure you he knew the subject of my visit and feared legal action and was conveniently absent. However, I would not have taken him to court and sullied our family name in front of the public in such a fashion. It's bad enough that Elizabeth is in love with a common chauffeur. As my sister's romance with Clark progressed—and I call it romance in deference to you, Dr. Watson—I promised to continue their support until Clark took over. And do not ask me why Clark never provided one guinea of financial assistance. Bankers."

The barrister stood up, gripped the lapels of his coat, and paced around the consulting office.

"You must understand, I simply wanted to put the fear of God in him. When I found out he would not or could not meet with me that night, I left. Then I decided to leave him a note. I returned and tried his door. It was locked. I engaged a locksmith my solicitor had used on several occasions who was not above doing a bit of dirty work."

"Who might he be?" Richard asked.

"I told the Inspector about him. George Pratt's his name. I found him in his favorite public house and was fortunate to get there before drink rendered him useless. We went to Nigel's office. It took only a few seconds for Pratt to open the door. I left the note on Nigel's desk. I wanted to surprise him that I was able to enter his office unimpeded, you understand...give him a perfect shock. We closed the door and departed. It is all the truth...the complete truth. And what I know about chemistry and such you can put in your eye. And heaven forbid if I wanted to employ his nightshade poison to kill him, how would I know what to do?"

Steele stood watching them. But what he got from Richard completely threw him off balance.

Richard sat back in his chair. "Why should my sister and I believe you?"

"On my word of honor as a gentleman, sir, it happens to be the truth."

Richard stared with unconcealed skepticism. "God alone is the judge," Richard said.

Emma found her brother's self-important posture humorous. She knew what he was about to do.

"Your story, sir, smells rather strongly of prevarication," was Richard's opening salvo. "You expect my sister and me to believe such a patently anemic story as this: That you approached your brother-in-law in an innocent attempt to hold him responsible for financial support of your sister and niece. As you said, 'To put the fear of God in him.' And that you freely admit you found the cooperation of a disreputable locksmith upon whose testimony you are trusting for adequate legal corroboration."

Steele's face blanched. "I shall leave you and return with Pratt," he said, half rising from his chair.

"Rubbish! Don't waste our time, sir. Men like Pratt will say anything for a fiver. No, sir." Richard walked around the office playacting the barrister's role. "What actually happened was ugly and vile. You returned after leaving the deceased the note and discovered him working in his laboratory. His work had become his life. Absorbing. All consuming. You knew about Dr. Thornton's poisonous discovery, of which you claim little knowledge. He was proud of it and had explained it in sufficient detail to gain your tolerance. Dr. Nigel Thornton was busily at work when you entered, he offered you tea, you accepted, and at a convenient moment you turned his lethal discovery on your unsuspecting brother-in-law. He succumbed in a matter of seconds."

Steele jumped to his feet and exclaimed hotly, "I'll not subject myself to such grave allegations!"

"Sit down, sir. I have not finished. After you satisfied yourself that Dr. Nigel Thornton was dead, you rushed from the building, convinced it looked like an accident. But you forgot the teacups on the laboratory counter and that incriminating note containing your fingerprints. You expect my sister and me to swallow your story?"

"But it is—"

"You had the means, the motive, and very clearly the opportunity, regardless of George Pratt's involvement, to commit the murder of Dr. Nigel Thornton, your brother-in-law, husband of your dear sister."

Bristling with offense, Steele started, "I am telling..."

"Your profession," Richard went on, jabbing, "would call this a closed case, would it not?"

"Yes, but I—"

"Yes, but this, and yes, but that. I want you out of our sight. You are beyond redemption, sir. God help you."

Richard stormed out of the office.

Emma rose to her feet. Mr. Steele attempted to stand, but she motioned for him to remain seated. After she closed the door, she returned to her seat and asked, "Mr. Steele, why are you here?"

"If you and your brother...well, at least if you are as good as Holmes claims you to be, then my only defense is to find the actual murderer." He added emphatically, "I did not murder my brother-in-law."

"Very well then, sir. Here is a pencil and paper. Where can we find this George Pratt? Also, where is this pub he frequents?"

After he scribbled the answers, Emma removed the note from her desk and moved to the office door. She opened it, and the exhausted barrister rose unsteadily to his feet.

"Is that all?"

"Mr. Steele, I doubt very seriously if my brother and I can be of any assistance to you in this appalling business. However, if we decide to take an interest in it, for Dr. Thornton's memory you understand, then we shall be in correspondence with you. A very good night to you, sir."

She opened the outer door, and he left without a word.

Emma returned to the parlor displaying a broad smile. Geoffrey, Richard, and Mary were in conversation.

"You were brilliant, Richard...simply brilliant. You should be a thespian."

Richard sat back in his chair. "Steele was convincing except for two words."

"I know," Emma said. "Nightshade poison. Very suggestive. Here's George Pratt's address, his pub, too."

"Em, you know solicitors and barristers. The shyster brigade...actors, the whole lot."

"Had he not mentioned nightshade," Emma said, "I would've been rather inclined to believe him. Only Gordon, Dr. Mull, and Dr. Hazeltine know it was nightshade."

"I do hope Steele did it and is convicted," said Mary. "I need Henry, and the sooner the better." She dabbed her eyes. "I better be going. Richard, you promised to send the telegram."

He patted his breast pocket. "I shall do it tonight before I find this George Pratt. I've thought of a devious project for him. I'll see you home. Let's give Em and Geoffrey some privacy."

During the carriage ride to the Palmers' near Beeton Park, Richard held Mary close as she cried quietly. He did his best to diminish her perception of the danger Henry faced in Wales. But he wanted not to overcompensate. Henry's danger was real, and Mary had to possess a sound understanding of it.

Mary berated herself to Richard for considering Henry's guilt at the outset.

"Don't fret, Mary," he said, patting the telegram in his pocket. "Henry will get this in the morning. Perhaps even yet tonight. His love is Gibraltar. Don't worry unduly."

She kissed his cheek before he handed her down from the cab. The constable on watch gave him a thorough going over, then opened the door for Mary. She waved to Richard as he departed.

Richard found Petey standing at the telegraph office with his hands thrust deep into his pockets.

"Mr. Watson, 'm glad ta see ya. Waitin' fur Alby ta take o'er. Found out that blondie fur ya. Named McMannus. Here." The boy pulled a scrap of paper from his pocket. "See. 'Elen McMannus—British ta me eyes, but talks German better 'n 'em Germans."

"Good work. Is there anything else?" The boy shook his head. Richard slipped the boy a handful of coins. "Be here tomorrow morning. Now, be on your way home lest your mother gets worried. I'll wait for Alby."

"Shud be here soon. 'Morrow, then," Petey said and left at a run.

After Richard sent Mary's telegram, Alby arrived, freeing Richard to get to the Crown and Lion pub on Darlington. In the warm, stuffy pub, full of chatter, he was directed to a shabby little man seated at the end of the bar. He settled onto the stool beside George Pratt, and within moments they were talking. He gained Pratt's confidence after buying him a pint of scrumpy and a pork pie. Soon the two men were having a chinwag like old chums. Richard arranged to have the locksmith arrive at surgery in the morning, tools in hand, for a well-paid caper. He slipped Pratt a five-pound advance payment; the locksmith's hand closed around the money, his eyes roving through the pub.

"Carlisle, ye say," Pratt said, his hand guarding his money.

"Ten o'clock tomorrow. One-twelve Carlisle Street. I'll make it worth your time."

CHAPTER 19

"Very well. Don't tell me." Fiona slammed the motorcar door after the drive to the pub. "Father'll tell me."

"Please, Fiona, stop pestering me about it. I told you it was all very good, but I have much to sort out."

Henry closed his door and joined her in front of the Cock and Bull. She stood on the pavement with her arms crossed.

"They're waiting."

"Not until you tell me."

"I'll tell you tomorrow. I need time to think."

"No."

"Fiona," he said, placing his hands on her elbows.

"Henry." A man yelled, coming across the street. "Henry."

"Evan, old chap."

"Fiona. Lookin' wonderful as always," Evan said, offering his hand. "Lucas and Kynan are inside waiting to see you. Saw Thadd. He might be here, too." Evan started to the door. Fiona remained stiff, arms still folded, not budging a single step.

"Fiona, please."

She uncrossed her arms and walked through the doorway past Henry and shot him a look. Inside, Lucas, Thadd, Evan, and Kynan surrounded him with their handshakes, slaps, and hugs, resembling a rugby scrum. The pub's din died as everyone watched the reunion of the town's finest and strongest colliers and quarrymen. It took only a few moments for the other men in the three-hundred-year-old public house to join the scrum, leaving Fiona standing to the side. She watched the commotion with muted pride, still seething about the secret, eyes roaming, excluded from the throng.

"Back here," Kynan said, as he walked toward a dark alcove at the rear of the pub. The group moved slowly toward the tables where the men's wives stood. Fiona fastened herself onto Henry's left arm, and they threaded their way around tables and past the ancient soot-blackened hearth as townspeople welcomed him. The wives hugged him, and after fresh pints of stout were delivered, toasts offered, and social pleasantries exchanged, the men gathered at one end of the long wooden table, laughing and remembering rugby matches and childhood adventures while the women chattered about their children and wifely concerns. Fiona tried to remain close to Henry, listening to two conversations and a part of neither, a rare experience for her.

Finally, Henry leaned to her, nudging, recalling a memory centered on Fiona. Instantly she seized the opportunity, entering into the revelry. Another round of stout and more toasts and recollections, and soon Fiona was challenging the men to a tournament of darts.

"Road to Burma," she exclaimed, looking at Kynan, the serious darter among them. The men scrambled noisily to their feet and followed Fiona as their wives watched.

The dartboard hung on a pockmarked wall. Two gaslights hissed. After several minutes of practice Fiona started the game. The wives encouraged their men and after several games were on their feet, and the players were getting into it. Lucas and Kynan were in the lead when Fiona followed and on her last throw hit the double bull.

Henry stepped to the line, smiling at Fiona's luck. He had not had so much carefree fun in years, and he allowed Fiona to kiss him excitedly. Then she looked up, startled, at the stranger who suddenly clamped his large hand onto Henry's shoulder.

"Dr. Dafies," Krajic sneered, "or are you da goot referent Palmer?"

Henry faced his tormentor while his friends stood, unaware that an evil force had suddenly entered their happy gathering. Beside Krajic was another man from the train whom Henry remembered as Muellerschon. His face displayed a hard smirk. Richard's admonition filled Henry's mind, warning him to remain sequestered in the dormitory on the hill. Henry felt a sudden coldness and stood still as a stone.

Krajic brought his face close to Henry's. His foul breath from rotting teeth was the kind mouth salts would not cure. Hunter and prey looked into each other's eyes.

"Come vit us, Dr. Dafies," Krajic said, still gripping Henry's shoulder.

"The darts," Henry muttered and walked to the dart holder on the wall. As he slowed past Fiona, he spoke to her from the corner of his mouth, "Get your motorcar started. Now!" He fumbled with the darts and returned to Krajic and Muellerschon. He saw Fiona slipping through the crowd towards the door. She looked back anxiously.

"Come," Krajic ordered.

Lucas demanded, "Who's this?"

"None uf your beezness."

"They've been threatening me, Lucas," Henry said as he fell into step behind Meullershohn. Krajic followed and after him, Lucas, Kynan, Thadd, and Evan. Their wives remained near the dartboard, fearful and confused.

When Henry passed near the bar, he stopped, turned, and sent his fist into Krajic's stomach, doubling him over. When the German straightened, three darts protruded from his belly. Henry lowered his shoulder and lunged into Krajic, driving his tormentor back against the bar. Lucas balled his right fist and struck Krajic's face. He thought he felt the man's front teeth give way; the German's head snapped backward between the beer taps. The pub owner backed away, then whipped his towel from his apron, looped it under the monster's chin and trapped his head between the taps as Lucas delivered a blow to the anarchist's stomach. Krajic choked as his arms and legs flailed, his bull neck straining, helpless.

"Run, Henry," Lucas said. "We'll deal with 'em."

Henry moved towards Thadd and Kynan, who were grappling with Meullershohn on the wooden floor. The German was getting the drubbing of his life and pooling around his head was his blood, mingling with spilled ale, glass, and coal dust. Henry headed for the door and saw Evan extract the darts from Krajic's middle. Lucas pummeled him as Evan pressed the bloodied darts to Krajic's throat.

Kynan yelled, "Lucas, move!"

The two men yanked Meullershohn to his feet, bent him forward, and drove his head, like a battering ram, into Krajic's middle. For a moment, they thought Krajic's back snapped, but he had more fight left. He groped in his coat for his gun. Evan drove the darts under the anarchist's jaw. Lucas wrenched the gun away and Kynan twisted Meullershohn's arm, nearly breaking it before he could grasp the gun he concealed inside his coat. Thadd wrenched the gun free and struck Meullershohn's head with it. The man slumped forward, unconscious.

Outside, Fiona was revving the engine, eyes dark in fright. Henry jumped in beside her.

"Fast! I must hide!"

Fiona sent the motorcar down the high street of Blaenllyn towards the hills and collieries. Henry looked back and saw his friends dragging the two stalkers by their ankles onto the dirt street. A crowd poured from the pub, and a figure ran in the direction of the constabulary.

"What are we doing?" Fiona cried.

"Where can I hide?" The motorcar bounced over the ruts, heading up the winding hill past Number Eight. "I can't go back to the dormitory. They know I was there. I'm sure of it." He recalled the dark figure outside the window of Fiona's home. "They probably know I was at your home, too."

"What's all this about?" Fiona shouted, yanking on the wheel.

"Are they still working Number Twenty?"

"How should I know?"

"Let's go to Twenty."

"Who were those monsters?"

They raced past numerous turnoffs. Number Eight. Number Fourteen. They rumbled past Number Three and eventually into the murky valley near Copley's sheep farm. Fiona had to reduce speed along the road that now had quickly become a serpentine path of cinders barely wide enough for a lorry. They bounced over decaying wooden tram rail sleepers that were now unused.

"I'll stop if you don't tell me."

"When we get to Twenty," Henry shouted, holding onto his seat. "This soup is getting worse." Fiona squinted through the engulfing murk as they slowed to a crawl.

"Crank up the windows."

"You better tell me, or I'll leave you at Twenty to rot."

Number Twenty had been the first of the Rhys shafts. It was the remotest one among the Rhys operations. Tucked between Bull Hill and Shafton, it stood alone, a dead end. The road to it narrowed. Weeds and vegetation were visible in the arc headlights. Fog swallowed the motorcar's beams as they inched blindly forward.

"We missed it," Fiona said in the quiet.

She stopped and shifted into reverse. Carefully she steered the Fiat back along the road curving behind her. Henry opened his door, hoping to see the road's edge through the fog, but he saw nothing but darkness.

"Why don't they put lights on the rear of these contraptions?"

"Be quiet, I'm listening. Hear the cinders falling over the edge? There's a precipice on both sides."

"I know that, Fiona."

She inched the motorcar backward. Then she stopped.

"I'll check my side."

Henry eased himself from his seat and into the fog. Suddenly he had no footing. Cinders cascaded down the slope, and he clung to the open door.

"We're on the edge. Don't move back! Go ahead a piece and try again."

He held his door open and dragged his foot along the edge as the motorcar chugged slowly forward. Fiona opened her door, too. "The path might be impassable." The two were silent, cursing the loud engine.

"Good on this side," Fiona called. "Do you have room over there?"

"A little." Henry stepped onto the path and got to the rear of the motorcar. He clung to the metalwork. "I need a torch."

"This was a bad idea," Fiona said. "Perhaps we should spend the night here."

"Don't move. I'm going back to check the road."

The motorcar was wet with cloying moisture. Fog blanketed them. Henry could taste it as he moved from the edge of the ridge path. He found a large wooden splinter from a sleeper and poked along the darkness at his feet.

Several minutes later Fiona heard his gravelly footsteps as he called out, "We'll be fine. I'll guide you. Slowly now...go very slow."

He sat on the rear of her motorcar with his feet on the path. As they moved, he thrust the wooden splinter at the sides of the path, testing and listening for tumbling slag.

"Stop." He checked more of the road and returned. "Just a little ways more." They inched into the blackness behind them, Henry poking and guiding, Fiona steering and trembling. Slag and cinders fell away. "A bit more."

An inch of path either way separated them from a fatal plunge to the chasm below.

A few seconds later, he called out, "Stop."

He edged his way along the narrow footing beside Fiona until he was standing in the arc light beams. Fog billowed.

"I'll walk in front of you. I'll stay in the center. Follow me."

Fiona shifted the gear box and the motorcar inched forward following Henry—a ghostly guide ahead. Several times they stopped to allow him to probe the edges of the path with his splinter.

"Alright. Slowly, Fiona," Henry said. Then, "Drat it. I lost the stick. I'll use my feet."

"Careful."

They moved slowly for several hundred yards, stopping numerous times for Henry to clear the path of wooden sleepers, barrels, crates, and other debris. Finally the path enlarged into the expanse Henry remembered as the marshalling area near the tipple.

"The supply shack should be to the right," Henry called. Fiona steered her motorcar onto the wide area. "Stay there, Fiona. I need to feel around." A minute later he emerged from the fog and stood in the swirling arc beams. "It's there. We'll spend the night here."

She shut down the engine and extinguished the arc lights.

"Where are you, Fiona?"

"I'm getting picnic blankets. Say something, Henry, I can't see you."

"I'm here...over here. Here. Here."

Suddenly, she collided against him. "Ow! Your chest's a rock."

Fiona handed him the blankets, and he grasped her hand as they felt their way to the abandoned shack. He ran his hand across the damp wood until he found the door. "It's stuck." He kicked it and it creaked. Another kick forced it open, and they edged inside, bumping into things.

"Here's a place," Henry said. They knelt down and felt around. Tossing aside a few stray cinders and coal lumps, they reclined beside each other, breathing the smell of damp and rotting timber, listening to the unpleasant stillness. They sighed. They had been holding their breath during their ordeal.

"Now, Henry," Fiona said, "that explanation."

CHAPTER 20

"Says here that the Royal Geographic Society is planning an expedition to Kathmandu, led by Messrs Clive Farleigh and Trevor Clark," Dr. John reported from the morning *Times*. He reached for the last of his toast. "He's one of the banking Clarks, it says. I believe Richard did a painting or two for him. Not long ago, as I recollect."

"I don't know, doctor," Mrs. Mac replied, pouring more tea into his cup.

"Says that their last RGS expedition was to South America. Had my fill of primitives when I was in Afghanistan. Wasn't pleasant, I can tell you. I'm quite happy here in modern civilization." He folded his *Times* to read another article.

"Aye. The way London is a growin' these times, ya just walk fer a block er two if ya wanna see heathens."

"Where are Richard and Emma?"

"They breakfasted early and left. Didn't say where. Emma tuck a big present with her, though. Pink ribbon 'n bows."

"Please...in...come," Mrs. Einbecker said with embarrassment, wearing a plain dress and apron, fussing with her hair. "Hildy. Hildy," she called and gestured for Emma to sit on a small sofa.

Hildy scampered into the room. "Dr. Watson, is this for me? You promised."

Emma drew Hildy to her. "First of all, Hildy, how are you feeling?"

"The pain is bad sometimes."

"Let's have a look. After that, you can open your present."

She looked away as Emma removed the bandages and examined the wound. The swelling was diminishing. She applied an aloe mixture, then redressed the wound with fresh gauze and tape. Hildy's eyes were on the large gift resting on the floor in front of her.

"Open your present, Hildy."

"What could it be?" Hildy asked excitedly.

She tugged at the ribbons with her free hand and tore away the wrapping paper. She hesitated before lifting the box lid. "A bear. It's a bear."

Emma helped her remove it from the box, and the girl hugged it, looking towards her mother, stroking the fur against her chubby cheek.

"It's called Paddington Bear," Emma said as she stroked the girl's back.

"Paddington Bear," Hildy echoed.

"I'm happy that you like your Paddington Bear."

"I do. Oh thank you, Dr. Watson. I'll keep him forever."

Emma withdrew the stolen photograph from her shopping bag. "Mrs. Einbecker, do you recognize these people?"

The woman examined the photograph, and Emma saw recognition appear in her eyes. "Ja. Dis woman. Rount here mit Krauss. Alvays mit Krauss. Him I dunno. Nefer before saw. Brandenburg Gate, ja. Berlin."

"Hildy, do you remember telling me about a mean woman who had a terrible odor?"

Fidgeting and engrossed, Hildy said, "Paddington Bear likes it here. I want to take him to my room. Maybe I can show him to Werner."

"Hildy, I want you to look at this picture. Is this that mean, stinky woman?" Emma held the picture in front of her. Hildy pulled a face.

"Uh-huh, she's the mean lady. I don't like her." She paused and looked at Paddington Bear. "Can I play now?"

"Of course." Emma smiled as Hildy scampered across the room.

"Her arm and hand are healing nicely. And thank you for your help."

Emma collected her things, left the Einbecker apartment, and turned towards the stairs on her way to visit the Haas family. When she arrived at the next floor, two painters were cursing and gathering their buckets and brushes.

"Bloodiest thing I e'er seen. Keeps comin' back," one of the painters fumed. The other painter elbowed him and removed his cap when he saw Emma. "Beggin' yer pardon, ma'am. I didn't mean fur yur ears to hear. 'Cept we keep paintin' o're this stain 'n it keeps turnin' color."

Emma stepped towards the wooden doorframe of Herr Krauss's apartment where the men had been working. She studied the discoloration.

The men departed as Emma rapped on the Haas door directly across the hall. Mrs. Haas was surprised to see her. The woman looked nervously at her son, who was resting on the settee.

"Doctor?" she exclaimed.

"Guten Morgen, Mrs. Haas. I was examining Hildegaard Einbecker, and I thought I would pay you a visit. How are you getting along?"

"Ah... am goot. Bettah, danke." She glanced over her shoulder again.

Emma watched Gunther slowly stand up in obvious agony.

"Gunther, what happened to you? May I help?" Emma asked.

His mother and he exchanged glances. He moved towards the doorway, his arm hanging in a homemade sling.

He said weakly, "Got inta fight at pub. Been hurt vorse."

"That was a rotten bit of luck. May I examine you?" Emma asked as Hildy bounded up the stairs and knocked on a neighbor's door.

"No. Thanks," he said with a painful headshake.

"Here is my card. If you need medical attention, you may visit me any time. Understand?"

He nodded and winced.

After a chilly, awkward moment, Emma concluded she would not be invited inside. Reaching into her shopping bag, Emma asked, "Have you ever seen these people before?"

Gunther turned on his heels and disappeared. Mrs. Haas shook her head, unconvincingly. She closed the door without a word.

Emma walked across the hall and examined the stains on the doorframe. "My word, violet. I wonder..." She placed her bags on the floor and snapped the hasp of her medical case. She removed a sterile scalpel and a waxed envelope and examined the stains more carefully. Emma whittled several deep samples from the wood and placed them in the envelope using sterile tweezers. She noticed how the stain had permeated the wood. She strongly suspected it was the poison from Dr. Thornton's laboratory. Raising the open envelope to her nose, she smelled the odor of fresh paint with a tinge of foulness; her face puckered. She secured the samples and instruments in her bag and decided to make an unplanned inquiry of Krauss's other neighbor.

She knocked and eventually a young boy Hildy's age opened the door. Unsure if he could speak English, Emma ventured, "Hello."

"Hello," he replied.

"I am Hildy Einbecker's doctor," Emma enunciated slowly and clearly, pointing downstairs towards the Einbeckers' apartment.

"I know about you and Paddington Bear," he said in fine English. Then Hildy came into view. She was clutching the bear as she left the boy's apartment.

"What is your name?"

"Werner."

"Do you know Mr. Krauss very well?"

"No," he answered, rubbing his ear.

"Does he like children?"

"He doesn't like nobody," Werner said, glancing towards the Krauss apartment and tugging his knickerbockers.

"Do you know Gunther Haas?"

Werner's face brightened. "He kicks the ball with me sometimes."

"He does? Do you know he is injured?"

"Krauss hurt him."

"Mr. Krauss hurt Gunther?"

"Everyone heard them. They were angry and we could hear the fight."

"Where?"

"Here."

"Your apartment?"

"No. In that apartment," he said, pointing to Krauss's door. "It was real bad."

"Mr. Krauss and Gunther are friends?"

"I don't know. Papa told me to stay away from Mr. Krauss."

"Can you tell me if you or your parents noticed a bad smell near Mr. Krauss's apartment?"

"Uh-huh." The boy wrinkled his nose.

"When did you notice it?"

"Days ago, maybe."

"Do you recognize the people in this picture?"

"That one. She's a friend of him."

"Who?"

"Mr. Krauss."

"Thank you, Werner. You're a very good boy. May I visit you again sometime?"

"Do I get a present, too?"

"Perhaps," Emma said with a smile. She shook his hand and left the apartment building.

Emma noted Petey across the carriageway, where he watched for Krauss and telegrams. Seeing her, the lad wiped his hand across his mouth, the Irregular's furtive signal of acknowledgement, and she tugged her ear, indicating she had seen him, too. Then she caught an overcrowded horse-drawn tram at the crossing, heading to Westminster and Scotland Yard.

She glanced back at Petey. Emma tensed suddenly, gripping the hand rail. As the tram pulled away, she saw the man who had followed her to Rundell's Toy Shoppe running for the tram. The conductor shouted, "Full. Ain't yer got eyes?" She saw him stop in the middle of the carriageway, looking in every direction for a cab.

CHAPTER 21

"Fiona. Wake up. The fog is lifting."

The fog-dampened mine whistles in the valleys hours earlier had not stirred her. She moaned and rubbed the sleep from her eyes.

"You must return home. No doubt your parents are panic stricken." Henry remained at the window. The retreating fog unveiled edges of lush valley mantled in cowslips and wildflowers. "Haven't slept. Just watching for the Germans and thinking."

"You do look a fright." She got up onto her elbow and rubbed her aching back. Their eyes met for a long, meaningful moment. "I'm sorry about—"

"I should've told you about Mary from the beginning. We covered it all last night, didn't we? And then there's Richard."

"Didn't you know I've always ...well..." She spoke against his gaze. "Please don't tell him how I presumed upon you so shamelessly. Tell no one. I'm so very embarrassed." She warmed to his tender smile. "Richard never wrote to me in Paris. Not once."

"Nor I."

"Only Emma. She wrote of your successes at university. Nothing about your engagement."

"It had to be kept—"

"I know that now. Her letters spoke of Richard's art and his flirtations with writers and artists and entertainers. People change in three years. It's obvious that he's now a rather rakish bon vivant, and I don't mind telling you I got my fill of them in Paris. I almost became engaged to a French scamp...an aristocrat. Wealthy as Croesus." Fiona brushed her skirt and sat up. "I need to secure a curatorship at a museum and marry. Not for money. Lord knows I shall inherit enough. It's my career and my life. Isn't it odd? It was Richard who sparked my enthusiasm for art and antiquities. Now our common interest has sent us in rather opposite directions, hasn't it? His fame. My anonymity. He's forging a life. I'm trying to begin one. I should think he hasn't given me a thought since I went to Paris... surely not

181

with all his glamorous liaisons. I must use my education in art history and curatorship, musn't I? I need to finally settle. Not because of Father's wishes. It's what I desire most. It's all rather incompatible with Richard's life, don't you see?" She chewed on her lip.

"Fiona, who did you talk most about during our day out in Aberystwyth? It was Richard, I'd say." Henry waved her silent. "He worships you. And his flirtations? I know them all. Ha, all of the ladies are hangers-on. He sees them for what they are. His relationships have the life expectancy of a fruit fly. He's a bright light in the art world and that attracts women, doesn't it? I know him better than anyone, and I can tell you his adoration of you has never diminished but grown. You know him to be brash and fearless. He is, of course, except around you. Don't tell me you never noticed his special tenderness toward you? His shyness? A certain reticence? His reserve?"

"Reticence? Reserve? Richard?"

"If you ask me, I'd say he's afraid to express himself to you. He can recite Shakespeare, but disclose his feelings to you?" He paused. "Can you keep a secret?"

Fiona nodded.

"His love for you finds its fullest voice in his art. He has a dozen or more sketchbooks filled with drawings...only of you. I've seen most of them. And what artwork it is! We sit in his studio talking about rugby and all as he sketches you from memory. He has a devastating oil painting hidden. I saw it. It's a breathtaking work. The two of you are picnicking on the banks of the river Blaen...by the old oak where we always fished. It's far better than any Renoir I've ever seen. And...there's an unmistakable sparkle on your ring finger."

Fiona sat motionless on the blanket. "Richard," she murmured.

"Do you love him?"

"I think I always have."

"Has he ever told you of his love?"

"Never."

"And you?"

Fiona kicked a lump of coal on the floor. She picked it up.

"I thought so. You're just like him, aren't you? All talk. All bravado, adventure, daring in all things except with the very person you cherish most. It's like you two are so terrified of causing the other to slip away that you fail to grasp."

Henry looked at the vast green landscape unveiling from the fog.

A sweet, warm breeze swept through the shack, lifting her spirits and thoughts of Richard. She glanced at her watch. "It's past ten!"

Henry helped her to her feet.

"Gracious!" she exclaimed, pointing to the back of the shack where a wall should have been. "If we had gone only three or four feet more last night, we would have... Good Heavens. I'd better go home. I'll bring you food." She rubbed her tangled hair vigorously. "And a pillow and father's rifles. You'll be safe up here."

"The Germans know your car. They'll follow you." He grasped her shoulders. "Fiona. They saw you. Stay at home and remain secure. Contact Lucas or the lads if you need to get something to me. God knows how long it'll be until the Germans find me."

They went outside to her motorcar. Fiona climbed in and he closed her door. He cranked the engine once; it sputtered and began chugging. Walking behind her, guiding her with signals, he maneuvered her back onto the tramway path.

"Stay hidden, Fiona, and tell my father and mum I'm fine."

He watched as she waved. The motorcar slowly bounced along the path that curled behind Bull Hill. He ran to the bend and saw her reappearing at the farthest turn. She rounded the bend and disappeared.

He stood there gazing in all directions and listened to the distant bleat of sheep. A lamb replied and a dog yelped, probably Mr. Copley's border collie. He turned towards the sound. There was no movement except for pockets of fog being drawn away by a gentle wind. He kicked a lump of coal over the edge and watched it tumble down the crags. He found another lump and kicked it along as he walked back to the shack, warmed by the morning sun breaking through.

Inside, he found several wooden crates and fashioned a seat by the window facing the tram path to the shack. Most of the window glass was gone, and he struck the remaining shards from the frame with a stick. Henry tested the wall with his shoulder, and it appeared secure.

"What's Mary doing at this moment?" he said into the silence. "She's probably at work."

He pictured her in her office, imagining her desolation. He wondered about his telegram and realized he should have reminded Fiona to arrange for someone to check for it. *Perhaps someone will think of it on their own.* He resigned himself to a long wait. Resting his head against the chalky windowsill, he wondered how Richard and Emma were doing.

"Emma, who is this?" Gordon Lestrade asked, looking at the photograph.

"Dr. Gregory's wife with her brother, Colonel Rainer Schmidt."

"Schmidt?" He glanced at Emma, then back to the photograph.

"I visited the girl who was injured by the poison. She told me that a woman had frightened her the night of Nigel's murder. And the woman had a foul odor about her. Little Hildegaard says the woman in the photograph and the smelly woman that night are one and the same—Mrs. Gregory."

"Just a moment Emma. Are you..."

"Listen to me, Gordon," Emma said impatiently. "The handkerchief you have in your evidence room has 'JSG' embroidered on it. 'JSG'...Jutta Schmidt Gregory. Furthermore, Hildegaard's mother and a neighbor boy saw this photograph and claim they have seen her visiting Krauss."

Lestrade examined the photograph again. "Where did you get this?"

"Dr. Gregory's office. He doesn't know it's missing."

Emma went on, eagerly opening her medical case and placing the waxen envelope on his desk. "And here...look, smell...be extremely careful, Gordon. Don't touch its contents."

Lestrade lifted the flap using his pencil and blew into the envelope to open it.

"Paint chips from Krauss's door frame. They're stained with the purple poison," Emma said. "Smell it."

He did. Lestrade jumped to his feet. "Smells like it. It's a stink you don't soon forget. Let's have Dr. Mull analyze this."

Dr. Mull's eyes peered above the top of his spectacles as they entered. "Inspector...Dr. Watson."

"Here. What is it?" Lestrade asked and handed over the envelope. "Caution. Possibly poison chips inside is my guess."

"Poison chips?"

"I need you to determine if the nightshade poison is in those fragments. How soon?"

"Immediately, Inspector. Especially if Dr. Watson examines one chip and I the other."

"Good."

The doctors separated to opposite ends of the small granite counter where two Leitz Ortholux microscopes were positioned. Emma and Dr. Mull prepared the specimens as Lestrade stood beside Emma. He caught her fragrance. She adjusted the optics and the motions of the platen, her delicate fingers twisting the platen controls. "It looks like belladonna to me."

"Yes, quite," Dr. Mull said. "Permit me to show you the specimen of the poison. We shall perform a direct comparison."

Dr. Mull opened a large locked cabinet and removed a glass slide containing the poison collected from the crime scene. Emma joined him at his microscope. The odor from the sample was faint, yet its power to nauseate remained. Holding her breath, she examined the original specimen.

She replaced her pince-nez. "I've seen enough. Dr. Mull?" Emma said, allowing the doctor space at his microscope.

After a minute or so, Dr. Mull sat up, lowered his spectacles onto his nose from his forehead, and announced, "Identical in every way except for the solvent migration from the paint."

"Log these samples into tentative evidence, doctor," Lestrade said. "They were taken from a Mr. Krauss' doorframe." Lestrade ushered Emma into the hallway.

"I was followed again today, Gordon. The very same man."

"I shall have Coyle escort..."

"That was not my intention. Just thought you should know. I'm troubled by something else, however. Curare."

"Emma, I shan't have you being followed. Coyle is on duty. It's settled. Now, what about curare?"

"It's very difficult to obtain curare. The university may possibly have a supply of it, but frankly, Gordon, it's quite rare. None of the usual chemical vendors and suppliers of biologicals have any quantity at all. Houghton Biologicals promised to let me know if they can find a source."

"That rare?"

"I believe we should inventory the poisons and check the records at the university and we should do it quickly. And furthermore, I think Dr. Mull should comb through the laboratory books and formulae for any reference to curare. Perhaps there is more evidence to be collected."

"I agree. Help yourself to tea. I'll return in a few minutes."

Lestrade returned with three men on his heels: Harry Coyle, Dr. Mull, and a young laboratory assistant.

"I've arranged a carriage. Shall we?"

The men followed Lestrade and Emma to the side entrance and a liveried carriage.

"Emma, you and Coyle will search for curare in the laboratory," said Lestrade. "Dr. Mull and his man will examine the laboratory notebooks. I'll check the purchasing records for any transactions concerning curare."

They swarmed within the university laboratory, methodically searching for the poison or any record of it. Emma and Coyle had the easier task and were soon finished, having found no evidence of the poison in stock. Lestrade was reviewing the business records of the department and would be occupied a while longer, so Emma seized the opportunity to return Dr. Gregory's missing photograph to Mary.

"Emma, we must talk," Mary whispered. They huddled at the tea shelf in the corner.

Emma raised her shopping bag. "I have the photograph."

"Wonderful. I don't know what we should do first." Mary rubbed her forehead. "No... give it to me. Dr. Gregory is out. Wait here." She hurried away with Emma's shopping bag and returned greatly relieved.

She stepped close to Emma and whispered from the corner of her mouth. "I think Dr. Gregory is the killer."

"Surely you are joking."

"Jealousy. I was talking to Celia Norris in Dr. Gregory's outer office an hour ago. His door was closed, but we could hear everything. They were having words."

"Who?"

Mary raised a finger to her lips. "Mrs. Gregory was there. She noticed her picture was missing. I thought I'd surely die. Dr. Gregory wanted her to see a physician for some reason or other, and he accused her of traveling to Germany with Dr. Thornton. She burst from his office and brushed Celia aside without the faintest apology. He followed her out and has not returned. I think he killed Dr. Thornton because he was jealous. Celia told me that Dr. Gregory was eager to have Dr. Thornton return from Germany...almost angry about Nigel's absence at the same time his wife was in Germany. Dr. Gregory went to Waterloo Station to collect Mrs. Gregory from the train, and he said to Celia that he might collect Dr. Thornton there as well. He said they were traveling together. Simply awful!"

"Extraordinary. But Dr. Gregory wouldn't be sloppy. He surely wouldn't've left the crime scene in such a state. Also, he's old. He couldn't've overpowered Thornton."

"At least, not by himself. He did it somehow. I'm certain of it. Maybe Crane was involved, too."

"Is Dr. Crane conducting a class at the moment?"

Mary glanced at the clock. "In his office, I suspect."

"Good. Now a small favor. I want you to find out if Henry or Dr. Thornton ordered a new distillation apparatus recently. You mentioned you'd check on that."

Mary exclaimed with sudden embarrassment, "It slipped my mind."

"First, introduce me to Dr. Crane."

"It's almost time for his next class."

The women walked down the corridor to his office. Emma reviewed in her mind the account of Evelyn Moxely's fabrication of a love affair as a ploy to deflect Dr. Crane's romantic attentions.

Mary tapped on the door glass. "Doctor, it's Miss Palmer. May I come in?"

"Yes," he spoke in a weak voice caught in a cough.

She led Emma into the stuffy office. "Dr. Crane, this is Dr. Watson. She has interviewed everyone except you regarding Dr. Thornton's death. I shall withdraw so you may have privacy. Good day, Dr. Watson," Mary said and shook Emma's hand, giving a convincing impression that they had met only moments ago.

Emma gave Dr. Crane an assessing glance. She labeled him a classic pedant, the very opposite of Henry: sallow complexion, sparse brown hair, a stained waistcoat that appeared slept in, pencils displayed points up from the breast pocket, and tired eyes that squinted from too much reading. As a young man he was the sort usually targeted by bullies. His weak chin and sad eyes appeared to invite domination.

"Dr. Crane, from my interviews with everyone, especially Dr. Gregory, I have learned you are certainly held in the very highest regard. It is a pleasure to meet you." She hoped to disarm him.

He did not look at her. "Thank you, Dr. Watson."

Emma had no time to squander and knew uncovering causes of enmity always produced a reaction, caution—even withdrawal. "Doctor, may I ask why you were upset with Dr. Thornton?"

"I was not upset with Dr. Thornton," he answered in a monotone through his teeth.

"Dr. Crane, during my interviews, it was mentioned that you were upset with him and Dr. Davies. Not to put too fine a point on it, doctor, why?"

He paused and pulled at his lower lip. "Perhaps whoever said that is referring to my concern that Dr. Thornton laughed me out of his office when I reported that Evelyn Moxely and Dr. Davies were engaged."

"Why did you care?"

"The university has rules, you know. Fraternization."

"When did you fall in love with Evelyn Moxely?"

"What?"

"You will admit that you did love her?"

"If I had, it is my business entirely. It means nothing." He beat his pencil on his desk, nervously avoiding her gaze.

"I find it strange that you were so upset over Miss Moxely's alleged engagement with Dr. Davies when, in fact, you were in love with her yourself and presumably prepared to violate the selfsame university rule."

Dr. Crane stared at his crooked bookcase. The words were difficult as he surveyed his books. "It has no bearing on Dr. Thornton's death."

"I have noticed a lot of new and expensive equipment in Dr. Davies' laboratory. I was quite honestly surprised by it. I assume your own laboratory has been similarly modernized. It was my classroom years ago."

His eyes met Emma's for the first time, but only for a moment. "Davies gets all the new equipment. The problem with this place is they're too miserly.

Thornton would not permit me to buy anything. How can I do effective research and teach under such conditions? I ask you, doctor. I complained to Dr. Thornton. All that concerned him was his research and Davies. It's unacceptable, I say. I leave Liverpool and come to this. They promised me new equipment, a research assistant. It makes me furious when I think about it. Whenever Davies wants something, new equipment, specimens, chemicals, he gets it. I complained to Thornton."

"And?"

"Nothing."

"Why do you suppose Dr. Davies always got what he needed and you did not?"

"It's beyond me, Dr. Watson."

"Were they chums?"

"Thornton and Davies? Oh, no. Cordial but not chums... especially in recent weeks."

"Why recently?"

"All I know is that Thornton was pressuring Davies. I don't know why. However, Davies and Thornton, as far as it matters, had not been themselves. Actually, both seemed...nervous. Thornton must've pushed him too hard and he snapped. Frightful. I must say that I'll never understand human nature." His gaze returned to the bookcase.

"Did you know that Dr. Thornton was working with poisons?"

"No. Well, the talk is that some type of poison was applied to his arm."

"I was unaware that you were researching poisons here."

"I certainly am not. I can't speak for Thornton or Davies."

"What about curare?"

"Strychnos toxifera?"

"Yes, curare."

"Thornton died of curare poisoning?"

"Sorry, professor. I didn't mean to imply that. When I think of a rapid-acting poison, curare, among others, comes to mind."

Someone knocked at Dr. Crane's door.

"It's Miss Moxely, doctor. Your next class is waiting."

"I'll be there in a moment." He looked at Emma. "Strychnos toxifera. That's not my field, and I'm surprised that Davies and Thornton were involved in such research...particularly Davies. He must have snapped. Who knows what any of us are capable of?" He pulled his glasses onto his forehead and rubbed his eyes. "This is my worst class of imbeciles. You must forgive me, Dr. Watson. I must go."

"I shall explain to Dr. Gregory about your need for a modernized laboratory." Emma stepped into the corridor. "After all, I want my children to attend here, but not under these deplorable conditions."

"That's terribly civil of you, doctor. I cannot endure until the new building is constructed. I must have—"

"What new building?"

"The Clark Science Center. It will take four years to build, they say. All Mr. Clark's money."

They advanced down the hall to Mary Palmer's office.

"Good day to you, Dr. Watson. Again sometime."

"All the very best." She watched him disappear at the end of the corridor. She glanced at Constable Graves and entered Mary's office.

"What about the distillation apparatus?"

"No orders. Nothing. How did you get on with Crane?"

"Interesting. You'll be joining us for dinner, I trust? Mrs. Mac's preparing your favorite."

"I adore everything she prepares. What is it?"

"I'll keep you guessing. I must find Gordon."

Emma withdrew and found Lestrade with Evelyn Moxely reviewing purchasing records.

"Anything unusual?" Emma asked.

"Nothing," Lestrade said, leaning back to take a rest. "The oddest things are weekly purchases of live grasshoppers and crickets."

"Grasshoppers and crickets?" The question hung in the air.

Lestrade found a typical entry and pointed. "See. Nine consecutive weeks. All live."

"Miss Moxely, do you know anything about this?" Emma asked.

"The box arrives and Dr. Thornton takes them home. Never kept them here." Evelyn rubbed her arms with her hands. "Gives me a right case of the chills."

"Upon my word...live grasshoppers and crickets," Emma murmured.

CHAPTER 22

"Aye, we been awaitin' fur the gel for most of 'n hour now," Mrs. Mac said. "We shud eat's, what I say."

"Let's begin," Dr. John commanded. "Been smelling the aroma from your kitchen all afternoon. And no further talk of Henry's case at this table."

Richard protested. "Father, I've had a breakthrough concerning Krauss and..."

"Mind me, not at table." Emma looked at Richard, wide-eyed at the potential good news. "Mind me now."

Emma assisted Mrs. MacIntosh with the food. They passed hot bowls and plates and talked of rugby, weather, a new play at the Garrick and Schubert at the Royal Albert.

"My compliments as usual, Mrs. MacIntosh," Geoffrey said, shoveling more onto his plate. "Pot roast is superlative."

"Ta. 'Tis Mary's favorite. Hoped it would lift 'er spirits."

Afterward, Emma helped Mrs. Mac tidy the table while the men retired to the parlor. She was eager to exchange the events of the day with Richard and learn about his breakthrough. Sensing Emma's inattention to the chores, Mrs. Mac nudged her arm and said, "Off with ye, now. I'll finish things."

Emma rushed to the men; her father was already settled in his chair with his newspaper and port. She sat beside Geoffrey and caught the end of Richard's discussing Krauss. He lit his cigar and sat forward on his chair, keen to talk with Emma.

Geoffrey hugged her. "Dear, it's unbelievable!"

"I'll wager you've not heard the like," Richard said.

"Tell me," Emma demanded.

"Pratt picked the locks...Krauss's and McMannus's. I found her passport. McMannus isn't her real name." He pulled a slip of paper from his pocket. "Her German passport says she's Maria Steuckl. They're all Nachtgeist. Mrs. Gregory, too." Richard puffed his cigar and swept away the blue-grey smoke.

"Files, telegrams, letters, all connecting them with Nachtgeist. The whole bloody lot of them."

"Jolly good work!" Geoffrey said, hugging Emma with one arm, but she politely twisted herself away, far too absorbed in her brother's discoveries.

"More, Richard," she demanded.

"First, I took Pratt to check the locks in the laboratory. He said that only one was picked... the one directly into Thornton's office from the corridor, just as Charles Steele claimed. At least that part of Steele's story is true. Then I had him pick Krauss's lock."

"Yes? And?"

"Em, it's unbelievable what I found."

"Stop toying. Tell me!"

"I discovered volumes of correspondence and Nachtgeist files. At McMannus's, too. I saw notes from Rainer Schmidt, receipts for train tickets to and from Bremen, telegrams to and from Milos Krajic, and even a master scheme of anarchy in England and Europe. And I saw technical gibberish between Dr. Thornton and a Dr. Leopold Hoeltzer from a German chemical company. You'd know better about that, Em. And, Geoffrey, I noticed a manual on satanic worship. Mycroft was correct. They are a cult."

Geoffrey stared. "Worshiping Satan! May it never be!"

"And the missing container of poison from the laboratory cabinet? It's at Krauss's flat. A circular glass jar filled with a violet substance stinking to high heaven."

"How much did it contain?"

"Full... or nearly so. About the size of my fist."

"Enough to kill or injure a hundred people," Emma guessed.

"I went to the Yard, but Lestrade wasn't there. Gordon must get a search warrant for McMannus' and Krauss' apartments. Mycroft must see it all. And Emma, you'd be able to decipher all the technical correspondence. It's all in German. It should be very instructive." He flicked the cigar ash into a silver tray. "We're coming to the end of the matter, I say."

Emma recounted the identification of Mrs. Gregory and her discovery and analysis of the paint fragments.

"My theory has Mrs. Gregory killing Dr. Thornton, then fleeing to Krauss's flat with her soiled glove and handkerchief. She encounters Hildy and pushes her away. Then Krauss exercises caution, and they dispose of the items in the dustbin. She probably pinched the Number Sixteen notebook and the jar of poison. There you have it."

"Brilliant, I must say," Geoffrey said.

"I talked with Dr. Crane. Strychnos toxifera came readily to his lips."

"What's that?"

"Curare. There are no records of curare in the laboratory. No record of any purchases." Finally she allowed Geoffrey to pull her closer to him.

"There it is, Em. Gordon gets the warrants, gathers the evidence, and arrests those Huns."

"It'll come to a head tomorrow. Then Henry can come home. I'll call Lestrade now." She left and returned shortly. "Gordon's at Southampton."

"Ah-ha, following our abduction ruse. Tomorrow, then," Richard said. "I think I'll enjoy a good night of sleep."

"Emma, let's get some fresh air," Geoffrey said, coaxing Emma to her feet. "A stroll to Beeton Park?"

"Good night, Richard," Emma said as they went off, hand in hand.

"Why didn't Mary join us tonight?" Richard asked himself, dousing his cigar and staring at his dozing father.

"Wake up, old man. Hurry. Wake up," Geoffrey shouted, shaking Richard's bed. "Mary's missing. Wake up."

"Huh?"

Geoffrey grabbed Richard and pulled him from the bed. "We can't find Mary. Hurry. Get dressed. Em's frantic. Chop-chop."

"Mary's missing?"

"Emma and I walked through Beeton and went to see Mary. The Palmers had assumed she was with us. Mrs. Palmer fainted."

"Go on."

"Emma tended to her. Then we went to university. The main door was unlocked. Emma found Mary's purse under her desk. She searched the ladies'...no sign of her. We talked to the guard on duty, and he said Mary had left hours ago with her mother and aunt. The description of the women he provided brought Mrs. Gregory and McMannus to your sister's mind."

"Does Lestrade know about this?"

"Emma's telephoning him now, but she thinks he'll still be in Southampton."

"Good God, Geoffrey. Should've considered Mary's vulnerability. That note of hers. I'm a damned fool. She should've had a constant escort. Should've told Lestrade. Blast it all."

The two men joined Emma downstairs.

"Geoffrey told me everything. Where are we going?"

"Lestrade's back. We'll meet him at university," Emma said. "Geoffrey, I think you should return to the Palmers'. Stay there until you hear from us."

The three squeezed into the hansom. A few minutes later when they saw another cab, Geoffrey left the twins. Their hansom rumbled on to the university. They hurried into the building and found Lestrade waiting. His men were swarming in Mary's office and the laboratory, fingerprinting and examining everything in sight.

Emma, Richard, and Lestrade went into the department meeting room. They sat anxiously at the conference table as Emma presented her discoveries and theory that Mrs. Gregory and McMannus had kidnapped Mary.

"What better way to flush Henry into the open than to capture his fiancée?" Emma said.

"Fiancée?" Lestrade said, taken aback. "Why didn't I know?" He pounded the table. "Had I known, I'd've assigned a man to her." Lestrade watched them, anger in his eyes. "You two knew."

Richard pushed on, describing the horrifying Nachtgeist documents and the poison-filled jar he had discovered in the Germans' apartments. He nervously rubbed his goatee and finished, "And now Mary's been kidnapped."

"I want to see evidence," Lestrade said.

Richard exploded: "How much evidence do you need? You saw Mary's purse. Where's your head, man?" He kicked a nearby chair across the room.

Lestrade shot to his feet. "Don't you raise your voice to me, Richard."

"Mary's abducted, you half-wit!"

"Not Mary," Lestrade said, controlling himself. "I want to see all this evidence you claim is at Krauss's."

"You don't believe a thing I say, do you, Gordon?" He grabbed Lestrade's lapels. "Look, we're wasting time. I would've been better off taking this to Mycroft."

"Take your hands off me. I'll have you in Belmarsh if you ever—"

"In prison, will you? After Emma and I do your work for you?"

Emma stepped between the men. "Richard. Gordon. It's late. We're all very tired and worried."

"You pay attention, Richard. I have to get search warrants for those apartments. You know that. This'll take time...pperhaps several hours. I'll issue a bulletin for Mrs. Gregory, Krauss, and McMannus. What more do you expect of me? Give me all the addresses."

"You can see we are nearing the end of this," Emma said placatingly, tearing paper from her brother's sketchbook. "I pray that Mary is unhurt. Here. The addresses."

Emma and Gordon walked into the hall leaving Richard behind, very angry. When she returned to the meeting room, she found him standing by the slateboard brushing chalk dust from his sleeve. He had written *curare* in large letters. Abruptly he looked at his pocket watch.

"I wonder if Petey is still on duty... or Alby. No matter," Richard said. "You remain here, Em. If you must leave, make sure you tell one of the guards. And make certain you're escorted wherever you go. I'm going to the telegraph office." He went past her without another word.

An hour later, Richard returned and called down the corridor, "Emma. Emma." He heard his voice caroming off the cold walls.

"In here," she answered from the meeting room.

"I caught Petey as he was about to rush to Carlisle. Krauss boarded the nine-forty to Cardiff from Paddington."

"He's going for Henry," Emma gasped.

"Petey says Mrs. Gregory and McMannus must have sensed the boys were following them. Somehow they lost them at Picadilly this afternoon. The boys returned to their stations, and the women haven't been seen all evening."

"They must be the ones who kidnapped Mary...absolutely."

"Rainer Schmidt telegraphed Krauss to kill Henry," Richard said as he tossed his sketchbook onto the table. "That's why Krauss left for Wales. And the telegraph operators are Nachtgeist!"

"Are you sure?" Emma stared. "Goodness, you're bleeding!"

"I confronted the telegraph operator. He took a swing at me and I cold-cocked him. Petey ran for a constable. I looked around and found a folder of the telegrams. There was a book on satanic worship. The constable and I dragged the telegraphist to the Yard, and I pressed charges." Emma examined his bleeding knuckles. "The last telegram was to Krajic," he said. "Krauss told him that Schmidt had authorized him to kill the bird and that he was on his way to assist."

"You translated all that?"

"The telegraphist did quite nicely with my hand on his throat."

Emma left the room, motioning for her brother to wait. She returned with a clean damp cloth and bathed her brother's hand. "No bones broken," she said.

"We must be careful. You're linked to Henry as surely as Mary is, you know. After all, you've been followed on two occasions that you know of."

"We can't retreat into a shell," Emma said, folding the bloodstained cloth.

"Of course not, Em. But we must be wary."

They heard footfalls echoing in the corridor. Lestrade appeared.

"Come with me, I'm going to Krauss' apartment. Then to McMannus' and the Gregorys," he said, waving search warrants. His face was sour. "Seven more people are infected. Two men and five women. Someone slopped the poison on the door pulls at Babbage's Chocolate Shoppe on York and Swan's pub on Derby."

"They're within a block of the German building," Richard said.

"Did anyone see who did it?"

"No. The anarchists have begun their work."

"They're testing it on the public," Emma said. "A little of that chemical does terrifying damage."

"But," Richard said, "they don't know how much to use. They'll probably use too much rather than too little. Right, Em?"

"That's what worries me."

Lestrade was pacing, his face anxious. "They may know more about the formula than we think. Hurry."

Emma collected her purse and Richard's sketchbook.

The Scotland Yard carriage raced through the deserted streets, cutting corners and frightening several derelicts. They rushed into the German apartment building and up the stairs to Krauss's apartment. Lestrade knocked several times. There was no answer. He pounded the landlady's door. While they waited, Emma pointed to the purple stains, even more vivid, and to the gouges where she had removed the samples.

Mrs. Haas appeared at her door and was startled to see Emma. Lestrade thrust the search warrant in front of her eyes. She left for a moment and returned with a key. Trembling, she opened Krauss' apartment door. Lestrade, a sergeant, and two constables entered, followed by Emma and Richard. They ignited several gaslights and searched the rooms for Mary.

"Em, look at this." Richard opened a file with his pencil, careful not to obliterate any vital fingerprints. "Scientific stuff. Give it a going over."

Richard and Lestrade opened several more folders.

"Here are the Bremen tickets, the telegrams, it's all here," Lestrade said.

"Now Gordy, give this a look. Tell me if Mycroft might find this fascinating reading."

Richard opened a large file containing Nachtgeist's three-year plan of anarchy across Western Europe and England. Richard read the labels. "England, Wales, Scotland, Norway, France, Holland, Belgium, Spain, Italy."

Lestrade sat down with the file on his lap.

"Richard, Gordon, here's a document from Schmidt to Krauss. It's in German and I'm a little rusty, but it concerns Henry," Emma said.

"Sir," Sergeant Hanes said timidly.

"Yes, sergeant?" Lestrade did not look up.

"I grew up with my grandparents, sir, and—"

"What of it?"

"We changed our name to Hanes from Heinz when the old folks moved to England."

"I thought you were British to your boots."

Emma handed the sergeant the correspondence. "Translate."

Sergeant Hanes quickly scanned the handwriting. "Oh my, give me a few minutes. There are some odd words here."

Lestrade stood up and returned the plan to Krauss's desk. "You say there is an equivalent amount at McMannus'?"

"A little less, but similar," Richard replied. Then pointing, he added, "There's the poison jar. Not as full as this morning."

Emma turned over more technical reports, then shook her head. "I don't see anything here that might suggest curare. This file contains formulas exchanged between a Dr. Hoeltzer and Dr. Thornton. I need more time with this."

"I think I have the essence of this, sir," Sergeant Hanes said.

"Go on, Sergeant."

"Yes, well. As you say, it is from a Schmidt to a Krauss. He's informing Krauss that Dr. Hoeltzer thinks Dr. Thornton is a fool. It appears that Dr. Thornton is in Germany at the time of this message—Bremen actually."

Emma asked, "What's the date, Sergeant?"

"The seventh of this month."

Emma and Richard glanced at each other. He grabbed a folder of receipts. "See, that was during Thornton's alleged holiday."

"Anything else?"

"It appears that Dr. Thornton is there in Bremen and his experiments are not successful. They have a suspicion that Dr. Thornton did not discover some type of formula as he claims, but a Dr. Davies probably did. It goes on to give Herr... pardon, Mr. Krauss authorization to offer Dr. Davies fifty thousand pounds to work with them to create a poison. Whatever this Davies developed must be important to Nachtgeist. It says if Davies does not cooperate willingly that they are to threaten him. And if threats do not work, then they are instructed to kidnap him and take him to Bremen. Mr. Krauss is being ordered to cooperate with Mrs. Gregory and kill Dr. Thornton. They are to make his death appear to be accidental. That's all."

"Gordon, now do you see why Henry took flight or maybe was kidnapped?" Richard said softly, resisting the chance to pounce on Lestrade for doubting Henry from the start. "And look here. The receipts for Mrs. Gregory's passage to and from Bremen as well as Dr. Thornton's. Observe their departures and arrivals. They traveled together... same compartment."

"Secure this apartment. McMannus is next," Lestrade ordered. "Maybe Miss Palmer's there."

Richard grabbed Lestrade's arm. "Wait a minute. Em, do you see any indication of curare?"

"Not a single reference to it. But Dr. Mull should look this over in detail. I believe he can read German."

"Curare must be in there somewhere," Richard said.

"To McMannus," Lestrade said, stepping into the hallway.

They heard Mrs. Haas crying and muttering in German in her flat.

"Just a moment," Emma whispered. "She's saying something. Sergeant Hanes... translate." He pressed his ear to the door.

"She's crying and praying that God would deliver her son from evil and keep him safe... something about an injury and a prodigal son."

"Now," Lestrade ordered.

The group sped to Helen McMannus's apartment and found more of the same evidence, including a personal diary that Sergeant Hanes studied, discovering an interesting entry.

"She's expressing frustration over Dr. Davies' continued refusal to cooperate," Hanes said. "She's calling him a blind dumb patriot of a skeleton empire. She writes that he received his final threat the night of the murder."

"That diary will be most helpful to us," Lestrade said. "But we don't have any more time to spend here. Secure this apartment, Constable. Sergeant Hanes, Richard, come with me to the Gregorys' home. First Emma, I want to deliver you to Carlisle Street. This might be a very long night, and I'll probably require your scientific skill tomorrow. Moreover, Dr. Gregory knows you. I want you kept at a distance."

"Perhaps you'll find Mary there," Emma said, more in hope than belief.

CHAPTER 23

"What fool at this ungodly hour..." Dr. Gregory grumbled as he fumbled with the lock, finally opening the door.

"Dr. Gregory, I am Chief Detective Inspector Lestrade of Scotland Yard. I must speak to your wife."

Dr. Gregory stared. "You certainly have your nerve at this hour."

"Mrs. Gregory, if you do not mind, sir."

"What do you want with her?"

"That's between Scotland Yard and Mrs. Gregory. Now, may we come in?"

"Why should I let you in, Inspector whatever-your-name-is?" Dr. Gregory crossed his arms over his sizable middle.

When Lestrade produced the search warrant, Dr. Gregory capitulated and led the way to the parlor. He struck a match and soon the gaslight was hissing. Looking, touching, Richard moved systematically about the room, which was adorned with Germanic carvings, paintings, photographs and icons.

"The problem, Inspector?"

"We must speak with Mrs. Gregory immediately."

"Impossible." Dr. Gregory scratched his belly through his nightshirt.

"Impossible?"

"She's in Edinburgh."

"Hanes, have a good look around. Now, Dr. Gregory, how long will your wife be in Edinburgh?"

"Four, maybe five days. Touring with the local German Society."

"I want your wife's address in Edinburgh."

The professor sprawled defiantly on the divan. "No."

"You refuse me?"

"I don't have it. She promised to contact me from Edinburgh upon her arrival."

"When did she leave London?"

"Late afternoon."

"I want names and addresses of members of her German Society. Anyone who would know her itinerary."

"I don't know her German friends. Why must you speak to my wife?"

"When did you see her last?"

"This afternoon."

"Time?"

"Can't say. I can assure you, sir, I shall be speaking with my solicitor tomorrow and shall register a formal complaint with your superior unless you explain your interest in my wife."

Richard saw Lestrade turning angry red.

"We have a few questions to ask your wife. Important questions." Lestrade went on. "I shall be communicating with Edinburgh police. Be warned, doctor, your lack of cooperation will be in my report. If you're connected with the matter we're investigating, then I can assure you that your intransigence will aggravate your punishment."

"Intransigence? Punishment? I can't give you what I don't have." He retrieved his pipe from a piperack. "Again, why must you speak to my wife?" Dr. Gregory lit his pipe and bit down angrily on the stem. Spittle rattled.

"Now, Dr. Gregory, do you know the whereabouts of Miss Mary Palmer?"

"Miss Palmer's whereabouts? Next you'll be asking for the names of pickpockets working Oxford Circus. And I suppose—"

"Where is Miss Palmer?"

He waved his pipe. "With her parents, I should think. How in this world should I know?"

"Miss Palmer has been abducted, doctor."

Dr. Gregory stared. "What?"

"When did you last see Miss Palmer?"

Dr. Gregory glanced nervously at the clock on the mantlepiece. "About mid-afternoon. Abducted?"

"Did you observe any strangers with Miss Palmer today?"

"None."

"Are you certain of that?"

"Absolutely positive."

"Any strangers in your department today?"

"I wouldn't know." He stared at his pipe, as if it would offer answers. "You suspect my wife. You suspect me. How dare you? I am grieved to learn of Miss Palmer's abduction, but I can tell you we know nothing."

Dr. Gregory got up and started for the door. "Now, if you do not mind, sir. It's late. I have classes tomorrow." He opened the door.

"Chief Inspector," Sergeant Hanes called from the top of the stairs. "Nothing. No Miss Palmer."

"You expected to find Miss Palmer here, did you?" He stabbed with his pipe towards the Scotland Yard carriage. "Out. You shall be hearing from my solicitor."

Lestrade brushed by him and the door closed.

"Hanes, watch him from the shadows over there. I'll arrange a plainclothes from the Thomas Street Station to relieve you as soon as possible. Now to Mycroft's."

Lestrade pulled Mycroft's door chain vigorously for several minutes. Richard was beginning to doubt if Mycroft was inside. Perhaps he had fallen asleep at the Diogenes Club across the carriageway. Then they heard a shuffling at the door and Mycroft appeared, half-awake. He invited them inside, and they summarized their discoveries for him. Mycroft telephoned a restricted number and ordered someone to obtain photographs of Mary from her parents and dispatch them to Dover, Portsmouth, Bournemouth, and Southampton in case the Germans attempted to spirit Mary to Germany.

He walked about in his robe, rumpled and strangely lethal. "That girl will be tortured. Have you been keeping Emma away from this mess?"

Richard glanced at Lestrade. "She's at home."

"You're right. She's at home. Never toy with me. She is as deeply involved in this enterprise as you two are. I've had her followed, and she keeps slipping away from my man. You never could control her."

Mycroft looked from the window overlooking a sleeping Pall Mall.

"About Rainer Schmidt?" Richard asked.

"Be quiet. I'm thinking." Mycroft stared from the window. When ready, he turned and sat at his desk. "What about Schmidt?"

"You told me he was the brains of Nachtgeist."

"You're wasting my time."

"Can we charge him with murder?"

"Of course not. We have no extradition agreement with the Kaiser. Now get out of here and mind what I've told you. And pray that Miss Palmer is not maimed, if she survives, that is."

On their way to Carlisle Street, Richard asked, "Gordon, if Schmidt was in London, we could arrest him, couldn't we?"

"We could. You can be sure he won't set foot 'round here."

The carriage stopped and Richard alighted.

Richard forced a smile and watched the carriage drive away. He paused with his hand on the door pull and heard the rooks in the tree tops calling in the night. An overpowering restlessness took him. He walked across the carriageway and headed towards Beeton Park. As he walked, he argued with himself. Near Beeton he was struck by a sudden insight. He headed toward the university.

Ten minutes later Richard arrived at the telegraph office across Forbes near the science building. He scribbled his message for the telegraphist, and a minute later he was on his way home. Richard knew he was now obsessed, but he was convinced that someone had to do something both daring and risky.

When he arrived home he heard a stirring on the settee.

"Richard, I've been waiting for you," Emma said, her voice husky with sleep.

"Go to bed, Em. Mrs. Gregory is in Edinburgh, but I don't believe it. Mycroft knows everything, and the man who was following you was Mycroft's agent... it was for your safety. And I just sent a telegram."

"To whom?"

"Colonel Rainer Schmidt."

"Good heavens, you aren't serious?" Emma sat up on the settee.

"Yes."

His sister yanked his arm. "Have you gone mad?" Her face twisted in anger.

"We must get him on our soil, Em. Then Gordon can arrest him."

"This is utter madness! Mycroft will be unhinged." Anger raged on her cheeks. "What did your telegram say?"

"I said: Sister near death. Asking for you. Hurry. Keeping vigil at St. Bartholomew's Hospital. Dr. G."

"Dear God in heaven."

Richard grasped her elbow and tried to redirect her towards the hallway to her room. "You need some sleep, Em."

"Take your hands off me," Emma spat, twisting her arm free.

"I'm going to my studio. I have to think."

"You should've thought to ask me before you sent that telegram. What's your plan? Tell me. Go ahead. Tell me your plan. What do you expect will happen? I don't think you have a plan, Richard."

"Emma. I need to think—and pray."

"Pray? Pray? You should have prayed for wisdom before you did this. You always expect God to save you from your stupidity!"

Richard started up the stairs. "This evil is poised to engulf nations, and it's started already with ours. Put out the lamp and go to bed, will you?"

Emma glowered at him. "Too far this time, Richard. Too far."

"We must capture Rainer Schmidt here, in London...on British soil. Lestrade can then charge him with murder. Otherwise, Mycroft's hands are tied. *Where th'offence is, let the great axe fall.*"

"Oh, shut up." Emma watched her brother climb the stairs. She needed to lash out at him once more, but the anger caught in her throat. He did not look back.

CHAPTER 24

The man's hand grasped Fiona's wrist, pulling her into the livery near the Rhys Company Store.

"Lucas! What are you..."

"You're supposed to be 'ome."

"I was checking the telegraph office. This came in for Henry," she said, waving the telegram. "From Mary. Have you taken him breakfast yet?"

"The Huns got mended at the infirmary and are lookin' everywhere. They'd recognize you. Your groundskeeper told me they been up 'round your place yest'rdy."

"Lucas, you worry too much."

"Come with me. I saw your car 'round the corner. Figured your father drove."

They turned at the chug and rattle of a fast-approaching coal lorry, black lumps tumbling and bouncing onto the dirt street.

"It's them Huns! The biggun's drivin'," Lucas said and stepped into the dusty street, watching the lorry head into the hills. "They stole it."

"Look!" Fiona cried, pointing. "They turned at the fork. They're goin' towards the collieries and Henry." Fiona ran to her motorcar.

Lucas ran towards the constabulary as Fiona's bright red Fiat skidded through the crossing and raced along the high street towards the hills.

The Germans enjoyed a significant lead, but Fiona had confidence in her motorcar and her skill. Another advantage propelled her. She knew the hills better than many of the local men—certainly better than the Germans. She put her foot to it. Her Fiat's canvas top was snapping and ruffling in the damp morning air.

The motorcar bounced over the rutted road. She veered onto the road fork and raced up the hill. Around the first turn she saw the Germans from the overlook.

Fiona accelerated and easily took the next turn, becoming airborne before the Fiat landed on the road beneath her. She gripped the wheel and prepared for the next turn, choking from the lorry's dust.

With the object of her anger in view, a growing rage filled her. She knew the ridge routes would begin narrowing a mile or so ahead. But what would she do when she caught up with the lorry? Her motorcar was no match.

"Follow? Pass? What?" She pounded the steering wheel with her palms.

She slowed the motorcar behind the lorry through a sweeping outer curve.

She kept her distance, completely enraged.

Lumps of coal were hitting Fiona's Fiat. She heard a shattering sound and knew a chunk had hit the torch glass covering her arc lights. Several more hairpin turns were coming up, and she settled for a moment, knowing there was nothing she could do but remain close and, she hoped, somewhat hidden. A straightaway lay a mile ahead. It led down towards Copley's sheep farm before climbing to a sudden sharp bend where the road became the abandoned tramway along the ridge. She would surprise the Germans along Copley's.

Fiona rasped into the next turn as the lorry was disappearing around another blind curve. She reduced speed. The Fiat chattered around the bend. On the other side she saw the lorry still in its turn. Her Fiat was exposed to them.

The German passenger pointed in her direction.

"One more turn before Copley's. Get behind them."

Her chance to pass them lay ahead, and she prepared for it, heart pumping. How had the Germans discovered Henry's hiding place? If they knew that much, then they must have an idea of the terrain. Her special advantage evaporated.

Fiona steered the Fiat Zero through the curve and sped within a few feet of the bouncing lorry. Coal chunks pounded her motorcar. She bobbed and ducked as coal ricocheted off the Fiat's bonnet and windscreen. As the two vehicles approached the straightaway, the Germans edged their lorry to the right, cutting her off. Fiona steered left and accelerated, but had to brake as the lorry lurched into her path and accelerated down the hill towards Copley's farm.

The German passenger was barking directions to the driver as the lorry wove a side-to-side course down the hill, holding her back. Dust and coal projectiles were dangerously close now, bouncing into her face and off her arms. When the lorry hit a sharp depression in the road, a large coal chunk hurtled towards her. She closed her eyes as the windscreen shattered, glass shards showering into her lap and passenger seat. Her knuckles whitened in fear, but there was no blood.

The valley floor was flat with pasturage. She gambled she could safely pass. The engine clattered in protest as she accelerated through the thick dust cloud and emerged on the lorry's left side near the rear wheel. The two vehicles raced onto the broad expanse and the Germans bashed her Fiat. Metal ground against metal, ripping and sparking and shredding. It was hopeless. She was being forced off the road.

She pumped her brake pedal. The lorry jumped ahead. The Fiat's front fender tore off. She steered for the center of the road, the tires showering grit and dirt. She began the climb up the hill as the road narrowed into the treacherous ridge route. She gained on the Germans again, getting in behind them. Krajic steered the lorry from side to side, taunting her to pass. Fiona now waited and watched. They were approaching the dangerously narrow path. She gripped the wheel and spat road and coal dust from her mouth.

Fiona inched the Fiat to the right, goading the Germans into cutting her off, teasing them into taking the turn at the most perilous angle.

"Ha!" Fiona shrieked as the lorry took the bait.

The road narrowed and the lorry took the ridge path at high speed, bouncing and swaying. Cinders, coal, and slag flew in all directions. The Fiat crashed into the rear of the lorry. Fiona accelerated and sent her motorcar into the lorry's right rear wheel. The Fiat's metalwork buckled and twisted. Krajic applied the brakes. The Fiat's tires spewed cinders and dirt as the lorry skidded half off the path. Fiona braked, then aimed her rattling motorcar past the lorry and onto the narrow ridge path. There was blood and wooly flesh on the road. Copley's sheep scattered down the hill.

Fiona clung to the steering wheel and hoped Henry would be keeping watch and not traipsing somewhere in the hills. One cold fact throbbed in her head: there was no way to escape except back along the same ridge route.

Fiona bounced and clanked the Fiat over the tramrails nearing Bull Hill. She remembered being there in the night fog. She spat more grit from her mouth, and within moments she saw the shack and Henry running outside.

She drove the Fiat onto the turnoff, onto the narrow, grown-over path, then up to the front of the shack. Henry was standing aghast, mouth agape. Fiona aimed towards the path for a speedy departure, then turned off the engine.

"What in the name of all that's holy?"

Fiona sat stunned and mute. She stared ahead, exhausted. She picked broken windscreen glass from her lap.

"What happened?"

"I ran the Germans off the road at the turn above Copley's," she managed, coughing now. "They were coming to get you. They stole one of the big lorries."

Henry got Fiona from her car. Her legs went under her. He carried her into the shack and lowered her onto the blankets.

"Here, take a drink." She managed to hold the jug and swirled water in her mouth. She spat onto the floor.

"Go to the window and watch. The Germans may get the lorry back onto the road somehow, or they may come on foot."

"You're supposed to stay home."

"Give me a moment, Henry." Fiona poured water over her head.

She grabbed a rifle, stepped to the window, and aimed it towards the path along Bull Hill. "Should I stay here or venture back down to the Germans?" She put the gun down and shook her wet hair.

"You're staying here for the present, Fiona. I must go back to London and fight... as soon as possible."

"Fight? You've got a fight right here! I stopped at the telegraph office this morning. Here's a telegram. Came in last night. From your Mary."

He read it and shoved it into his shirt pocket. "I'm needed back there. I have information that could be vital to my case. You know how tirelessly Richard and Emma are trying to help. I should've thought about all this before I fled London."

Fiona watched him. "I-I don't know what to say to you. These past few days have been... I just want you to be safe." She grabbed his forearm and squeezed. "You can always—"

"Look," Henry said. "The lorry!"

Henry dashed to the half-unhinged door and jammed it closed. He rearranged a few old crates near the open end of the shack and motioned to her.

"Get behind these. You aim at the window, I'll take the door."

They listened to the threatening chug as it approached.

"We might die here, Henry," Fiona said, over her rifle.

"I know."

He readied his rifle, testing the action, feeling the cold oily smoothness of it. He watched the doors over his gun sight. The heavy lorry drew steadily closer and louder. The shack's timbers rattled, vibrations shivered through the floorboards.

Fiona looked at him. He sighted along the black, polished gun barrel, his face oddly calm. Fiona shifted her gaze to her own target, beyond the glassless window.

The lorry stopped and the engine coughed into silence. They waited, holding their breath. Henry could hear his pulse.

"The window. I have the doors," he said again.

The lorry's door opened. Boots ground on cinders. Then, nothing. Henry pictured Krajic surveying the scene, assessing, planning. The rifle stock became slippery with sweat.

Footsteps crunched across cinders and slag. Henry and Fiona waited.

Then suddenly: "Henry. Fiona. Are you in there?"

Fiona gasped, then screamed, "Lucas!"

Henry whispered, "Be quiet. They might have him at gunpoint."

The crunching footsteps stopped at the feeble doors for a moment before kicking them from their hinges. Lucas stood in the doorway, bathed in sunlight.

"Are you alright?" Lucas peered into the shack.

"We're fine," Henry said, helping Fiona to her feet.

"Did you see the Germans?" Fiona asked.

Lucas chuckled. "They were inside the lorry, afeared to shift 'eir weight. I pushed 'em over the edge down ta Copley's. Your father'll dock me for doin' 'at, I'm afeared."

"Are they dead?"

"Nah. I saw 'em get out after it rolled over. It'll take'em all morn ta get anywheres and ya know they can't climb up 'ere."

"Henry wants to go back to London," said Fiona, brushing at her grimy clothes.

Lucas nodded thoughtfully. "Good. I would if I were you."

"Why?"

"Henry ain't fightin' sittin' up 'ere, is he?"

"I must go to the train station," Henry said.

"Take the lorry. Leave it at the station. I'll get it." Lucas turned to Fiona and pointed to her roadster. "Does 'at contraption still go?"

"Of course it still goes."

"We'll foller ya down 'n I'll ride with Fiona 'n help her explain things to her father."

Henry gathered Fiona into his arms and embraced her.

"Thank you, Fiona. And thank your father." He kissed her cheek and strode out to the lorry.

Fiona settled into her mangled Fiat. After setting the rifles inside and swiping away the windscreen glass, Lucas got into his seat. They watched Henry drive off.

Fiona slowly accelerated her damaged Fiat onto the old tram path. "Are you sure the Germans can't climb to the ridge?" she asked.

CHAPTER 25

Mrs. Mac groused about the disruption to her breakfast routine as Richard sat at the table studying his sketches and sepias. They were strewn over its polished surface.

"I n'er seen the like. The good doctor eatin' in the kitchen 'cause you got insp'ration. Here, least have toast."

"No thanks, Mum. Later." He fussed with sketches and photographs he had been reviewing for hours. It had come to him during the night, too bright to ignore. Fresh energy marshaled inside him.

"Em," he said, when she entered, "it's about time."

"I see you haven't finished your early morning grumble," Emma jabbed, still smoldering about the telegram to Colonel Schmidt. But her training took in the dark smudges of sleeplessness under his eyes.

"Marnin', Emma. Yur father's takin' breakfast in the kitchen," Mrs. Mac announced, shaking her head in disgust.

"Just tea, please."

"Tea. Just tea. Why did ah expect diff'rent?"

"Look at these." Richard tossed three sepias in front of Emma as she took her seat. She set aside charcoal sketches Richard had on the table, then regarded the sepias with little interest.

"Just three hunting photographs."

"Here's your tea, Emma," Mrs. Mac said.

"Curare, Em. Curare."

"Curare?" she snorted, filling her teacup.

"Look at this one. Do you see a familiar face?"

He slipped a sepia print across the table. She adjusted her pince-nez.

"Just naked natives and a couple of hunters."

Richard leaned towards her. "Look at that man."

She stared at the bearded man. "Who is he?"

"Pretend he's not wearing a beard," Richard said.

Emma shook her head. "Sorry."

"Trevor Clark."

She examined the photograph again. "My yes. I see it now." She tossed the sepia back to her brother. "What of it?"

He sailed the photograph back to her. "Don't be dense. What are they holding?"

"Blowpipes or..."

"Blowguns, Em. Blowguns!"

Emma slumped back against the chair. "Blowguns."

"Curare. The natives dip the points of their darts in curare and blow—"

"Are you thinking that Trevor Clark is responsible for Thornton's death?"

"These are the prints he gave me as reference for the paintings I did for him. He's a weapons collector...an obsession."

Emma sipped her tea.

"But access to curare?"

"What do you see in his other hand?"

"Darts."

"A quiver of darts."

"Of course! Nigel would be an impediment to his affair and eventual marriage to Mrs. Thornton. And we can assume he possesses curare, which we know was the means of Thornton's death. But when did he have an opportunity?"

"I plan on finding out...today if possible. I believe my plan can work. You said that Clark was donating money for the new science building." Richard leaned forward. "Plans for the new science building were found at the crime scene. If I had his money and influence, especially funding the new building, I could probably see Dr. Thornton anytime I wished."

Mrs. Mac entered, looking agitated. "Mr. Palmer is in the parlor in a right state."

The twins went to him immediately.

"How are you faring, Mr. Palmer?" Emma inquired. "Pray, be seated."

"News on Mary?" Richard asked.

"No, I'm afraid. The missus and me are at our wits' end. Truly we are."

"Take heart, sir." Richard smiled. "No less than a representative of the Crown is taking personal action on Mary's behalf as we speak."

"Two Coldstream Guards were at our home during the night. Wanted photographs of Mary."

"Please breakfast with us, sir?"

"No thank you. No appetite." He removed a paper from his vest pocket. "We received this telegram and I came here straightaway. Henry's coming home to fight."

Richard took the paper and unfolded it as Emma sat on the settee beside him. Richard read aloud:

> "Dearest Mary,
> I love you more than life. Troubles here
> in Wales. Coming home. 7:10 tonight
> from Shrewsbury to Paddington. Hope
> Richard is at station. Full of fight.
> Love Henry."

"I'll be there," Richard said, looking up. "Who knows about this telegram?"

"Just me and the missus. I must return home. Forgive me. The missus, you know." Mr. Palmer made for the door.

Richard took out his pocket watch. "I have much to do today before I meet Henry at the station. I'll be the one to give him the news about Mary."

"Good. Hide him in your studio. Gordon won't search it again."

"You stay here and help Father. If there is any news of Mary, it'll be sent here."

"Where are you going?"

Richard grimaced.

"Mr. Trevor Clark."

"Clark's a pompous jackass," Richard declared with elaborate disgust on his face. "Please pass the potatoes."

"Not one of your favorites," Dr. John laughed as he arranged his dinner plate.

"As a client he was impossible to work with, getting in the way of my painting, and he was completely condescending today. Where's Em?"

"She's finishing with the Clifford woman. I very much appreciated her help today. There's influenza about."

"Any news about Mary?"

"None."

The door chimes suddenly jangled.

"Good heavens. P'rhaps it's about Mary," Mrs. Mac exclaimed and started for the front door.

"Why did you see Clark?"

"Curare. The official cause of Nigel Thornton's death. I remembered the paintings I did for him. Brazil... all from his Amazon adventures with the RGS." Richard paused, his fork poised over his potatoes. "Blowguns."

"Good Lord, Richard." Dr. John's eyes flashed. "Curare darts! Are you suggesting—"

"I visited him on the pretext that I wanted to photograph the three paintings I did for him... The Amazon Trilogy. Actually, I should have done that a year ago when I finished them, but I hadn't the time. I had to endure the snob for an hour."

"Cut from his father's cloth, I'd say."

"I got his permission to visit Clark Green. You know the place...on the overlook near The Downs? I had a jolly good look around. He had blowguns on the wall of his study. Above them, in a glass case, were twelve darts arranged like a fan." Richard leaned towards his father. "Four of them were missing."

"Why, do you suppose...?"

"I took one of the darts. I thought it might be useful for a chemical comparison. Assuming they had been dipped in curare," Richard said, testing his Bordeaux.

"You handled them carefully, of course." Dr. John said.

"Of course. And I nicked Clark's journal. For fingerprint samples." Richard speared a small boiled potato. "I talked to the butler, and soon I was in Clark's workshop. The butler had Clark's personal valet escort me to the place. It's a detached building with a covered walkway so he won't soil his fancy Italian boots. His hobby is gunsmithing and sword making, you know. That workshop is larger than most homes here on Carlisle. It's old, and attached to it is a larger livery where Clark keeps his motorcars and carriages.

I discovered the four missing darts standing point down in a beaker in the workshop. That murdering cur!"

"In a beaker? Then he leached the curare from the tips."

"The valet wouldn't leave me alone. Don't touch this and don't touch that. But fortunately, one of the footmen arrived and announced he was needed in the servants' quarters. Finally I was alone in the workshop. I quickly photographed the beaker and darts before I packed them in my camera box. I nicked several of his spanners for more prints. I'll wager his prints will match those on the second teacup and the teapot lid. Everything's at the Yard getting analyzed. Gave them to Harry Coyle. Remember Coyle?"

"Richard," Mrs. Mac interrupted. "Emma wants ye ta know 'at Gunther Haas is in the waitin' room. The boy's in a terr'ble state. She says she'll call ye if ye be needed."

"Mrs. Clifford, I'm certain you will be very much improved in three days. You come back then. Three days, remember?" Emma opened her office door to discharge the woman.

Motioning to Gunther Haas, Emma said, "Gunther, please come. Have a seat. It's not your dear mother, is it?" She quickly assessed his condition as he shuffled in, wincing in pain. His eyes were shadowed black.

"Nein... ah, no. Doink vell," Gunther said, easing himself into the chair beside Emma's desk.

"What is troubling you, Gunther? You look rather unwell. Your arm."

The young man glanced around the office. "You doctor... I-I trust. Been kind to mama. Arm hurts."

"Let's have a look. Remove your sling."

He moaned as she carefully rolled up his shirtsleeve.

"Gunther. You should've had me examine you yesterday!"

His forearm was swollen, and Emma could see, without touching it, that it was broken in at least two places.

"Please, doctor, arm not vhy I come here."

"We can talk later, Gunther. We must deal with this broken arm immediately. I'll have my father assist me. Don't worry, he's a doctor, too."

"Please, doctor, I..."

"Father. Father. Hurry," Emma called. She helped the young man onto the examination table. He protested mildly, but his pain was tormenting him.

"What's the matter?" Dr. John asked, looking around the door.

"This is Gunther Haas. Gunther, this is my father, Dr. John Watson."

"My word, son, you have a broken arm."

"He was in a pub fight."

The boy shook his head. "No. Not pub fight. I fight mit mine neighbor."

"Don't worry, son," Dr. John said, "we'll give you some ether, and you'll sleep while we fix it."

"But I don't tink..."

"Gunther, stop. Your arm must be set immediately. You'll not feel any pain. Now, we must remove your shirt."

"Dr. Vatson, pleeez..."

"Gunther, you'll be fine. I must cut your shirt from your arm." Emma grabbed scissors and snipped while her father prepared the ether. "We can talk later. Lay back on the table."

"Maybe you should do ether and I should..."

"No, Father. I'll set the arm."

"You dun't unterstand."

"Relax, old son." Dr. John placed the ether cloth and glass barrier over the young man's mouth and nose. "Breathe deeply."

Soon Gunther slipped into unconsciousness, mumbling, "Palma, Palma, Palmmm." Emma paused. She glanced at her father. But now the worst break of her career demanded her undivided attention.

"Emma, this looks like a nasty one to me. Saw my share of these in the Second Afghan War. Are you sure you don't want me to..."

"Father, I'll do it," she said, very much in command of herself. Emma explored the break. "I think just two breaks here and here, the ulna. We should get one of those new x-ray machines for this work."

"How long has the boy been like this?"

"Two days."

"Then it's already started to knit. You'll have to..."

"Re-break it."

Emma went to the supply cabinet and placed morphine, a syringe, cotton, gauze, and tape on a movable table and pushed it near Gunther's arm.

"Richard," Emma called. Within moments he arrived in surgery. "Medium splints." He checked the storage room in the back as she examined the breaks.

Without looking up, Emma said, "Put the box there," and nodded towards the table. "Get a mask for yourself...and a scope. Richard, watch Gunther's pressure. You know what to do."

"Did he say anything important?" Richard asked. Emma's fingers pressed along the ulna and radius while she imagined the spatial relationships of his broken bones.

"Could be Palmer, but it'll have to wait. I want to get this done before we talk to him."

Emma exerted pressure on Gunther's forearm. She directed her entire seven stone and ten pounds onto the two breaks. Her feet left the floor as she lunged downward. The boy's arm yielded with a muffled snap.

"I must be leaving soon to collect Henry."

"You'll make it."

"One twenty-five over sixty-six," Richard reported.

Emma applied pressure again, but this time nearer to Gunther's elbow.

"That'll be a bit of tricky," Dr. John cautioned.

"I know, Father. Would you prepare the plaster, please?" Emma grunted and lunged. She examined the alignment with her fingers, then pushed and examined once more. She positioned the heels of her hands on the ulna and lunged again. She relaxed her fingers again, reexamined the break. The bone had slipped into position. She glanced at Richard.

"Cease ether. Pressure?"

"Holding."

"Remove the cuff and go," Emma ordered.

Richard placed the cuff on Gunther's chest and exited from surgery.

Dr. John returned to the table.

Emma administered morphine to her patient and prepared Gunther's arm with gauze and cotton, wrapping the splint into position. Her father handed Emma a metal bowl containing wet plaster. She began to fashion the cast. There had never been a time when preparing a cast had not reminded her of her brother's sculpting. She envied his skill as she scooped the white paste onto Gunther's arm. She troweled and smoothed from elbow to wrist.

As she sculpted the plaster, Emma pondered over the young man's involvement with Nachtgeist. *How deeply is he immersed in this devilish cult, and how was he recruited? He could not be older than eighteen.* Why should she care? Emma reviewed all of the ugly facts she had learned about Nachtgeist. Gunther groaned. She smoothed the final application and repeated under her breath, "Hate the sin...love the sinner."

She had not noticed her father leave until he returned carrying a tray of tea with three cups.

"You read my mind."

He placed the tray on her desk. "That's good work. I've never seen it done any better."

She tidied the instruments, placed the syringe and needle in the autoclave, and joined her father preparing tea at her desk. They sat sipping from their cups and watching Gunther. They waited for him to regain consciousness. *What secrets are hidden in the boy? And what of Palmer?*

CHAPTER 26

Richard chewed on his unlit cigar while he paced along the Paddington Station platform. He carefully noted the other men waiting on the platform. He wondered who might be Mycroft's agent or worse, Nachtgeist.

A derelict stumbled onto the platform, spilling an odd collection of garbage from a sack. Everyone looked at the man. His teeth were brown and his tattered clothes were filthy. Gnarled fingers trembled as he gathered up his worldly goods and refilled his sack. He muttered to himself.

Richard helped the man retrieve a brush, a roll of paper, rusted scissors, matches, several cigar butts, and a shoe.

"Ta, kind sir." The man spoke clearly. "Be quiet and listen to me, boy."

Sherlock!

"Mycroft's man is standing there by the pillar. Not sure about Nachtgeist."

"Right."

"Get Henry. I'll divert. Don't look back."

Sherlock stumbled with his sack towards Mycroft's agent.

Richard peered down the track and noticed the train's torch, a mere pinpoint in the faraway darkness. The stationmaster announced the arrival of the train from Shrewsbury.

The engine came into Paddington trailing billows of smoke and soot. The bell clanged three times as it screeched to a halt. Richard counted the carriages. Eleven. Steam billowed as Richard tensed.

Then Henry alighted.

"Run! Follow me," Richard shouted. They headed down the stairs. Richard heard a commotion on the platform above.

They dodged through Paddington Station and darted to the carriageway. Fortunately there were many hansoms in queue. They jumped into the third cab, which was Richard's habit in situations like this. The drivers of the first two hansoms cursed Richard's breach of etiquette, but he hoped other passengers would take the first two cabs and Mycroft's man would be drawn into following one of them instead.

"Carlisle and King," Richard called to the driver, who cracked his whip in the night air. "Hurry. Double the fare."

Richard forced a smile. He had now to deliver his horrible news. If only Henry could be told of Mary's abduction by inches. "You should've returned with me from Straithairn."

"Sorry, old chum. Believe me, I know."

Richard paused. "Listen, Henry…"

"What was all that about back there?"

"One of Mycroft's men. Sherlock dealt with him."

"Sherlock?"

"Look at me, Henry," Richard said. "Mary's missing, and we fear she's been abducted."

"Abducted!" When his voice came, it was in overwhelming misery. "Who? When?"

"I suspect Nachtgeist."

Henry wept.

Men did not cry. Most men never allowed other men knowledge of their hurt. But Richard and Henry were different. Their roots were deeply fraternal, with no secrets. Richard could only imagine the enormity of his friend's anguish. He wondered how he would respond if it were Emma who had been kidnapped instead. But Mary's kidnapping was real, and Henry's anguish was real.

Richard said, "We'll find her, and I'm going to need you, old fellow."

Henry braced himself. "Alright. The details."

"Cooee, Gunther. Cooee. It's Dr. Watson," Emma said. "Open your eyes. Good. You're doing fine. Gunther, open your eyes again."

The young man was groggy and blinking at the ceiling.

"Say hello to us, Gunther."

"Ah…Hal-lo."

They waited. Gunther groaned, more fully awake.

"Good. Do you recognize me, Gunther? I'm Dr. Watson. I mended your broken arm. You'll be fine. How do you feel?"

"Ah...I...dunno."

"This is my father, Dr. John. Do you remember him?" Gunther nodded.

"Speak, Gunther. Tell me that you remember him."

"Ja. Remember."

"Very good, son," Dr. John said.

"Arm better?"

"You'll be fine," Emma said. "I'd like you to sit up."

Dr. John lifted the end of the sectional examination table. He angled it for Gunther, inclining him into a sitting position.

"There, my boy. How is that?" Dr. John asked.

"Ja, but...I haf no money."

"No charge, my boy," Dr. John said, patting the young man's leg.

"Here is some tea. Drink it," Emma said, steadying the cup to his lips. He sipped at first. Then he gulped, and Emma refilled his cup. Color returned to his cheeks.

"Gunther, would you like to talk with me?" Emma asked. "Do you have something to tell me?"

He sipped more tea. "Tank you."

"What did you want to talk about?" Emma held a cloth to his chin.

He looked nervously at Dr. John.

"Would you like to talk with me alone?"

He nodded.

Dr. John squeezed Gunther's leg. "Very well. You're in good hands, my boy."

"Now, Gunther. What is troubling you?"

"Fery bad people here. My people. Germans...not all Germans. Some bad Germans."

"Yes. I understand. There are a few bad Germans."

"I've been fery bad. Mama's been prayink fur me. She knows I've been bad."

"What do you mean, Gunther?"

"She knows Krauss is bad. He got me to run fur him. Doink things fur him. I know about da poison dat hurt mama and Hildegaard."

"You do?"

"I know da vomen and Herr Krauss put poison things in dustbin. Voman used poison to kill man."

223

"Do you know the woman?"

"Gregory." He sipped his tea.

"Go on."

"I got mad at Krauss. Dat poison hurt mama and almost killed her. I hate him. Ve fought and see vhat happened." He looked at his broken arm. "He made me vatch apartment. It started hurting real bad, everyvhere... inside and outside."

"I can imagine."

"And last night he made me vait in place I nefer been before. I vaited dhere with box he gave me. Dhen Gregory and Maria came with lady."

"What is her name?"

"Palmer. She was strugglink. Dhey took her in bedroom and closed door. I heard cryink and slappinks. Den dhey called me to brink box. Da voman vas cryink and...she...vas naked. Dhey didn't vant her runnink avay. Dhey vanted me to tie her. Dhey slapped her. Slappinks. Slappinks."

"Did they injure her?"

"She vas cryink. I tied her to chair like dhey wanted, and tried not look at her. Dhey vere askink about man. Vhere he was. Alvays vhere he was. Da vomen gave me her clothes and told me to throw dhem away. She vould never need dhem were she goink, dhey said."

"Did you?" He shook his head. "What was in the box Krauss gave you?"

"Rope."

"Then?"

"Ve left her tied up and vomen laughed at me. I vas embarrassed and dhey teased me about seeink naked voman. I vas hurtink very bad. I put voman clothes in box and Gregory voman yelled and pushed me into door. My bad arm. She told me go avay. I took box home and hid. All day been vorried. I brought box. I thought you know vhat to do."

"Where is it?"

"In vaitink room."

"Mrs. Mac," Emma called.

Her eyes were wide as she looked into surgery.

"Gunther has a box in the waiting room. Fetch it please."

Emma drew up a stool and sat, weakened by the news.

"Here 'tis," Mrs. Mac said.

Emma lifted the lid and saw Mary's familiar skirt and blouse. Even her shoes. She pressed her hand to her mouth, fighting for composure. Gunther reached out and touched her shoulder.

"Father!" Emma shouted, her voice shrill. "Gunther, where are the women?"

"In pocket."

Emma removed scrap paper from his torn shirt.

"313 North Cambria. That's near the university."

"Emma, what's wrong?" Dr. John eyed Gunther with suspicion.

"We know where Mary is. Mum, please get a cab. Now Gunther, I want you to stand up for me. Help him, Father." He was unsteady for a few moments, then he gained his legs.

"Gunther. Go directly home. You must only tell your parents that I fixed your arm... no charge. Do not tell them about Miss Palmer. Do you understand me?"

"Ja, doctor. You hurry. Bad vomen haf bad frogs. Many jumpink bugs."

"Frogs...bugs?" Emma asked, suddenly alert.

"Some red...some green unt orange. Vomen say poison frogs. Dhey told me not touch."

"Are the frogs in cages?" Emma asked.

"Ja, unt vomen said frogs vere goink to kill lady."

Emma recalled hearing of such frogs—Poison Arrow frogs—from rainforests in South and Central America. Their skin exuded poison.

"Of course!" Emma said.

"What?" Dr. John asked.

"Thornton was probably studying poison frogs for his formula," she said, thinking it through. Thornton needed live crickets and grasshoppers—frog food. She adjusted Gunther's sling. "Go. Not a word, mind you."

Mrs. Mac met him in the waiting room and assisted him out.

"Mum, while you're outside, please have Lloyd bring the carriage around."

"What is this about Mary?" Dr. John asked.

"She's being held captive by Mrs. Gregory and McMannus near university. I'm taking her clothes to my room. I need time to think. Please call me when Richard and Henry arrive." Tears came. "Father, please have Gordon here as soon as possible."

Once in her bedroom she placed the box on her chair, sat on the edge of her bed, and wept. The thought of Mary's death skewered her. The notion of depravities caught painfully in Emma's throat. And she would soon require unflinching calm. She gathered her spirits and prayed.

Afterward, she went to her dresser and lit the spirit lamp. She leaned over the ewer and splashed water onto her face and patted it dry with a flannel. A hand mirror revealed a calm and determined face.

The sound of horses at the back of the house drew her to the rear window, and she saw Richard and Henry alighting from a hansom. Richard paid the driver and slapped the horse into a gallop. He paused and looked warily around the alleyway.

Emma hurried down the hall, through the kitchen to the back door near the scullery and larder. She opened it to Richard and Henry.

"I know where Mary is, Henry. Come."

They hurried through the house, with Emma shouting, "Henry's here! Henry's here!" Mrs. Mac and Dr. John appeared. They all got together in the parlor.

"Emma, tell me about Mary." Henry's face was gaunt.

"I know where she is. Near university. I hope she's still there. Wait. This is important." Emma hurried to her office and returned with Gunther's scribbled note. "Here. This is where they're holding her."

Henry read it. "Nigel Thornton's apartment!"

"Are you sure?" Richard asked.

Henry stood up. "I'm on my way."

"Wait a moment, Henry. Sit down," Richard said. But Henry paced, cracking his knuckles.

"Father, when'll Gordon be here?" Emma asked.

"He won't. There's been a terrible gun battle in Wales, near Blaenllyn. It was concerning your case, Henry," Dr. John said, his eyes worried. "Gordon's in Blaenllyn now."

"My case!"

"Scotland Yard said he left for Blaenllyn hours ago. Special assignment."

"Lloyd's waiting with the carriage," Mrs. Mac said, looking in on them.

"We'll have to do this without Gordon," Richard said.

"Is she hurt?" Henry's knuckle cracked.

"I don't know," Emma said. "Mrs. Gregory and McMannus were guarding her. Richard, please get my medical bag from my office."

"Medical bag? Mrs. Gregory!"

"It's a very long story, Henry. We don't have time."

Emma went to her bedroom and packed fresh clothes into a Gladstone. Henry shouted for her to hurry. She grabbed Mary's shoes from Gunther's box and tossed them into the bag, then made her way to the front of the house.

"What's that for?" Richard asked, pointing to the valise.

"Never mind." Emma moved by him to the front door.

Dr. John and Mrs. Mac watched them climb into the carriage. The coachman coaxed the horses into a turn in the middle of Carlisle, and they charged down the carriageway and out of sight.

"I don't know if I can take much more o' this," Mrs. Mac said, hands to her mouth. "If it be all the same ta ya, sir, I'll do some prayin' in me room."

"Of course. We must pray."

CHAPTER 27

During the fast carriage ride to Dr. Thornton's apartment, Emma explained Gunther's story without the more alarming details of Mary's ill treatment and the specter of Poison Arrow frogs. Richard and Henry were on the ragged edge of rage. Richard punched his seat. Henry cracked his knuckles and looked out the windows. Emma doubted she could restrain them.

"May God have mercy on whoever crosses you two," she murmured.

Richard nudged Henry. "I'll get out first. You help Emma. Hug the buildings. Stay in the shadows." Then he shouted to the coachman, "Pull over now, I say!"

"Not at three thirteen yet," Lloyd said, pulling the carriage over to the curb. "It's up a piece."

"Wait." Richard got out. Henry handed Emma down, then her bags. They slipped into the shadows and crept along a block of sandstone flats.

"Have you been here before, Henry?" Richard asked.

"Couple times."

"Third floor?"

"No. First."

"Back exit?"

"Only on the ground floor, I think."

"We'll be quiet and I'll listen at their door. Then we'll break in."

The trio skirted several steps, a bicycle, and dustbins.

"Which window?" Richard asked.

"That one. No curtains."

"Good. The lights are on. Shadows on the wall. Someone's in there."

Richard studied the street. Only a young couple walked along on the opposite side.

Richard opened the front door. They climbed the stairs. "Which flat?"

Henry pointed down the hall to the right. "Number four."

They stopped near the door.

Richard tested the doorknob. "Locked."

He motioned for Henry and Emma to give him room. He hurled his body against the door. The old door lock held, but the door hung shattered. Henry helped Emma over the rubble. The two German women were struck dumb. Henry heard Mary screaming from the next room. Emma lunged for the door and found it unlocked.

"We're here, Mary," Emma shouted. "Henry, you're staying out until I say so."

"Emma!"

Emma thrust her bags into the room and closed the door behind her.

"Mary, I'm back, dear."

"Henry, where's Henry?"

Mary's face was pale with the dark, staring look of shock. She was trembling.

"He's outside with Richard."

"You left me, Henry! You ran away. I hate you, Henry Davies."

Emma opened her medical bag. "You don't mean that."

Emma untied Mary's bonds and questioned her during a rapid examination. Her face was bruised, lower lip cut, dried blood on her lips and nostrils. Her eyes were red and swollen.

Emma looked around. Two large glass containers held small, colorful frogs.

Mary's voice steadied. "They said they're poisonous. Ridiculous. They threatened to take me someplace and set them free on me."

Emma concentrated on the examination.

Richard and Henry forced the two women to lay face down on the floor. The Nachtgeist pair were cursing in German. Mrs. Gregory punched McMannus. Several neighbors dressed in robes and nightshirts looked fearfully through the broken doorway.

"Scotland Yard. I'm Inspector Watson. Return to your flats. Everything is under control." Richard tapped Henry's shoulder and nodded towards several boxes in the corner. "Watch these shrews while I have a look."

Inside the boxes he found correspondence and scientific memoranda to and from Dr. Hoeltzer in Bremen. He flipped through several files and discovered Dr. Thornton's personal diary. He scanned the last several entries, glancing towards Henry and back again, re-reading them once more, finally handing the diary to him.

"Read what Thornton wrote while I watch these harpies."

Henry looked at the entries and shook his head.

"He really hated me, didn't he? The Germans had paid him for a poison formula... that's why he was pressuring me...all for a formula that he couldn't create and I refused to develop." Henry tossed the diary in the box.

Emma opened the door.

"Henry. Your bride-to—" Before Emma could finish, Mary pushed by her and into Henry's arms. He gathered her up and kissed her. Emma stood watching as they clung to each other.

Emma lugged her bags into the room and removed a scalpel, brandishing it in front of the two women. She handed it to Richard and retrieved pieces of rope from Mary's prison. They tied the women's hands behind their backs.

"Help us, Henry," Richard called. They tugged the German women to their feet and passed neighbors milling in the hall. Bilingual profanity filled the air. Inside the carriage, Richard had them kneel on the floor. Henry helped Mary and Emma inside.

"Back to Carlisle!" Richard shouted.

Emma screamed, reaching for her ankle and discovering blood. "She bit me!"

Mrs. Gregory was clearly deranged, hurling abuse and protests, predicting England's collapse and eventual subjugation to Nachtgeist.

"Are you alright, Em?"

She examined her ankle as best she could in the dark.

"I'll need a tetanus."

The carriage slowed to a stop along the alleyway behind the Watsons'.

"You ladies go. Henry and I'll deal with this pair."

Emma limped up the steps to the door and called inside, "Mary's here!" Richard and Henry removed the German women from the carriage.

"Mary, dear gel!" Mrs. Mac said. She hugged her. "Our prayer's been answered!"

Dr. John entered the hall, tying his robe. "You gave us a right scare."

"I was terrified, sir," she said as he hugged her. Richard and Henry hauled the German women inside.

"Good heavens, Richard. Who are these women?"

"Father, Em's injured. In the larder with them."

They forced them to lie face down on the dirty floor.

"Watch them, Henry, while I see to Em."

Richard returned smiling. "Emma's fine... no stitches. Got her tetanus. Let's get these Germans into surgery. I have a plan."

Mrs. Mac wrung her hands. "Dear God in heaven."

As they entered the surgery, Emma and her father were arguing.

"Father, I know what I'm doing. Please prepare the sedatives." Emma tugged a second examination table into place.

"This isn't right. We can't keep them here," Dr. John said.

"Father," said Richard, "we must keep them here until Lestrade returns from Wales or..."

"Or what?"

"We need some time. We'll explain in a few minutes." Emma spoke over the profanities the two German women were spewing at them. "The sedatives, Father."

"Which hypnotic are you prescribing? Chloral hydrate? Sulphonal? Barbitone?"

"Barbitone."

Dr. John prepared the barbitone syringes and handed one to Emma. She gripped Mrs. Gregory's arm and delivered the injection into her vein. She watched as Mrs. Gregory's cursing abated, and finally, sleep.

Seconds later, both Germans were unconscious and the surgery was quiet.

Mrs. Mac broke the silence. "What'er'll we do now?"

"They're wicked," Mary said, her face contorted with repugnance. "I never imagined women were capable of such evil."

Henry drew her to him. Quietly she confessed her fears, what the kidnappers had promised she would soon experience, including ritual perversions and a final sacrifice with frogs on an altar somewhere in London. Mrs. Mac left the surgery holding her ears.

Emma moved a chair and Mary sat down and cried. Everyone was stunned. Mary's revelations purged her heart. Emma prayed that her friend could one day purge her memory.

After she had collected herself, Dr. John pointed to the kidnappers. "You can't leave them here, Emma. And we have our office hours tomorrow. The Yard must be told about them."

"Richard and I'll talk this over. Mary, please telephone your parents. Use my office telephone. You, too, Henry."

"And you go to bed, Father. This'll be sorted out in the morning." Emma fluffed her hair nervously.

"Never in all my years with Sherlock did we ever have to resort to…"

"Father. You're forgetting the Boynton murders," Richard said, smiling. He placed his arm on his father's shoulder, urging him to the door.

"I don't want to see these women in the morning."

"I must treat this one's wrist. Then we'll contact the Yard," Emma said.

Dr. John left, tugging at his robe.

Emma removed the homemade bandage from Mrs. Gregory's right wrist and examined the injury. She glanced up at her brother.

"Just like Hildy and Mrs. Haas. I daresay it's the poison." She examined the infection more closely. "Gangrene?"

"We must plan our next step, Em. I have an idea."

"My next step is to treat this wound. I see additional lacerations on her other hand. They're infected. Looks like a few slivers of glass are deep inside. And you should've thought about next steps before you sent that telegram to Schmidt," Emma said tartly. She placed a container of saline, cloths, cotton, gauze, tape, iodine, and bandages onto a table. She studied the embedded glass slivers.

"Might be fragments from the distillation apparatus."

Henry and Mary came out of Emma's office. They were surprised to see Emma at work on Mrs. Gregory's wrist.

"Dear, you go on. I'll be with you in a moment," Henry said and kissed her. "What happened, Emma?"

"Thornton's version of your formula."

"Look at the infection. My formula wouldn't…"

"See," Emma said, raising the German's hand. "Slivers of glass. From your distillation apparatus, Henry!"

"What poison?"

"Belladonna. Enough questions. Go to Mary and allow me to treat these wounds."

"She needs to be hospitalized," Richard said as Henry left.

"Should've been days ago. It's very advanced."

"Her husband should be notified." Richard watched his sister bathe the wound with saline.

"Go."

"Just a moment, Em."

"Go."

"What if you admit her to hospital? Wouldn't she be kept heavily sedated there?"

"Look at this wound. Her ugly mood is most likely due in part to the pain and God knows what else."

"There you have it."

"I'm busy here, Richard, or haven't you noticed?"

"Listen. You'll admit her to St. Bart's tonight. My telegram to Schmidt was perfect after all. Don't you see? We'll get Schmidt...maybe at the train station...perhaps at hospital. With all the evidence we have, he'll never see the Kaiser again."

"Schmidt could be at hospital this very moment. Have you thought about that?"

"Impossible...tomorrow morning at the very earliest. I checked the schedules."

"You dolt. He could've taken the Kaiser's private coach for all you know. Leave."

"Admit her to hospital after you're finished. I'll visit Dr. Gregory and give him the news. Hope Schmidt and Gregory haven't talked." Worry crossed his face.

"Very well. He needs to be with his wife, regardless of what happens."

"I shall. After that I'll go to the Yard and have them keep watch at hospital."

"She'll need me to stay with her. You return here and..." Emma paused as she was excising the poisoned tissue, "...and if Father refuses to continue watch over McMannus in the morning, then you must do it. Move her to my bedroom. The sedative will dissipate in about four hours; she'll need more then. You know where it is and what to do...Barbitone, three cc's every four hours."

"Henry stays in my room tonight."

"Go. And be careful with Dr. Gregory."

As she removed more infected flesh, she wondered if Dr. Gregory would cooperate.

How could Dr. Gregory live so long with this woman and not be a part of Nachtgeist? How could he condone her involvement? And would seeing his wife in such a condition cause him to thwart any effort to arrest her and Rainer Schmidt? If he has been in correspondence with Schmidt, Richard might be walking into their ugly midst. Father's pistol...

She turned to remind her brother before he left, but heard only horses on Carlisle cobblestones.

"I'll wager he didn't take the pistol," she said aloud, swabbing iodine into the wound.

CHAPTER 28

"Dr. Gregory," Richard said. In the dark night a stray dog yapped out.

The professor stood disoriented; his grey robe hung on him.

"Dr. Gregory, sir. I am Richard Watson, remember? I was..."

"You were here with that inspector."

Gregory stood in the shadowed doorway, out of the damp wind. Something in his left hand caught Richard's eye, but it was too dark to know what it was.

"Dr. Gregory. Your wife is not in Edinburgh."

"She never called me."

"Doctor, you should know the poison that killed Dr. Thornton somehow contacted her wrist."

"Poison?"

"My sister is admitting her to St. Bartholomew's."

"Your sister?"

"Dr. Emma Watson, sir. Are you all right?"

The professor swung open the door and stepped aside.

"You must get dressed and come with me. I shall escort you to St. Bart's."

Dr. Gregory led Richard into the unlit parlor. He fumbled for a match and lit the gaslight mantles above the fireplace.

"Have a seat," Dr. Gregory said. He went to the kitchen.

Richard looked around the Victorian room. His interest in a German landscape above a grand piano was interrupted by the old man entering, a telegram in his right hand. He thrust it towards Richard.

"Can you explain that?" He rubbed his eyes. "It's from my brother-in-law. He'll be here tomorrow. You say St. Bart's. I've telephoned them several times. Jutta isn't there."

Richard read the telegram out loud. "Arrive tomorrow at 5:17PM. Will meet you at hospital. Tell Jutta am on way. RS."

Dr. Gregory sank into the settee. "How did my brother-in-law know about Jutta before I did?"

Richard reread the telegram, noting the arrival time.

"I should think he will arrive at Waterloo," Richard mused, watching as Dr. Gregory distractedly kneaded the object in his hand.

"Do you feel strong enough to accompany me to St. Bart's? My sister is at her side. Your wife is heavily sedated. The wound is quite serious."

"Scalded, you know. The kitchen at her club. I told her to go to the doctor. Wouldn't hear of it. Wouldn't allow me to examine it. You said poison...same as Thornton's?"

"Yes, sir, I'm sorry to say."

The professor looked at the dark papered wall; he sat unmoving. Richard waited.

"It must be very bad," Dr. Gregory said at last, flexing his hand. "I know where I went wrong."

"Wrong?"

"That German Society."

Gregory ran his hand over the brocaded settee fabric and fiddled with a thread. He kept squeezing what was in his hand. Richard guessed it was leather by its texture.

Dr. Gregory stared at the cold fireplace. "She discouraged me, you know. I was interested in learning more about Germany. I hoped to go there with her again some day...to see the Germany she knew. I wanted to attend the meetings with her. But there was always some excuse. She would say, 'The meeting is just for the women tonight.' Or, 'A German speaker will be there and you'll not understand a word.' This or that...always something...so eventually," he said, looking up, "I stopped asking. At first I thought it was odd. Then I began to think she was seeing another man." Richard edged forward on his chair. "Can you imagine? I believed she was having an affair with Nigel. God rest him."

He was too fatigued to show embarrassment. He glanced at the grand piano covered by a garish fringed shawl.

"She could play the piano beautifully, y'know? She could have been on the stage. Oh yes...she could have become well known. Jutta wanted to give concerts when she was younger...when we met. Beethoven...Liszt...and Bach. Ah yes, Bach."

He closed his eyes, lips moving to silent melodies. Richard sat watching, catching these musical echoes. The mantle clock ticked away its fate, then suddenly broke the silence with its chime. Dr. Gregory's hand squeezed rhythmically.

"Yes, sir. Her Bach was triumphant, transcendent...Heidelberg School of Music. Honors." He glanced sharply at Richard. "Poison, you say."

"It's rather alarming, sir. Your wife is a member of a German cult."

"Yes, the German Society."

"No, sir. Nachtgeist."

Gregory purpled in anger. "It's him, isn't it?" He pointed to a picture of Colonel Schmidt. Richard nodded. "He seduced her into Satanism, you know." Dr. Gregory closed his eyes. "I should have stopped her. I knew he was evil. Not at first, though."

"I'm afraid your wife is strongly connected with Dr. Thornton's murder. She abducted Mary Palmer."

"Dear God. Are you certain?"

Richard waited.

"Oh my, Jutta," he breathed. "What's our future now?" He bravely pulled himself to his feet, groaning as he stood up. "Very well, sir. Stiff upper lip and all that. I must go to her. Give me a few minutes to make myself presentable."

As he shuffled past Richard, he dropped the object from his hand. Richard caught it.

"Jutta's," Dr. Gregory said.

Richard unrolled the supple leather. It was a companion to the black right hand glove in a locked drawer in Scotland Yard's evidence room. He put it in his coat pocket.

"I shall wait for you, sir. I have a cab outside."

Dr. Gregory left Richard in the parlor. The clock on the mantelpiece chimed the hour, and Richard surprised himself with a sudden observation about the room. There were no photographs of the Gregorys together. Only photographs of Colonel Schmidt alone or with his sister populated the tabletops and niches. He looked at the photograph beside him. Brother and sister stood holding hands. Alone the pose was of little import. But combined with the others, it appeared they were lovers. Richard looked closer. The brother and sister bore no resemblance to each other. And their demonstrated affection was not that of siblings. *Are they lovers? Are they married?* Could such an arrangement have gone undetected by the professor?

"Right," Dr. Gregory said from the stair landing. "We must do what we must."

They left the bleak house, home to the professor and his wife and a shrine to Colonel Rainer Schmidt—her brother or lover. Richard helped the professor into the hansom. The horse started towards St. Bartholomew's Hospital.

Dr. Gregory watched his home disappear in the dark street behind the cab. During the journey Richard explained what might happen at hospital and the possible capture and arrest of Colonel Rainer Schmidt. Dr. Gregory pledged his cooperation, and Richard trusted the man. He steered the conversation to the Schmidt family in Germany.

"Mrs. Gregory's family should be informed about her hospitalization."

Gregory shook his head. "They had all passed on before I ever knew her. All Jutta has living is her brother."

"Well done, sister. I shall wait at her side. Her husband is on his way," Emma said and sat down exhausted on a straight-backed chair at Mrs. Gregory's bedside.

"We done the best we cud. Every bed in the place is filled, but ya gotta still keep 'em three 'ere." The nursing sister pointed to three female patients farther down the wardroom.

"They'll be fine. At least you moved most of them out, and Mrs. Gregory is first by the door. I imagine Scotland Yard will be here soon. Thank you, sister."

The sister departed and left Emma staring at Mrs. Gregory. Emma knew that she had done all she could for her patient. She looked at this woman in peaceful repose and wondered what other malevolence she had been involved with. To Emma, the woman's evil lowered the whole of womankind as well as civilized society. She pondered her own efforts to serve God through her medical missions in the slums, in her professional practice, and in the cause of women's rights, while this woman sought to honor her god through savagery and lawlessness in the name of Nachtgeist. The thought of it nauseated her.

And what other brutality was on Nachtgeist's schedule? Who else were agents of the cult? Emma watched the busy sisters and nurses in the hall. Could one of their number be a cultist? "How preposterous," she said out loud, before she could catch herself.

A woman groaned five beds away. Emma went to her and reviewed her record—an appendectomy eight hours ago. She mopped the perspiration from the woman's forehead and pressed a cold damp cloth to her neck and face. The woman moaned, aware only that someone cared and was near. Emma checked her pulse and incision. The bleeding was not excessive. She offered her a sip of water. The other two women were resting quietly and, by their records, were indigents. They had no family or loved ones. They were women of whom polite society was either critical or insensitive, pretending they did not exist. Emma knew women of this circumstance, impoverished, lost. Husbands no doubt had died or had been cashiered, or they had cruelly discarded them, leaving them helpless. They lived on the street, or worked at hard labor patching clothes. Or sorting refuse. Long hours of servitude. Emma stood beside each woman's bed, offering her prayers.

She returned to her chair beside Mrs. Gregory. Should the police have an opportunity to capture Rainer Schmidt in this room, few patients would be at risk. And when would Schmidt arrive? She hoped her brother was correct concerning the train schedule. What about Gordon's mission in Blaenllyn? She prayed he was not in any danger and wished he would return soon. More questions: *When will Dr. Gregory and Richard arrive? Might Richard be in danger?* If Schmidt had arrived at the Gregorys' home before Richard, then... Emma halted with alarm. She closed her eyes and prayed for him as the wind rattled the nearby window, whistling through the cracks.

"Thank you, sister," Richard said at the women's wardroom doorway. Dr. Gregory went past him to his wife's bedside. Emma stood aside.

"Your wife is resting comfortably as you can see, sir," she said.

Dr. Gregory stood with his hand on his wife's shoulder. He took her unresponsive hand. His eyes watched her, and Emma tried to discern what he might be thinking. A terrible anguish dwelt on his features. "Jutta. Jutta." Then his eyes found Emma.

"Please have a seat, Dr. Gregory," Emma said softly. But he remained standing, stroking his unconscious wife.

"It's my professional opinion that Mrs. Gregory came into accidental contact with the poison in Dr. Thornton's laboratory. Her condition is stable, but I must await Dr. Hazeltine's opinion for a final diagnosis. Gangrene is present, and the poisoning has reached a rather advanced level. I don't believe it is life-threatening. But the wound had been self-treated, and she should have received professional attention much sooner."

"She told me she scalded herself in the kitchen."

"I excised the infected tissue and neutralized the poison. But I must refer this case to Dr. Hazeltine. We must be patient."

"Of course, Dr. Watson. I do believe I'd better sit down now."

Richard moved a chair near the man and helped him settle into it as comfortably as possible.

"Is there anything you require?" Emma asked.

"No."

"Then I shall leave you with your wife for a few minutes."

"Thank you."

"I shall be in the hallway should you require me."

The twins moved into the corridor and conferred near the wall.

"Schmidt's arriving tomorrow in the late afternoon," Richard said. "I must contact the Yard about this, but Gordon's in Wales. Only he can handle this situation properly."

"Agreed."

"We must keep Mycroft out of this at the moment. He'll have to concern himself with the international implications soon enough. Agree?" Richard asked, rubbing his whiskers with both hands.

"The important thing, Richard, is getting the Yard prepared and your looking after the McMannus woman."

"Very well then. You'll be here all night?"

Emma nodded. "Mrs. Gregory will survive. I must remain here."

"You need rest."

"I'll be fine. Go."

"Here tomorrow morning then. Telephone me in surgery if need be. I'll spend the night watching McMannus."

"Three cc's of Barbitone every four hours."

Richard hurried from the hospital and ordered his waiting cab to Scotland Yard. The wind strengthened, and Richard could smell rain. When he arrived, sheets of it were slashing his carriage. He sat in the night officer's waiting room, fidgeting and feeling the constant eyes of the desk sergeant and constable on him. The sergeant had informed Richard that Officer Coyle was still on duty. Suddenly two constables entered, tugging a bloodied, handcuffed belligerent into the room, and manhandled him through a second doorway. They were drenched from the downpour and left a wet trail across the floor. Minutes later, Coyle emerged through the same doorway, shaking his head. Richard jumped to his feet.

"Harry, any news?"

"Sit down, let's talk." The room had a slight echo, and Coyle motioned for Richard to lower his voice to a whisper.

"Doc Mull says 'er's enough p'ison on 'at dart ta kill a man. Terr'ble stuff that. And 'em prints on the beaker 'n spanners all match. Is surely confusin' what ya expected ta find."

"Confusing?" Richard said too loudly, twisting his head towards the desk sergeant who was still watching over the top of his spectacles.

"Them prints on 'em tools 'n beaker don't match them what's on the journal. Them same prints on 'at journal don't match what's on the teacup 'n lid neither."

"Harry, you're telling me that none of the prints match? You're saying my theory that Clark put the poison in the teapot is wrong?"

Richard was exhausted. He ran his hand through his damp hair.

"'At's not what am sayin'."

"What then?"

"'Em prints on the journal book don't match 'em what's on the teapot lid and cup. 'Em prints on 'at journal book don't match what's on the beaker 'n wrenches. But am sayin' 'em prints on the beaker 'n tools match 'em what's on the lid 'n cup."

Richard sat up, jolted. "Clark's journal has his prints all over it. Correct?"

Coyle nodded. "Assumin' 'at journal is Clark's. But we'd haf ta fingerprint 'im ta be sure."

"Yes, yes, of course. But whoever touched the teapot lid and cup also touched the beaker and the tools. Correct?"

"'At's what Doc Mull says. We find 'at person 'n he'll be our man, most likely. But who?"

The question hung in the musty air.

Richard closed his eyes. "Very rummy this. A moment, Harry." Muted shouts and curses drifted from an interrogation underway inside the building. The desk sergeant shrugged his shoulders at Coyle as Richard scratched his goatee. "When does Gordon return?"

"'Round two t'morrow at Paddington."

Richard explained the events surrounding Mary Palmer's kidnapping, the two German women, and the expected arrival of Colonel Rainer Schmidt. He asked Coyle to have plainclothes officers at St. Bart's when Schmidt arrived and a Black Maria available.

Coyle shook with eagerness or fright or a combination of both. He was to be an integral part of Scotland Yard's primary case! Richard got up and Coyle followed.

"Harry, can you handle all the arrangements without Lestrade?"

"Am yer man," Coyle said. "Where are ya goin'?"

"Harry, I know the murderer. Tomorrow." He hurried from the building.

"Gor, blimey!" Coyle exclaimed as he stood, his chest expanding with excitement. He turned to the desk sergeant and received another shoulder shrug as he headed out. Coyle knew he had a great deal to arrange, and he had visions of a promotion skipping in his brain.

CHAPTER 29

"Nearly forty minutes and surgery will be open. What about her, Richard?" Dr. John asked angrily, tossing his morning newspaper on the table.

"We'll take her to Em's room."

"Emma's room?"

"This is the day, father." He reached for the teapot and hesitated—a change of mind. "I need coffee. Mum, would you be kind enough to brew some coffee...strong?"

"Acourse, Richard."

Dr. John glared at his son. "Emma's room?"

"Mum can look after her, and when she begins to regain consciousness, she can alert you for another barbitone."

"Alert me? More hypnotic? There is no medical reason—"

"Father, the woman's a criminal. She'll probably be hanged or at least imprisoned for the rest of her life. She's an anarchist...part of the Nachtgeist lot that even frightens Sherlock. No ordinary terror, this. I'll tie her to the bed. You simply sedate her when Mrs. Mac..."

"What about me yer sayin'?" Mrs. MacIntosh entered with a pot of coffee.

Richard explained the plan and the vigil the housekeeper would keep.

"Father, the Nachtgeist are poised to wreak terror on England. They've already infected nine people. We saw their plans of anarchy, beginning here in London. It's our duty to stop them."

"One day," Dr. John said. "One day only." He dipped his toast in the egg yolk and returned to his newspaper. "Ah, yes," he said, tapping the page. "I wanted to point this out. It's a piece about Blaenllyn. Says here Scotland Yard is there investigating a shooting. Says there was a motorcar crash leaving two injured, one dead, and one of His Majesty's Secret Detail is near death. I hope Lestrade wasn't injured."

"I was at the Yard last night. He's returning this afternoon. What else?"

"The murderer got away and was last seen at the station catching a train to Shrewsbury."

"Shrewsbury." Richard said. "He's returning to London. I wonder if that's Krajic."

"Krajic?"

Richard finished his coffee and got up. "I'm going to move McMannus." Richard waved him off. "I'll take care of it."

He bound her to his sister's bed, then got his camera case. Moments later he was on Carlisle Street locating a hansom. He headed to St. Bart's. Emma was awake when Richard entered, her face grey with fatigue. Dr. Gregory sat beside his wife's bed. Quietly Richard summarized the facts he had learned from Harry Coyle. Emma wished him well as he left.

"Clark Green, near the Downs," Richard shouted to the driver.

The hansom cab jostled for an hour in tangled traffic before reaching the road to the vast Clark estate. Richard got out with his camera case. Marble steps brought him to the double doors, which offered ornate glass and brass trim. Before he could knock, the door opened to a footman. His look suggested Richard should have used the tradesman's entrance.

"I am Richard Watson. I was here yesterday taking photographs of three paintings I did for Mr. Clark." Richard waited, expecting recognition. The footman remained mute. "Unfortunately, one of the photographs did not develop well, and I'm here to take another image."

Then Mr. Clark's valet descended the grand staircase. He welcomed Richard. "More photographs?" The footman stepped back, and the gentlemen's gentleman ushered Richard towards Mr. Clark's study.

He watched Richard unpack and arrange his equipment on the Persian carpet.

"I must've had a bad photographic plate last visit."

"Photography is fascinating. May I help?"

"Is Mr. Howell on the estate today?"

"I should imagine he is. Why do you inquire?"

"My sister met Mr. Howell at the Thornton home the other day. He showed her Mr. Clark's automobile. She's been raving about the Rolls Royce. I thought Mr. Howell could show it to me."

"A Rolls Royce Alpine Eagle. It's a fine motorcar." Then the valet looked slant-wise at Richard. "Your sister is a friend of the Thorntons?"

Richard sensed a hidden anger, perhaps wariness, at the Thornton name.

As he secured the camera onto the wooden tripod, he decided a truthful response would encourage more information from the valet.

"Oh no, sir." Richard shook his head. "Quite the opposite. Dr. Thornton was a professor of hers at university. My sister simply visited the home to pay the briefest of respects. Mr. Howell was present and insisted on showing off this motorcar."

"Howell's life is women and motorcars—especially that Alpine Eagle." The man stepped closer. As Richard was adjusting the aperture, the valet said in a conspiratorial tone, "If you ask me, there's something going on over there."

Richard fussed with the camera. "What do you suppose is going on?" Richard elevated the tripod.

"I must say that I'm ashamed of my employer and his chauffeur."

"Ashamed?" Richard began focusing.

"Mr. Clark has been staying with Mrs. Thornton off and on for the past several months now. And Mr. Howell is no better." Indignation surged. "He delivers Mr. Clark to the Thorntons and gallivants with the daughter at all hours. Sometimes their parlormaid, too. T'ain't right. We all think it's sinful. I confronted Mr. Clark with it and I nary got the boot."

"I'm happy that you didn't," Richard said, from under the black hood.

The valet angled closer to Richard and whispered, "Just between us. Money is the root of it. It sure ain't looks. I've seen Mrs. Thornton and the poor girl—plain, she is. Both are, really. Howell's a man of the world. You should've seen some of the high-toned ladies he would bring around here in Clark's motorcars, their fancy clothes and noses in the air. I tell you, there's money in it somewhere. Clarks have a way of finding money like a compass finds north. I say it's common, garden-variety greed."

"Dr. Thornton was a professor, a life commited to modest finances. Surely you must be mistaken."

"Ah, but rumor has it the professor discovered something...I don't know...some type of potion that'll be worth more than a bob or two. I can say that much. I was dusting off Mr. Clark while he was on the telephone. Bragging about it, he was. I heard it."

"That explains Mr. Clark's interest," Richard said. "But why is Howell so interested in such a girl?" Richard took a photograph of the painting.

The valet looked around, then lowered his voice.

"Mr. Howell is Mr. Clark's stepbrother. A bigamist he is."

"A bigamist?"

"When Howell was on the seas, he had wives in every port. And when Mr. Clark travels on one of his frequent adventures with the Royal Geographic Society, Howell accompanies him and arranges assignations whenever and wherever. I do believe Clark drove his saintly mother to her grave. I believe it. All us do."

"Fascinating. Now, do you think Howell would show me the Alpine Eagle?"

"I'll inform him of your wishes, sir. I'm sure he will, but not a word about what I told you."

"Mum's the word," Richard smiled. "Clark is one of my wealthiest patrons."

When the valet left, Richard waited. It was not long until the study door swung open.

"I understand you wish to see the Alpine Eagle," Mr. Howell said enthusiastically. "You are Dr. Watson's brother then?"

"Yes, indeed. I'm finishing up here. I'd love to see that Alpine Eagle my sister has been talking about."

Howell swaggered around the Clark study.

Richard started to store his photographic equipment. "Would you mind handing me those plates?"

Howell grabbed one from the floor and handed it to Richard, who took it, careful of Howell's fingerprints.

Howell gathered three more plates from the floor.

"Would your sister care for a drive in the Rolls?"

"She would, indeed." Richard collected his lens brush, his shroud, and closed the case. "I thank you for your help, Mr. Howell."

"Call me Burton. The Alpine Eagle then?"

"Thank you. I understand you are acquainted with the Thorntons," Richard said as Howell guided him to the motorcars.

"Mr. Clark is fond of Mrs. Thornton. Old friends, I think."

"And I take it that you are old friends with her daughter . . . what's her name?"

"Elizabeth...a convenience." Howell offered a knowing look.

Howell turned the incandescent lights on, revealing three gleaming motorcars. Richard had never seen such beautiful motorcars. He thought of them as moving sculpture. He touched each one as Howell led him to the Alpine Eagle.

Without prompting Howell recited every specification of the motorcar. "Get in."

Richard gripped the steering wheel and examined the interior. "I must say this is elegant...sumptuous."

Howell traced the sweeping curve of the fender with his finger. "Beyond my means, I'm afraid."

"The Thorntons will have a struggle, will they not?" Richard said.

"Struggle? Struggle financially?" Howell laughed, "Oh no, no, no. The old man made certain they would be well taken care of."

"How can that be? Dr. Thornton was a poor professor."

"It's all hush-hush. They'll be very wealthy as a result of something Dr. Thornton discovered." Howell polished the mirror with his handkerchief and gazed at his reflection.

"Discovery?"

"Mr. Clark knows the particulars. It's something medical. Elizabeth says it's quite revolutionary." Howell polished the motorcar's mirror-like metalwork. "Mr. Clark might marry Mrs. Thornton someday. She'll be well cared for."

Richard opened the door and got out. "Good for him. Where does that leave you... Burton?"

"What was that?" Howell asked, preoccupied with his image in the sparkling grillwork.

"I'm sorry. I must be going. I can understand why Emma was so impressed by the Rolls."

They returned through the house, and Howell escorted him to the waiting hansom. For Howell's benefit, he directed the driver to Carlisle. After the cab had turned in the street and progressed a block or two, Richard shouted, "Scotland Yard and hurry."

"Richard, ya can't be comin' in here like you was Lestrade, havin' us do analysis when'ere ya want," Coyle whined from behind his desk. "Ya must be daft er summink."

"Harry, Dr. Mull must fingerprint these photographic plates immediately. I'll warrant the prints on them'll match the ones on the teacup. If you crack this case while Lestrade's out, whom do you think they'll promote?"

Coyle brightened. "Gimme the plates. Wait 'ere."

"Harry, hold them by the edges."

"Acourse I know 'at. I tweren't an Irregular fur nuffink." Richard opened the door for him. "Have some tea. Just made it mese'f."

Richard poured a cup and sat down. He closed his eyes and sipped. He whiled away the time by imagining Howell at the Old Bailey hearing his death sentence pronounced. Without trying, he fell asleep.

Richard awoke, blinking hard, gathering his wits.

"Ya been sleepin', Richard," Coyle said, laughing. "Acourse you know Dr. Mull."

Richard got up and shook the doctor's hand.

"Tell 'im, doctor."

"We have the murderer. The prints on the photographic plates match those found on the beaker, the tools, the teapot lid, and cup...even the roll of blueprints. Do we know the motive?"

"Money," Richard said. "The potential of great wealth. We also know the means."

Coyle inserted, "Curare, acourse."

"Yes, but I'm struggling with the opportunity. There are no witnesses. Absolutely nothing to indicate our suspect was in the vicinity of the crime scene."

"Who is our suspect?" Coyle inquired.

"Burton Howell. He's the personal chauffeur to the owner of Clark's Merchant Bank."

"Very good work to the both of you," Dr. Mull said and withdrew to his laboratory.

"Opportunity, ya say," Coyle said. "We can look through Lestrade's files for a clue."

"Harry, I don't have time to read files. I believe you should get an arrest warrant and charge him with the murder. It's Howell based on the fingerprint evidence."

"I'll begin the proceedin's, 'n while 'at's happenin', I'll check 'em case files what's on Lestrade's desk," Coyle said.

"I'll be at St. Bart's with Emma. You know what to do this afternoon."

"A detail of guards. Plainclothes and a Black Maria."

"Keep it hidden somewhere."

Richard left Coyle's office.

Coyle guzzled the last of his tea, excited at the prospect of arresting the leader of Nachtgeist and Dr. Thornton's assassin. He looked up as Officer Muldowney opened his door.

"Did you hear?" he asked, stone faced and grave.

"Ain't heard nuffink."

"The man Lestrade was chasin' 'n Wales jus' shot 'n killed two of our own tryin' to board a train at Shrewsbury."

CHAPTER 30

The hospital was quiet.

"It's half four," Emma yawned to Richard. "Where are the police?"

"Bloody Coyle," Richard said, scratching his goatee.

Dr. Gregory stood up, his face colorless and haggard. They had discussed the situation from every possible angle with him, and the old academic had pledged cooperation. He went to the window at the far end of the women's wardroom and gazed towards Beeton Park and St. Mark's Cathedral.

"The Yard should be here by now," Richard said.

At that moment, Henry and Geoffrey entered the wardroom.

"Geoffrey, you wouldn't mind if I asked you to lie a little? We want you to pretend you're a surgeon assisting Emma. You'll be Dr. Halsey. You speak German. You can help translate if required."

"Of course. But I must say I'm far from fluent."

"Dear, you need a proper surgeon's robe. Give me a minute." Emma left the wardroom.

Richard removed a pistol from his pocket and handed it to Henry. "You've used this before. Six rounds so make them count, old fellow."

Henry hefted it. Two female patients watched him guardedly as he made for Dr. Gregory at the far window. As he approached, the old man's legs buckled beneath him. Henry caught his arms and guided him to a nearby chair.

"Here, try this one," Emma said, handing Geoffrey a white robe. He slipped it on. "Perfect, Dr. Halsey."

Emma and Geoffrey gathered chairs near the bed while Richard stood outside in the corridor, checking his own gun, referring to his pocket watch repeatedly. Sisters and doctors studiously ignored him, conscious of special circumstances in the women's wardroom. Henry and Dr. Gregory talked quietly near the window.

"Mr. Watson," a man said, coming towards him along the corridor. "Mr. Watson?" Richard nodded. "I'm Officer Muldowney. Lestrade sent me."

Richard shook the officer's hand. "It's nearly five o'clock. Where are your men?"

"Lestrade wanted me ta tell ya that Krajic's in London. Murdered two of our men in Shrewsbury. They was runnin' fer the movin' train 'n Krajic shot 'em deader 'n Cromwell from the baggage car."

"Where are your men?"

"Arrivin' soon."

"Soon. They should be here now. Lestrade's in town?"

The officer nodded. "Officer Coyle wanted me to tell ya 'at he arrested Mr. Howell 'n he confessed. But he's claimin' his employer put him up ta it. Paid him for the dirty business. Big money he sez. Coyle's gettin' a warrant fer 'im, too. Coyle sez the university security guard saw some fancy motorcar parked near the school buildin' the night of the murder. A big, what ya call it, Alpine something er t'other. None of us thought nuthin' of it 'til Coyle found the report in the files."

Richard took Muldowney's elbow and led him into the wardroom.

"Henry, you're free," Richard said. "Thornton's killer confessed. Trevor Clark's chauffeur. He's trying to implicate Clark. Officer Muldowney here says so."

Henry got to his feet and helped Dr. Gregory out of the chair. "Thank God," Henry murmured.

Emma and Geoffrey joined the scene as Officer Muldowney stood back, pleased that he was associated with a happy outcome instead of tragedy and suffering.

Someone cleared his throat from the wardroom doorway.

"Gordon," Emma exclaimed, smiling, relieved.

"It's ten past," Richard said, approaching Lestrade, extending his hand. "You survived Blaenllyn, but not by the look of you. I'm sorry about the loss of your men, Gordon."

"That Krajic's ruthless, and very quick, Richard. Stay on your toes." He forced a smile. "You've got me into a tight spot with Director Wallace. He's furious. I had to tell him about Schmidt. Told him someone lured the German here and Coyle got wind of it. If Schmidt slips through our fingers—"

"We'll get him and he'll hang," Richard said firmly.

"Wallace ordered me to bring Mycroft into this."

"You didn't, surely?"

"No, Richard. You can have that honor."

Lestrade turned to Dr. Gregory and extended his hand. "Dr. Gregory, I am sorry how this turned out. Terribly sorry, sir."

Dr. Gregory nodded but said nothing.

"Richard...Emma, you should know that I've dispatched a detail to your home to wait for Helen McMannus to regain consciousness."

"Very well, then," Richard said. "Colonel Schmidt should be arriving at Waterloo within the next ten minutes. Perhaps a few minutes to alight. Five minutes for his valise. Five minutes for a cab or carriage. Fifteen minutes to travel here. He should arrive at approximately six. What's your plan?"

Everyone sat down except Lestrade. "Henry, I'm afraid I have rather bad news. Lucas Griffin is dead. Krajic shot him."

Emma gasped. A painful silence fell over the room.

Henry was stunned. He stared at Lestrade incredulously. Then only anger remained.

Lestrade recounted the appalling events that had ended Lucas's life: how Krajic had stolen his pistol from the constable's office; how Krajic and his henchman used a stolen lorry to chase Fiona and Lucas out of town on the Aberystwyth road; how Krajic shot Lucas in the back during the pursuit; and how Lucas had slumped against Fiona, causing her to lose control of her Fiat and plunge headlong onto the soggy bank of the River Blaen. The Germans assumed that the couple could not survive the crash and returned to Blaenllyn to catch a train to Cardiff. Fiona remained unconscious until Blaenllyn's constable and three Rhys colliery men arrived. They confirmed Lucas's death at the scene and transported Fiona to the physician. Her legs were broken. She was delivered to Aberystwyth hospital, where she underwent surgery.

Hearing about Fiona caught Richard in a rush of emotion. "Fiona."

"I talked with her briefly," Lestrade went on quietly, trying to smile. "She said she should've pushed them over the hill when she had the chance. I didn't ask her what she meant. She fell asleep."

Gordon looked questioningly at Emma.

"He loves Fiona," she whispered.

Richard covered his face. Had he been alone, he would have driven his fist into something... anything.

"Where's Krajic?" Richard asked, his voice lethally quiet.

"In London, and I can assure you we will apprehend—"

"Apprehend him?" Richard said. "I'll kill him."

"Not if I get to him first," Henry said.

Emma placed her hand on her brother's arm. "Go on, Gordon," she said.

Lestrade moved on. "Figured you'd like to know that Trevor Clark admitted to paying Burton Howell for Thornton's murder. But they didn't use the curare from the darts you nicked. Howell owned a small amount from his travels to Brazil. He was a seaman, you know. The evening of Thornton's murder, Howell delivered the roll of plans to Dr. Thornton and poisoned him. He had prepared the tea while Thornton reviewed the drawings. That was before she arrived," Lestrade said, pointing to Mrs. Gregory.

"How did she know about the poison formula?" asked Richard.

"I told her," Dr. Gregory said.

Everyone turned.

"I was so thrilled with the breakthrough," he said, "that I kept her informed of the developments. All quite innocent, wasn't it? But she probably passed on the information to her brother."

Lestrade went on. "The records we found indicate that she was in Bremen with Dr. Thornton as they discussed the formula with a Dr. Hoeltzer. He's Nachtgeist, too. Hoeltzer had concluded that Thornton was not the brain behind the formula. He found Henry's name mentioned somewhere in Thornton's personal notes. My theory is that Mrs. Gregory saw Thornton fall to the floor nearly the instant she applied the poison to his arm. But it was the curare, of course, that had been in his blood circulation for some time. She wrongly assumed the poison formula did him in. Then she took the poison and Henry's notebook to Krauss. I'm sure we'll find their prints all over them... the jar of poison, the notebook, and the laboratory cabinet. Krauss probably forced her to return the notebook to the lab later that night...after they disposed of her glove and handkerchief. He retained the jar of poison for testing before sending it to Dr. Hoeltzer."

"Testing?" Geoffrey asked.

"Practical testing...at the chocolate shop and the pub. Remember?"

"Why return my lab book?" Henry said.

"Krauss probably wanted the death to appear self-inflicted," Richard put in. "Perhaps a human experiment gone amiss. Krauss knew if the notebook was discovered missing, it would appear to be a theft, which it was after all. And nobody knew about the jar of poison."

"I didn't know about the poison," Henry said to Lestrade.

"Nachtgeist had confidence that Dr. Hoeltzer could perfect the formula with the jar full of poison to study. And Henry?" Lestrade looked solemnly at his friend. "For several days they thought they needed you for the formula. But Dr. Hoeltzer claimed he could complete the development without you. I'm sorry, Henry, but they decided to kill you. It's all in the files. I don't mind telling you that you left Blaenllyn just in time, old chap."

Henry paled.

"And the frogs?" Emma asked.

"Those little devils? Mull says Thornton had been studying their poison for use in the formula. He found records of it in the books. Colorful little things. Mull called them Poison Dart frogs."

"Some call them Poison Arrow frogs," said Emma. "The poison's on their skin. Mary needn't know."

Richard had a thought. "Clark should've consulted his solicitor, you know. Thornton might still be alive if he had. Any discoveries or patents made by any professor are the sole property of the university. Right, Henry? So Thornton's formula automatically becomes the school's intellectual property. The formula would not accrue to Thornton's estate and hence, Mrs. Thornton. They should've known that."

"Greed can cloud one's common sense, wouldn't you say?" Geoffrey said.

Richard looked at his watch, his face set. "Schmidt's on his way."

Quietly they discussed the possibilities of a confrontation with Colonel Schmidt. They settled on a plan they believed had the best chance for success with the least risk to hospital staff and patients. But Lestrade and Richard expressed fear that if Krajic became involved, there would be violence in the extreme.

Lestrade said. "I have guards at all of our exits here, and my Black Maria is out of sight in the alleyway across Norfolk." He stood up and walked to the window beside Mrs. Gregory. He waved and raised the blind up and down several times. "My man'll be watching. When I signal, he'll bring the wagon to the main entrance."

"What about Harry and your three men here? Schmidt'll know these blokes aren't doctors."

"Harry has a young, clean face," Emma said. "Let's have him get into a hospital gown. I can bandage his head, and he can lay in the next bed."

"This is a woman's ward," Coyle fussed.

"Good idea, Emma," Lestrade said with a grin. "Coyle, you're a sick woman. I order it."

"And the other three can wear surgeon's robes," Emma said. She went to the supply room.

"Henry," said Richard, "we have to assume that Colonel Schmidt has seen a picture of you. Hide in the room directly across the hall. If you keep the door ajar, you should be able to see a good deal. If I think you should join us, I'll motion for you." Henry nodded and patted the pistol in his pocket. "And, of course, if all hell breaks loose, you're on your own."

Emma returned with the robes and dressing gown, and Officer Coyle undressed behind the screen. She bandaged his head to disguise his features, and he climbed into the high hospital bed and slipped his revolver under his pillow. His fellow officers laughed, fumbling into their surgeon's robes, and Emma reminded them of the impending danger.

Richard checked the time. "He's on his way." The group waited, everyone sitting but Richard, who paced like a panther in the corridor. Nurses bustled, carrying trays and maneuvering carts.

A sister cried from the hall, "Dr. Watson! Dr. Watson!"

Richard motioned to her. He glanced at his watch. Ten past six. "Dr. Watson is in there," Richard said, pointing.

Emma met the young sister in the doorway. "Dr. Watson. There's a Colonel...I forgot..."

"Schmidt?"

"Yes, my goodness. A Colonel Schmidt is demandin' ta see his sister."

"Tell him that Mrs. Gregory's surgeons will see him in the waiting room in a few minutes. Is he alone?"

"Yes. Has me in a right state he does."

"Collect yourself, sister. Be calm. I'll be there with Dr. Halsey."

The girl nodded and hurried down the corridor.

"Geoffrey, let me do the talking in German. You can support me when needed." Emma glanced around and took a breath. "Ready, Dr. Halsey?"

Emma and Geoffrey walked down the corridor to the reception and waiting room.

"Are you Mrs. Gregory's brother?" Emma asked. She recognized him from his picture. He was alone.

The tall, handsome man advanced towards her. He walked with a slight limp. He was the embodiment of German manhood. Prussian strength was in his jaw and his unflinching eyes.

"I'm Schmidt."

"I am Dr. Watson," she said, meeting his eyes with appropriate warmth and extending her hand.

He did not take her hand. "I will now see my sister."

Emma offered her own authority.

"You speak English very well, Colonel Schmidt. This is Dr. Halsey."

He shook Geoffrey's hand. "My sister!"

"Would you care to be seated so we can discuss your sister's unusual case?" Emma asked, motioning to the chairs.

"Sitting since Bremen."

Emma wanted him in a softer mood when he arrived in his sister's room.

"Colonel Schmidt, I am sorry to say that your sister is very ill."

"Yes. Yes. I know this is hospital." His glance was an inferno of self-importance.

"We are doing everything we can for Mrs. Gregory." Emma touched his arm, which he pulled back.

Without a warning an altercation flared with the nursing sister in the reception area behind Emma. Schmidt's face brightened. He shouted in German towards the commotion. Geoffrey and Emma tensed when two men strode toward them. She recognized one of the pair—Krauss. But the other man was the most massive, powerful man she had ever seen. She took in his coarse features and her insides tightened.

The three men had a few brief exchanges in German. Looking at Geoffrey, she knew this was an alarming complication, that things hung in the balance.

Emma tried hard to remain calm. Then she spoke with as much authority as she could muster.

"Colonel Schmidt. Dr. Halsey and I are preparing your sister for surgery. We cannot delay." The Germans appeared surprised.

"What is problem?" Schmidt asked.

"It is rather complicated and very unusual."

"Yes. Well?"

"Your sister is suffering from an unusual poisoning."

"Poisonink?" Schmidt's eyes shot to Krauss and back to Emma. "What you know about poisonink?"

Emma knew her words had startled Schmidt, awakening concern in him.

"It appears to be the same poison that killed a local professor several days ago. Frankly colonel, we have conferred with experts on the Continent and America. Nothing like it has ever been seen. It is very deadly and powerful."

The Germans' expressions were frozen.

"It has compromised her liver function," Emma said. "She is being prepared for the operation. She is unconscious and will remain sedated throughout the procedure. Dr. Halsey here will be assisting me."

Schmidt's gaze shifted to Krauss and Krajic. "Have da authorities been notified and investigatink?"

"I honestly do not know. I am a physician. I do not deal in such matters. But I should think I would have heard about any investigation."

"What about your gufernment? Have they been contacted?"

"I am certain I would have heard."

Emma watched Schmidt's face.

"I want to see her," he said.

Emma stood a little straighter. "I am sorry, Colonel Schmidt. You may see her after the operation."

Schmidt stepped past Emma.

Geoffrey and Emma edged closer together. The anarchists conversed in German before giving her their full attention.

Emma could not wait any longer.

"Colonel, you must wait here. I understand your desire to be with your sister. But the procedure will not be long, and it is the policy of the hospital to keep family away until the patient recovers from the operation and anesthetic. The hospital's rule was not relaxed even when our late queen had to undergo surgery here. Please have a seat. Dr. Halsey and I will come for you when the operation is over."

"How long it take?"

"Perhaps thirty minutes."

The anarchists conversed in German, then Schmidt faced Emma. "Thirty minutes. We wait. Do good job."

Emma left with Geoffrey at her side.

Once into the corridor, Emma exhaled. "The giant is Krajic. We're lucky Krauss talked Schmidt into remaining in the waiting room. We must tell everyone. Lestrade should prepare his men on the street if Krauss and Krajic decide to leave."

They turned into the wardroom. She motioned for Henry to join them. Everyone gathered in front of Emma.

"Ready for the worst possibility?"

Lestrade dispatched an officer to alert his men outside. Emma referred to her brooch-watch. "Mrs. Gregory should be regaining consciousness soon."

The officer returned and everyone stood at the sickbed, watching the clock in apprehensive silence.

CHAPTER 31

"Thirty-nine minutes," Schmidt declared coldly.

"Your sister is doing well," Emma said as she and Geoffrey approached the Germans. "Her heart rate and blood pressure are good. She remains unconscious. A number of doctors are at her side because of the unusual nature of this case. You may see her now."

Colonel Schmidt's eyes softened. "Very good, doctor." He finally extended his hand. "My friends come, yes?"

Emma thought it far better to contain the anarchists.

"Of course, they may. Follow me," she said, patting his arm. He did not withdraw it this time.

Emma led the men into the corridor. "Dr. Gregory is with her. He is quite distraught. He has had no sleep. And I can only allow you to stay a few minutes."

"Of course, doctor."

The men followed her into the wardroom to the foot of Mrs. Gregory's bed. Dr. Gregory rose and weakly greeted his brother-in-law. Richard finished taking her blood pressure and stepped aside, concealing his face from Krajic.

"How is dear Jutta?"

"She has had a very difficult time of it," Dr. Gregory said. "But these doctors, and especially Dr. Watson, have saved her life."

Schmidt looked at Emma and nodded. He introduced Dr. Gregory to Krauss and Krajic by name, and they greeted him respectfully. Richard waited, nerves taut. Mrs. Gregory moaned, eyes closed.

Emma placed her hand on the woman's forehead. She knew the extra stimulus would accelerate her consciousness. Lestrade moved to the window and raised the signal blind, as Emma motioned for Schmidt to stand at the other side of the bed. Dr. Gregory stood near his wife.

"She is emerging from the sedative," Emma advised. "She will be in some pain. Might be somewhat delirious. It is perfectly normal." She stroked the woman's forehead.

The woman turned her head on the pillow. "Wake up, Mrs. Gregory. Can you hear me? I am Dr. Watson. Wake up. Your husband and brother are here. You are doing fine, Mrs. Gregory."

The woman's head turned towards her brother, she groaned deeply. Schmidt stroked her shoulder and spoke to her in German.

Richard urged Geoffrey to join him a short distance from the group. "Translate for me."

Geoffrey nodded. "'Jutta, wake up,' he just said. He's telling her he's at her side."

Mrs. Gregory opened her eyes and saw Schmidt standing beside her. She stared at him, recognition slowly flickering. She groaned to him. Something she said wiped the smile from his face.

"Tell me, Geoffrey," said Richard.

He whispered, "She called him darling and she hoped he would save her. She said, 'I love you.'"

Schmidt glanced anxiously at everyone before he went on. Then he spoke once more. Even Richard could hear the tension in Schmidt's voice.

"What's he saying?" asked Richard.

Geoffrey leaned a shade closer. "Just that he's her brother and over there is her husband."

The woman's eyes remained on Colonel Schmidt. She reached for his hand as she replied.

Geoffrey whispered. "She wants him to take her to Bremen to be together. She hates England."

Colonel Schmidt's guardedness came through as he continued.

"Yes. Yes, Jutta," Geoffrey translated. "We'll go to Bremen when you're well."

Schmidt was silent, his expression tight. Then Mrs. Gregory turned her head on the pillow and faced Emma. Her eyes widened. She shrieked. Then she assailed Emma in German.

Colonel Schmidt straightened, scowling.

Geoffrey looked at Richard. "Trouble! She said that Emma had kidnapped her and Maria and she has Palmer. Emma put her to sleep with a needle."

Richard noticed Kraus and Krajic retreating. Schmidt leaned over

Mrs. Gregory, who began cursing and ignoring Dr. Gregory at her side.

"She's hallucinating." Emma said.

Schmidt put his hands on her shoulders. "Yes, Jutta," he said in English. "Rest." He looked suspiciously around the room.

"Not hallucinatink." Her fury was fierce and scalding. "Dhey have Palmer and Davies, too. I saw dhem!"

German eyes darted everywhere.

Schmidt tried to keep her prone, but she sat up and slapped Emma across her face. Her pince-nez landed on the floor. The woman's hand struck her so abruptly that there was no time for Emma to turn away. As her head came back, Mrs. Gregory struck her again.

"We haf to escape," cried Mrs. Gregory.

Emma sent shock to her brother. Anger painted her face. She was fearless when angered, and now there was no caution in her.

Richard motioned to Henry with a hidden wave behind his back. Henry entered. Schmidt covered her mouth with his hand. Everyone sensed another eruption.

Then Krajic saw Henry.

Comprehension rushed into his repulsive face. He saw the empty beds, the three female patients, the clothes chests at irregular intervals, water pitchers, the metal bed pans, folding dividers leaning unused, and the window at the far end of the room nearly thirty yards away. He elbowed Krauss, and alarm registered in him, too.

"Mr. Krajic," Henry said, moving forward.

Krajic grabbed Krauss and shoved him at Richard before running for the window. The three sick women shrieked in their beds, one hiding under the covers. Henry yanked Krauss off Richard before taking after Krajic. Krauss found his balance and swung hard at Richard. Krauss' fist landed under his jaw, sending him stumbling backward against the wall. Richard shook his head, clearing it, and in an instant lunged at the German, feigning a rugby tackle. Krauss bent to absorb Richard's shoulder. Instead Richard drove his fist upward to the German's chin. The powerful blow snapped Krauss' head back. He staggered, grasping Richard's waistcoat for support, and the two men tumbled to the floor.

Schmidt scrambled across Mrs. Gregory's bed trying to escape, but

Lestrade wrestled him to the floor as Coyle rolled out of his bed, and held his pistol to Schmidt's head, but he was determined to flee.

Krajic tossed a chair through the window and kicked another into Henry's path, but he jumped over it and was on the German, grappling and punching. Krajic lifted a small table and rammed it into Henry's chest, sending him stumbling backwards. Krajic kicked glass shards free from the ground floor window and jumped out. Henry scrambled to his feet and followed.

Additional officers arrived from the hospital corridor and joined the melee around Mrs. Gregory's bed. Richard was pummeling Krauss' bloodied face. The officers waved their truncheons at Krauss. Richard clambered to his feet and ran across the room to the window.

He shouted, "They're headed to Beeton."

"Muldowney, Beeton Park," Lestrade shouted.

The officer raced from the room.

Richard returned and helped pull the Colonel to his feet. Schmidt was kicking and twisting until Richard pressed the barrel of his pistol into the anarchist's nostril. Schmidt's eyes widened.

Lestrade shouted to the officers, "Secure Krauss in the wagon. Then come back for this one."

Two officers dragged Krauss from the room.

"Roll her over," Emma said to Geoffrey, her voice filled with heat. She tore some gauze and tape and wrenched Mrs. Gregory's arms painfully behind her. She tied them together while Mrs. Gregory spewed profanity.

The two officers returned for Schmidt and grappled him down the corridor to the Black Maria. Richard and Lestrade went to the window. They saw Henry and Krajic running across Dennison and Muldowney pursuing them with his gun drawn. They returned to Mrs. Gregory and pulled her from her bed, following the men down the corridor.

They heard a gun shot.

Then another.

Outside, Richard and Emma left Lestrade, Coyle, and Geoffrey to deal with Mrs. Gregory, and ran to a crowd gathered around a brewery dray and its injured Clydesdales.

"Hurry, Em!" They forced their way through. Constables were pushing people back. One of the two Clydesdales had just been shot. Richard saw a man's mangled legs and feet protruding through the spokes of the front wheel. The rest of his body was under the dray's side, crushed into the ground. "Good lord, Em."

"The fool came a runnin' into the crossin'," the driver said desperately. "T'weren't nuthin' I cud do. Sally hit 'im. Trampled 'im somethin' terr'ble, and I were in the air 'n me wagon twistin' under me awful. I had ta have 'at constable shoot ol' Sal. The t'other one's fine."

"Are you injured?"

"Just a scrape here 'n 'ere. But poor ol' Sal," the man said, looking pitifully at the dead horse. "Easy now. Easy," the driver shouted at the dozen or so men trying to right the dray. "There's a bloke under 'ere."

The wagon creaked and slopped beer. The higher they raised it, the more beer poured out. Men slipped and fell on the slick cobbles, but they finally tipped the wagon onto its wheels as several kegs split completely open. Emma and Richard rushed to the unfortunate man who lay in a pool of ale and blood.

"It's Schmidt!" Emma felt for a pulse in his neck, shook her head and stood up.

Lestrade elbowed his way through the crowd. "Coyle said Schmidt broke loose." He looked down at the mangled body. "Blimey, he didn't know what hit him, did he?"

A gunshot came from Beeton. Three more shots sounded. The crowd dispersed away from the crossing. Women screamed and gathered children into doorways. Richard and Lestrade sprinted across Dennison towards the park. Emma followed as best she could but was quickly left behind. She stopped, unbuttoned her shoes, and sprinted.

"Keep down...we don't know where the shooter is," Lestrade said as they crossed onto the grass.

"Muldowney's down."

Running to the fallen officer, both men could see Henry and Krajic wrestling on the grass near Beeton Lake a hundred yards or more away.

"They're fightin' for the gun," Muldowney grunted in pain.

"Three shots or four?" Lestrade yelled.

"Four," Richard said, and Muldowney winced agreement. His blood-covered hand gripped his thigh.

"All his, or did you get off a shot?"

"I didn't shoot."

"He has two rounds left," Richard said, scrambling to his feet. "Give me your gun, Muldowney. I'll go round to the shed behind them. You go that way," Richard said, pointing to the fight.

Lestrade nodded. "Stay low."

Emma arrived, her stockings shredded. She dropped to her knees beside Muldowney. "Where's Richard going?" she asked as she attended Muldowney's wound.

"You two get out of here," Lestrade ordered. "Crawl back to the street. Now!"

He watched Richard progress from one tree to another as Henry and Krajic wrestled. Lestrade ran toward the fight.

Henry and Krajic were fighting for the gun in Krajic's hand. Their faces were bloodied; Krajic was missing several teeth, and he was repeatedly driving his knee into Henry's stomach as Henry kicked and scrambled to pin Krajic to the ground.

Richard watched Lestrade get to within fifty yards of the men; his gun leveled, but there was no safe target. He slipped behind the shed and lost sight of the struggle.

Lestrade now crawled towards the men. Krajic's fist hammered through Henry's defenses, but Henry still gripped the gun with both hands. The German was about to lose control of the weapon. He punched Henry's face, then had both hands locked on the gun. Henry was dazed and Krajic wrenched the gun free. He rolled to his feet, raised the gun towards Henry, then saw Lestrade.

"Drop it, Krajic."

The German aimed at Lestrade and fired. Lestrade dropped to the grass as Krajic's round tore into the trees. Birds took flight. Krajic ran for the far side of the shed, knowing he had only one round left. Henry flung himself behind a tree. Lestrade found cover behind a boulder.

Richard slinked behind Krajic and barreled his gun into the German's spine, reaching for Krajic's pistol. "Not so fast!" Krajic's gun fell to the ground as he stumbled. When he clambered to his feet, Henry was standing in front of him. He drove the heavy revolver into Krajic's temple, knocking him unconscious.

Richard glared at his friend. "You should've left some of him for me."

Lestrade snapped the handcuffs on the German's wrists. The smooth click-click sound of each cuff's metal-against-metal brought a smile from Henry. "Finally," he said.

The three friends brought Krajic around and walked him towards Emma and Officer Muldowney, who were making slow, limping progress towards the hospital. Geoffrey joined Emma and assisted the wounded officer.

Dusk gathered around them as they reached the carriageway. They watched a mortician's wagon driving away with Colonel Schmidt's body. Only the brewery dray, the dead horse, and the surviving Clydesdale remained in the crossing, with the driver soothing her.

Once Krajic was secured in the Black Maria, Richard, Henry, and Lestrade entered St. Bartholomew's and watched Emma finish treating Muldowney's wound. An hour later, she attended to Henry and Richard. Later, they climbed inside Lestrade's carriage, beginning their trip to Carlisle Street in silence, exhausted.

Geoffrey uttered, "Thank you, Lord."

Everyone said, "Amen."

Then Emma began to laugh. So infectious was her laughter that soon they were all laughing in release.

"I just remembered," Emma said, "the look on Schmidt's face...when Richard shoved the gun barrel...up Schmidt's nose." Laughter broke out again.

Henry's swollen face became a quiet mask, and the laughter died.

"Lucas died for me, didn't he?" Henry said. "And his family. Oh dear God, Margaret and the boys..." He closed his eyes.

"And dear Fiona," Emma said, looking at her brother. She recalled how Fiona's letters to her always inquired about Richard and his art and his romances. Emma read the romantic interest between the lines. And there were those private sketches of her Emma had found once in her brother's studio. "I pray her legs will mend properly. We really must bring her to London for proper care."

"I must go to her," Richard said, staring out the carriage window. "Henry, we must go to the funeral together and then visit her."

As the carriage slowed to deliver Henry at the Palmers' home, he asked, "Are the lads still forming a rugby team?"

"Indeed," Geoffrey replied. "Saw Cyril and he asked again about you. I signed up."

"I'm in," Lestrade said.

"I wonder if there's a spot for me," Henry said.

Emma glanced at her brother and found him beaming.

Richard gave Henry a broad smile. "Welcome back, old fellow."

OTHER EXCITING HISTORICAL MYSTERIES BY
J. BROOKS VAN DYKE

Available Exclusively From
MULBERRY LANE BOOKS
www.mulberrylanebooks.com

THE COROT DECEPTION
WHEN DECEPTION BECAME AN ART FORM

J. BROOKS VAN DYKE

$15.95

281 Pages

978-0-9886033-3-2

London artists are getting murdered. The killer leaves behind an odd signature. And when Richard Watson, an artist, discovers the corpse of his gallery owner, he investigates, pitting himself against the ruthless killer. Is Richard next on the killer's list?

Against a backdrop of women's suffrage activism, art collectors' avarice and J.P. Morgan's power, Richard Watson and his twin sister, Dr. Emma Watson, a suffragette physician, search for clues in the Edwardian art world and posh estates of 1910 London. Steeped in the principles of criminal detection they learned from Sherlock Holmes, the twins are drawn quickly into a web of deception, a close friend of the Watsons, joins the hunt for the killer, Richard's life gets complicated. Will romance divert his attention from the cunning assassin?

$16.95

263 Pages

978-0-9886033-0-1

Through meticulous research and vivid imagery, J. Brooks Van Dyke, popular author of the first Watson Twins Mysteries, No Ordinary Terror, has woven together another page-turner packed with period detail, absorbing intrigue, awakening romance and baffling murder. He has once again proven himself to be a master of historical mystery which delights readers and Sherlock Holmes fans worldwide.

From the Eternal City of Rome to the remote outpost of Roman-occupied Judea comes a fresh new mystery series by J. Brooks Van Dyke which evokes the feel of the ancient world in the final days of Christ's life. Like his other mysteries, Van Dyke's Empire of Secrets evolves into a hotbed of intrigue, espionage, romance and bitter betrayals as he transports his readers to the political upheavals in Judea in 33 A.D. in the final days of Christ's life. Like his other mysteries, Van Dyke's Empire of Secrets evolves into a hotbed of intrigue, espionage, romance and bitter betrayals as he transports his readers to the political upheavals in Judea in 33 A.D.

Caught up in the same conflict, Gaius Secundus, a recent graduate of Rome's military academy, has been dispatched to Judea to find his older brother's assassin. In his desperate search for truth, Gaius uncovers a deadly plot that rocks the ancient world, throwing the young Roman centurion into turmoil and a spiritual warfare of his own.

Author of the Watson Twins and Gaius the Centurion Mystery series